THE APEX BOOK OF
WORLD SF

"Each story pushes past established boundaries, bringing readers experiences that are unique and familiar all at once."
Publisher Weekly

Also from Apex Publications

The Apex Book of World SF 1

"These stories deserve to be heard!"
—Frederik Pohl

The Apex Book of World SF 3

"**The Apex Book of SF** series has proven to be an excellent way to sample the diversity of world SFF and to broaden our understanding of the genre's potentials."
—Ken Liu, winner of the Hugo Award
and author of *The Grace of Kings*

The Apex Book of World SF 4

"Important to the future of not only international authors, but the entire SF community."
—*Strange Horizons*

THE APEX BOOK OF
WORLD SF

EDITED BY
Lavie Tidhar

An Apex Publications Book
Lexington, Kentucky

THE APEX BOOK OF WORLD SF 2
ISBN: 978-1-937009-35-9

Edited by Lavie Tidhar
Cover Art © 2015 by Sarah Anne Langton

Published by Apex Publications, LLC
PO Box 24323
Lexington, KY 40524

www.apexbookcompany.com
First Edition, August 2012
Second Edition, August 2015

To Charles A. Tan, for help above and beyond. Charles, this book's for you.

TABLE OF CONTENTS

TABLE OF CONTENTS, CONT.

INTRODUCTION
BY LAVIE TIDHAR

When we first set out to put together and publish *The Apex Book of World SF*, none of us thought it would become quite what it became. Success is relative, of course—but we were in turns amazed and gratified as the anthology took off, receiving wide-spread exposure in the genre world, initiating conversation—even ending up on more than one university curriculum!

At the same time as the book came out, I launched the World SF Blog, initially intended to be a promotional tool for the anthology, but very quickly it took on a life of its own. The site now publishes a regular stream of articles, essays, interviews and even short fiction, all on a daily basis (you can find the site here: http://worldsf.wordpress.com/). Charles Tan joined to help me run it, and somehow, between blog and book, we seemed to have hit on a new wave of interest in, and enthusiasm for, the science fiction and fantasy coming from outside of the traditional Anglophone world of SF. Whether we helped create the wave, or merely rode the top of it, I can't say—nor does it matter, as long as the wave is there and still going.

To my mind, though, what we are doing simply reflects a wider change in the SF world. In this volume, for instance, we have a story from Finnish author Hannu Rajaniemi, whose debut novel—written in English—has done tremendously well on publication. Here, too, is mega-star in the making Lauren Beukes from South Africa, whom I got the chance to see win the Arthur C. Clarke Award in 2011.

In this volume, too, we are very lucky to have a story from Polish grandmaster Andrzej Sapkowski, whose novels are beginning to be translated into English and winning a wider readership everywhere. And here, too, I have tried to address the imbalance that was present in the first volume, and which I lamented in my last introduction—namely, to introduce more African and Latin American writers into the next volume

I am extremely grateful to Daniel W. Koon for his help with the two Cuban stories and much else, to Wu Yan for his help with securing another Chinese story—this one by Chen Qiufan—for this volume, and for Charles Tan for services above and beyond the call of duty. And none of this would have been possible without the support and enthusiasm of our hard working publisher, Jason Sizemore, whose faith brought this project alive.

There are more original stories in this collection than in the last one, and more stories, period—a whopping twenty-six this time around!—featuring writers from Africa and Europe, Asia and Latin America, Australia and New Zealand and the Middle East. I hope you enjoy them as much as I did.

Lavie Tidhar
London, 2012

ALTERNATE GIRL'S EXPATRIATE LIFE

ROCHITA LOENEN-RUIZ

Rochita Loenen-Ruiz is a writer from the Philippines now based in the Netherlands. Her short stories have appeared in *Fantasy*, *Weird Tales*, and *Interzone*, amongst others.

I n springtime, her garden yielded a hundred wisteria blossoms. White English roses climbed the pergola. *Digitalis purpurea*, lavender from the South of France, mint and thyme, rosemary and tarragon, basil and sweet marjoram—they all grew in Alternate Girl's one-hundred-percent super-qualified housewife garden.

Across the street, excavators dug up large swathes of grass.

"They're building a new complex over there," her neighbour said. "I heard the farmer who owned that land went off to live the life of a millionaire."

Her neighbour babbled on about yachts and sea voyages and Alternate Girl stood there staring while the machines went about their business of churning up grass and soil. She wondered what it would be like to be crushed under those hungry wheels, and she flinched at her own imagination.

"A pity," her neighbour said. "I sure will miss the view."

Alternate Girl murmured something vague in reply, and went back to tending her flowers.

She wondered if the farmer was happier now that he had his millions. Would wealth and sea voyages make up for severed ties and the erasure of generations of familial history?

She pulled out a stray weed, and scattered coffee grounds to keep the cats from digging up her crocus bulbs.

She shook her head and headed back indoors. She'd only known two kinds of lives, and in neither of them had she been a millionaire.

Most expatriates pursue a model life. This makes them a desired member in their adopted society. They appear to assimilate quickly, adapting without visible complications to the customs of the country in which they reside.

On the surface, they may appear contented, well-adjusted, and happy. However, studies reveal an underlying sorrow that often manifests itself in dreams. In dreams, the expatriate experiences no ambivalent feelings. There is only a strong sense of loss. It isn't uncommon for expats to wake up crying.

    — **On Expatriate Behaviour, Mackay and Lindon** —

IN HER DREAMS, ALTERNATE GIRL fled from her life as an expat. She sprouted wings and let the wind take her back to the gates of her hometown.

Even in the dreamscape, she could smell the exhaust from passing jeepneys. She could taste the metal dust in the air. The moon shone on the gentle curve of asphalt, cutting through dusty thoroughfares, creating long dark shadows on the pavement. Metal tenements jutted up from the land, pointing like fingers at the night sky.

By day, a constant stream of drones strove to keep those buildings together. Every bit of scrap metal, every piece of residual wiring was used to keep the landscape of steel and concrete from breaking to pieces. For all its frailty, for all its seeming squalor, there was something dear and familiar about the way the streets met and turned into each other.

Even if her life was filled with the cosiness of the here and now, she could not shake off the longing that thrummed through her dreams in the same way that the thrum of the equilibrium machine pulsed through this landscape.

Towering above the tenements was the Remembrance Monument. Made of compressed bits and parts, it contained all the memories of those gone before. Each year, the monument reached higher and higher until its apex was lost in the covering of clouds. When she was younger, she'd often imagined she could hear the voices of the gone-before.

Above the pulse of the Equilibrium Machine, above the gentle susurrus of faded ghosts, she heard a cry. High and shrill, it emitted a hopelessness Alternate Girl remembered feeling.

It was the same cry that pulled her out of her dreams and back into the present. She turned on her side, pressed her ear against her pillow, and stared into the darkness.

This is my home now, she told herself. *I am happy as I am. We are happy as we are.*

Never mind her personal griefs. Never mind her longing for that lost landscape.

Would you like a chance to revisit the past or to visit the future? Optimum Labs offers you the chance to take the leap in time. Our company is 100% customer satisfaction guaranteed. Unlike the scams out there, Optimum Labs offers you the real thing.

Alternate Girl stared at the screen. Each day the spam mail showed up without fail. Same time stamps, same recipient name, all from anonymous senders.

Who sends this mail? she wondered. And did everyone in her neighbourhood receive the same mail with the same time stamps every day? If she had the courage to reply, would she receive an answer from all the anonymous senders? Her hand hovered over the delete key.

If you sent garbage to the landfill, it got buried underground, but what about garbage in the ether? Did it float around silently on the airwaves? Would all the spam and the deleted mail come back to haunt her in the form of ether pollution or some such specialised name?

While she sat there, the speakers gave off a faint ping. She clicked and waited as the new message filled her screen.

Happy Birthday, Alternate Girl! Today is a milestone for all of us. You have successfully completed one hundred weeks of expatriate life. In recognition of your hard work, a reward has been issued to you at the designated station. Report in as soon as you can and don't forget to register at our renewed website. Greetings from Memomach@metaltown.com

Alternate Girl squeezed her eyes shut. She opened them and stared once more at the message on her screen.

Could it be what she had been waiting for all this time, or was Mechanic finally calling her home?

Most expatriates express mixed feelings regarding their origin.

3

Many of them harbour a secret fear of losing touch with the collective memory. While they seem content with their new lives, repatriation is a common subject of conversation. For the expatriate, to return raises a complex response.

One of the subjects of this study worded it this way: "Return is something I fantasise about and desire. But at the same time, it is something I am afraid of."

Choosing to build a new life in an unfamiliar land represents a leaving behind of the collective, and while there may still be remnants of a shared life, the expatriate faces uncertainty. What if he or she has lost the ability to pick up the threads of their old life?

— On Expatriate Behaviour, Mackay and Lindon —

HER FIRST RECOLLECTION WAS OF Father's eyes shining down at her from his great height. Light filtered in through drawn shades and she could see an outline of buildings from where she lay. It seemed as if there were a thousand busy bees buzzing inside her skull. Beside her, someone moaned. She shivered and echoed the sound.

"There, there," Father said. "No need to be frightened."

"Father," he said pointing to himself. "Metal Town." He gestured to something beyond her vision.

She repeated the words after him, and listened as he murmured sounds of approval.

"You're progressing very well," he said. "Soon, I'll take you to Mechanic."

He shuffled away, out of her line of sight. She heard a thump and another moan, and she called out anxiously.

"Father?"

"I'm here," Father said. His voice was soothing and she drifted away into a kaleidoscope of screeching metal and the crescendo of another voice wailing out Father's name.

When she woke, the curtains were drawn back. From where she was, she could see black metal struts and the carcasses of vehicles piled on top of one another.

From far away, came the hum of lasers and a low bass thrum that she later discovered was the Equilibrium Machine. A man bent over her; his face was shiny and round and she saw metal cogs where his ears should have been.

His fingers felt cold and hard on her skin.

"Just like one of them," he whispered. "If I didn't know any better, I'd say you were one of them."

His words made her uncomfortable, and when he took her hand she pulled it away.

"Don't fight it," he whispered. "Fighting only makes it worse."

She felt something sharp and burning on her skin. Wet leaked out of her eyes. She couldn't move.

"You'll be fine," he said. "It's all part of the process."

STARING AT THE MESSAGE ON her screen, she wondered if Mechanic considered this as yet another part of the process.

"Leaving is a part of the process," Father had said.

"While we may long for return, we also know that having left we are already changed."

She looked around at her cosy nest, stared at the brilliant blues and greens of her living room, at the paintings of sunflowers and butterflies, and she wondered whether she would be able to go back and surrender to a life spent waiting for harvest.

Outside, the digging machines had fallen silent. She looked up at the clock. It was half past twelve and the men who drove them were probably off to lunch.

Extract from Notes on the creation of Alternate Girl: 2001 hours
Original model expired at 2000 hours.
Harvested from prototype AG 119-2:
Pulsebeat, bodyframe, eyes, memory, emo chip
2021 hours
Applied Mechanic's new plastics to bodyframe. Installed chip, memory, pulsebeat, eyes. Molding of face follows, arms, legs, and other parts. Assembly proceeded as planned. Pliables applied.

2065 hours

Awareness installed. Test successful.

2070 hours

Emo chip installed. Test successful.

2098 hours

Memory chip activated. Trace and recall function activated. Registration complete.

THERE WAS A PARTY WHEN she passed the 4000-hour mark. Father beamed, and Mechanic looked happy and hopeful. Metal Town's citizens came in reply to Mechanic's summons. Of these, she loved most the ones who rolled in on lopsided wheels and who smiled and chirped code at her.

When she tried to chirp back, they encircled her and projected their enthusiasm in signals and bleeps that she couldn't put into proper words.

"You are one of us," the chirpers said. And she felt welcomed and included.

Father beamed at the compliments he received.

"Yes, I am proud of her," he said. "Our first success," Mechanic said. Alternate Girl wondered at his words. Had there been others then? If she was the first success, where were the ones that had failed?

The chirpers moved away and she was surrounded by tall and gangly ones who took her hands in theirs. They ran their fingers up and down her arms, peered into her eyes and asked her questions about her training. Mechanic beamed and looked on. He sipped oil from a can he held in his hand and bowed his head and gestured towards her.

Where were the words to tell a powerful being that you had no wish to be looked upon and admired as if you were a foreign object placed on display?

Foreign. It struck her then. She lifted her hands, marvelling at the elasticity of her flesh. Of course, she was foreign.

Notes on progression:
AG 119-2 perfectly adjusted. All systems normal. Social skills optimal. Sequence failures, nil.

In the weeks that followed, she passed through various tests. A model housewife, she learnt, was dedicated to maintaining a perfect home and garden. She perused hundreds of pages of magazines culled from God knew where. Housewives by the hundreds, all extolling the virtues of various cleaning products, household goods, cooking sauces, oils, liniments, lotions, facial creams, garden products, and intimate apparel. The array of faces and products dazzled her.

"Will there be others like me?" she asked Father.

"If all goes well," he replied.

"What about you?" she asked.

"When the time comes, the old must give way to the new."

She waited for him to continue. Wanting to know more, wanting to understand what he meant by his words.

"You're not old," she said.

He touched her cheek and shook his head.

"I shall tell you more soon," he said.

These hours spent with Father were precious to her. He was patient with her attempts to put to practice the things she had learnt.

"You must learn control," he said. "You are far stronger than others think you are, but control will serve you better where you are going, AG."

"When they take me away," Father said, "I want you to remember that it's part of the process we all go through."

"Why would they take you away?" she asked.

"In the order of things, old models must make way for the new," Father said. "But even if I go, my pride and joy live on in you, AG. Eight thousand hours old and going strong. You are our future."

"Where are you going?" she asked.

"I'll be there," Father said.

She looked to where his finger pointed and saw the Remembrance Monument.

"When the time comes, I will be harvested as others have been before me. My memories will become part of the monument. There are those who say that when the end of time comes, we will unfold our bodies, regain our memories, and find ourselves changed into something more than machine."

"Will I be harvested, too?" she asked.

"I don't know," He cupped her face in his hands. "You are our first success. We don't even know what you'll be like when you're as old as we are."

"Can I have your memories?" she asked.

He didn't answer. Outside, Mechanic's men tramped through the streets of Metal Town. Someone screamed.

Harvest, the word whispered through Alternate Girl's circuits.

Father flinched, closed his eyes and bowed his head.

"Will it hurt?" Alternate Girl asked.

"I don't know," Father replied.

But she knew he was lying. She wondered what happened at Harvest and whether it was indeed a natural thing as Father had said. She visited the Remembrance Monument, and tried to make sense of it all. Its cold walls gave back a reflection of her face—so unlike the faces of her fellow citizens.

She thought of a life without Father, and there were no words for the grief she felt.

"Take me then," she said to the Monument. "If you must take Father, then you must take me, too.

But the monument stayed silent, and no matter how hard she listened, there were no messages or codes from the beyond.

AFTER THAT, SHE GREW MORE conscious of how the machine men made their daily trek to the walled buildings. They went in the same as they came out. The drones monitored the streets, gathering up residue and scrap metal. It seemed to her that each one had a duty to perform, a routine task to follow.

Mechanic had found no routine for her yet.

"Learn all you can," he had said on one of his visits. "You will be our first ambassador. The model housewife, a perfect expatriate. They will love us because of you. Perhaps they will finally remember us and we will be reconciled with the original makers."

"What about Father?" Alternate Girl asked.

"He does his part," Mechanic said. "You must do yours."

She didn't like the uncertainty of his answer, but she had learnt not to say so. Instead, she nodded and listened and took in the knowledge he fed to her.

There must be a way out, she thought.

It was the first time she thought of escape.

The Expatriate Choice as subject of this study reveals the following common causes for expatriation:

Economic. Some expatriates choose to live or work in a different country or society for the sake of material gain.

Social. Some expatriates choose to live or work in a different country or society because they see this as a means of increasing their stature in society. Others choose exile for the sake of love.

Political. Some expatriates embrace voluntary exile as a means of protest against the ruling body of their home country.

—Observations of Expatriate Behaviour, Mackay and Lindon—

ALTERNATE GIRL FOUND THE RIFT IN the barrier a week after Mechanic's visit. It was late at night, and she had chosen to take one of the roads leading south. She ventured further and further away from the heart of Metal Town. The moon cast its light on the road before her and she could see the long shadow of herself stretching out and mingling with the waving shapes of wild grass and brush.

She was deep in thought when the sound of wheels swishing on asphalt caught her attention. She saw a flash of light, and then she was at a barred gate. Through the bars, she could see the outline of cars and buses flowing in a rush away from her. She stared at this vision of vibrant and full-bodied creatures, and she understood that they were relatives of the disembowelled who lay stranded in the many garages around Metal Town.

On her way home, she was conscious of the spy eye stationed atop the Remembrance Monument and, passing close to it, she heard a faint murmur that sounded like voices whispering through the scaffolds of the Monument's steel ports.

The recollection of screams played back in her memory and she stopped. One day they would take her, too. She'd be joined to the Monument regardless of whether she desired it or not.

Across the street, she saw Mechanic. Moonlight glinted off the chrome of his head, and he gave a slight nod when he saw her. She could hear him muttering to himself as he crossed to where the tin houses of the Numbered Men leant against each other like pale reflections of their owners.

Alternate Girl wished she had the courage to run up to Mechanic.

"Please," she would say. "Please spare Father."

But she already knew his answer.

"Our duty is to the original creators of the monument," he'd told her once. "It is our task to harvest the bodies and to store the memories of the gone-before. It is all for the greater good, Alternate Girl. We all have our duties to perform. Your father understands his place in all of this."

Memory, its storage and the passing on of it, is essential to the inhabitants of Metal Town. What function does the Remembrance Monument have, if not to store the memories of the gone-before? At the heart of Harvest is the preservation of the spirit that is Metal Town.

—excerpt from A Celebration of Memory by Sitio Mechanics—

FATHER WAS SILENT. HE DRAGGED his feet when he walked and complained about his joints. She tried to cheer him up, but all the while her mind circled around the question of escape.

"They'll be coming for me soon," Father said. His speech slurred and he sat down and leant his head against the back of the chair.

"Mechanic wants to create a partner for you," he whispered. "He wants someone created in your image. An alternate man designed to fit the perfect housewife."

"Father," she knelt down beside him. "If I told you we could get out and not have to come back, what would you say?"

He laughed.

"Don't you think anyone has tried that before? Why do you think the monument keeps growing, AG? Our masters created us to stay in Metal Town, but there were always those who tried to escape. Everyone comes back to Metal Town, even those who leave with Mechanic's blessing."

"But there's a road out of here," Alternate Girl insisted. "If we leave, at least we'll have a choice."

"They'll always catch you," he whispered. "Metal Town allows no exemptions, AG. Right now, you are one of a kind, but what's been made before can be made again."

He closed his eyes and leant back in his chair. She could hear the slow whirr of his heart, and she felt more frightened than she had ever been.

"Why did you make me this way?" she asked. "You could have made me a drone, if this is all the life I'm meant to have."

"Do you think a drone's life is of less value than yours?" Father asked. "Memory and hope is all that lies between you and the life of a Numbered Man. We come home when our time is at an end. To be joined to the original dream of our creators is a privilege, not a curse."

"I'm sorry," she said. "I'm sorry, Father. I didn't mean for it to sound that way. But please, please, won't you at least try?

Without you, I might just as well be a Numbered Man."

"Escape is never without a price," Father said.

But she only heard the capitulation in his voice.

Copy of Memo as lifted from Mechanic's desk:
Received: 23.11, Remembrance Monday
Re: circular number: 792-A-1B3Rae
Release Request: Alternate Girl
Status: Under consideration

They left Metal Town early in the morning. In the quiet dark, the thrum of the Equilibrium Machine was magnified a hundred times. Avoiding the street lamps, they kept to the shadows as best they could.

"I'll slow you down," Father had said.

But she wouldn't leave him behind. And so they crept along behind the piles of junk and strip metal.

Their feet slipped on smooth steel and made clunky sounds in the silence. They waited, but when no-one came, they slid on forwards until they reached a surface less finished than the one they'd left behind.

"We're almost there," she whispered.

She could hear his joints creak in the silence, and she reached out a hand to help him.

"I'm fine," he said.

And then they were out in the open. Beyond them, the road opened up and curled southwards to where the rift in the barrier had expanded.

The rising sun cast a golden glow over Father's face, and it seemed as if he were made of light.

They were headed towards the rift when from behind came the sound of pursuit. The roar of Mechanic and the clunk of boots on the hard surface of the road.

They raced down the blacktop as the sun made its journey to the apex. Alternate Girl ran, propelling Father onwards with a fresh surge of energy. The earth shook, and Alternate Girl slipped and lost her footing.

"Get up," Father's voice whispered in her ear.

"Run," Alternate Girl gasped. "I'll slow them down."

"I'm not letting them take you," Father said.

The Equilibrium Machine shrieked, and Alternate Girl cried out as Mechanic loomed before them.

"What did you think to gain?" Mechanic asked.

What did I hope for? Alternate Girl wondered.

"Let her go," Father said. "I will do as is required of me. Only let her go."

"Do you think you still have the power to intervene?" Mechanic asked. He kept his gaze locked on Alternate Girl.

"No," Father said. "I realise there is no forgiveness for what I chose to do. Still..."

Mechanic raised his right hand in a silencing gesture.

"Forgiveness is not up to you to decide," he said. "Whatever follows lies in the hands of this girl you have created. She is ready to leave this place, and I am sure she will be an asset to the Expatriate Programme."

Building bridges and abolishing barriers is central to the Expatriate Programme. Ignorance leads to misconceptions and stereotypes, hence the lumping together of certain groups of expatriates. It is hoped that the Expatriate Programme will give rise to mutual understanding and acceptance of each other's differences.

Participants to the Expatriate Programme are given the freedom to appropriate what they deem necessary in order to achieve the central goal of total integration.

—**Understanding the Expatriate Programme, Mackay and Hill**—

She'd found her partner on the other side of the gate. It had seemed simple enough to follow him home and to allow herself

13

to be embraced and joined to him. That union made it possible for her to slip seamlessly into the pattern of his everyday life.

All the knowledge fed into her came to good use, and their lives entwined as if by rote. She became the housewife, and he, her model mate.

How he spent his days was a mystery to her. She imagined him spending all day behind a desk in an office somewhere. She thought of him lost in a maze of paperwork, one of the hundreds of thousands of Numbered Men wearing the same coloured shirt, the same suit from the same local haberdashery, the same haircut from some local barber, the same coat, the same tie. She imagined all of them, working together towards the same goal.

How many numbers have you added up today? That's how Alternate Girl imagined their conversations went. *How many more numbers before you meet your quota?*

"If I do as you wish, will you return Father to me?" she asked Mechanic.

"Already, his body is good for nothing but the harvest," Mechanic said. "But I can give you the essence of him. How you choose to restore him lies within your grasp."

She turned the chip over in her hand. For all that it seemed small, it contained the entirety of Father's memories as well as the history of their lives.

"A simple matter to appropriate a body," Mechanic's words whispered in her head. "You won't even need to tell him what you're doing. Let him fall away into an eternal dream, so Father may return."

"Won't he feel pain?" She asked.

"A relative thing," he said. "Such things are unimportant and the outcome relies on your ability to do what must be done. You have done well, AG. Allowing you to regain Father is a small reward."

The chip felt hard and hot in her hand. She'd made sacrifices working towards this goal, subjugated her will in order to build a life beyond the shadows of the Remembrance Monument. Already, she couldn't remember the name of this man whom she'd shared a bed with for one hundred weeks.

Should she feel regret or remorse for what she was about to do?

She had no answer to that question. All she could think of was Mechanic's admonition, she could only hear his voice telling her that she was free to do as she chose. If she chose to erase her partner's life for the sake of regaining Father, it wouldn't matter if she could no longer return to Metal Town.

She listened to her partner's key turning in the front door, listened to the sound of his footsteps in the hall, listened for the familiar creak of his joints, and turned to welcome him home.

Mr Goop

Ivor W. Hartmann

Ivor W. Hartmann was born and raised in Harare, Zimbabwe. He publishes *Story Time*, an online magazine of African fiction, and co-edited the anthology *African Roar*. He won the Baobab Prize for *Mr Goop*.

Tamuka hated Mr Goop; it wasn't as if it was really his anyway. He had the unfortunate distinction of being one of those kids. The ones with poor parents who could not afford to buy their children Geneforms of their own. Just this morning before class, in the translucent, dome-sealed playground, Tamuka had yet again been a victim. Well, at least he had not been alone this time: two younger kids and their inherited family Geneforms had also endured the playground circle of laughter and cruel taunts.

Mr Goop stood motionless outside the classroom; Tamuka could see its vague shadowy humanoid outline through the frosted glass wall. The adult-sized Mr Goop was too big to be allowed in the classroom. While everyone else in his class had their small—and very cute—Geneforms dozing on their desks or sitting quietly on their shoulders, he had Mr Goop standing outside.

Mr Goop. Tamuka shuddered at the name given to the Geneform by his grandfather, Manenji Zimudzi. A bad joke, Tamuka had been told when he had asked him. One that Grandfather had made when he had first bought it in better days, long before Tamuka's father was even born, about it being a genetically manufactured lump of goo, which became a walking Mr Goop. And the name had stuck. It would respond to no other, no matter how hard Tamuka had tried to train it.

Tamuka then thought of Grandfather, alone on that mountain top in Nyanga where they had buried him last year. Tamuka wondered if Grandfather was lonely up there, and vowed to nag his mother into going to visit him. The truth was that he really missed Grandfather; he was the one person who always had time for Tamuka, no matter the hour or the problem. But during all the commotion that had surrounded Grandfather's death—Mother in floods of tears, Father being strong for her—no-one had bothered to ask Tamuka how he felt about it all.

"Tamuka, what is the name of the English Isles' capital

city?" asked his teacher, Mrs Mudarikwa, breaking the spell of memories that surrounded Tamuka.

"London," blurted Tamuka.

The class around him erupted in laughter. Mrs Mudarikwa, a wizened old lady whose wrinkles probably outnumbered the dunes of the seaward deserts, motioned for silence. But then she gave him that look, the subtle one reserved for her brighter students that showed a slight disappointment, that always left Tamuka feeling very disappointed with himself.

"No, Tamuka that used to be the capital until... Who can tell me?" Mrs Mudarikwa asked, once the laughter had subsided. A dozen eager hands shot up and she chose Tiny, of all people. Tamuka groaned inwardly. Tiny really was a small lad, not that it stopped him from becoming the ringleader in Tamuka's Geneform circle of humiliation.

Tiny glanced at Tamuka, a smirk plastered on his pixie face, then he turned a solemn face back to Mrs Mudarikwa, "The great floods of 2040, Ma'am, forced the permanent relocation of the English Isles' capital city from London to Birmingham."

"That is correct, and can you tell me why the Great Floods occurred?" asked Mrs Mudarikwa.

"In 2040, due to the exponential runaway effects of global warming," Tiny replied promptly, "the entire continental western shelf of the Antarctic caved into the South Ocean and melted. This created, in addition to the 70 metre rise by 2020 from the melting of the Arctic and Greenland continental ice shelf, a total 90 metre rise in global sea level and the loss of over 1,710,000 square kilometres of the Earth's low-land seaward areas." Tiny smiled proudly. And at that moment, Tamuka couldn't decide who he hated more, Mr Goop or Tiny.

AS TAMUKA CRUNCHED HIS WAY HOME between the disused railway tracks, he fiddled with his oxygen mask. Mr Goop followed silently behind him, and of course it didn't need a mask, gene-tailored as it was for the Earth's current environment amongst other things. *Like being able to virtually live forever,* Tamuka thought irritably. As with all Geneforms, Mr Goop was of limited intelligence, but it certainly knew enough to sense Tamuka's moods, and remained a constant five metres away. Tamuka could feel Mr Goop's quiet presence behind him, as he had his entire life. He could not, in fact, imagine what life might be like without Mr Goop. Tamuka had no brothers and sisters, nor would he ever, with the one-child family law.

In the low late afternoon sun, the rusted railway tracks shone like two lines of spun gold. On either side, Tamuka could see through their transparent domes and into the rear of the rich suburban houses of this area. From where he walked, they all looked to him like big bubbles housing other dimensions of existence, which could only ever be glimpsed by peeking over high walls, and through bright laser security systems. From behind a row of thorny acacia trees that jutted from a dome to his left, he could hear the sound of splashing water and children's laughter. Unable to help himself, he leapt from the tracks, down into the thick vegetation that thrived in the high carbon dioxide and low oxygen environment. He battled his way to the plastic-steel wall, leant against it and listened carefully.

Mr Goop stopped walking and waited patiently in the hot sun. Tamuka closed his eyes and imagined the happy sun-soaked scene behind the wall; he could almost smell the chlorine in the water.

"You are unauthorised to be near these premises," bellowed a disembodied voice, "Please vacate the immediate area in twenty seconds, or become liable to arrest and prosecution."

It scared Tamuka so badly that he jumped backwards, deep into a very dense and thorny wait-a-bit bush that he had already so-carefully avoided. As Mr Goop plunged off the tracks to get to him, Tamuka kept very still. He could feel blood starting to drip, warmly, where the small needle-sharp thorns had painfully punctured right through his sun-screen coveralls and school uniform. *Well, it wasn't called the wait-a-bit bush for nothing,*

Tamuka thought. The trick was to keep very still and remove each thorn-studded, vine-like branch, one by one. The property had to belong to a really rich and important person to have such a security system. Tamuka tried to stay calm, but his breathing was hard and deep, steaming up the clear oxygen mask. At least he had remembered to strap the vulnerable oxygen line underneath his clothes before leaving the school airlock. And so far, he could hear the steady hiss of the mask: no thorns had penetrated it.

"Nineteen."

Mr Goop reached Tamuka, its grey skin paler than usual, and began to gently remove the thorny branches, one by one.

"Eighteen."

Mr Goop had done this before, Tamuka could see. There was no hesitation in his movements.

"Seventeen."

Tamuka was mentally racked by visions of armed and armoured men, jumping from fliers in the sky to capture him at any moment.

"Sixteen."

There was a measured haste to Mr Goop's actions now; Tamuka could tell that it knew, in its way, what could happen if Tamuka was arrested.

"Fifteen."

The surface of the wall began to hum and several holes opened like pupil irises along the top. From these apertures sprung robotic necks with camera heads, which swung themselves around and whined into focus on Tamuka and Mr Goop.

"Fourteen."

Faster now, and with no thought to the thorns that were scratching his own skin, Mr Goop started on the branches wrapped around Tamuka's head.

"Thirteen."

New holes opened along the wall and out popped several sleek, gun-bearing robot arms. Beams from their blue lasers roamed Mr Goop and Tamuka's bodies like glowing beetles.

"Twelve."

The last branch finally came free and Mr Goop hauled Tamuka over its shoulder and sprinted up to the tracks. Though the countdown had ended, the robot cameras and guns continued to track them.

Mr Goop did not stop when it made the safety of the tracks, or when Tamuka flailed to be let down, or even when its own breathing became ragged and its footfalls heavy. Tamuka lay helpless in its strong grip, wondering at Mr Goop's reaction. Surely they were safe now.

Still, he had been twelve seconds from a fate possibly worse than death; the faster they went and the further they were, the better for him. Tamuka then had a flash of what might have happened had he not been with Mr Goop. *What use would a normal kid's Geneform have been,* he thought? He would certainly have been arrested, or worse.

Mr Goop set Tamuka gently down by the front entrance to their apartment block before collapsing in a heap. It gasped for air like a stranded fish, but just as Mr Goop did not speak, it did not sweat either—none of the Geneforms ever did. Digging for the remote digikey in his schoolbag, he looked upwards and squinted at the thin clouds whipping past floor one hundred and twelve. Their apartment was one of ten thousand in the government housing block. They were on the ninety-second floor. *Just below the cloud-line,* Tamuka thought grumpily, not that they could have seen anything anyway, set right in the middle of the block as they were, with no external windows. Their block was officially called Tsvangirai Heights, after some ancient, long dead prime minister, back when this was a country, not a state, called Zimbabwe.

Tamuka found the digikey, pulled it out, and waved it at the thick glass doors. They swung silently open to the air lock chamber beyond. Tamuka ambled in slowly, giving the tired Mr Goop enough time to rise and join him. If Mr Goop was locked outside it would be denied access until a registered owner came to fetch it.

As usual, there was no-one home when they arrived. After tending to Tamuka's cuts and scratches, Mr Goop opened a cup of Instacook noodles and set it out on the kitchen counter. Then it climbed into its capsule in the adjoining scullery and closed the hatch. It wanted to be left alone then. Tamuka stood in the kitchen and munched on the now-steaming hot noodles, while absently staring out of the fake windows.

Out there, if you believed the windows, it was a late summer's day and a brisk wind blew leaves around silently. The wind swooped down from the thick European pine forests just past their back-garden fence. You could turn the sound on, even the smells with some of the newer models he had seen on display in the mall. You could also change the scene with those new ones. Not these ones though; these were all standard issue and came with the apartment. They had one built-in scene: Remote European Countryside. Throughout the whole apartment all you could see were these damn forests, cows in rough-walled fields and the odd blackbird. Not forgetting, never forgetting, the damn scarecrow in a wheat field outside Tamuka's bedroom window.

Ever since he could remember, he had been absolutely terrified of that damn scarecrow. That was before he was old enough to realise that none of it was real, or could ever be real anymore, not even in Europe itself. However, even when he had finally caught on, the irrational fear remained and he was even more scared than before. Eventually, against government policy, he had pinned up a large picture of an extinct puppy over the window. The picture was still there, and his parents let it stay, even though it would mean a fine if it was ever discovered. Tamuka vaguely remembered that the "windows" had something to do with the psychological-well-being of the approximately thirty thousand inhabitants of Mbare, which was his block's informal name.

Tamuka knew the unofficial name used to belong to a high-density suburb that existed here once, when this had been the capital city—not just the state capital city—Harare. The current Mbare was the first of the really big housing blocks to be built in the United Federation of Africa. The proper name for the block was an Arcology. Every basic need was met within the arcology, apart from their schooling. Tamuka wasn't sure exactly why school was outside Mbare, but it was also something to do with that psychological-well-being stuff. Inside Mbare was a huge interior mall, thirty storeys high and filled with all the shops, cinemas, playgrounds, gyms, sports grounds, restaurants, nightclubs, lakes, and parks one could ever need. Quite a few of the adults—including his parents—worked here, too. Some had never left the arcology and were quick and proud to say so.

Although the idea of forever living in Mbare was not for Tamuka, he could understand why others could do so. It was, he supposed, like living in one huge, close-knit village. People could know you, and you them, for your whole lifetime. Families often made deals to move their apartments closer together. Tamuka's closest friend, nicknamed Chinhavira, was surrounded by no less than twenty apartments, all belonging to members of her extended family. They were strict traditionalists and her father, Mr Tonderai Mpofu, held a senior position in the Tsvangirai Height's People's Council. Chinhavira already had an apartment that was being rented out until she married. It seemed to Tamuka that she had no choice either in her parent's choice of apartment, or her future genetically-selected, arcology-born marriage partner.

Tamuka slurped the last of his noodles down, opened the atomiser by the sink, and threw the cold cup inside. He flicked the lid down and it automatically locked in place with a vacuum hiss. A muffled bang came from inside as the cup was atomised and sucked away. Gone, forever. Like his grandfather, even if his parents said he was with all their ancestors, watching over all their living family.

"Can you hear me, Grandfather?" Tamuka whispered, half expecting, half dreading an answer. The apartment remained silent.

"TAMUKA!"

His mother's call jerked Tamuka rudely awake on his bed where he had fallen asleep while reading. He leapt up and tossed the digital screen-reader to the bed. Quickly, he wiped his face and straightened his clothes. It would not do for mother to know he had been asleep, on top of whatever else was obviously bothering her. He hurried out of his bedroom; if she had to call twice, there would be hell to pay.

Mrs Kundiso Zimudzi was a formidable woman when stirred to the occasion. His father often said that it was this fiery quality that had drawn him to her in the first place. But the look Tamuka got as he rounded the corner into the kitchen made him wish his father had found another, less dangerous quality. Most people did not recognise the danger signs — distracted by her jet-black eyes and slim elegant eyebrows, neatly shaven head and skin the colour of burnt wild honey. Her short body was fit and generously proportioned. Her bland grey domestic worker's coveralls were always touched with a bit of colour and individuality. Today, Tamuka noticed that it was in the form of a fake but beautiful golden scarab beetle brooch. All these attributes could — if you did not know her well enough — keep you distracted until she suddenly had you at her mercy. Tamuka knew her all too well.

"Perhaps you would like to tell me why Mr Goop is in the capsule and won't come out when I call?" she asked. She placed her hand on her hip and Tamuka's danger meter shot up about ten points. She hardly ever did that!

He took pains to be totally honest, and yet very careful. "I'm not sure," he replied tentatively, "we had some trouble on the way home and Mr Goop carried me; perhaps it's just tired...?" He turned away, trying to look anywhere except at his mother.

24

"Not boring you, I hope?" asked his mother lightly.

Of course, what she was really saying was, if you don't look me in the eye right now and fully answer my questions, there's going to be hell to pay. He turned and looked her squarely in the eyes. It was no easy task.

Tamuka relayed the whole day's events in one long breath, and had to breathe deeply afterwards. His mother was silent, another rare thing; she regarded him carefully as though seeing him from a whole new perspective. Although she said nothing, her eyes glistened more, he thought, before she crossed the kitchen and enfolded him in a tight hug.

"Don't you ever be so foolish again, Tamuka," she whispered but held him even tighter for the longest of moments. And just then he wasn't a big boy of twelve, embarrassed by parental displays of affection. He was a little boy who'd had a big scare. He cried a little and his mother hummed sympathetically while gently swaying from side to side.

"Your father is working a double, up at the air docks," his mother said, after she had slowly broken their embrace. She then bustled around the kitchen making dinner. Presently, she turned to him, "Now hold on, what do we have here?" She whisked out his father's blue lunch box from behind her back. "Methinks, young sir, that your father would be rather pleased to see this. Why don't you take it up to him?"

Tamuka wiped away his tears and grinned excitedly. "But what about Mr Goop?" He realised he hadn't even considered going without it.

"Don't worry about Mr Goop for now. You go on, and I want you back in an hour for dinner, that's one hour only, mister." Tamuka turned and ran down the short hallway to the front door.

"And don't forget to put your coat on, it gets very cold up there after sunset," his mother called out after him.

Tamuka had forgotten, and dutifully put on the coat before slamming the door open, and then shut. *What a day it's been so far,* he thought as he eagerly ran down the corridor—from the morning's humiliation to the afternoon's ordeal... and now he got to go and see his father at work—without Mr Goop. It was a strange feeling not having Mr Goop in his shadow. A bit scary even, but he felt wonderfully grown up, just like a short adult really. He stopped running and a few people passed by. He nodded hellos, and felt even more adult when they nodded back.

"THANKS, SON," MURMURED TAMUKA'S FATHER as he manhandled a small crate into position inside a much larger one. Tamuka placed the lunch box in his father's work bag, which hung on a nearby hook. In the dim light of the cavernous warehouse underneath the rooftop runway, his father, Mr Tapiwa Zimudzi, sweated profusely. It ran down in sheets over his enormous bare barrel chest, staining dark his light green labourer's coveralls, which was knotted at his waist. Standing at over six feet eight, his father was as huge as his mother was diminutive, one of his arms alone was as big as both Tamuka's legs put together. Tamuka had sometimes heard laughter when they all walked together in the mall, but normally all it took was one look from either of his parents to shut that person up. His father had a square face and blunt, craggy features and could not really be called handsome—until he smiled. He, too, sported a clean scalp. *One that shines like a polished cannon ball and is just as hard,* Tamuka thought.

"Tamuka, are you here at all, son?" asked his father, as he hefted another heavy crate.

"Sorry, Father, it's been a long day," Tamuka said, hanging his head.

"So I heard from your mother," his father said. He paused for a moment to gently lift up Tamuka's chin. "Look, it's not like I don't know how rough it can be for you at times. I do remember what it's like to be twelve. Now, this kid that's been bothering you... Tiny, is it?" Tamuka nodded gravely, and his father continued. "Have you thought that perhaps Tiny has never been alone without his Geneform, and yet here you are

26

now without Mr Goop." Tamuka's eyes widened as he realised what his father was saying.

"That's right, here I am, alone!" Tamuka said, hatching the beginning of a verbal attack that he could use at the next taunting session.

"You got it, kiddo. And if you are wise, Tiny might just never bother you again," his father said and ruffled Tamuka's short spiky dreads as he ambled past.

"You must understand how important school is, Tamuka," he said while wrestling with what seemed like a very heavy crate. "When your mother and I were growing up there was no schooling, only day to day survival. Now when I was twelve, I—"

"—Was in a mass exodus that crossed the seaward wasteland deserts, walking five thousand kilometres to return to the homeland of our ancestors, during which time you met mother. Yes, I know the story," Tamuka cut in impatiently, still plotting exactly how he would aim his verbal darts.

His father unexpectedly burst out laughing and soon had Tamuka in a fit of sympathetic giggles, although he was not altogether sure why his father was laughing. Their laughter attracted a glare from a management type, standing over a computer terminal at the far end of the warehouse. His father choked his laughter down to snorts of air through his nose, but grinned happily at Tamuka before he resumed working. Eventually their laughter died down to a long comfortable silence, in which Tamuka just watched his father at work. As always, he marvelled at the way his father seemed to effortlessly flip up the crates and position them within the larger crate.

Tamuka knew those crates were probably very heavy; he'd never managed to budge one. They were all shapes and sizes. His father had once explained to Tamuka that in his mind he held a map. One that he created by first looking carefully at the smaller crates designated for the larger one. He then played a quick game in his mind. In this game he played every possible combination of smaller crates to fill up the larger crate. When he won the game with the best possible arrangement of small crates, he had a final mind map. This meant, added to his immense physical strength, he loaded up the crates with an incredible speed and efficiency that kept him gainfully employed.

His father's job, like his mother's, was a position normally reserved for Geneforms or the rare and expensive robots. His mother cleaned apartments, capitalising on those who could not afford either, while his father was assigned to deal with items requiring special care during packing, such as the delicate but heavy ion metal sculptures that were the specialties of the Mbare artistic community, or anything to do with Mbare's Mayor, the shady Mr Isaac Gondo. So his father was never lacking for this type of work, and it afforded him some liberties since he was nearly indispensable. Liberties such as Tamuka being allowed here while he worked, without much objection from his manager. Still, Tamuka knew, the wages were hardly great, and his parents struggled each month on their combined income to pay the mortgage, something they had both taken pains to explain to him at various points in his life. Mostly as the final "No" when he incessantly nagged them about having a Geneform of his own.

"I think you'd better think about going home in a bit, Tamuka," said his father. "It's best not to make your mother wait too long. Even today."

"But, Father!" Tamuka started, and he wanted to protest further, but his father simply looked at him briefly. And wordlessly he said, it's time to grow up son, not too much, just a little, enough to show you are worthy of our trust. So Tamuka kept quiet, and his father carried on packing crates. Timing it carefully, Tamuka quickly nipped in, hugged his father and then scampered off. He thought he could feel his father's glance and loving grin, warm on his back. But he did not need to turn around; it was enough to just feel it there.

MR GOOP WASN'T LOOKING AT ALL well when Tamuka got back

to the apartment; its skin was even paler, almost translucent. It still refused to come out of its coffin-sized capsule, but at least the hatch was open.

"See to Mr Goop," his mother said from the kitchen, "Before you even think about having dinner."

At first, Tamuka just stood near Mr Goop's capsule, but when he saw tears roll down Mr Goop's expressionless face, it all fell into place. Tamuka immediately crawled inside the capsule with Mr Goop, something he had not done for years. It was much smaller than he remembered. But he managed to eventually wriggle his way into a snuggle on top of Mr Goop's chest. Once there, he lay still and waited for Mr Goop's reaction.

With a slight sniffle, Mr Goop wrapped its arms around Tamuka, just as it had done many years previously. Tamuka sighed happily. He realised that it had been afraid for his life. For Mr Goop truly loved him in its own special way. The idea of losing Tamuka must have been a great shock and, followed by the strenuous sprint to get Tamuka home and safe, Mr Goop was simply tired and upset.

Tamuka felt quite adult, not only for realising what ailed Mr Goop, but also for being adult enough to put another's feelings above his own and take the best course of action to help. His mother poked her head in and smiled at them.

"Dinner on the table when you want it," she said and left them alone.

Tamuka had the notion that this was probably the last time he would be able to fit into the capsule with Mr Goop, so he decided to enjoy the moment a little longer, and right then he felt as if he would burst with his love for Mr Goop. And one day probably, he dreamily mused, so would his own child.

But perhaps sooner than that, Tamuka could ask to go to school without Mr Goop.

TREES OF BONE

DALISO CHAPONDA

Malawian Daliso Chaponda is a stand-up comedian as well as a writer, with shows such as *Feed This Black Man*, *Don't Let Them Deport Me*, and others performed in Canada, South Africa, and the UK. He was a Writers of the Future finalist in 2002 and has been short-listed for the Carl Brandon Society Parallax Award for the following story.

1

The sound of his bedroom door being opened woke Katulo. "What is it?"

"It's Chama, he's dying." Eyo's voice was an agitated whisper.

"Get the clinic ready."

Eyo hurried off and Katulo dressed. He snatched his walking stick and stepped into the humid night. This had been the hottest summer Burundi had seen since 2072. In the last two weeks, Katulo had treated a record number of patients for dehydration and *angazi* fever. As he walked, he tried to call up a mental image of Chama. He could vaguely recall a loud boy with mud-brown skin who had been terrified of syringes. Chama's father was the chief of the village police.

When Katulo neared the clinic, he heard shouting: "We can't wait for that stupid old man." He recognised the voice.

"Just wait. He's coming," Eyo replied firmly.

It made him proud that his apprentice was standing up to someone twice his size—especially a person as intimidating as Osati. Osati's nickname since his teens had been "the leopard". It suited him. He was tightly muscled, and his motions gave the impression he might lash out at any moment. Eyo, on the other hand, had a body that looked like a collection of twigs.

Osati swallowed his response when he saw Katulo enter.

The clinic was a circular hovel with little space. In the daytime, patients were received in the yard outside. Eyo and Osati stood between two unpolished wood cabinets and the sleeping cot. Lying on it, Chama's body looked like slaughtered game.

"Fill a basin with water," Katulo ordered. Eyo scrambled to do as he had been instructed. Katulo turned to Osati. "Bring me bandages and my operating kit. You remember the layout of the clinic?"

Osati nodded. He had been an apprentice five years earlier but had left prematurely. Katulo still felt anger at his decision. He had shown so much potential. His memory had been impeccable, and he had been able to make terrified patients relax with only a few words. He would have been a gifted healer.

Katulo worked intently for the next twenty minutes. He cleaned and sterilised the wound in Chama's side before stitching it closed. The boy's breathing went from shallow sporadic bursts to a smoother, though still uncertain, rhythm.

"Will he live?" Osati asked.

"Maybe, I have done all I can. How did this happen? This wound was not caused by an animal." It was a single, deep, horizontal slash. A machete?

"It was those Hutu bastards," Osati spat. "I swear by my ancestors they will pay for this."

The oath made Katulo flinch. "What happened?"

"They attacked us for no reason. We were at a rally in Bujumbura." It was because his passion lay in politics that Osati had left Katulo's tutelage. "Some Hutus were watching us and laughing. We ignored them. After the rally Chama, Dengo, and I were walking back here alone and they attacked us."

"Where is Dengo?"

"He is coming. I ran here carrying Chama. "

"You ran here all the way from Bujumbura?"

"We were about half way."

Still, that was a two-hour walk without carrying a wounded man in your arms. Katulo now noticed that Osati was covered in sweat and blood. His lips were parched and his breathing was irregular.

"Sit, I will bring you some mango juice."

"I have no time. The people of the village must be awoken."

"Why?"

"They nearly killed him. You said he may die."

"And rousing the village will do what? Impress the ancestors so much they will help Chama?"

"You joke about this?" Osati's disgust was unconcealed.

"If your friend lives it will be because of me. Do me a

favour in return. Let your anger cool. There is nothing you can say tonight that you can't say tomorrow. After the wedding..."

"After this, the wedding will be cancelled."

"Love is a good reason to postpone anger. The opposite is not true." His words were just aggravating Osati. "Please, hold off. After the wedding I will go to Bujumbura and speak to Minister Kalé. With his help we shall apprehend the ones who attacked you and deal with them. You, Dengo and Chama will all testify."

"Kalé is one of them; it's a waste of time."

"Kalé and I have been friends three times as long as you have been alive. Kalé is wise and his word is respected among the Hutus."

Osati dipped his head but he was clearly insincere.

Katulo sighed. "I'll tell you how he's doing at the wedding."

Osati left without a word of thanks.

"This is called an anaesthetic," Katulo said as he put the half-empty bottle back into his operating bag. "It dulls the body's responses to pain."

"You want to teach me now?" Eyo was flustered. He was looking out of the window.

"What better time is there to teach?"

Eyo pursed his lips. He shifted uncomfortably. "It... it's late. I'm tired."

"What is the truth?"

"I told you..."

"The truth might change my mind."

"I want to see what Osati does. I think he will wake up some people and they'll talk about this."

"I should have known. Learning is more important. Long ago healers used to have to rely on—"

"You can teach me any time."

As good as he had been at soothing people, Osati was better at working people up into a frenzy. Katulo didn't want Eyo to be exposed to that. He tried a different approach. "Have you ever seen a Waking?"

The question took Eyo by surprise. "No, of course not. I am not yet sixteen."

"I will let you go now, no teaching, and if you go straight to bed, then tomorrow, when all the other children are sent away, I will make sure you can stay and watch."

"Really?" The idea of watching a secret meeting paled in comparison to the chance to see a mystical ceremony.

"Do you promise?"

"I promise." Eyo's index finger mapped out a cross shape over his chest.

Katulo knew that Eyo had no idea what the origin of that gesture was. The worship of that tortured white saviour had faded from Burundi. "Good. You may leave."

Katulo continued cleaning up. He got out an old rag and mopped up the blood. When he was finished, he threw it and Chama's rent shirt into the dustbin. Finally, he blew out the gas lamp and returned to his house. It took a long time for him to get back to sleep. When he finally managed, he dreamt.

2

As with most young boys, obedience did not come naturally to Katulo. When his father had told him to stay behind with the women and other children, he immediately chose to do the opposite. He was too clever to be fooled by his father's placatory, "They need you to protect them." Katulo was fourteen, two years away from his initiation ceremony. He was too old to stay where it was safe. When he asked about the fighting, his father always told him, "You're too young to understand." This angered him. He knew this was about those Hutus. Fenke at school was a Hutu. He was stupid and Katulo knew it wasn't his fault. He couldn't be blamed for being born that way. The fighting is because the Hutus are stupid. What was so hard to understand about that?

When his father and the other men had left, Katulo sneaked

out of the village and followed them. He stayed distant enough that he was not seen. He was a good tracker. He shadowed them for over three hours until they reached a small primary school. Its faded sign depicted a laurel wreath wrapped around a shield and words that were too rain-washed to read. Katulo hid amongst some bushes and watched the adults go into the school.

Waiting was boring. This entire escapade had been far less exciting than Katulo had hoped.

He waited for twenty minutes, passing the time by counting how many bugs and birds he saw. He created an imaginary conflict—birds against bugs. Every bug he saw gave the bugs ten points and every bird he saw gave their side the same. A clumsy ladybird that had tumbled from a leaf had just put the bugs sixty points ahead when he heard a loud bang. He heard three more abrasive explosions and knew they were gunshots. His father and the others had probably been ambushed. Katulo ran forwards instinctively. He advanced with no thought for how he planned to defend his father. He just couldn't let it happen. When he reached the school, he pushed open a set of double doors and ran in. Inside, he heard terrible sounds.

The noise woke him up. This was the point where the nightmare usually ended. Sometimes it would be later. He had not had the dream in a long time, but Osati's rage had brought the memories back. *It was those Hutu bastards. I swear by my ancestors they will pay for this.* "It cannot happen again," Katulo said aloud. Afterwards, he was unsure whether he'd said this to reassure himself, or as a prayer.

3

Weddings in Azamé village were huge. Even poor families slaughtered at least two goats. The Gomozis were a wealthy family so the wedding was even grander. Celebration began at sun up and would keep going through the night. There was loud music, hot-blooded dancing, and the smell of roasting meats saturated the air. Freshly baked pastries and honey-dipped treats were pulled out of ovens and children's faces were soon coated in sticky syrup. There was much laughter and boisterous jesting. The most acclaimed storyteller in Burundi told a wild tale of Hyena the trickster. It had no moral; it was simply for enjoyment. The couple wore costumes that were dyed in multiple colours. Dozens of well-wishers surrounded them.

Normally, Katulo was in the midst of any celebration, pushing his antique body to the limit by asking pretty young girls to dance. If necessary, he would dance using his walking stick for balance. But today, even with all the pomp and energy, it was impossible for him to relax and enjoy himself. His mind was with the wounded youth in his clinic, and his eyes were drawn to things he would not normally have noticed. The Marulas, a family with Hutu blood, sat separately from the rest of the guests and nobody approached them to give greetings. Also, Osati, Dengo, and a group of their friends walked around pulling people aside and talking in whispers. After the whispers, nods of agreement would follow. Even people who usually had no time to listen to Osati's denunciations of the Hutus were moved by his words. Chama's injury had made his solicitations much more persuasive.

Katulo was tempted to leave but he was the last person in the village, in all Burundi, actually, who could perform the Waking ceremony. He had tried to teach many of his apprentices how to do it but had been unsuccessful. Even when his father had taught him, the skill was almost forgotten.

Eyo approached Katulo twice to make sure he would not change his mind about letting him watch. This, at least, amused Katulo. He had to admit that he drove Eyo harder than his previous apprentices. Katulo was increasingly aware that he did not have much longer to live. With his previous apprentices, he had stuck to teaching medicines and physiology, but there were other things Katulo wished to pass on. He had seen so many amazing things. He had been there when Burundi won the 10,000 metres in the Olympics, beating the Kenyans and Ethiopians. He had listened to Wana Maisu's final concert. He had survived two droughts and one epidemic. He had also seen Africa become fully independent as Europe and America were torn apart in a succession of wars. He had been part of the Second Revolution and treated President Peneka himself for gout. He had listened to the visionary president blabber to conceal his nervousness. There were so many memories, small things as well—some that he esteemed more than the things worthy of history books: how good it felt to run naked in the forest, the unique taste of roasted groundnuts when eaten after love making, the amazing things he'd learnt about his mother when she finally spoke to him as an equal.

Every morning, as he and Eyo ate breakfast, he would begin. He would tell the boy the history of Burundi, myths, proverbs, and stories. He told Eyo dirty jokes—oral tradition that would be a crime to forget—with the same passion that he taught the boy herbal remedies and anatomy. Eyo never complained. It was hard for him to absorb a lot of what Katulo taught, but he tried. He deserved the privilege of seeing a Waking ceremony.

After the wedding vows, the father of the bride called Katulo. The young boys and girls were taken away to eat boiled sweets and spiced cassava. "Not him," Katulo objected when they tried to take Eyo. He winked at his apprentice, which elicited a huge grin.

Katulo took out his ceremonial mask, put aside his walking staff, and walked unsteadily to the bride and groom. The mask was not actually needed for Waking, but it was tradition. The mask depicted a buffalo's head. The horns were brass and the face was carved out of wood. There were gaps for the eyes and the mouth. When he was standing a few steps in front of the married couple, Katulo spoke loudly. His voice was richer and more musical when he performed the role of Waker. "A river is a droplet of water; a mountain is a tiny pebble; and the two of you are all of Burundi. This union is not only between two people but between two souls and two families. Your love will forever change the community. It will enrich us when we are frightened, sustain us when we are lost, and our community will continue to grow. You will bring us the future but never forget that you are connected always to the past."

The bride and groom had been told what to do when he said these words. The groom cradled his new wife's head between his palms and leant forwards. Katulo lifted his arms in the air and opened his senses to their kiss. He let himself feel the moment. At the same time he thought of his marriage to Owuro when he was twenty-six. He let himself relive the rush of adrenaline and the tremble in his lips before he kissed her. He pictured Owuro's light olive skin and long braids. He thought of her crooked smile and mischievous eyes. He remembered the taste of her wedding kiss—light cinnamon and cloves. His flesh tingled. He felt the earth around him as if it were part of his body. He let his memories seep into the ground.

Between the wedding guests, wispy figures appeared. The mirages were all embracing and kissing. They were misty at first and then gradually became fully visible. There were twelve couples in total. Some were barefoot and almost naked, while others were adorned with tinted cloths, beads and bangles. Most of them were young but there was a grey-haired couple hugging each other near the bride and groom. It was not only images that were Wakened. The air was suddenly full with the sound of lovers' giggles and frenzied exhalations. Scents of perfume, coconut, and crushed flower petals tickled every nostril

One or two of the guests began to weep. Wakings were intense because everyone watching experienced a measure of the action. That is why young boys and girls were chased away.

Every guest, for a minute, felt the passion and desire of the distant past. Katulo's gaze focused on one couple. The woman was wearing an elaborate headdress that denoted her as a storyteller, and the young man with her had a proud, regal face and a thick moustache. It was strange to see the younger version of himself. No matter how many times he performed Wakings, it was the hardest part to get used to. His younger self was smirking with self-confidence. Owuro looked so young and so beautiful. Katulo wished he could step forwards and touch her. She looked so real.

And then, in a breath, she and the rest of the spectres were gone.

The father of the bride was the first to snap out of the silent awe that enshrouded everyone in the grove. He bowed deeply. "Thank you, Waker."

4

Katulo did not stay for the rest of the reception. He wanted to get to Bujumbura by nightfall. He said his good-byes and summoned Eyo. If the boy was disappointed at having to leave the festivities, it did not show. He obeyed immediately and a little nervously. He seemed frightened. At first Katulo was sure he was imagining it but, as they walked, Eyo continued to glance at him from time to time. He would look away whenever Katulo looked back. At first Katulo ignored it but, after they had been walking for an hour, he lost his patience. "I am the same person I was yesterday?"

"I know," was the timid reply.

"You are looking at me like I am not human."

"I'm sorry."

"I'm not angry with you, Eyo. What is on your mind?"

"Nothing"

Nothing? This from the boy who usually asked "why" with irritating consistency after every statement Katulo made. "If the

Waking is bothering you, you can ask me about it."

Eyo hesitated. Katulo did not insist. He waited.

"Th...Those were g...ghosts?"

"Yes," Katulo replied. "But they were not ghosts of dead people. They were ghosts of past moments. Everything is changed by the passage of time. When a river passes over rocks it wears them down in a unique pattern. A man who knows how to look can tell you many things about the river and the rocks because the mark they leave is unique. It is the same for actions. Everything we do changes the land. When we sang at the wedding, when we danced, even now as we walk, our steps are changing the earth. The land remembers."

"So they were not real ghosts?"

"They were echoes of the past."

"It was amazing."

Katulo smiled and then felt a tide of sadness. "Yes, it was. But I may be the last Waker in Burundi."

"How can that be?"

"Waking is not a skill that is easy to pass on. A person can only be taught to bring the past back to life if they can already feel the echoes left in the land."

"How did you learn?"

"I learnt in secret, back in the days of the white outsiders. Worse than the things they did to our governments were the things they did to our beliefs. They forced our people to worship their God and learn their ceremonies. They called our ways devilry and superstition. My father was a spirit speaker. There had once been many like him, but the white outsiders killed many of them. My father kept the old ways alive by hiding, and people would travel far to ask him for advice or to see him when they were sick. He taught me how to Wake and begged me to pass on the skill."

Shame threaded through Katulo. He and Owuro had never been able to have children and he had not remarried after she'd died. The failure of every apprentice he'd tried to teach Waking

to, made him suspect that sensitivity to the land was heredi-
tary. His determination not to betray Owuro's memory might
have doomed the ancient skill. So much of the old knowledge
was already gone. Most of the medicines Katulo used were
European, taken out of glass bottles and plastic vials instead of
the earth and trees. They were purchased in what little trade
still occurred between Burundi and Europe. The white outsiders no longer had concrete interests in Africa. They were too
busy rebuilding to care about much else.

Whatever nostalgia Katulo might have, he had to admit the
medicines they sent worked better than the saps and herbs his
father had taught him to use. His father had considered it a be-
trayal when he chose to learn white medicine, but he had
needed to make a living. The only way to get a job at hospitals
in Bujumbura had been with a degree in Western medicine. His
father had raged and called him a disgrace. Long ago, Katulo
had promised himself that when he had children, he would be
more understanding but the closest he had ever had to children
were his apprentices.

5

They arrived in Bujumbura in the early evening. It was still
hot but winds from the north brought temporary relief. The city
streets were full of filth and litter. Broken glass, crumpled papers, rotting food, and empty plastic bottles clogged the drain-
pipes. Every time Katulo visited the city it looked worse. Eyo
and Katulo passed many rickety beggars and malnourished
prostitutes. *Why do people want to live here?* Katulo pondered.
The answer was bright in Eyo's eyes. The boy was staring at the
buildings with delight. In his mind, he was surely concocting a
fantasy life in the city. The city had large stores with diverse
wares and water that sprang from taps at the turn of a knob—
much more enticing than dreary village life.

It had been a long time since Katulo had last seen Kalé.

They had become friends when Katulo had lived in the city, working for a private clinic. Back then, the wounds Burundi had suffered at the turn of the century seemed to have healed. Things had progressed to the point that a friendship between a Hutu and a Tutsi was no big thing. How had the old resentments come back? Was it because they were left alone and not consciously minded?

The central city was almost entirely populated by Hutus. The Tutsis lived in outlying ghettos. It had not always been that way. The Tutsis had once been the majority. Katulo still remembered the way to Kalé's home. They walked from the poor to the rich district. The buildings looked just as decayed and the streets were just as squalid. In some of the windows though, electric lights were on. They passed one house in which music was playing. To be able to use electricity for entertainment was an indicator of great wealth.

When they reached Kalé's home, a security guard told them, "The Minister is not here. He is at a party." The guard refused to give them directions but Katulo remembered the house that had been playing music. He backtracked with Eyo until they reached it. The door was open. They walked upstairs. The house was crammed with people. A servant handed them both bottles of beer. Eyo looked from the bottle in his hand to Katulo.

"It's all right. I won't tell anybody." Eyo smiled and took a big gulp. His face contorted at the bad taste.

"It gets better," Katulo assured him.

He looked around the room. It would be hard to find Kalé. He wove through the tightly packed group. At the end of the room he saw two young men who were seated at a table that seemed to be the epicentre of the celebration. One of them had probably got married, or maybe they had both won some sport? Faces Katulo could recognise surrounded them. He had seen them in newspapers though he wasn't sure of their names. Someone at that table would surely know where Kalé was. As he went to the table, Katulo realised he should probably congratulate the two youths being honoured. He stopped a staggering man with a pimpled nose. "What is this party for?" he asked.

The man laughed and Katulo inhaled the stench of beer. "You don't know, Old Father? Yesterday, some of those Tutsi animals were making trouble. Those boys there beat them down good. Made them run like the cowards they are."

Katulo suddenly could not breathe. The man was still talking but he could not hear it. Shock filled him with a sensation like panic. No. No. No. No. It couldn't be. Out of the corner of his eye Katulo saw someone approaching him. It was Kalé. He had a thick grey beard and the curls on his head were white. His facial expression was taut with urgency. "What are you doing here?"

Katulo could not answer. Eyo answered for him. "We came to see you."

"You can't be here. I'll talk to you outside." Kalé was a large-bodied man. What was once a boxer's frame of heavy muscle was now composed of layers of fat, but he still looked menacing. Once outside, Kalé instructed Eyo, "Wait here. We need to talk alone." He grabbed Katulo by the collar and dragged him into the darkness of an alley. "Do you know how foolish it was of you to come here? You know what might have happened if you were recognised?" Kalé paused. The concern gave way to a smirk. "Still, it's good to see you."

"What would have happened? Would I have been beaten for being a Tutsi, too?"

"I know you are angry, but that in there is just politics. The anti-Tutsi groups are very popular. Those boys are guests of honour and for show. They don't have any real power."

"They have to be punished." Katulo's voice had risen in volume. "That's why I came here. They nearly killed someone."

"Nonsense, it was just immature childishness."

"Right now he's in my clinic."

"I am sorry, Katulo."

"You should not be the one saying it. There is a lot of anger and it could escalate into disaster. Those two have to be put on trial."

"Impossible."

"Chama may die."

"I told you, it's political."

"They are savages."

"They did not start it. Those Tutsi boys were causing trouble."

"Those 'Tutsi' boys?"

Kalé looked down, embarrassed. "It's complicated. You live in the rural areas. It's simpler there. Here, there has been unrest. Tutsi labourers refusing to work, demonstrations, things like that. People are fed up."

"That gives them the right to assault people who are protesting peacefully?"

"Peacefully? They were throwing stones, breaking windows."

"Did they hurt anyone?"

"They could have."

"They will, Kalé."

"Is that a threat?"

"Think, Kalé. The ones from my village who were attacked are thinking 'revenge' now. They will do something, something very stupid, and they will make someone else start thinking revenge. It will keep going like that until it loses control."

"Then stop them."

"How? They were the ones attacked. It has to be those boys in there."

"Then we will leave it alone and hope it passes."

"How can you say that, Kalé? You and I are maybe the only people old enough to remember what it was like."

"This is nothing like that."

"Maybe it started like this and if people had just tried to take control of it..."

"You're just fantasising, Katulo. You were also a boy. You had no idea of the political and social forces that caused the fighting. You only saw the results. Burundi was a child then. We are older now and things will not lose control."

"Two boys who almost killed another are being congratulated instead of punished. I say it's already out of control."

Kalé was now visibly irate. "Look, I've already said..." He started to leave.

"Wait." Katulo placed his palm on Kalé's ribs. "I understand there are a lot of political things at work. You aren't in charge of the policies your party makes, but what if I could get the boys who were protesting to apologise? Could you get those boys, if not to stand trial, to at least apologise? That would not pacify everyone, but it might be enough."

Kalé thought for a moment. "I don't know."

"Can you at least try?"

"All right."

"Thank you."

The two old friends exited the alley and parted ways.

"Did it work?" Eyo asked.

"I don't know. We need to return home immediately."

"You said we would stay here tonight?"

"I thought we would, but not any more." Katulo remembered Kalé's words: You know what might have happened if you had been recognised?

"It is late," the boy pleaded.

"It took us five hours to get here. It's what, seven now. We can make it before midnight. If we get tired we can make camp on the way and walk the rest of the way tomorrow."

"Why can't we—"

"We have nowhere to stay."

6

In Siranja forest, Katulo saw Eyo was lagging behind. "All right, we'll stop here."

Relieved, Eyo let his pack drop to the floor.

Katulo began picking up fallen branches. "I'll get a fire started and set up camp."

"A fire?" The gaze Eyo gave Katulo was one that suspected

him of insanity. In the heat it was an understandable reaction.

"All I have is dried fruit. I thought you might try and catch some game."

Eyo agreed. "I am hungry."

"We should have taken food from that party before we left."

"Why do people like beer anyway?"

"You get used to it."

"Why would you do something so unpleasant over and over again until you got used to it?"

"Good question."

Eyo took out a hand spear and went off in search of game. Katulo set up the tent. He realised now that he had placed too much hope in Kalé. He had thought it would be so easy: Kalé would use his influence, the boys would be tried, and then everything would calm down. "Even an eighty-nine-year-old man can be naïve," he mumbled.

Eyo returned after half an hour. In his hands he carried a dead rabbit. He tossed it beside the fire Katulo had roused, and then sat. "There is something about this forest?"

"What do you mean?"

"The trees don't look right. They're so pale, thin, and tall. They seem like they are moving even when there is no wind. Also, when I was hunting, I felt something... I don't know... sort of... sad."

Katulo was instantly more attentive. "Are you sure?"

"Yes. What is it about this place?"

"There is a story that says that long ago when the gods still walked the earth there was a great divide between them. The gods split into two groups and fought a terrible war for a hundred years. The continents were torn apart. The war ended with a great battle right here. Thousands of gods were slain. After the battle, the blood and rotting flesh of the dead germinated the earth and trees sprouted that had trunks of bone."

"They do look like bones." Eyo reached out and touched the bark of one of the towering trees. "Do you believe the story?"

"All stories have some truth in them, but also some that is not true. You said you felt sadness?"

"It's less now that I've stopped hunting, but it's still there. I feel like I want to cry but I don't know why."

"I feel that, too, whenever I enter this forest."

"What does it mean?"

"Something terrible did happen in this forest once. I do not know whether it was between gods or between men but the land here is weeping. I told you that the land remembers everything. Something left a stain here."

Eyo nodded and quietly reached through his bundle. He took out a knife.

Katulo debated whether to say what was on his mind. Part of him told him not to hope—not to dare hope... "It means something that you can sense the sadness in the land."

"What?"

"Maybe you can learn to Wake?"

"Me?" Eyo's body was a string pulled taut.

"It is a small chance," Katulo said firmly. He did not want Eyo to get his hopes up.

"Can I try now?"

"No."

"What better time is there to learn?"

Katulo laughed. "All right, you can try, but do not expect anything."

"What do I do?"

"You were about to skin the rabbit. Go ahead."

Eyo's left eyebrow perked up.

"I am not trying to trick you. All Wakings need two things to make them happen. One is an action. The other is a memory. You cannot Wake anything you have not done. It is not enough just to have watched. I could not, for example, Wake a birth because I have never given birth. Do you remember the first time you skinned an animal?"

"Yes."

"Tell me about it. Tell me everything you remember."

"It was at my uncle's farm. It was just a chicken. My brother lopped off its head with a machete. I knew chickens did not die immediately but it was something else to see it. It wriggled and flapped its wings. Blood poured out of its head; it should have been red but I remember it being dark—nearly black—and smelly. I wanted to run away but my brother was watching. He wanted me to run so he could laugh at me..." Eyo broke off. "Oh, I just realised. I plucked the chicken; it's not like a rabbit."

"It's close enough. Think of as many details as you can about that chicken. Think of what the feathers felt like and how slippery the blood made your fingers. Remember what your saliva tasted like. Think of that moment as though you were reliving it, and as you do so, begin to skin the rabbit. It is hard to do, but to Wake, your mind must be totally in the past and totally in the present. The old memories in the land want to live again but you have to be a conduit."

It was hard for Katulo to try to describe what he did when Waking. So many things were happening in his body when he performed a ceremony that it was impossible to break them down. Katulo saw Eyo close his eyes in an effort to concentrate harder. "No. If you close your eyes you are blocking one of your senses and focusing too much on your memories. The present moment is just as important. You must see the rabbit in front of you and everything you are doing.

Eyo opened his eyes and the knife slit the rabbit's throat. He cut a line across its abdomen. Katulo watched intently, and he felt with his other senses. He felt in the land for any shift. *Of course it won't happen,* he warned himself. Eyo stuck his finger into the rabbit's lacerated belly and pulled, at the same time he pushed the blade right under the fur. Eyo continued through the motions of skinning and Katulo realised nothing was going to happen.

"It's..." he began but then stopped. He felt a slight shift. Nothing large, but for a moment he felt a burst of nausea.

Eyo stopped. "I guess I can't do it."

"You just did," Katulo said. He was winded.

"You don't have to say that."

"I'm not lying. You did it. I can't believe it."

"I didn't see a ghost."

"That comes much later. You Woke an echo of the revulsion either you or some other boy felt the first time that they skinned an animal. I could feel it." He was now shouting with joy. He embraced Eyo hard. He had passed on every other skill he knew in one form or other, but he had never been able to find an apprentice for the most valuable. He realised now just how much he had underestimated Eyo because he had not seemed naturally bright. It took him longer to grasp simple concepts than other apprentices. Katulo had tested each for their capacities to Wake but he had not even considered testing Eyo.

Katulo began planning to cancel all other instruction for Eyo. Every lesson would now be about Waking. The rest could wait. Tomorrow, they could... And then Katulo stopped dreaming. Tomorrow he had a more important task. Tomorrow he had to try and use reason to stop violence from returning to Burundi. Harsh memories slipped back into his conscious mind. *No,* he thought, reaching forwards and taking the now skinned and skewered rabbit from Eyo. He thrust it into the fire. There was a spark and a sizzle. Right now, he decided, he would just celebrate; he would laugh and eat well with Eyo. Let all the pain and tears come tomorrow.

7

When they got back to the village, the first thing Katulo did was check on Chama. He still was not conscious, but his breathing was easier. He let Eyo sleep—the boy had found it difficult to sleep in the forest—and went looking for Osati. He expected him to be at the market. It was the place where most people would be gathered on a Saturday morning. When he reached the market kiosks, his theory was confirmed.

Osati stood on a makeshift podium of six upturned crates. He shouted loudly and his arm gestures punctuated his every word. "Too long we have been pushed down," he yelled. There was a chorus of assent. Some listened to him as they shopped but most of the people stood still and listened closely. "Because of history we have stayed quiet. Over and over we are reminded of what our fathers did to their fathers as an excuse. They forget what their fathers did to ours. But why should I expect anything to be fair. That is childish of me. After all, there have been no free elections in twelve years. After all, the high positions of the government are all occupied by Hutus. After all, when there is a drought their families get relief while ours have to struggle.

"We have not always been weak and subjugated. We once had influence and Tutsi children could walk with pride. Our children..."

Osati continued on the theme of children for a few minutes and then ended by promising that a new future for Burundi could be shaped. There was clapping and chanting when he finished. Katulo had to admit Osati's words were stirring. Osati walked through the crowd shaking hands. People looked at him with the reverence they would give a prophet.

When Osati saw Katulo he smiled. "I would not have expected to see you here. You've never come to see me speak before."

"I didn't want to encourage you."

"You've finally given up hope that I'll give it all up and decide to be a healer?"

"Maybe."

"How is Chama?"

"He's recovering. Not conscious yet."

"I must apologise to you," there was a fervour in Osati's voice. "When I brought Chama to you, I was tired and angry. I did not treat you with respect."

"I understand."

"I have been angry with you for a long time. At the wedding, when you did the Waking, I realised part of me resented that you never could teach me that skill."

"I pushed you too hard."

"You were right when you said the wedding should go on," Osati admitted. "We needed that beauty in this time of struggle."

Katulo felt bothered by Osati's use of the word "struggle." His former apprentice fancied himself as a hero, leading Burundi boldly to a Third Revolution. "There are some things that I also have to admit you are right about," Katulo conceded. "There have been no elections, and the government is mostly Hutu. You are right that changes are needed, but this is not the right way."

"What way do you think this is?"

"Violence."

"Did you hear me say one word about violence?"

"You were throwing stones in the city."

"We hurt nobody. Chama is the one lying in your clinic."

"I went to see Minister Kalé."

"And what did he say?" Osati's voice was rich with contempt.

"He will get the boys who attacked you to apologise publicly, if you apologise publicly for the vandalism."

Osati laughed raucously.

"It would just be to calm things down."

"Things don't need to be calmed down. I can't believe you expected me to agree to this. Maybe if they are put on trial."

"Maybe later."

"Go away, Katulo. Stick to tending patients in your clinic."

Osati started to turn away.

"If you had only been alive during the massacres."

Osati whirled, filled with rage. "It always comes back to that with you old people. Oh, oh, our terrible past. Oh, the lives lost in the massacres. It's the past. What? We should be docile and let ourselves be ground under the boot of the Hutus because of a memory? "

"You can't know how bad it was. When I was fourteen I followed my father and some men to a school..."

51

"I mourn for all the dead but I am not dead. These people here are not dead. Right now, right here, we are being oppressed." A woman standing nearby clapped her hands at Osati's words. Osati turned and delivered her all his attention.

Katulo leant heavily on his walking stick. *What did I expect when I came here? That he would agree? No. I knew this is what would happen, but I had to try anyway.* Katulo walked away from the market slowly. His body felt more exhausted than it had in a long time.

8

When Katulo walked into the clinic, he knew with just one look at Chama. He walked forwards and pressed a finger against his pulse. It was as he had feared. Chama was dead.

How could it have happened? He had been recovering, but Katulo knew as he thought this that nothing was certain after a wound like Chama's. A sudden seizure or a spasm could change everything. *If I had only been here,* he cursed himself. *Why did I have to go to that bloody market? Maybe I could have...*

The thoughts faded away and Katulo let go of his walking staff. He crumpled to the floor. His eyes were focused on Chama's corpse. He knew what he was meant to do next. Contact the family, tell them what had happened, say those empty words of condolence, and then... what? Osati would find out. The rage of the villagers would be at a peak. And then... what? Suddenly, he was fourteen years old again, standing in the corridor of the primary school. He felt dizzy. He wished he could hide somewhere no-one could find him. If only he could disappear with Chama's body and if no-one knew, if it had never happened, if he went into a dark cave far away, if no-one ever found out, if he never told anyone, if maybe...

The door opened. "...I thought I heard you. I didn't know where you..." Eyo saw Katulo on the floor. He crouched beside him. "Are you all right? Did you fall?"

Katulo spoke slowly. "Go to the home of Chama's family. You must tell them..."

Eyo looked at the corpse. "When... How?"

"Go."

Eyo grabbed hold of Katulo's arms and tried to pull him up.

"Just go." He said the words harshly.

The wind blew the door shut after Eyo had left.

Katulo sat there for a long time. His only movement was the rise and fall of his chest. Inhale. Exhale. Inhale. Exhale. His mind was only partly in the clinic. The rest drifted into the past as it did when he was performing a Waking. His muscles sagged, pulling down his bones with their weight. Sweat made his clothes stick to him. His head spun. An hour passed.

The door flew open. Eyo ran in. He was gasping. "You have to come." He saw Katulo was still on the ground and his face filled with shock. He repeated himself. "You have to come. Osati was at Chama's father's house. When he found out, he started shouting and people came to listen. Then... They are going to Bujumbura."

Katulo was still not responding.

"Chama's father. He opened the police station. He gave them guns."

Katulo looked up now.

"They said they will take Chama's killers by force."

Katulo could see it as clearly as if it had already happened. There would be shouting and screaming. The police would be called. The mob would be angry, scared, and carrying guns. The police would be nervous, angry, and carrying guns. Someone would shoot first. It wouldn't matter which side. There would be a death, Hutu or Tutsi. And that would just be the beginning. It would begin in Bujumbura and spread to the rest of the country. Rage, beatings, killings, accusations, running, hiding, homes being burnt down... things that people swore would never happen again. And he could do nothing.

"You have to come," Eyo said for a third time. "Please."

And what can I do? Eyo was looking at him with so much hope. Eyo, who symbolised his own hopes to pass on the skill of Waking. "I will come," he said at last. His skills as a healer would be needed.

He got up. "How long ago did they go?"

"I ran here. They were on the way to the police station."

"We won't be able to catch them, but if we hurry, we will arrive in Bujumbura just after them."

Katulo wished there was a car they could take but the only car in the village had no gasoline. Burundi's petrol reserves had run dry over a decade ago. Katulo accepted Eyo's help to stand up. He and Eyo collected up his medical supplies and stuffed them into a leather bag. Katulo went to his house and packed the extra bandages he kept underneath a closet. Beside the boxes of medicines, he saw a machete. He used it occasionally to garden behind his house. It made him think of Chama's wound, the catalyst for the violence that was sure to happen later. He picked up the machete and stuffed it into the bag.

9

Osati and four hundred and seventeen men and women from Azamé village were shouting in Bujumbura's streets by the time Katulo and Eyo arrived. They were demanding the killers of Chama be brought in front of them. Twenty of them were carrying guns and the rest had rakes, machetes, spades, and broom handles. Osati was standing on top of a cart shouting, "We want them. Bring them out."

There were hundreds of other people there, too. "Go away, you Tutsi scum," Katulo heard someone shout. There was a group of Bujumbura citizens facing the villagers. Many of them were also carrying makeshift weapons. Osati tried to make his way through the entropy. His walking stick was knocked from under him. He started to fall but Eyo caught him and the wooden staff. They continued through.

A shrill whistle sounded. It announced the arrival of a third group. The police. They were wearing riot gear and holding up batons. A few were holding up guns. One of them spoke through a megaphone. "Go home, go home now."

The presence of the police added more volatility to the already tense masses. Unease rippled through the mob. Eyo shouted something but Katulo could not hear him through the din. Katulo saw a woman whose son he had treated for tonsillitis, crouch. She had two sons, a six-year-old and a ten-year-old. When she stood up, she was holding a stone. She flung it and it struck the side of a face. In response, a wooden pole rose and was brought down on the head of a Tutsi villager. Beside the man the pole had struck stood a man with a gun. He pointed it. The trigger was squeezed. The bullet tore through the shoulder of the man holding the pole.

Katulo reached into his medical bag. He had wished it would not be necessary but this was only the beginning of the bloodshed. Soon, people would begin to die. There was only one thing Katulo could do. His hand was trembling. He grabbed the hilt of the machete and he pulled it out. He opened himself to the land. He felt the streets around him and reached into them. He pulled out the past. In his mind, he was fourteen years old again, out of breath and desperately afraid his father was dead. He was sprinting down that school corridor again, with every step getting closer to those terrible sounds: shrieks and gurgles and wails. At the end of the corridor, opposite a sign that said "EMERGENCY EXIT", there was a half-open door. Katulo looked in and he saw a pile of bodies. They were tiny, frail children's bodies stacked up like bricks of flesh and bone. The children who were still alive were standing in a line and clutching each other. Katulo saw his father and the other men walking down the line. He saw his father push a uniform-clad six-year-old Hutu to the floor and swing his machete. He did not slash her only once. He lifted it again and then brought it down over and over again. Hacking.

55

The revulsion and confusion Katulo had felt returned to him. He had run away. He had hidden in the forest, wept alone, and then returned home before nightfall. He did not mention what he had seen. When he saw his father again, he hugged him and pretended he had not been there. He had never mentioned that day. He had decided never to let that memory control him but now he had to let it. It suffused him. But the memory was not enough. Katulo had never killed so the land could not Wake unless...

His fingers tensed against the machete's hilt and with an abrupt swipe he brought the blade down against Eyo's neck. He saw shock in Eyo's eyes for a split-second and then the blade crushed his apprentice's throat. Blood sprayed and dripped down the blade onto his clenched fingers.

All around Katulo, people gasped. Suddenly, smoky figures had appeared in their midst. Most Wakings called a few. Forty or fifty spirits was the most Katulo had seen at a Waking. But the streets of Bujumbura were deeply scarred. Wounds that had been closed and ignored for seven decades ripped open. Screams deafened Katulo and all around, echoes of viciousness were reanimated. Hundreds of spectral men appeared in the streets strangling each other, lashing bare backs with vine whips, stabbing, shooting, and rejoicing. Near one wall, a vague figure lifted a baby and smashed its head against the wall. On the floor in front of some Azamé villagers, a man in a soldier's uniform raped a woman with the sharp end of a kitchen knife. The living watched with horror.

The Waking was not restricted to the streets. Throughout Bujumbura men and women saw monstrosities. In a bar, laughing patrons were choked into silence when six figures materialised in front of them. Five of them stood around a single man and were beating him mercilessly. In one house, a couple's conversation was interrupted by the appearance of a man kneeling on the floor with his face in a mound of dung. Behind him, another man was laughing and pressing a gun against his temple.

There was a loud bang and the kneeling man died.

There was blood, so much blood. The living could smell it so strongly they could taste it. They felt the rage and desperate lust for revenge consuming the awakened spirits. Some of the living ran to escape the horrors they were witnessing, but in every street they ran into there was more. Old pain and old death celebrated at being rekindled. Forgotten cruelty ran rampant.

Katulo stood looking, not at the spirits around him, but at the broken body of Eyo. The corpse lay in front of him, eyes and mouth still open. His neck bone was exposed. Somewhere in Bujumbura, a group of terrified people watched an echo of Katulo's father murder fifteen schoolchildren. Katulo did not care about that memory any more. What he had done was the only thing in his mind. His body quaked and his voice cracked. He howled like an infant, hating every person in Bujumbura, but none as much as he loathed himself. The rampage of the spirits continued for an hour. Katulo was blind to them. When they finally disappeared, he, too, was gone.

10

The murderers of Chama were never punished. There was no trial, but there was also no slaughter. The Azamé villagers returned home.

Katulo was never seen again. Some said he had died but no body was found. At marriages, harvests, and initiations there was no longer a Waking ceremony. Waking was now a part of legend like rainmaking and giants.

If Katulo had lived on, it cannot have been for long. There were occasional rumours that he had been seen walking alone in the streets or by a river in ragged clothes. One of his ex-apprentices said that he had seen Katulo one morning, bent over the place where Eyo had died. He could not be sure. The old man he had seen rushed off. Where the old man had been, between gravel and weeds, a slender white sapling had been planted.

THE FIRST PERUVIAN IN SPACE

DANIEL SALVO
TRANSLATED BY JOSE B. ADOLPH

Peruvian Daniel Salvo is the creator of *Ciencia Ficción Perú*, a website devoted to science fiction. He is a writer and researcher in the field of fantasy and science fiction and has written the first survey of Peruvian SF. The following story appears in English for the first time.

Anatolio Pomahuanca had reason enough to hate whites. Hundreds of years ago they had invaded and conquered his world and reduced his forbearers to the sad condition of serfs or second-class citizens. There were historic changes like independence wars, rebellions, and revolutions. But, be it as it may, whites were still those who ruled and decided everything in Peru and throughout the rest of the world. "Now we live in a democracy, we have made great progress in human rights and integration," they proclaimed. Anatolio smiled crookedly every time he heard such used-up and false sayings. Weren't the president, the military and the priests white? Had anyone ever seen a native holding a decisive post? If he could, he would have spat on the floor. All whites were shit.

He couldn't spit because of where he was: a metallic, softly illuminated cubicle full of controls and screens. It was the command post of an orbiting spaceship. Like all spaceships, it belonged to the United Nations. Its mission was routine—to measure solar winds—but this time it had an additional element: Anatolio Pomahuanca, the first Peruvian in space.

Everybody considered his appointment to the ship's crew an honour; although he had no illusions. His tasks as maintenance engineer were like those of an attendant at a gas station. The ship, built with the best of the white's technology, was an enormous automatic mechanism destined to follow a precisely sequenced program of instructions. In truth, he and the rest of the crew were mere passengers. The navigation and registry instruments would do it all.

He yawned. His brief turn at the command bridge would soon be over. He had completed his assigned tasks. To check a screen, to verify a measurement, report some co-ordinates... all activities that led nowhere. *They have to keep me busy somehow,* he thought bitterly.

The captain of the ship and chief of the mission entered the cabin. He smiled winningly at Anatolio, who nodded. An indifferent expression on his face, he rose.

"Everything okay, Pomahuanca?" asked the captain in perfect Spanish.

Anatolio hated whites in general, but more so those who tried to win his confidence or his friendship. It was always easy to notice their intentions, the false mask of respect hiding the contempt whites felt or, even worse, their pity for Anatolio's race.

"Everything in order, captain."

"Up to now, you've done very well. It's a great opportunity for a young engineer to be a part of this mission. A lot of Peruvians would like to be in your place."

"Oh, yeah?" Anatolio knew the whites were incapable of catching the contempt in his words. He knew the whites really considered them an inferior race, a sort of animal that, in the past, was exploited without pity but now had to be better treated. But they would never accept them as equals.

"Of course, Pomahuanca. You have shown the ability of the true Peruvian man to take part in the exploration of space, to go upwards and always upwards, as Jorge Chávez, your aviation pioneer, said."

"What ability are you talking about, captain? Of the ability to work in a mine? Of the ability to push a plough? Of the ability to be a servant in the home of a white?" Anatolio, without meaning to, had ended up screaming the last few words.

The captain kept smiling. Anatolio sighed. In the past, when Anatolio had asked the same questions of other whites, there had been different reactions. Some left silently, others insulted him. Anatolio preferred the insults because they at least expressed what they felt. The captain belonged to the worst: those who believed there was already a harmonic conviviality between whites and natives as a result of centuries of history that had erased past wounds. In books and official speeches there was no more talk of invasion or conquest; now it was all about the meeting of two worlds or two cultures. He thought it incredible that the whites also believed their lies.

"There are—whites, as you call them—who also do jobs like those you described. Anyway, work dignifies us all."

"But we always get those jobs! Do you let us be presidents, ministers, or ambassadors?"

"Everything in its own time, Pomahuanca. I am sorry that things were different in our common past, and that we now have to carry that burden..."

"What burden do the whites carry? Is being entrepreneurs, big landowners, or generals a burden? To drive luxurious vehicles is a burden? To appear in the media? There are no changes, captain; we are still the conquered and you the conquerors."

"Then how do you explain your presence here, Pomahuanca? How do you explain your education, completely free, with the highest quality standards and in the best universities? Your healthcare? According to your logic, only the whites, as you call us, should be on this mission."

Anatolio Pomahuanca shook with anger and hatred. He closed his fists while, out of his mouth came the thoughts that had been growing in his mind ever since the mission had begun. They could do what they wanted afterwards, they could sanction him, degrade him; at least he'd had the pleasure of telling this captain what he really thought of the mission.

"Because I am an ornament! A symbol! Because you needed me in order to say you sent a Peruvian into space! So that everybody could believe that "harmonic conviviality" thing!"

The smile on the captain's face disappeared. His eyes became small decoloured slits, parallel to the lipless long hole that was his mouth. He furled his hearing appendages as he stepped to the command dashboard. Except for the blue crest his species displayed on the head, his scaled skin lacked any pigmentation. The few earthlings who had survived the wars of conquest of the invaders from space had been right in calling them whites.

"You can leave, Pomahuanca, Be ready for your second shift," said the captain, waving him off with his membranous hands.

Eyes in the Vastness of Forever

Gustavo Bondoni

Argentinean writer Gustavo Bondoni grew up in Buenos Aires and spent some of his formative years in the United States. His stories have appeared in *Jupiter SF*, the *StarShipSofa* podcast, *Expanded Horizons,* and elsewhere.

Every few moments, one of the lights would blink. It was for only an instant and almost unnoticeable because of their sheer number, but Joao De Menes was watching intently, defying the devil-eyes to come closer. If they did, he would show them the power of a Portuguese right arm.

Magalhaes had laughed at him, simply saying, "If you fear the Indians' camp-fires on the coast so much, perhaps you should take all the watches tonight," and had then ordered the anchor dropped.

The captain might be an arrogant fool, but Joao knew the truth: those eyes were watching and weighing, the eyes of hundreds upon hundreds of hungry demons, waiting for the foolish Europeans to sail their ship beyond the edge of the world.

He didn't know what lay beyond the end of the world. Some men told of a magic mist that you wandered around in forever, with no exit and no heaven, while demons feasted on your spirit. Others simply said you dropped off the edge of the planet, straight into the fires of hell. Still others spoke of eternal blackness, impossible torment.

Whichever was true, there were demons, and those demons possessed eyes that stared down at the ship malevolently from the cliffs that marked the edge of the world.

And every once in a while, one of them would blink.

DAWN BROKE LIGHTLESS AND DRIZZLING, but Magalhaes was adamant: a boat was lowered and a fearful crew selected. It was impossible to fault the captain's courage—he was the first to nominate himself—but easy enough to resent his cruelty. Of the ten men selected, five were the strongest on the *Trinidad*, while the other five were the most superstitious. Magalhaes was convinced that they could be cured of their foolishness by force, and exposure to the fact that what they believed to be demons were, in fact, just natural phenomena.

Predictably, De Menes was amongst them. He hadn't even

bothered to go to sleep following his watch because it was obvious that he would be on the boat. He boarded sullenly, ignoring the wind-driven spray. That wasn't what was bothering him; his concern lay in the fact that he had no inkling as to what devils might await them on the barren patch of rocky land ahead.

The place looked innocuous enough: an empty brown and grey shore with low cliffs broken by periodic inlets. But De Menes knew that daytime often found malignant forces dormant, waiting. They were still there, of course, but they wouldn't show themselves, just feel out the sailors and take them in the night when their power went unchallenged.

They landed without incident and Magalhaes led them a short distance inland and halted in front of a fire pit surrounded by the bones of a small animal. He pointed at it, looked straight into De Menes' eyes, and laughed. "Here are your demons, Joao. Hungry savages, from the look of it." Turning to the rest of the men, he said, "Be wary, they can't have gone far. This fire was burning an hour before dawn—I marked it especially."

The men shifted uncomfortably. All were well aware that being harpooned by seal-hunters who'd never seen a European before would only destroy the body, as opposed to the eternal ravages that falling into the clutches of a demon supposed, but it made no difference to them. Death was what they feared, and they would worry about their immortal eternities at a later time. They stood straighter, attentive to the approach of any savages.

The natives they'd encountered along the interminable coast they'd sailed down to get that far hadn't been particularly aggressive, but it was never advisable to let down the guard. Everyone who'd ever boarded a ship bound for spice or glory had heard the tales of fearsome ceremonies, strange rituals in pitch-coloured jungles and unholy banquets in which Europeans had been served as the main course.

They need not have worried, however. An hour after sunrise, a small group of natives approached them from behind an outcropping of rock. They walked slowly, their skin just slightly darker than the pale brown grass that their passage seemingly did nothing to disturb.

As they came nearer, the sailors could discern that every member of the group, composed of three women and two men, was as bare as the day they'd been born, their skin covered with some kind of thick grease or paste, a bright red colour. Presumably, this must have kept out the winds that, this far south, were cruel even in the spring—and would be deadly in winter.

The three women walked boldly to the group of Spanish and Portuguese mariners and spoke in their own language, a tongue that sounded harsh and hollow to De Menes, as desolate as the moaning of the ever-present wind. There was no threat in their gestures. The men were unarmed, and the spokeswomen seemed unsurprised to see them.

Magalhaes turned to Herrero, a Spaniard who could understand any tongue, no matter how uncivilised. Rumours, given strength by his dusky skin and quick temper, told that the interpreter's affinity for the tongues of the savages was due to him being half-savage himself. Others said it was a gift from the devil. However he'd come about it, though, the ability had proven both useful and profitable on the journey so far. "Stay ashore and learn their tongue. I will have the ship send you a boatload of supplies. De Menes and Carrizo will stay with you." Herrero nodded.

De Menes said nothing. He should have felt fury at the captain for belittling his beliefs once again, but there was no anger within his soul. He'd known what was coming, felt as though he was walking a predetermined path with an already decided ending, albeit one he could not see. All he saw when he thought about it was the greyness of impenetrable fog, an indeterminate future.

He simply walked behind Herrero as the linguist selected a campsite. This was not hard to do: the whole hillside was dotted with pits, each of which held the remains of a discarded campfire.

The rest of the morning passed peacefully. Herrero had

wandered off and was seated in the centre of a group of natives, gesturing, laughing, offering gifts of beads and other trinkets which seemed to go down very well with the natives. Soon, they were gesturing for Carrizo and De Menes to join them.

The two sailors did as they were told. De Menes sat down gingerly between a greying old man and a woman, who could not have been more than twenty, with jet-black hair. He tried to keep his eyes away from the exposed anatomy of the locals, but the circular seating arrangement made that difficult. Carrizo stared openly, but none of the women seemed to mind.

Herrero was already making progress with the language. Interspersed with the gesturing, there was now a word here, another word there, which seemed to please their hosts, who tried to correct his pronunciation and laughed at his efforts.

One woman, however, was paying no attention to Herrero. The girl De Menes had sat beside seemed to have eyes only for him and stared the entire time. At first, he thought it must simply have been the close-up view of his light skin and strange clothes, but he soon realised that the girl had not even glanced at the equally exotic figures of Carrizo and Herrero.

He smiled at her and placed one hand on his chest. "Joao," he whispered. Her dark eyes invited him to speculate about the rest of her, and he tried desperately to keep his own gaze locked on them while she spoke.

"Teuhuech," she replied, placing his hand on her own chest. He pulled it back quickly as she said something else, a rapid-fire string of words in her own language, delivered in a husky monotone. The man on De Menes' opposite side chuckled.

At that moment, a couple of men from the *Trinidad* arrived, carrying sacks of provisions. "Your tent is down in the boat. If you want to sleep under cover, I'd suggest you get it. We aren't coming back up here."

Grumbling, but relieved to be able to escape from the strange natives for a few moments, Carrizo and De Menes walked down the hill. Herrero, of course, was much too important to be bothered with menial tasks. They joked with the oarsmen as they pulled the poles from the boat. "Magalhaes says we'll be back tomorrow or the next day. He wants to sail beyond that outcropping—" the man pointed to a peninsula some leagues away "—to see whether we can replenish our water."

De Menes' heart sank. They would be alone, without even the comforting sight of the flotilla to keep him sane, on a small spit of land at the edge of the world. But he would not give the tyrant the satisfaction of begging to be allowed back on board. He gestured Carrizo to pick up his half of the burden and set off towards the campsite.

The wind, already a desolate howl, had picked up even more as they began to pitch the tent. By De Menes' reckoning, it was about three in the afternoon, and there were still hours and hours of late spring sunlight remaining. And yet the sunlight seemed weak, thin, as if its force was being drained by invisible fog. De Menes shivered.

The girl, Teuhuech, realised he was back almost immediately, and joined them just as Joao attempted to position the final tent pole. He watched her walk in their direction, unable to ignore the fact that there was a young and supple body beneath the red paint.

She playfully took hold of the tent pole, her surprisingly strong grip resisting his efforts to tear it from her grasp, and his attempts to twist the pole without making contact with her skin only made the native girl laugh.

Finally, she relented, allowing De Menes and Carrizo to finish erecting their tent, a medium-sized piece of canvas suitable for three men. When it was done, she smiled and crawled inside. De Menes tried to look away, but Carrizo had no such qualms. He stared at the indecently exposed flesh and then turned to his companion and winked lewdly. "I would go in after her, my friend, but I don't think that would make her happy. You, on the other hand, should hurry before she changes her mind."

De Menes gave him a dark look. While he wasn't a saint, by any means, and certainly wasn't averse to the occasional dalliance with a native girl, this one's single-minded determination made him nervous. It was impossible to shake the feeling that there was something deep and disturbing lurking just behind those smiles. Maybe it was just his dread at having been abandoned by his ship at the edge of the world with nightfall approaching fast. But he felt his soul and his immortal existence were at the mercy of forces no mortal could ever hope to control.

He shook his head and returned to the circle where Herrero was still holding court. The Spaniard complemented his limited—yet still impressive, considering how little time he'd taken to create it—vocabulary with wild gestures and vocal sound effects. His audience sat in rapt attention.

"I'm telling them the story of our Atlantic crossing," he explained. "Although they seem to believe that we're sorcerers from the sky, because they saw the sails of our ship, and think it looks like a bird."

De Menes nodded and sat on the cool ground, squeezing between two of the local men who'd arrived in their absence. The red paint did little to cover them, either, but it was still less distracting than having Tehuech beside him. As the story went on, more men arrived, none aggressive, all painted red. The girl, disappointment evident on her face as she saw his new seating arrangements, sat straight ahead of him.

The long afternoon's anaemic light soon gave way to an eternal twilight, and the men began to drift to the nearby fire pits. Soon, the demonic eyes once more lit the hills, but this time De Menes sat amongst them. He wondered what else walked the night, connecting the dots between the warmth and light.

The sailors were left to their own devices as night came down and the last vestiges of the day's warmth and cheer were swept away before the howling wind. De Menes had difficulty believing that the savages could bear the chill without clothes, and found himself wondering whether they insisted in that same lunacy during the winters, which he imagined must be merciless in those latitudes.

Their own fire was an unimpressive affair, built close to the tent and casting a small ring of light from which De Menes refused to venture even to relieve himself. He could feel the demon lords watching them from the darkness, present in every shadow and trying to find the doorway that led from their own grey and boundless kingdom into the world of the living.

Knowing sleep would be beyond him, he'd offered to stand guard. So he sat with his eyes open long after Carrizo and Herrero had drifted into snoring slumber. He cringed at each sound, ready to defend himself, but, when the demon crawled into his tent and took his hand, he could do nothing but follow it out.

It led him endlessly across the stiff grass to the embers of another of the bonfires. By its light, De Menes saw that no demon held his hand, but that Tehuech had brought him there. He knew exactly why. She was still naked, but she'd also scraped off the paint.

He pulled his hand away, trying to remember the way back to his own fire and the security of the tent, but fear had made him an unthinking being, a sheep led to slaughter. He turned back to the girl, and a movement above her breasts told him that she wasn't completely bare. A necklace of stone and shells and driftwood danced above her breasts.

Seeing where his gaze lay, she smiled. "Joao," she said. She removed the necklace and held it towards him with both hands, saying something incomprehensible, and then "Joao," again.

He shrugged and bowed, allowing her to pass the offering over his head. It caught on one ear, but was soon in place around his neck.

"Thank you," he said, and she smiled back, understanding the meaning, if not the words.

Joao felt more relaxed. Having accepted her gift, he felt that it would be all right to return to his camp. He turned away from the fire, the afterimage of the embers dancing in his eyes.

He waited for them to subside, for his night vision to return.

But, instead of disappearing, the moving lights came into sharper focus, resolving themselves into points of light just beyond the ember's illumination. Eyes that stared unblinkingly back at him, seemingly an arm's-length away. De Menes recoiled from those eyes, his steps taking him straight into Tehuech's waiting embrace.

He knew the fire was all that kept them away, and that the girl was all that kept the fire alive, and that the creatures of the netherworld were not there to interfere, but to bear witness to a consummation.

THE FOLLOWING DAY DAWNED BRIGHT and clear; memories of the previous night burnt away, but De Menes was still surprised to wake inside the tent. He had no recollection of having returned, and his memory of the rest was blurred as if veiled in grey fog. But it had not been a dream: the clicking of his new necklace as he crawled out of the tent assured him of it.

"Come on, sleepyhead," Carrizo chided. "The sun's been up for an hour, and Magalhaes is back. He found some more savages a little further west, and they seem a bit more advanced than these. We have to pull up the tent and return to shore."

The manual labour allowed De Menes to temporarily forget about midnight rendezvous and ghostly eyes and, as he approached the sea and its waiting boat, he felt an enormous weight lifting from him. Each step felt lighter than the last.

A small party awaited, natives mixed with sailors. The savages even helped to load the boat, only asking a few trinkets and some cloth in return for their unnecessary help, which were given gladly—too often, the sailors had had to fight natives who took a dim view of outsiders. Tehuech, amongst the local group, said nothing and kept her gaze on the ground.

Finally, as De Menes was about to step aboard, one of the older women came forward, and said something to Herrero.

Herrero listened, and turned to Joao. "I'm not really sure what she said, but I think it was, 'That man wears a wedding circle,' and she pointed at you. Do you know what she's talking about?"

De Menes hung his head. "I think I do." He pulled the necklace back over his head and walked to where Tehuech was standing, heart heavy with dread and remorse. He held the jewellery out to her, but she made no move to take it and refused to meet his gaze, eyes resolutely turned away. Finally, he left it at her feet and stepped back. Still, she gave no sign of acknowledgement.

Joao walked back to the shore and boarded the boat. None of the savages made any move to stop them.

AS THE *TRINIDAD* LEFT THE hills with eyes far behind, the crew began to taunt De Menes, asking what had happened, and attempting to get the details of what they imagined must have been one of the more sordid escapades of the journey. But he refused to elaborate and the speculation soon passed into the realm of wild orgies and fantastic pleasures.

De Menes heard none of it. The lewd shouting seemed to him a far-off whisper. As the ship advanced, it grew fainter and fainter.

Even the ship itself seemed to be fading. It had sailed into a fog which became thicker as they sailed through it. The *Trinidad*'s prow became a ghost of itself, and soon, even the mainmast, scant metres away, seemed a spectre.

A small tremor of panic coursed through him as he realised that the deck beneath him was no longer solid, but made of ethereal mist, but he simply shrugged it off. Understanding had replaced fear, and a broken trust was suitably punished. Perhaps the endless, featureless grey at the end of the world would not be as bad as the visions of fire and torment that the hell of his own land promised.

And perhaps, just perhaps, he would be called upon to bear witness in some distant future, thereby remembering what it was like to tread upon the grass at the end of the world, and share the love of one of its guardians.

THE TOMB

CHEN QIUFAN
TRANSLATED BY THE AUTHOR

Chinese writer Chen Qiufan is a graduate of Peking University and a prolific short story writer. He is the author of the novel *The Abyss of Vision*, and winner of, amongst others, the Dragon Award. The following story appears here in English for the first time.

This is the entrance; and the exit, of course.

The dim blue light slid across the cold, wet, rocky ceiling and faded into the deep darkness. Between the indistinct here-and-there stood a mouldy wooden counter, the type found in an old-school by-the-hour hotel, with the bell, the chair, the registry, and the man.

A hand as skinny as an insect was wiping the metal plate with a black cloth clipped between the fingers. The man, hidden in the blue shadow, breathed upon the plate once in a while till the engraved words shone:

"That seeing they may see, and not perceive."

"DING." THE BELL QUIVERED ON the counter. The face lifted immediately—the fine wrinkles bathed in the blue light—and gathered into a smile. "Hello, sir. My name is Chen, code V0817. A pleasure to serve you. Are you passing by or assigned here, please?" He straightened his legs, his back slightly bowed and his hands curled on his breast, rubbing against each other and jerking like a pair of mating arthropods.

No answer.

"Hmmm, confidential? No problem. Please register." He opened a purple book and drew out a rusted pen. The edges of the blue pages had grown black.

Again, no answer.

"Want to look around? Okay. Let me introduce some lovely neighbours to you." Calmly, he closed the book with a loud snap, removed the keys from the wall and staggered into the darkness while holding onto the rock wall.

"You liked the words on the plate. Well, that's from the Gospel of Mark, chapter 4, verse 12. No, no, I'm not a Christian. Religion no longer matters if you are already in hell. You said you call this place 'Alice's Rabbit Hole'?"

Chen was deep in thought, his skinny fingers scratching a few scraggly lines into the wall like a long musical score without any notes. *Must've been from section B.*

The British are the only ones into such silly fairy tales. The Greeks called it "The Prison of Hades," Argentineans, "The Library of Babel," and Americans, "Zion," which is Biblical, but more likely they took the name out of movies. With all these names, all of them mourned the past glories of their civilisations.

Only the Chinese did not.

Against their five thousands years of tradition, the Chinese showed amazing courage and candour this time.

They named this world—"The Tomb."

I've lived in The Tomb for ten years, twenty, or perhaps longer?

THE SLIDING FINGERS WERE STOPPED by a bulge on the wall. He came back to his senses, stopped, and showed a pleasant smile.

"Sir, this is our Room 1, the magic hut of Mrs Shi." His hand was poised to knock, but he thought it over, put his hand down, and pulled out a key. "Shhhh... I think we'd better just take a peek instead of frightening her."

"You know, the people here on the outskirts of section V have all been assigned here because the old level could no longer hold so many..." Hmm, what's the word? The critically ill? The diseased? But Mrs Shi never considered herself ill. She's just living in a spiritual world.

How fantastic that experience is: the teapot tilts to pour not water but an arc of whiteness; everyone's playing the puppet game; all she can see are mechanical poses and expressions, then it all disappears, or else the eye sees through walls, furniture, or bodies and pauses at another corner. The world is like a badly degraded copy with too many dropped frames, its beauty only glimpsed in jerky, broken bursts. Chen licked his lips.

"Multiple regions in Mrs Shi's lateral cortex were 'filtered,' so she can't perceive moving objects. Bodies and objects flit into her vision like ghosts. It was very difficult at first; her screams almost became our time piece. Heh-heh."

Wheresoever is physical phenomenon, there is delusion; but whosoever perceives that all phenomena are in fact no-characteristics, perceives the Tathagata.

"She considered this her sin and kept praying to the Buddha for relief."

When all phenomena became no-characteristics all of a sudden, the human race wasn't ready. When the Tathagata was perceived, thus came one. How ironic.

He sighed. *When was it? Ten years ago, twenty, or longer? Was it war? An unidentified virus? Or divine retribution? Forgotten, all forgotten.*

All we knew was that the visual cortex regions of the brain were severely damaged, a phenomenon known as "Filtration". In the post-Filtration world, one-third of the population died of brain damage; one-third became insane and committed suicide; only less than one-third survived and eked out a living on the ground, immersed in toxins and radiation. To protect themselves, the survivors built huge burrows and lived off underground water and food reserves. Several small wars followed as people competed for resources before the synthesiser was invented. Thereafter, the burrows were expanded, networked together, until even the continental networks were connected. Social and economic systems were re-established, and the Cult of Satan spread and extended into the arts.

Chen closed the door quietly. "She's searching for peace in the darkness, like everyone else." His fingers resumed the progress to the next door. He looked at the visitor, *Hmmm, an ordinary grey suit, an ordinary pale face, what kind of filter does he have?*

EACH VICTIM HAD HIS OWN filter. No-one realised this frightening fact until five years after the Filtration. It was discovered at the end of 20th century that "vision" is a brain process involving the active interpretation of stimuli from the environment. There was no noticeable gap in our visual field despite the existence of the scotoma on the retina, a region with no photoreceptors. The visual system interpolated and filled up the blind spot through a precise and complicated process, and created the illusion of "reality". In other words, what you see is not what you get. Filtration selectively destroyed the brain regions responsible for the formation of vision such that the world through filtered eyes was significantly altered, not unlike the filters used in photography, and thus the symptoms were named "filters" as well.

Room 2. "Mr Wei's luckier than the others." He knocked, but the door creaked and swung itself open. "Wei, this is our new neighbour. Come on, shake hands with him. Right, you'll take care of each other."

He waved and closed the door with a click.

"Wei is a blindsighter. Large areas of his V1 visual cortex were destroyed. The prevalence of that is 0.03 percent. Did you notice that he gripped your hand immediately when I told him to shake hands with you, and that his blink reflex was intact when I waved? But he thinks he's blind. People with these symptoms can perceive light, shape, and simple movements and react accordingly, but they resolutely deny that they can see."

Useless trash gets special privileges, what a world...

He let out a sly grin. "Aren't the blind luckier than the seeing, here?"

"Why do I know so much? Ho-ho, didn't they tell you where this is?" Chen stopped at another door. "Not your fault. It was a long time ago."

"Mr Wang must be sleeping. He usually stays up all night working. But you can check out his works." He opened the door softly. A rotten stench filled the air. "Oh, the sun is gone, but time continues."

In the dim light, broken chunks of plaster were scattered around the room, their phosphorescence like bones in a graveyard. Inspected closely, these were fragments of female bodies, plump breasts next to slim calves, chubby hips connected directly to pretty heads. Quite a terrifying sight. The only thing the pieces had in common was a lack of proportion and symmetry, like failed genetic experiments that had been abandoned.

"Mr Wang used to be a sculptor, you know, before. His filter is 'planarity'. The world is two-dimensional in his eyes. Even an elephant looks like a piece of paper. And objects can only be identified from certain specific angles; that is, he can't distinguish a disc and a sphere from above."

Chen stepped on the white splinters. The snaps and crackles, like breaking bones, haunted this room day in and day out. Mr Wang's hope, modelled with those distorted Venuses and Aphrodites, was smashed along with them, as well. A lone easel stood in the corner. Chen touched the panel and wiped away the thick layer of dust, revealing a sketch of the face of a middle-aged man. The proportion and expression were both surprisingly accurate, despite empty spaces where the irises and pupils should have been. Like a soulless stone face.

"The beauty in his eyes has already been filtered. This sketch was a requiem for himself."

Chen stared at the sketch thoughtfully. When he discussed the painting, Mr Wang's tone, like that of a deserted wife, gave him a headache, but that face... The fingers ran over the high forehead, along the brow bone, across the tall nose ridge, and fell into the deep philtrum and the pair of bow-shaped lips, and then held the full chin. He sighed. It had been almost unbearable.

He rubbed his fingers, and looked at the visitor again. *Hmmm, an ordinary black suit, an ordinary yellow face, what kind of filter did he have?*

"THIS IS THE HOME OF THE obsessed. They were either infatuated with the filtered world, or denied the existence of the Filtration. While others re-adapted to the world with the assistance of rectifiers, they were sent to this, ho-ho, Shangri-La, for the peace of their heart."

Chen flung his head back towards the rocky ceiling as if he could look through the layers of infinitely dark rock to see the vast underground world, complex like neural networks. On those prosperous new floors, humankind was attempting to modify itself. Fresh flowers would bloom on the summit of the evolutionary tree, to wither or to fruit?

What about us? Are we left to ourselves, in this crack of Hell, to live or die in due course?

No. "I am their watcher. I will lead them back to light." He sounded resolute, full of sanctity and pride.

But, but what kind of filter do you have, indeed? Chen's hands twisted together, rubbing and writhing.

He hurried his steps, scraping one door after another, his fingernails screeching along the wall.

"Miss Ji in Room 5, the 'stranger' filter. She lost the ability to recognise faces and lives in a world of strangers. Everyday, after waking up, she spends half a day habituating herself to the new weeping face in the mirror...

"Mr Lv in Room 7, hippocampus and adjacent cortex damaged. His short-term memory lasts for 1 minute and 23 seconds only, so his life is sliced into episodes each lasting 1 minute and 23 seconds, just like the name of his filter—'debris'..."

All those familiar feelings flashed through his memory, various misfortunes, the same destiny, the past filtered to nothing, patched and woven together again this day. *Just like me...*

No, I'm different. Chen shook his head, hard, and strode forwards. *I am their watcher.*

FINALLY, AT THE END OF the cave, a grand door blocked the way, with a small 'c' etched on it.

"I'm sure you've found that the cave dead-ends here. I dug every single one of these rooms with my own hands and left the last one for myself. I can see all the doors, watch all the people, all..."

The rapturous hands paused in the air like a conductor pausing at a rest. His mind slipped again, remembering a proverb: Man turned into an animal, digging one exit after another in the burrow to protect itself, but he can never walk out of the burrow. That's from Austria, a dead country.

But why should I walk out?

"Don't you want to come in?" He put on his routine smile again. The door banged open, deep darkness soaking everything except the faint fluorescence on the ceiling. "I'll show you my private collection."

He danced on, light-footed, sliding and swirling in the dark room, his voice flying like a moth.

"Do you know the 'dark burrow' filter? This name actually originated from Anton's blindness, and the symptoms are very similar: blind without realising the blindness." He paused for a moment. "I was like that, living in my fictional world, even the rectifiers couldn't help me..."

Great Anton, no, the Sovereign Dark Pope, grant us lightness and hope, the sacrifice of the black mass will be offered immediately.

In the blue fluorescence, by the line of dome-shaped containers, his form fluttered about, and his hands kept on stroking the glossy domes.

"Are you feeling dizzy and weak? Ah-ha, it's suppressing your neural transmission. Soon, soon it'll be all right.

"Soon..." He fished about for something with great effort. With a crack, a strong electric arc flashed behind Chen, revealing a strange machine: two long thin tentacles stretched out from a jumbo-sized fruit blender, wriggling like snakes.

"You know, when I was assigned here, I tried to communicate with them, learning to match the hallucinations in the brain with the reality, but I failed, and I almost broke down from the failure." Chen began to hyperventilate, huffing like the bellows of a broken organ, his breaths imbued both with nervousness and excitement. "Man is too self-centred, too attracted by the present, the past, the undamaged world, even if it is just an illusion. But I couldn't. I needed release. Finally, the forbidden Society of Compound Eyes opened up to me. You must have heard about it, yes, the so-called 'evil cult.' That, that is all true..."

Chen's breath came even faster, breaking up his sentences.

Oh, the Society of Compound Eyes, the loneliest child of the dark Church of Satan, but also the one with the mightiest dark power. We, the three million 'dark burrow' filter owners, were called to serve the sole truth: only with compound eyes will we see again. Each compound eye needs many ommatidia, each ommatidium needs...

Another blue-white electric arc flashed through; the collections in the dome-shaped containers glittered: the twists and turns of the gyrus, the creamy sleek texture, and the deep fissure running through the centre.

All human brains, like plump, translucent fruits.

The damaged brains with their individual symptoms are the ommatidia. The dark science of the Society of Compound Eyes enabled those with the 'dark burrow' filter to wear these ommatidia, even though they were still seeing only a distorted world. But just as one can piece together a complete dollar bill from many bills damaged in different ways, when the number of ommatidia reached the threshold for a full compound eye, the 'dark-burrow' sufferers would see the light again. So, in all the rumours, they were called...

"Ho-ho! I am the so-called Filter Collector." Chen howled with laughter, grabbed the two tentacles on the machine, and stabbed forwards violently. Brilliant sparks burst at the end of the tentacles, lighting up Chen's face. On his face, where the eyes should have been, there were two deep, dark holes, all the more ferocious on his twisted face.

The air smelt of ozone. Chen grabbed in front of himself with his hands. Nothing but air.

"Stop!" He rushed out, running in the deep tunnels, stumbling. The scenes in front of him started to flutter and blink as though he were wearing the filters of his tenants again. The escaping human form suddenly became himself, then a stranger, and then swiftly faded away like a ghost. The cave walls started to flow, forming a shimmering picture. He ran with all his strength in front of the picture but could not advance a step. His shivering legs finally dragged him to the ground, where his body, devoid of all strength, collapsed, just like the dying Mrs Shi, Wei, Mr Wang... All those tenants who had gone missing one after another, with just their naked brains remaining in this world. Only the useless Wei died intact.

He kept on chasing.

ON THE BLUISH GROUND, THE waving shadows and the hurried steps chased each other, fighting, intertwining, and finally tangling into a shapeless mess.

Chen fell down with a thump, two bottomless eye sockets staring at the counter and beyond.

"I just wanted to try your filter! I just wanted—" he sobbed. "—to see, see the real world. I can see nothing but this..."

His sobbing bounced back and forth in the cave, pounding on the doors of the empty rooms. It seemed as if no-one had ever come, and no-one had ever left. A tomb of his own.

The voice died out far away. That's the entrance, but not the exit.

Author's Notes:

[1] *Tathagata:* see *The Diamond Sutra, Section V, understanding the ultimate principle of reality.*

[2] Cult of Satan: Satanism first emerged in the 12th century. The main ceremony is called the Black Mass.

[3] Blink reflex: an involuntary defensive neural reflex to protect the eyes.

[4] The Burrow: Adapted from Franz Kafka, *Der Bau (The Burrow).*

[5] Anton's Blindness: Also known as Anton's syndrome or Anton-Babinski syndrome, discovered by Gabriel Anton in 1899. Patients who suffer from it are completely blind but deny that fact, and often experience hallucinations.

[6] Anton Szandor Lavey: founded the Church of Satan in San Francisco on April 30, 1966, one of the most important branches of Satanism.

THE SOUND OF BREAKING GLASS

JOYCE CHNG

Singaporean writer Joyce Chng is the author of online serials *Oysters, Pearls and Magic,* and *The Basics Of Flight*. Her novel *A Wolf at the Door*, featuring werewolves in Singapore, is published by Lyrical Press.

NOW

Well, this is it.

I see. It looks old. Sure it's the right place?

I double-checked. Unit 1-10.

Wonder if he's in or not.

Nobody's answering the door.

Is he seriously crazy? A bit *siao*. I mean, all the junk outside. Some of it is positively ancient. A fire hazard, definitely. All the newspapers are yellow!

He's just a little eccentric, that's all. I mean, he's harmless.

The neighbours say that they keep hearing the sound of breaking glass at night. That's why they called us, right? They don't want people to get hurt. He's obviously a hoarder. Not sure if he's violent—

The neighbours also say that he likes hanging wind chimes made of glass bits on the black wattle trees outside the apartment block. Colourful glass bits, mind you, made of broken glass bottles and fishing string.

Okay, the door is slightly open. Want to go in? We are volunteers, right?

Ladies first.

It's so dark and musty. And what's that? Wait. Glass bottles. Look, Cedric, just look at all these glass bottles. Different colours. Green, blue, red, transparent. He must have collected them from the coffee shops and the dumpsters. So many bottles.

Ouch! There are glass shards all over the floor! Oh, wow. He really polishes them, doesn't he? All the sharp edges gone. So smooth, like pebbles.

He must have been a glass smith or something when he was a young man. Just look at these wind chimes. They glow in the light. Peridot-green, sea-blue, ruby-red. And the music they make. Magical.

One of the neighbours told me he hangs them out to entertain the fairies. Or spirits. Either way. Really weird stuff.

They are just wind chimes, Cedric. Very charming. I mean, he's obviously talented. Why doesn't he sell them or something? Why does he want to remain a karang guni man?

Maybe he just wants to remain a rag-and-bone man to collect weird things and entertain fairies as a hobby?

Cedric, you are so—Wait, I see something. Oh, God, Cedric, come over here. You have to see this.

Shit. I think he must have been dead for at least a day. I'm going to call the police.

I think he tripped, Cedric, and couldn't get up. There is dried blood on the floor. Head injury. Oh, God, this is so—

Calm down, Ling. I called the police. They should be here in about five minutes. They're bringing the ambulance, too.

It's already too late, Cedric. Too late.

OUTSIDE THE UNIT, THE WIND chimes stir in the breeze, twinkling in the twilight, inviting the fairies and other spirits to sing with them.

The music the chimes make is not the sound of breaking glass, but a gentle tinkle, almost like laughter born of a light heart freed from sorrow and bleeding hands.

THEN

He found the fairy tangled up in wire netting designed to trap birds.

It was a quiet afternoon, warm because it was the hot dry season, and quiet because he lived in an apartment block filled mostly with men and women of the same old age as him. The sunlight was an uncomfortably-bright orange, coating the brick walls with a golden glaze. The trees rustled—fruit trees: starfruit, belimbing, and jambu. He knew it was warm, because even the mynahs that feasted on both ripe and unripe bounty were conspicuously absent.

He was coming back from the neighbourhood coffee shop,

carrying his load of used aluminium cans and glass bottles. He had not been working for a long time now, preferring instead to collect newspapers, cans and bottles, all the disposable detritus of modern-day living in Singapore, in order to supplement his meagre income. He received about fifty dollars per month from all the collected objects, enough to buy himself simple daily essentials. The volunteers from the Moral Home Society would bring him food in the form of Khong Quan biscuits, Milo, and instant noodles. Sometimes, the good-hearted Malay lady who fed the stray cats would bring him vegetables and fruit.

Lugging his full bag of cans and bottles, he made his way to his unit. It was a small abode, filled with stacks of newspapers and used appliances, not yet exchanged with the companies who made money taking in recyclables. He had decided to live here, ever since his wife had passed away and he chose not to live in an old folks' home. He did not want to waste away in such a place. He no longer cared about his grown sons who had conveniently forgotten about him, except for in the Lunar New Year when they made a big show lavishing him with mostly useless gifts.

At first, he thought it was a bird—a mynah or a sparrow—caught in the thin wire nets strung up by the town council to deter any pests. They often did so, after receiving complaints from irate and tidy-minded people. He sighed, dropped his bag, and walked towards the nets. He loved birds.

The winged creature was struggling itself into a spin, thin leg caught in the net. Birds often died that way and he buried them under the trees. It made no noise though, just a determined flap-flap-flap of wings.

He reached out to hold the bird... only to find that the bird was actually a little girl. Or that it looked like a little girl, clad in a peach-pink gossamer—like spider silk, he thought, amazed—dress. She had brown sparrow-like wings.

For a moment, he gaped, then backed away. Jing. Evil spirits.

He was brought up with stories like that. Fairies and spirits were not often benevolent and kind-hearted in the myths and stories. They were chaotic little beings, mischievous at best, but more often capricious.

But he did not like seeing living creatures—jing or animal—suffering. Indecision warred with compassion. Compassion won—and he gently removed the thin wire netting from around the fairy's ankle. The fairy rubbed her ankle, soothing the abraded skin, a pained expression on her thin face.

"Wait here," he heard himself saying. "I will get some Tiger Balm for you." And so in he went into his little dim housing unit, grabbed the half-used container from the broken shelf and hurried out, thankful that the fairy was still waiting for him. She leant wearily against the lamppost next to the bird trap. Her eyes were closed.

He dipped his little pinkie into the pungent minty ointment, scooped up a fingernail-sized amount and applied it, ever so gently, to the reddened skin. Even fairies get hurt, he thought, as the fairy evidently relaxed and gave a soft wince of relief. She exercised her sparrow wings and cocked her head to regard him. Like a bird. She looked vaguely Chinese.

"Thank you," she said in a sweet piping voice, speaking fluent Cantonese. He blinked, surprised to hear his native tongue issuing forth from a little... fairy.

Before he could speak, uncertain of what to say, the fairy had already darted away, disappearing into the distance, a flash in the sunlight.

He certainly could not sleep that night, his mind filled with Cantonese-speaking fairies who looked like sparrows. Pulling himself out of bed, he began to sort through the bottles. He had a plan.

HE HAD BEEN A GLASS SMITH once, way back in the forties and fifties, when he was a young man, fresh from Guangzhou. He had apprenticed himself to a glass smith working in Zhujiang, then a rural area, now a thriving industrial town known for metal and steel work. He liked the look of glass, how it melted under extreme heat and how it would form into various shapes. How it shone under the sun.

He did not have the tools of the glass smith now, only a rusty hammer he had found discarded at the foot of the stairwell near his unit. With it, he began to break the glass bottles. He hoped the fairy and her friends liked the colours red, blue, and green. He had rejected the Guinness Stout bottles because the colour of the glass was too dark, not bright enough.

Without the proper tools, his hands grew raw, cut by the sharp shards. He had to use sandpaper (salvaged from a carpentry shop) to smooth the vicious edges and even then, his fingers bled.

Then he used fishing string (again, from the same carpentry shop—the boss liked to do a fair bit of fishing) and threaded the glass pieces with it, looping and tying them so that they stayed secure. It was delicate work. The fishing string was thin, like the bird trap wires. He rued his clumsy fingers, no longer nimble for such fine and delicate crafting.

In the morning he hung the first wind-chime up on the jambu tree, where he spotted yet another bird trap. The wind-chime tinkled in the morning breeze, glittering red-blue-green-transparent glass on the low-hanging branch.

"Uncle." A boy stopped in his tracks, his bicycle squealing to a halt. "What are you doing?"

"Entertaining the fairies," he answered, watching the wind chime sparkle in the sun.

For every bird trap he discovered, no matter how discreet and well hidden the officers of the town council had meant them to be, he made a glass bottle wind chime.

ONE EVENING, WHEN HE WAS about to make some broth out of instant noodle soup mix (the Malay lady had not visited him in some time, as she was busy with her family) the fairy appeared with another fairy. They carried, with some difficulty, a plastic bag filled with fried chicken wings. He stared as they placed it almost reverently in front of him before they flew off, laughing gaily. He cautiously peeled open the bag and the delicious aroma of freshly fried chicken plumed forth, bathing his face in an oily fragrant steam.

The fairies continued to bring food every week. They carried in pok choi, string beans, chye sim, and assorted root vegetables like muang kuang and sweet potatoes (his personal favourite—steamed or boiled). He did not know how they managed to collect all these vegetables. Perhaps they salvaged them from the wet market that sold fresh vegetables and produce. He was grateful for their kindness, for their generosity. In return, he made more of the glass-bottle wind chimes. His hands bled but he did not care. He woke one day to find that the fairy had left him a small tube of cream for cuts and bruises

THE WIND CHIMES SEEMED TO capture the attention of the apartment dwellers. Children often stopped and watched the glass bits stirring in the breeze. Sometimes they stole the wind chimes, and yet he did not get angry. Instead, he made more wind chimes, breaking the glass bottles at night and tying the glass shards with fishing string.

Some parents became concerned and they wrote to the town council about the weird and violent old man who broke glass at night. Please send down police, they requested urgently. Or people from the IMH. We are afraid he might hurt our children with his broken glass.

Trying to placate the residents and wanting to be seen to be doing its job, the town council sent officers to knock on the old man's door and slip warning notices through the gap, hoping he would read them. But he simply threw them away and went on making the wind chimes. The IMH—the Institute of Mental Health—sent in volunteers, too, but they were ignored by the old man.

It was two days before the Hungry Ghosts' Festival when the smooth glass pebbles started appearing in little plastic bags. He had noticed his unfinished glass shards disappearing a couple of weeks ago and was concerned because he had to make the wind chimes for the fairies. The glass pebbles intrigued him. Someone had smoothed the edges, made the glass pleasant to the touch. He made wind chimes out of these glass pebbles and hung them on the trees. The music they made was different from the sharp-edged glass shards. Softer, sweeter, lighter.

Like fairy laughter.

At night, he would sometimes catch glimpses of the wind chimes and the way they drew groups of stray cats who would just sit and watch the glass bits twinkle intermittently under the light of the streetlamps. Or there would be small little moths fluttering close to the wind chimes, drifting like white petals in the breeze.

More letters came from the town council. He shredded them and threw them into the gunnysack designated for recycling. All this happened during the weeks within the Hungry Ghosts' Month. He could hear the funeral wakes during the day and, at night, Buddhist chants wafting in the quiet-estate air. Oddly enough, he felt strangely protected and did not worry about hungry spirits haunting his abode. The food and pebbles still appeared as if on schedule and he was grateful for these little gifts.

CEDRIC. THE POLICE ARE HERE. We need to go.

Cedric?

Listen...

Can't you hear them?

THE WIND CHIMES ARE STILL THERE, singing in the breeze: still serenading the fairies, still warning of secret dangers.

A SINGLE YEAR

CSILLA KLEINHEINCZ
TRANSLATED BY THE AUTHOR

Csilla Kleinheincz is a Hungarian-Vietnamese writer living in Kistarcsa, Hungary. Besides translating classics of fantasy she works as an editor of Ad Astra, a Hungarian publisher of science fiction and fantasy. She is the author of two novels and a short story collection. In this anthology the following story appears in English for the first time.

I had learnt love with and for others, so when I met Iván, I almost knew what it was. I was confident enough to make the decision to leave the hospital and move to the country of curry and red plains. I visited my father for the first time in two years to tell him: I am moving to India with someone I met only three months ago, but I wish to spend all the following months to get to know him better.

I didn't expect his blessing; we never had that kind of father-daughter relationship. Rather, my visit was the work of defiance: I wanted to look into his eyes to prove to myself that I dared. He usually disapproved of my decisions, although he never explicitly forbade anything. He left me to discover the consequences. This time he never even waited for me to finish before he announced that I may not go with Iván. He spoke forcefully, almost like a normal dad would.

"Why not?" I asked and didn't look away because I had promised myself I would be brave and bear anything he might say.

He didn't answer at once, but the pity in his eyes jarred my teeth.

"Why not?"

"Because he will die in one year."

I watched my father, his face covered in grey stubble, his eyes that, even in my childhood, seemed tired—tired and as resigned as the planets that circle on the same route forever and know everything that can be known.

"Are you sure?" I asked. "Do you feel it? Even so, I don't care what you know."

"What should I tell you, Judit?" His gaze stole my breath from me. Cassandra must have had the same look as she faced the Troyans.

"Even so," I said, rising. "Even so."

I trembled. His study felt cramped.

Then I was standing on the doorstep, looking back. He was sitting in the same hunched pose, clasping his hands in his lap and regarding me with the same insufferable pity. I slammed the door and, in the next moment, was running down the stairs; another blink and I sat in my car, my hand on the ignition key. The time I had left behind caught up with me, swept through me, bringing the flotsam of rage and helpless frustration. I hit the steering wheel, and I couldn't understand why I hadn't hit my father instead, when he told me what he shouldn't have.

For even if I told myself repeatedly, *even so, even so*, hoping the undulation of words would loosen the knot in my belly, I knew he told me the truth.

Iván will die in one year.

MY FATHER WAS NO CASSANDRA. You had to believe him because he told the truth. We knew that.

Others thought this a gift, but they never knew the man beyond his reputation and they never got their prophecy. I wasn't even three when my mother left him. As his other women left him later. Not because he wasn't a good person or a suitable partner; he brought in a good income, he was nice and polite, never even raised his voice. But when his eyes turned to inhuman holes, showing the future, all the women fled. They tried to cope with it but it's impossible. You cannot live with someone who is sometimes older than the solar system.

I had visited him every two weeks but, as I grew up, it became less and less. After I divorced Gábor, I had taken up talking to my father, first on the phone, bouncing accusations back and forth, then more gently and in person, but once that faraway mist appeared in his gaze, I shied away for months. I didn't want to let him chip at my life.

You can never really get used to having an oracle for a father. You may forget it for a while, but then something happens to bring forth the strangeness. Often, he didn't even realise it. I remember once, when I was still in primary school, he stepped onto the crosswalk while the lights were still red. The horns blared crazily but when I held him back, he pulled me with him and said, "Not yet." He hurried like those who, unlike him, didn't know the exact time of their death. But his steps were surer. He knew that, until his appointed time, he was invincible. I looked up at him as I would upon a wonder. That passed, too. No big deal in being brave if you know you are invulnerable.

Now I know exactly what Mum must have felt when she took me and left him, finding that my father had ironed and folded her clothes beforehand. She knew she had to break away, but she also wanted to be held back. We all want that deep down inside.

So Mum entered the flat with the prepared words of goodbye on her tongue. The clothes were folded in neat piles on the sofa.

"I saw that he wanted to call me back," said Mum after my divorce, when we talked about the end of relationships. That time she was more like a friend. Not so much since. "I saw that his heart was breaking; he wanted to hold me back so much, but he knew what would happen and he didn't even try to change it. I couldn't forgive him for that for a long time. That he didn't even try."

At first, I didn't understand why my father never attempted to change fate. I tried to pry into it but he always dodged the answer by saying that he didn't see the future in order to change it, the same as I didn't control the lives of people I saw on television. After many years, I realised this was the only answer I would get. He cannot change the future, just tell it. He wanted me to know that. That was why his girlfriends had left him. That was why I said goodbye to him when, as we were talking, I saw the planets relay to him a sliver of the future. When you cannot fight fate, it is better not to know.

No, this is not entirely true. I asked him many times what he saw. I just stopped asking about Gábor.

As a teenager, I nagged him to tell me if I would pass my exam; would I be a doctor, a pharmacist, a nurse? No, no, yes. It had been a kind of vocational guidance. What could he tell me about Márton? Béla? Attila? When he told me whether the love affair ended in a nice or ugly manner, I realised I didn't need to know. I shouldn't know beforehand, never, because it is poison, a permanent ache, a constant search for faults and defects. Why wouldn't it work? Because of him? Or because of me? Which of us wasn't enough for the other?

I told my father to keep the messages of the planets to himself. For a while he complied, but I knew from the shadows crossing his face that he saw my future. I pressed my lips together and didn't ask. Perhaps it was defiance rather than the good sense not to let myself be controlled by my father's prophecies. I managed to refrain from asking. For a while.

When I married Gábor, I asked my father what I should expect. It was stupid but I wanted to be sure I'd done the right thing. I wanted affirmation. When he said, "Three years," I felt betrayed. I didn't invite him to the wedding. He still came; he stood in the back row and didn't come to congratulate us.

It really was three years. Whether there couldn't have been more time, or whether it was because I'd known from the beginning that I would have only three years with that man and had therefore allowed my marriage to slip through my fingers, I don't know. Perhaps my marriage had been dead even at the moment I said my vows.

After that I didn't ask him anymore. Not even now. He had decided to tell me because he had no other leverage to hold me back. To protect me?

Will Iván really die in one year?

IVÁN WAS A DOCTOR, TWO years younger than me. We both worked in Rókus Hospital, saw each other every day, and even if there was no time for intimate talking, we were never short of a quick touch, a hurried kiss on a flight of stairs where our colleagues couldn't see us. The day after I'd visited my father, I saw Iván briefly several times. Once he stopped for a moment to stroke me between my shoulder blades, then he continued walking. Words burnt my tongue: "I went to see my father and..." How could I end the sentence?

How could I tell him? I should. He should know in order to be prepared, even if he didn't believe me, even if he laughed at me. Maybe, if he took the warning as a joke, I would be able to see it more light-heartedly. "Ha-ha, what a strange bird my father is," I could say, and pretend.

As if I didn't know the future. Just like my father does.

At the end of my shift, I was close to snapping like a cord. I craved a cigarette so badly that when I finally got down to the garden and lit one, I realised only during my third that I couldn't remember smoking the first two. Anna from Surgery came after me, and asked me between two puffs:

"Why are you so nervous? You two had a fight?"

I don't think she was really interested. She had her own quiet lake-world; she never let anything from the outside disturb its water. Therefore it was easy to answer.

"Just my father... Now that I am over thirty, he's started to discipline me and he began with prohibition."

She nodded, finished her cigarette, and pressed out the stub.

"And you are really going to India?"

"Of course."

"Well, good luck! It must be more difficult for a nurse. To talk those weird languages. It's easy for Iván. Patients rarely chit-chat on the operating table.

She went in.

Sometimes I think Anna's calmness comes from taking it from others. Her remark hit me. Iván and I had planned everything perfectly. There was a hospital in New Delhi where we would work. It would be good experience for him, but for me...? Patients were patients everywhere, but Anna was right: I would have to talk to them; simply turning the sheets was not enough. Every doctor spoke English well, but my patients...? And the native nurses, my colleagues...?

Will I feel unwanted? Still, Iván will be there.

For how long?

The thought knotted my stomach. When Iván sneaked behind me and touched the nape of my neck, I jumped as if licked by fire.

"Let's go home!" I beseeched him, looking into his surprised eyes. "The sooner the better."

"Let's go then," he said. I liked his way of knowing the difference between the important and the unimportant, when fuss was annoying. He didn't expect an immediate explanation. He knew I would come around to that.

"Well?" he asked later at home, after ten minutes of silence and my nostrils had filled with his cinnamon scent. "What's the matter?"

"I am afraid of losing you."

He laughed—not with irony but with relief, as if my fear were a mere silliness not worth even a little consideration.

"What makes you think you will?"

"I went to see my father and..." I couldn't bring myself to tell the whole truth. "He forbade me to go with you."

"Aren't you adult enough not to let him dictate your life?"

"Of course I am but..."

Because it was easier, I talked about my father: what it was like to see him only every two weeks, how much he helped or didn't help as I grew up, how I wasn't sure I loved him at all. Iván listened devotedly like a child would, and at the end he generously said he understood. This annoyed me because I knew he knew nothing. I didn't tell him what my father said about his future.

UNSPOKEN WORDS HAVE WEIGHT. FIRST you barely feel them, then, as they proliferate you realise you cannot carry them anymore. You either release them or keep them in, in which case they start to press and pinch your heart. You feel the grip even if you are happy. Especially then.

I didn't tell Iván, partly because I wasn't sure, partly because I didn't want him to lose the light. He was happy. In a sense, so was I—but while I was laughing, caressing, loving, part of me peeled away from me and, watching us, said, "Not much longer."

It drove me wild. If you close yourself off to the future, the present seems richer. I felt every moment was perfect because there would be no more like it.

It's sweeter if you know it will end.

FOR TWO MONTHS WE CARRIED on like this, until we had only two weeks before the journey. It was the best two months of the five and also the worst. Then, one night as I was straddling Iván, looking down into his face, the knowledge became too heavy. He was calm and young after making love, and more beautiful than any other. He caressed my hip slowly and without thought.

I'd been saying goodbye for two months and knowing that I'd been doing it, and I had no desire for another ten months of leave-taking.

He watched me peacefully, vulnerable in front of the future. The dimness of the bedroom made it feel like a nest, but the words gathering inside me kept me from feeling comfortable.

"I won't go with you to Delhi."

His hand stopped on my hip.

"Why?"

I shook my head. I still didn't want to tell him.

"I won't go with you."

"But..." His hand fell down as if broken. After a few long moments, he blinked. "Oh. And when I come back? We continue?"

I turned away, stared at his books on the shelves. The ones I had read and the ones I wanted to borrow. Maybe from the library.

"We won't continue," I whispered.

We held each other, me crying, Iván caressing my back. We

made love again, madly, passionately, and at the end, I packed my things and left. Three times I turned back from the door to kiss him and every time it was harder to go. But I had to. I closed the downstairs door feeling ten years older. Nothing inside me, only the weight of emptiness.

THE FOLLOWING WEEK I LOCKED myself in the toilet several times to cry. In the end, I took some leave because if I saw Iván every day, I would turn back, go with him to the little apartment with the naked light bulbs that we had seen on the Internet, and to hell with what will happen in ten months time. I sat in my flat and waited until it was too late to do the paperwork needed for the journey.

Of course he called. Many times. He was sweet, his voice calm, but I knew that this meant nothing. The phone calls were full of awkward silences when only two wounds were bleeding at the end of the line. I knew more about how he felt than I did about my own feelings.

He didn't speak of his thoughts, but he spent long, strained minutes remembering our trip to the conference in Debrecen. What it felt like when I fell asleep on his shoulder while he was driving. I told him in turn about waking up when he touched my face—softer than anyone before had been. We recalled the morning stuck on that godforsaken train station because we got off a stop too early, how we sat on the grass-spotted concrete and watched the sun rise above the Hungarian Plain. It was then that we began spinning plans for the Indian trip, and the red light of the dawn had seemed to spill over tropical soil. On the phone, he asked about my mother's varicose leg and I sent word to his sister that there was a sale on skirts in her favourite shop.

We made everyday chit-chat because it seemed absurd that we were no longer a couple and soon he would leave my life for good, for there is no leaving as definitive as death. We laughed into the phone and sometimes I felt he was sitting very close to me, whispering in my ear—still we didn't meet. We didn't say our relationship had ended because it was different from breaking up.

He left for India and I went back to work. After a few months, I had to admit that breaking up was meaningless. I was still thinking about him, counting the days, and I was just as scared. The fear wouldn't lift until the year had passed, and maybe not even then. Sometimes you recognise things that are meant to be forever.

Then I saw my father on the tram.

I hadn't talked to him since I'd been burdened with his prophecy. My first thought was to get off the tram before he noticed me; in the end I shoved my way to him through the crowd of passengers and, skipping the hello, I said:

"You shouldn't have told me."

He started. He hadn't noticed me, and his face showed embarrassment—and maybe a little guilt.

"How can I keep it from happening?" I grabbed his arm.

"Put it off, you mean?"

"Don't play with me. You know very well what I mean! Turn it back, pre-empt it... I know what will happen. I can slow it down, right?" The passengers froze. They turned away with so much care that their attention filled us with tension.

"You can't slow it down; it is the future," he said and nervously glanced around. "Listen, can we get off?"

I laughed even though I didn't want to. The laughter choked me.

"You still want to control what and when you tell me?" I flicked my wrist. "Whatever. Let's get off!"

The tension followed us to the tram stop. I didn't wait for the people to leave the platform.

"I don't believe it is futile," I said. "Your prophecies... they cannot be gratuitous. They must be changeable!"

His eyes were tired.

"You want an answer from me? I only tell what I see. I

don't make up the future. I don't control it."

I pushed him hard, surprising myself as much as him.

"I don't believe you haven't ever tried!"

"I have," he said bitterly. His eyes showed some passion at last. "I have tried but in vain! The only way is acceptance or you go mad. That is my advice to you, as well."

I shook my head.

"I wish you hadn't told me at all."

"I'm sorry." He extended his hand, perhaps to draw me close, but we never felt easy enough around each other for an embrace. I stepped away.

"Or you told me to make me try..." I looked up, realising this was it. This had to be the reason. "I have to try, maybe..."

"Don't!"

"Then why?"

"Because I, too, can make mistakes!"

I shook my head.

"Then tell me what will happen to *me*! What will *I* do?"

A familiar face, yet confusing. Do I love him? Hate him? Despise him?

"It doesn't work like that. I cannot control what I see and what I don't. Don't you think I would have done it? Judit, listen to me..." He reached for me and this time touched me before I could pull away.

"Then tell me something, anything that will happen to me before the year passes!"

The next tram arrived. People shoved past us as they rushed towards the crosswalk. I saw his gaze darken.

He rubbed his face.

"One of your patients will die within six months while you are on your shift. I don't know exactly when. You won't hear her calling."

"Would I be able to save her?"

"I don't know. I'm not a doctor and I see only what I am allowed to see. Judit! There is no point."

"There is."

I left him there, without even a goodbye. I didn't care if he was right or wrong, but I knew my only chance was to reject his advice, to believe that fate can, indeed, be changed.

MY PLAN WAS QUITE SIMPLE: if I could change my own future, I could change Iván's. Somehow. Because I couldn't believe that fate was already written.

It was a test. On my shift I did rounds every fifteen minutes to catch anything serious that might happen. We usually didn't have critical-surgery patients; I was sure that if one of them crashed, there would be enough time to notice.

A few of them indeed had serious conditions, an old woman crashed in the corridor, but I was close by. A month passed, then another, and I became doubtful. What if the danger has already passed? What if the old woman who crashed was the one I had to save? Had I changed the future or not?

Sometimes I thought I could relax, but then came distress again; I didn't dare break my new habit for fear it would be the hour of the augured death. I began to understand what it was like to be my father: knowing and yet not knowing, waiting for something unclear with the certainty of the threat breathing down his neck.

I knew nothing about Iván's death, only the approximate time. I imagined him run over by a car, shot by a madman, having a heart attack despite his age, or getting sick from the Indian tap water. *Oh my God, he commits suicide because...*

Because I left him.

No, I told myself, and again: *no, no, no,* but the thought had already stabbed its hooks into me.

One evening was especially depressing. The sickly yellowish light of the nurses' room painted the walls, and the clock ticked. I was alone, and suddenly fear seized me because, in that moment, I was sure Iván would die because of me.

"It's late," said my father when he picked up the phone.

"How will he die?"

"Who?"

"You know who! Iván."

His sigh felt close.

"Judit, don't torment yourself with this! Won't you come over and talk? It would be easier to accept—"

"How will he die?"

"I'd rather not say."

Rage burst out of me.

"Because you are a coward! I don't believe this! You have your gift and just sweep it under the carpet? I don't think so! The world doesn't work like that. It's your choice not to do anything, but don't expect the same from me. I am not like you!"

"You make it more difficult than—"

"So what? It's my life! Even if you behaved like a proper father, my life wouldn't be yours to decide what I should do with it. Oh, fuck, I don't believe this! *Now* you want to protect me?"

Chilly silence. I had to press my hand against my forehead to cool my feverish brow. I could have said more: obscenities, accusations, suppressed hatred burnt my tongue and I bit my lips to hold it all back. I knew what I'd already said was more than enough.

"He will be hit by a branch," said my father at last, and he put down the phone.

"That's it?" I shouted, but the line was dead.

I sat with my cell phone in my lap. It tired me to move and when I finally stood, my knees trembled. I went out to check on my wards.

The corridor shone coldly as the night lighting reflected off the tiles. I had got my answer from my father and yet I felt empty. When I looked into the third ward I froze. I saw a patient with a pillow in her hands leaning over another patient, but the sight seemed abstract.

I don't remember moving.

I tore the pillow from the wizened old hands. She scratched my arm. "She wanted to kill me!" the old woman shrieked. "I saw it in her eyes, I knew it... she wanted to steal my money this afternoon; I had to hide it under my pillow."

I leant towards the dying woman's mouth—it was parched and smelt of age—but I was too late. I already knew it. I started CPR for I had to try. Only afterwards did I grab the old woman's trembling arm. She babbled on.

"She waited for me to fall asleep. As soon as I was asleep, she tried to take my money! I saw her hand! I wanted to make her sleep." She started to cry then. "I just wanted to make her sleep..."

The other two patients' eyes glistened in the darkness. Only for their sake did I refrain from hitting the old woman. I wanted to hurt her not because she was demented and had killed her bed neighbour, but because she had fulfilled the prophecy I wanted to thwart.

"You come with me!" I shouted in her face. I pulled her out of the ward as if I were a jailer. I had to report the incident. She was crying, but I didn't look at her.

My eyes were dry.

I TRIED TO WARN HIM. I called him in New Delhi. He immediately picked up the phone as if he was waiting for the call.

"Judit?" His voice was so eager and happy that it was hard to believe we hadn't seen each other for five months. How could one e-mail a week be enough? "To what do I owe the pleasure?"

"I missed your voice." As soon as I said it, I knew that was the real reason, not the warning. My whole body ached from missing him, and his absence smothered me.

"I missed yours, too." He paused.

"Listen to me!" I began. "If there is a storm... don't go for a walk, especially not under trees! And always watch for woodcutters thinning the branches. Take care..."

"What?" He laughed.

"I'm not joking. Take care with those trees!"

He didn't understand. I sputtered the warning again but I feared he didn't comprehend my words. He didn't believe me.

"Promise me!" I demanded.

"I do," he said, still laughing. "Okay. And what about you? Tell me, how are you?"

"I'm fine," I said, not wanting to chat. "Do you promise me?"

"Yes! I will be careful with the trees."

"Good. Bye!"

I put down the phone. A cigarette was already in my mouth. I couldn't remember taking it out.

Iván's voice had told me that he hadn't understood. He wouldn't keep his promise. Silliness, he would say, and even if he watched the trees on the first day he would realise it was pointless and forget about the stupid request. He would live like he did, walk under trees and, if he remembered his promise at all, he would only smile. Silly, pet, he would say fondly, and for a moment he would feel my face in his palm. That was all.

I wrote a letter to him, but it was already too late to start explaining my father's prophecies to him. Would I believe them if I hadn't been born into the family of an oracle?

My father wanted to ask for my forgiveness, at least that was what I deduced from the text messages that urged me to visit him. When he tried to call me, I didn't pick up. I deleted his e-mails—so he only wanted to talk, well, I didn't care. Maybe he was not the one who would kill Iván, but he knew about his death and not only stepped aside but wanted to pull me aside, as well.

"Your father called," said Mum one day when I visited her. She didn't look up from the stove. "He wants to talk to you."

They hadn't spoken to each other for a long time now.

When communication was absolutely unavoidable, they sent messages through me. They didn't hate each other; I think my father was afraid of my mother who, in turn, looked through him.

"My fault," I said. "He has been trying to reach me for a month now. Sorry."

"He didn't tell me anything else." Based on her voice I assumed she was smiling sarcastically. "He just asked me to tell you—visit him by all means—then said goodbye. I think he doesn't really know how to treat me. Will you put the cloth on the table?"

I took out the plates: a plain white for her, the blue one from my childhood for me that had cars, bicycles, and ships running along its edge.

"You don't know what he wanted?"

"I learnt long ago to leave his things be. You know the cost." Her voice was sour, as always, when she talked about my father. "If I am not cautious, I might get to know something."

"I see."

"Is that why you won't talk to him?" She glanced at me searchingly. "May I ladle you some soup?"

I nodded.

The bean soup was thick and hot, it burnt my tongue. It was good to sit in Mum's kitchen, although it has been a long time since I had last felt at home there. Lights were subdued, noises low: the cat purred in front of the stove, the washing machine rumbled softly in the bathroom. I was calmed not by the familiar plate, noises or the taste; the peace and harmony came from not speaking to my father. Suddenly we were on the same side and closer to each other despite our differences.

I finished eating sooner than my mother. I leant back and looked around the kitchen. It was cluttered, full of bric-a-brac, crochet left on the top of the fridge, books put down, opened on their belly.

"If Dad had begged you back, would you have gone back to him?"

She looked up surprised.

"What do you mean?"

"When you took me from him when I was small. If he had called you back... you said you wanted it... would you have gone back to him? Would you have stayed with him, even if he'd seen you leave?" I didn't add the question: would you have broken the prophecy?

Her mouth was pulled into a smile as if by a hook.

"It was so long ago, Judit..."

"Would you have gone back?"

"Maybe, I don't know. I wouldn't have taken it for long, even then."

She shook her head, more to herself than to me, and continued eating.

"It doesn't matter," she said at length.

I left it at that. Maybe she was right.

MY FATHER DIED. I HADN'T seen him before that, and I hadn't talked to him. I had erased his last message from my phone without listening to it; I learnt the news shortly after I had done that. I don't know what he wanted to say. I imagined a thousand messages, but I can't say if the real one was amongst them.

He had a heart attack. Perhaps he could have saved himself if he had called an ambulance, for he knew when he would die. But he did nothing of the sort. He simply lay down and waited for the last kick of his heart. A bottle of whisky and a big bar of hazelnut chocolate were prepared on the bedside table. The silver wrapping was torn just a little as if he had changed his mind.

I inherited his flat. I packed his things and I should have thrown them away but, somewhere between casting everything onto the floor and bundling it into a carton, a feeling overwhelmed me that the pullover I held in my hands was my father. And the books on the shelves, also. The used toothbrush, the leftover food in the fridge, the stuffed notebook on the table, the old guitar in the corner—all were him. Unmatched, incomplete objects that were not bound together by anything anymore. I tried to imagine my father in the pullover, the pen in his hands, his feet in his slippers, but I couldn't. My memories were leaking.

He had wanted to talk to me. For the last time.

If I had known...

I realised in the end that knowledge wouldn't have been absolution. If the only reason to talk to him was his death in a month, a week, a day, I wouldn't have been less of a stranger to him.

I stood in his flat, knowing where every object belonged and yet I felt lost. I had tried to understand him but had failed. It was too late for that now. But there was something I was still in time for.

I PURCHASED A TICKET TO INDIA. Just then, I didn't know when I would come back or how long I would have to stay for. I was only sure that I wouldn't budge from Iván's side. I didn't care what happened in a day, two days, three days or a month; I just wanted to be with him and not on another continent, alone.

He was waiting for me at Delhi Airport. The huge, multi-coloured and multi-smelling crowd in the waiting hall undulated between us, but it disappeared when I saw Iván—or I just pushed everyone aside, I can't remember. Our meeting was just as you would expect. I will skip that.

"I have been waiting for you," he said in the cool cab. His hand enveloped mine, holding me as he might hold a bird. "I knew you would come."

"Funny, I didn't know."

"I knew it for you." He laughed. "No, that's not true, I didn't know. But I am happy."

"And were you careful with the trees?" I asked.

"I haven't as much as peeked out, just like you said. This

warning was a clever idea; it made me think of you whenever I saw a tree. Smooth. Is that why you warned me?"

I was giddy from his closeness. I hadn't seen him in such a long time; all his features were new and yet painfully familiar. My fingertips remembered him more than my eyes.

I saw only his eyes and mouth as he talked. I noticed his dark tan, the scratch on his neck from shaving, his thinning hair. I was unguarded. I hadn't yet got used to taking care of him, although that was the reason I came.

In the sudden heat, as we were walking towards his lodgings, pulling my suitcases after me on the bumpy street, I didn't notice the people, the houses, the dirty motorbikes. The screeching, the honking din, the shouts, the singing on the street, the stench rising from the pavement; all of it came to me only later. I didn't see the truck turning the corner, nor the timber whooshing free.

Iván was looking at me, pointing at his house behind him.

"I had rats but I put out some poison," he said. "You are not afraid, are you?"

His eyes told me something else. I smiled and I started to answer this other, unspoken question and then...

The timber could have hit me but I only felt its draught. Iván fell like a bowling pin. His head... I am unable to write down what happened to his head.

I hadn't stopped it. I stood on the street that was suddenly filling with a loud hubbub; I smelt the stink and the spices and stared at Iván lying before me. I almost leant down but froze. I would have recognised his death even if I hadn't seen countless other dead before. I knew it.

The year had passed.

I understood nothing from the shouts around me. They spoke a strange language, strangers all. My suitcase was dotted with red, the feeling of Iván's touch was cooling on my hand.

The sounds fled; the scene became distant and memories attacked me.

First from the past: Iván, laughing when he tried to hide a pain; his touch on my belly; him shaking his hair from his face—then from the future: me, as I run away from all relationships; me who lets go because holding on hurts more; me, who will be the last oracle on this Earth for I won't bear a child for anyone.

I see me living alone, and when the gas remains on—accidentally or deliberately—I flare up without anything to feel remorse for, only that I have nothing and no-one to regret. It will be a perfect death, for I won't be alive before it happens. I won't even be old.

I trembled with the certainty, and then I was again standing on the pavement with two Indian women beside me who held my hands and talked to me in English. A large crowd gaped around us. Iván was covered with a tarp that had offered merchandise a few minutes ago.

I stared at the plaid tarp and still the tears didn't come. Only later, at the police station where no-one understood my pronunciation and mangled English and my stammer.

I don't recall how and when I made the journey back home.

THEY LEFT ME ALONE. PERHAPS they realised that my gaze was barbed wire and my silence a brick wall—at least they didn't approach me. They knew what had happened and talked about it, too; I heard the half-sentences float out of the nurses' room. Although I wished to see them fall shamefully silent as I entered, I waited in the corridor until the topic shifted.

I smoked a lot alone in the hospital garden. I noticed that the others went down separately whenever they could, while I was turning the sheets, giving shots, serving dinner. It was already winter, my fingers were chilled red and my feet were cold in my clogs because I only ever put on a coat, but I wouldn't go back until I had smoked at least two cigarettes.

"We will catch a cold," said Anna from behind me on one of the freezing afternoons.

I glanced back. She hadn't even put on a coat, just a sweater. She didn't seem to be cold; maybe she had spoken only to make me notice her. I made some space for her by the ashtray of the refuse bin. As she stepped closer, I grew dizzy for a moment. She was pregnant but she didn't know it yet: I saw her going on maternity leave. I kept silent for a while then said:

"All those cigarettes will ruin you."

She laughed hoarsely. "Look who's talking! You have more nicotine in your blood than haemoglobin."

I shrugged. I knew how I would die, and it wouldn't be from smoking. "Not yet," said my father from my memories as he pulled me across the street.

We were silently blowing out smoke.

"So what's going on?" I asked for the sake of asking.

"I have a room full of living dead," she said calmly. "I hope they hang on until Christmas."

I nodded. Rooms like that embittered nurses. Smiles and comfort lasted only so long. For half a year by my reckoning.

"I can take over if you like." It would mean hell for administration but it was all the same for me.

"No problem," she said and smothered the butt. "Are you coming? I have a kilo of tangerines, would you like some?"

I went with her to her floor. Their nurses' room was smaller but more snug. Someone had brought several pots of poinsettia, and I smelt the cinnamon bark hanging from a closet door. I closed my eyes. Iván's perfume also had a hint of cinnamon, and I realised that I missed his scent the most. I will remember his smell longer than his face.

We ate tangerines while Anna talked about making Christmas presents. She didn't ask me what I would give for Christmas and to whom, and this bothered me, although I had no inclination to tell her. When the time came to check the wards, I accompanied her because I felt that our conversation was incomplete.

The dead were lying in the room. They were still alive but

as I looked at them, I saw how they would die.

"You were right," I whispered to Anna.

"About what?"

I just nodded at them. I waited while she made her round. She stopped at every bed and asked how she could help. I was wondering whether I should tell her there were some who wouldn't live to see Christmas, but in the end I kept silent. I knew my father, and he wouldn't have given away information like that. There was a reason for that. When Anna came out to the hallway I just smiled.

"You are doing the same," she said as we were walking back.

"What?"

"You know it is only a matter of a little comfort for a few days, and still you won't give up." She stopped at the door of the nurses' room. "Well, bye."

"Bye." I didn't budge. Then: "I think you are pregnant."

The surprise in her face. The happiness. Who would have thought? I was amazed. Is that all? You tell a prophecy and you do good with it? Then the sudden prick: why hadn't my father told me anything happy?

"How do you know?"

I shrugged. "A feeling." I turned away and then I remembered what I had vowed. That I would never have a child. Ever. I was already sorry for saying anything at all.

"I have to go. My patients are waiting."

She nodded. "You seem to be in need of a nurse yourself," she said in her old, wry voice.

She had thrown me off my balance again. Her remark hurt, although I didn't really understand why.

I went back to my own floor. As I was adjusting the pillows under the patients to make them comfortable, I was chewing on Anna's words.

"May I have a glass of water?" The raspy voice jolted me out of my thoughts.

I looked down at the old woman, and a wizened prune of a face looked back at me. My vision blurred and in a memory — as if it were my own — I saw her recover from her operation and fall in love, then marry. I was shocked. Her skin was yellow, her eyes full of grit — not someone who has something waiting for her. And still.

I poured her a glass of water. My hand shook.

"Don't worry, love," I said as I handed her the water. My father kept prophecies to himself, good and bad alike, although the latter was more likely to be spoken. I could afford to tell the good news. A small thing but it is within my power. "Two weeks and you will be like new. You will even dance at your wedding."

She laughed. "Me? Oh heavens, no! Perhaps at yours, Judit."

Definitely not at mine, I wanted to say, but my throat constricted. The face of the woman looked younger from laughing, and I would be sorry to see her age again. Plus... My breath stopped. The stupidity and futility of prophecies was suddenly plain, and I was lost amongst the waves of my thoughts.

"Just believe." I put down the glass on the table and fled to the hallway.

I pressed my hands to my face. I knew that my father had wanted to talk about the future before he died. Was it good news or bad? I realised his message didn't matter. What I see in the future doesn't matter — for we are not unlike each other, the old lady and I. I know only a little bit more, and still I asked her to believe me. And what about me? Do I believe myself and what I have seen?

Or do I decide not to believe, and only believe what I wish for myself?

I clenched my teeth and hoped I had a little of my heart left still, for it has to feel. If it breaks in the process, it still has to feel.

I know the future. But I resist it.

I turned away from my past smelling of cinnamon, and while my clogs rapped loudly and quickly on the floor as I fled towards my room, my future melted at last and, salty and streaming, it overflowed.

THE SECRET ORIGIN OF SPIN-MAN

ANDREW DRILON

Andrew Drilon is a comics creator, writer, illustrator, and editor from the Philippines. He was a finalist for the 2008 Philippines' Free Press Literary Award and is a recipient of the Philippine Graphic/Fiction Award. He is best known for his experimental webcomic, *Kare-Kare Komiks*, and is a regular cartoonist for *The Philippine Star* newspaper.

So you don't know Spin-Man? Five-nine, lantern-jawed, starry-eyed Spin-Man? Spin-Man the Caped Cosmische, Spin-Man the Super-Cop, Spin-Man the Meta? Muscle-bound, brown-skinned, wrapped from beefy neck to toe in blue-and-gold spandex? Don't worry about it. It's okay. I don't blame you. Spin-Man was one of those forgotten heroes of the Dark Age of Comics, just before the Image Era of big guns and chains and Spawn and bloodstained alleys. The champion of the Multiversal Continuum, balls-out science fantasy, following in the footsteps of Jim Starlin and Silver Surfer and Jack 'The King' Kirby—Spin-Man was the last good Space Hero of the 90s and my number one favourite super-person. I'll explain.

Okay, this may seem unrelated, but hear me out first because it's important. When I was nine, my little brother and I went to the bargain bins of CATS as often as we could. After being picked up from school by our assiduous driver, Manong Eddie, who had been instructed to take no detours but had a soft spot for us boys; after an intermittent car ride, owing to the long stretch of traffic circling the vast perimeter of our private school; after a half-eaten merienda of adobo sandwich and Zesto Orange sent by our grandmother, God rest her soul; James and I would take it in turns (sometimes called out in unison) to remind our driver: "The main entrance of Virra Mall! We'll only be thirty minutes! Mang Eddie, pleeeese!" Then the drive past Uni-Mart, around the corner facing McDonalds, as we busied ourselves counting the money in our pockets, at times almost two hundred pesos when pooled together, until finally my grandfather's Altis slowed outside the mall's main entrance, and we'd thrust the car doors open and hop out, promising Manong Edie that we'd be waiting there at exactly 4.45, no later, cross our excited little hearts.

Running in, ignoring the cinema schedule by the entrance where five or six people always stood deliberating what to watch, we would brush past strangers and other boys in school uniforms, our trajectories plotted through the long air-conditioned corridors of the mall to avoid the various temptations that lined its capitalist halls (including the arcade) until we arrived at the shop of our hearts' desires. Its windows, covered with painted posters of masked men and women, sheltered under a primary-coloured electric display that announced its most hallowed name: CATS. (Comics And Then Some.)

For a moment, we would ogle at the comics on the New Arrivals rack, committing their covers to memory and silently promising to acquire them when we had more money, after which we would go directly to the bargain bins; James starting on the leftmost end while I worked on the opposite, thumbing our way through rows and rows of titles as if in a marathon, flip flip flip, until we met at the middle, ready to sort through two piles of bargain comics. We would debate on thirty peso copies of *X-Men*, *Avengers*, *Batman*, and numerous other titles, eliminating possible purchases by creating an agreed-upon hierarchy based first upon the title's character, then artist, then writer. On rare occasions when we came to a disagreement, we would split our money down the middle and dictate our own purchases, though most of the time, our tastes were in complete accord.

By the end of our ritual, a stack of five or six carefully-considered comics were rung up at the till and wrapped in the customary CATS plastic bag, complete with a crude drawing of Wolverine printed under its wonderful, acronymic logo. Manong Eddie would be waiting for us outside, as patient as ever despite the extra quarter of an hour of waiting, resulting in a drive home that transpired in complete silence, as James and I lost ourselves to the outrageous adventures of these fictional men and women.

James and I agreed: the world's greatest comic book artist was Jim Lee. I also liked Erik Larsen on Spider-Man; but his replacement, Mark Bagley, couldn't draw Carnage with the appropriate menace, in my view. At an early age, I had become acutely aware of the people who worked on these comics, and in my wildest dreams I imagined myself drawing the X-Men under the pen of my favourite writer, Chris Claremont. I spent hours scrutinising these comics, copying my favourite poses, memorising the costumes and learning the vagaries of super-hero anatomy; the intricacies of foreshortening and the convolutions of idealised musculature wrapped in spandex. James struggled to keep up with me, but in the end resigned himself to colouring my illustrations in deference to my burgeoning drawing ability. I suppose our tastes were still far from refined, and if you had told us back then that Neil Gaiman was far superior to Scott Lobdell, we would have argued you out of the room. As a nine-year-old who could draw Superman with a modicum of accuracy, I had pronounced myself an expert on these multicoloured worlds, and James was more than willing to share in my obsession.

James, in turn, proclaimed himself to be the real-world counterpart of Daredevil. He would sit in the corner of our room facing a crumbling dartboard, one hand over his eyes, a trained dart in the other, declaring: "I will hit a bull's eye using only my ears!" He rarely made the centre of the board, but when he did, it was a cause for celebration, and we'd jump around the room in a mock-battle between Daredevil and the vampire Morbius. For a while, I myself was intent on developing a keen psychic talent à la Professor X, but that ambition fell by the wayside when I failed to read my classmate's mind during a critical science exam. Fortunately, I had gained some popularity at school for my art skills, and in the end it was this ability that I cherished as my one and only superpower.

It was 1991, the year of the Pinatubo eruption, when James and I were invited to stay over at our Lolo Doming's house in Los Baños to finally meet our long-lost uncle: Tito Fermin. According to my mother, he had lived in the States all our lives, hiding as an illegal immigrant, and it was only that year, when he had married into an American citizenship, that he was able to visit the Philippines without fear of recrimination. Both James and I were eager to meet our uncle, having heard that he was a comic book artist; one who actually made a living conjuring up the four-colour worlds we were so fond of.

It was with some disappointment that we learnt the specifics of his occupation: Tito Fermin was a cartoonist for neither Marvel nor DC, but for a small independent company known as Echo Comics. They produced a grand total of four titles a month, one of which was a black-and-white superhero comic that, Tito Fermin said proudly, he both pencilled and inked. We were slightly more impressed when he showed us samples of his work, but though his art had the romantic quality of classic Tagalog Komiks, it lacked the inflated modern dynamism that we had grown accustomed to.

Regardless of his artistic prowess, Tito Fermin was a striking character. Long, shaggy black hair spilled down from his head and his face was rounded out by a full beard which, in retrospect, made him look like a Filipino Alan Moore. His eyes had the hint of a Chinese slant; he spoke in a low, sonorous voice that commanded attention and, as with our grandfather (who we'd nicknamed Santa Claus) you could rarely tell if he was smiling under that beard.

Tito Fermin spent most of our first dinner talking with Lolo Doming, the details of which I can no longer clearly recall; only the slurred American accent that possessed my uncle in the midst of his soliloquies on life abroad and the inscrutable grunts that my grandfather contributed to the discussion. Rain hammered through the trees outside, splashing against the windows and conversation, the warm yellow light of the chandelier washing over the lazy Susan that pivoted food around the dinner table. James and I contented ourselves with fielding questions from Lola Lita, who we had insisted on calling Lolita in spite of her good-natured refusals. We asked her what superheroes were popular in her time and she shook her head as she replied, "My heroes were movie stars, ballet dancers, and singers—Judy Garland, Irina Baronova, and Frank Sinatra. Those three are my favourites." And then she crooned a few lines from the song she always sang when she put us to bed, the song I will always remember her for:

No, there's nothing to be ashamed of if you stub your toe on the moon
Though it may be a blow to your pride, you're a hero because, well, you tried
So don't give up too soon, if you stub your toe on the moon

Perhaps, as a consequence, as we were falling asleep that night, James confessed that he had grown tired of Daredevil. "I want to be Silver Surfer now," he said. We contemplated the means by which James could acquire cosmic power and a silver board capable of space flight. I suggested that he find a way to contact Galactus while he mused on the existence of cosmic rays beyond our atmosphere, and after a while we simply lay in our beds for the thousandth night next to each other, our thoughts racing to find the path to James's goal until, finally, sleep overtook us.

Due to its distance from the city, Los Baños was a place that we rarely visited, and when we did it gave off the impression of being otherworldly, like a dream that never happened: bosky mountains stretching to the horizon, tiny three-floor shopping malls, the subtle incline on all the roads, sari-sari stores, the musky-sweet smell of Lolo Doming's cigars, trips to the video rental store, a rough-painted cement ceiling, flower-patterned bed sheets, non-cable television, wood-panelled walls, kare-kare stew, marble floors, and, best of all, discount bookstores with five-to-ten peso comics.

It was there, in the Book sale beside Carmela Barbershop, that Tito Fermin began to participate in our love for comics. He was leaving for the States the next morning and had been meaning to pick up a few Filipino Komiks to take with him.

James and I were simply excited to find more back issues of *Ghost Rider* and *Wild Dog*. The bargain bins were smaller, only three rows, but we commenced with our ritual anyway, thumbing through back issues, flip flip flip, until we each had our stack of comics to choose from. Tito Fermin surprised us by taking both piles and paying for them, more than thirty comics each and, as we walked out of the store suffused with happiness and gratitude, I silently calculated that he'd spent over five hundred pesos on comics, which was a huge amount at the time, at least to me.

And then lunch at Nilda's Restaurant, where we ate mushroom burgers while Tito Fermin quizzed us on our love of superheroes. A lengthy discourse ensued on the extended line-up of the X-Men, the convolutions of Peter Parker's life, the rogues gallery of Batman, how Hulk was too boring, how the Legion of Superheroes had too many members, how the Fantastic Four had too few, how Superman and Captain America were outdated; and more besides. He shared stories of his meetings with various comics' creators during conventions; of the long argument on the art of cartooning that he'd had with Gary Groth; the drink he had shared with long-time *Spider-Man* editor Tom Brevoort; and the time he had managed to procure a sketch of Superman, Batman, and Wonder Woman from Jim Lee.

The last one fired me up. There we were, sitting in a restaurant in the Philippines eating mushroom burgers—and we were right next to a man who had actually shaken hands with Jim Lee. Jim Lee! The phenomenal artist's artist, the person who'd redesigned all the X-Men costumes, the comic creator that I dreamt of one day becoming. Tito Fermin laughed at my ebullition and promised that the next time he met Jim Lee, he would ask for a signed sketch and post it to me.

As we made our way back to Lolo Doming's house, our uncle began to relate the difficulties he'd been having with his latest project. Echo Comics was intent on adding another superhero title to their monthly line-up, and they were looking to

Tito Fermin to deliver it. This was his concept: a superhero that policed the multiversal continuum, spinning from dimension to dimension in an eternal struggle with the Forces of Chaos.

"Spin-Man!" James interrupted.

Tito Fermin stopped and gave my brother a profound look. "Spin-Man?"

"Spin-Man. I don't know. I just thought of it. Do you have a name already?"

"Spin-Man," my uncle said, enunciating the syllables slowly, as if he were tasting them. "Spin-Man is a good name. I was thinking of calling him Omni-Man, but Spin-Man sounds much better. Would you mind if I called him that?"

"Yes!" James exclaimed, almost lost in delight. "I mean, no! I don't mind!"

It was unprecedented—my brother's idea was going straight into an actual comic book to be published in the States. His idea was going to be the name of the superhero, if not the title of the series. I was a little jealous of his moment of brilliance, but conceded that it was fair since he'd thought of it first. That was, of course, before things got out of hand.

"Can I be Spin-Man?" James asked, pulling on Tito Fermin's shirt sleeve. We had just arrived at my grandfather's house, and our uncle seemed lost in a daze.

"You mean his alter-ego? That would be a little like Shazam, wouldn't it?"

"Yes! Please? I can be a good character. I'll fight the Forces of Chaos."

James made a spinning move, grinding his sneakers against the pavement, and ended it with a punch to the air and a shout: "Spin-Man!"

Tito Fermin laughed. "All right, all right. You can be Spin-Man. What about your brother?"

By that time, I was foul-tempered and indignant. James had thrown a load of ideas at Tito Fermin, including Spin-Man's name, his costume, thoughts on potential enemies, and even a love interest. My jealousy was frothing at the mouth. I was an artist; a creative; I should have had more ideas than my colourist brother, but my mind was blank. I couldn't visualise Spin-Man. He was merely a figment, a cipher; I had no story to hang him onto. I struggled to keep my resentment in check, but when you're nine years old it's a difficult thing to hide. "No thank you, Tito Fermin. I think I'd rather draw Spin-Man. At least I'll make money doing it."

"You can draw it when you're older. I'll even ink you, if you'll have me." It was a promise that I knew would never be fulfilled. With that, Tito Fermin ruffled my hair and walked off to his room. As he moved away, I caught my little brother staring at me, and this is the face that I will never forget: James biting his lips, his eyes wide open, his expression a mix of guilt and apology, as if he had done something wrong.

That night, before we went to bed, he broached the topic one last time. I had ignored him throughout dinner and he had respected my silence, but after Lolita had tucked us in, he turned to me and asked, "Are you okay?"

"I'm fine," I said, though obviously I wasn't.

"You can be Spin-Man if you want. I can just tell Tito Fermin—"

"No thank you," I said, cutting him off.

And that was that.

I awoke late the next day. The sun was shining, the midday heat had begun to settle in, and my first thought was that I'd somehow overslept and missed Tito Fermin's leave-taking. My second thought was of James. There was no-one in the next bed, and I assumed that he must have been too bothered about my reaction the previous night to wake me. I put on my slippers and went downstairs. Santa Claus was asleep on his favourite couch, and Lolita was in the next room, sweeping.

"Good morning," she said. "Your Tito Fermin left early. He didn't want to wake you because it's your vacation, but he said that he loves you and that he'll keep in touch."

"I'm sorry about that, Lola. Have you seen James?"

"James?" she asked. She seemed puzzled. I rubbed my eyes and thought, *She must be going senile in her old age.*

"James," I repeated. "My brother."

She stopped sweeping and eyed me with suspicion. For a moment, she seemed to be considering what I meant, though it should have been obvious. And then she smiled. "Perhaps when you sleep tonight, you will see him again. Lunch will be ready soon."

I frowned at her. My grandmother was patronising me. Clearly, some sort of joke was happening that I was unaware of. I left the room and began to look for James. I had searched the living room, the terrace, the dining room, and the balcony before I began to wonder if James was playing an impromptu game of hide-and-seek with me. I pursued him through the house. I looked in bathrooms, closets, cabinets, and convenient hiding places behind doors, between bookshelves, and under beds. It was only when I noticed that his bag was missing; the bag that my mother had packed for him the day before we left for Los Baños; it was only then that I began to worry.

"James!" I called for him as I ran through the house. "Where's James?" I yelled at Lolita as she was putting out dishes for lunch. Lolo Doming walked in on us, scratching his head.

"What is he talking about?" he asked. "Who's James?"

I grew frantic, panicked. "James! My brother! This isn't funny!" I ran back to our room, looking for the pile of comics he had chosen the day before. There was only one pile. Mine.

"What's the matter with him?"

"I don't know."

I shouted. "I want my brother!"

Lolita ran after me. "What happened? What's wrong?"

"Where did he go?" I ran out of the bedroom and tossed my stack of comics down the stairs. "I want my brother!" I yelled.

Lolita bent over the comics. "You have no brother."

"James!"

My grandfather held me down. "Stop it right now!" he said. I struggled.

"James!"

I screamed. I cried. I went into hysterics. I must have blacked out because the next thing I knew, it was night time. My mother was there, in the bedroom, ready to take me home. "Where's James?" I asked her. I told her that his bag was gone, and that my grandparents wouldn't tell me where he was, and how could they not remember my little brother when she had tucked us in the night before?

She carried me and patted my back. "I know, honey, I know. Everything will be fine."

"I'm not fine," I sobbed.

"I know."

One interminable car ride later, I was home. I had secretly hoped that James had somehow got there ahead of us, that by some miracle of time and space, he was sitting on his bed or on his chair, waiting for me to arrive so that he could laugh at me and confess that it was all a joke. But when I entered our room, he wasn't there. Furthermore, the furniture had been rearranged; there was only one bed set, one chair, one writing desk, and a shelf where James's stuff should have been. Our superhero posters still covered the walls, but apart from that, I could find no trace of my brother.

I thought that I had already cried myself out that day, but as I stood there in our empty room, the tears began to trickle down my cheeks once more. Not tears of confusion or anger, but of grief. As I lay in my bed, my mother sat beside me, stroking my hair. "I don't know what you're going through," she said, "but I want you to know that I'm here for you. Okay?"

She pulled out an envelope from her bag. "Your Tito Fermin left this for you before he went to the airport. I hope you at least had a good time meeting him."

She left the envelope on my bedside table, kissed me on the forehead, and walked out of the room. "I love you, son. Rest well. I'll be here when you wake up."

I didn't want to sleep that night. I was exhausted, but I couldn't stand the idea of someone else disappearing while I slept. It occurred to me that I might have entered the Twilight Zone; that this was some horrible subconscious dream; that I would wake up in Los Baños and James would be there and everything would be as it should have been. My throat felt raw. My eyelids were heavy. But fear got the better of me, and after some time, I sat up in my bed and opened the envelope from Tito Fermin.

My hands shook as I pulled it out. There it was, in crisp, near-mint condition: a signed copy of *Spin-Man #1*, written and illustrated by Fermin de la Cruz.

The story opened with a scene featuring a young boy, James Jeronimo, reading a comic book. James was a normal boy, like you or me, who dreamt of becoming a superhero. The caption read: *At that precise moment, as James came to terms with his inflexible humanity, he felt an unearthly presence in the room.* The planets aligned. In an alternate dimension, a black mass crept over red skies, intent on devouring all life. James's eyes lit up as a display of coruscating energy erupted from his comic book, pulling him into a cosmic vortex. A wormhole opened up in the centre of the universe, and from its luminous recesses, a blue-and-gold figure emerged—Spin-Man, champion of the multiversal continuum!

Cloudy thought-balloons rose from Spin-Man's head: *Who am I? What is this place? I thought I was a boy reading a comic book, and now I have been summoned—to do what?* Then a vision appeared before him—black tendrils blotting out the sun on a world teeming with innocent life. Spin-Man's eyes narrowed. *The Forces of Chaos are threatening the continuum!* He activated his cosmic powers, spinning himself from the centre of the universe into an alternate dimension where, with the help of his cosmic abilities, he banished the Forces of Chaos into a black hole.

Spin-Man hovered over a crowd of green-skinned alien beings: inhabitants of the dimension he had just saved. *It seems that I have found my true purpose,* he thought. *Whenever Chaos threatens to engulf meaning in the universe, it will have to reckon with the might of Spin-Man!* Then a smile, a wink at the reader, and, under the last panel on the last page, the words "to be continued" laid out in bold letters.

Now, this is the difficulty of my story. By all other accounts, I never had a brother named James. No-one else seems to remember him. There is no birth certificate, no extra toothbrush, no extra bed in my room—not even a picture. But I remember him. I can see him in my mind. I remember his preferences, his lactose-intolerance, his Cyclops T-shirt, and his difficulties with Maths. I remember his birthday (June 15, 1983,) his favourite colour (green) his lucky number (4) and his best friend at school (Nicolo Suarez).

He was my little brother. He talked in his sleep. He loved Honey Stars and hated fruit-flavoured toothpaste. He was always our mother's favourite, and it had frustrated me that she always took his side. We watched *Ghostbusters* every Friday night, and on Saturday mornings we would get the garden hose and water-blast each other. We stole a book once, from the library—*The Illustrated Monkey King*—and it was James who eventually convinced me to give it back.

I remember him. But if I position this as true, then you'll think it absurd. I'm no scientist. I have no degree in quantum physics, no academic theory in my pocket, no hypotheses by which I can even begin to make you believe that he ever existed. I have no evidence, no proof. I only have what happened.

And now even that is just a memory: limited, intangible, decaying, and wide open to contention. If I die tomorrow, there will be nothing in this world to prove that James was ever real.

I kept *Spin-Man #1* in a Mylar bag, in its own drawer beside my bed. It had become the most precious comic book in my collection. Months passed before I came to terms with the reality of my brother's disappearance. My mother was very supportive. She took me to a psychiatrist and worked with me to uncover the root of my insistence on an imaginary brother. After the first few sessions, I learnt to stop openly asserting James's existence. With nothing to back up my claims, it was a losing battle. No progress was to be made on that front.

I kept trying to contact Tito Fermin. At first, they told me that he was too busy to talk to me, but I later discovered that he had moved addresses upon his return to the States and left no numbers by which we could contact him. I searched for further issues of Spin-Man, but was unable find copies in CATS or in any of the direct market stores. Apparently, they had never carried the title. I learnt later, from a 1993 issue of *The Comics Journal*, that Echo Comics had been a print-on-demand publisher that had struggled through low sales for two whole years before finally declaring bankruptcy.

In the summer of 1996, I found out that Tito Fermin had died. He had quit making comics three years earlier due to lack of money, and had become an automobile dealer in California. One night, he drank too much and drove his car into a copse of trees, which was where they found him three days later, wide-eyed with a long piece of window lodged into his head. We held a memorial mass for him in Los Baños. His body was buried in the States. He bequeathed a number of items to the family, amongst them a signed sketch of Spin-Man by Jim Lee, which was left in my care.

Years went by. I grew up. I had two girlfriends and one bad break-up. Peter Parker separated from Mary Jane, who moved away to become a supermodel. The X-Men's line-up shifted multiple times. Their Jim Lee costumes changed with each turnover until they could only be glimpsed in flashbacks and back issues. The Hulk grew smart, then dumb, then bald. Gotham City survived a plague, a major earthquake, and an army of ninjas. Superman died then came back to life. Green Lantern was corrupted, went rogue, died saving the universe, and was replaced by another Green Lantern. Spin-Man never made it past issue two.

I know this because, on the day after my graduation, I found a battered old copy of *Spin-Man #2* in a book sale bargain bin. James was on the cover, hovering in the void of the universe as the tell-tale blue-and-gold vortex, the one that had transformed him into Spin-Man, whirlpooled around him. In the comic, a black hole had turned sentient and was trudging across the cosmos in the shape of an impossible spider. The Forces of Chaos had returned. Spin-Man, as valiant as ever, rushed to combat the threat, but in a critical moment, the Chaos Spider spat a web of nebulae at our hero, disrupting his celestial abilities and forcing him to spin into another dimension.

Spin-Man awoke in a void, buffeted on all sides by peculiar purple rain. He bowed his head in shame. *I've failed,* he thought. *I've fallen into the unknown, somewhere beyond the far reaches of the multiversal continuum. If I don't find my way back, the Forces of Chaos will engulf the universe and all that I hold dear.* Spin-Man coughed. For a moment, his visage shifted into that of James, his human alter-ego. His eyes glimmered with hope. Spin-Man's course was clear. *I have to find my way back, no matter how long it takes.* With that, he launched himself into the void, away from the reader, as the words "never the end" appeared beneath him, like a promise. It was the last issue of Spin-Man to achieve publication. I swear, I broke down right there in the middle of the bookshop, holding onto that stupid little comic book. I realised, right then, that I needed to do something; anything, or else James would be lost forever.

These days, CATS no longer sells comic books. They've since turned into a specialty store for action figures, and though I visit it from time to time, the bargain bins I used to thumb through are no longer there. I still buy comics every Wednesday when I have the money. I keep track of my favourite superheroes' lives. For me they affirm that, despite hardship, some things may still endure. I've taken a course in Fine Arts, and I've been applying it to my comics' illustrations, working hard to improve to a professional level. As soon as I finish college, I'll send off applications to the major comic book companies. I'll get a job in the States, and when I've saved up enough money, I'll look up Echo Comics and buy the rights to Spin-Man.

Then I'll publish *Spin-Man #3*, and in that issue, Spin-Man will be at the edge of the universe, contemplating his path home. A blue-and-gold wormhole will appear before him. With superhuman courage, Spin-Man will activate his cosmic powers, jump through the vortex, and spin his way back into our world.

BORROWED TIME

ANABEL ENRIQUEZ PIÑEIRO
TRANSLATED BY DANIEL W. KOON

Cuban author Anabel Enriquez Piñeiro is a prolific writer of short stories, articles, and scripts, and has organised several conventions and workshops in Cuba. The following story, appearing here in English for the first time, has won the first prize in the 2005 Juventud Técnica SF competition.

Your hair, a centimetre or two longer, your skin maybe more tanned than the last time. Smooth, yes, like a shiny shell, without a single fold, without a scar. Me, on the other hand, my face could serve as the canvas for an astronavigation map: you could catalogue all my wrinkles by latitude and longitude. And locate all its globular clusters, wormholes, and black holes. There's room for the entire universe on my face.

You don't see my face. You have taken up residence on a spot on the terrace where you watch the stars fall—m-e-t-e-o-r-s, you make me repeat, letter by letter, helping me to spell it out with your hands. And even the perfume of the poplars in bloom seems to bother you. Serena-Ceti is a world without a future—you shake your fingers wildly and point at the night sky over the terrace.

Look up above, so many worlds to visit, so many twilights beneath double and triple stars, the chance to use hyperjumps to effectively live forever... an eternity of journeying between the stars. I struggle in vain to understand your words, your passion for those faraway lights in unknown and unreachable houses that inhabit the night; I am only five years old.

I run my fingers through your hands, as I did back then, trying to find some final assignment in them. But they are rigid, muteness, fingers that refuse to surrender the secret behind your need to transcend.

The Persephone docked for the first time on Serena-Ceti a few days after your confession on the terrace. How long ago was that for you? Three months, four...? It doesn't matter... For you it is time elapsed, time transcended. For me, the indelible image: the hydrogen smell of the aerotransporter that carries you to the spaceport; the shards of glass embedded in the soles of my boots (from the last glass lamp we would ever put in our hallway); the colour of helplessness on my father's face... You don't need any superior intelligence to understand what "stomping out of the house" means to a five-year-old girl, even if she's a deaf-mute. But I didn't understand then what it meant for you. Father did.

Father spends hours writing up his Academy lectures, the

crumpled papers piling up around him and his computer growing mouldy beneath the dust. He never sleeps more than two hours. He never rests. I think that he is afraid of falling asleep and aging at an accelerated pace. Or of falling asleep and dreaming of you. Father accompanies me to the pulse station in the capital to receive a message you sent barely a week after you left on the exploration ship, *The Persephone*, with that splendid annual contract as back-up exobiologist. I am twelve. You are exactly as I remember you. And your fingers speak with the same fluency as ever: *maybe, when you see this message I will be arriving home.* Funny how these transmissions keep coming from the Sorceress of Hyperspace. *You must be quite grown up, sweetheart.* And then, in gestures: *I'll bring you some glass rock earrings from Delta Altair to set off your ears with that short haircut of yours.* I am twelve years old, hair down to my waist, my ears marked with scars from the cochlear surgery and the rejected implants that have not cured my deafness. But you don't know. And in my naïve twelve-year-old eyes, that not knowing makes you innocent; and besides, I already know that you will be back in less than three years for my fifteenth birthday, and I will wear those earrings at a party and my ears will shine with the light from other worlds, from other stars, from the entire universe.

I waited a whole year when I turned fifteen. I watched so many twilights of our little sun and the conjunctions of the moons twice nightly. But not a single star came down from the sky. *The Persephone* arrived one random afternoon in the summer. I went by myself to pick you up at the spaceport. I'm sorry, Miranda, you said, with a quick hug and the same smile as ever. My calculation was off by a few minutes. You could not have forgotten the way. How far off was it this time...? Two minutes, five? That doesn't matter to you either. But I've turned eighteen and it would have been a miracle for me to still be so naïve. Something has changed dramatically in this lost little world during what has seemed like only three weeks to you. I can forgive you missing a lot of things in your absence: the operating rooms, puberty rudely taking over my body, the angst of my first unrequited love, the listless and frustrating experience of my first non-orgasm. But your absence from my successes was more painful.

Over my father's objections, I got a scholarship to study astronomy at the Academy for Physical Sciences in the capital. No more nights of tiptoeing through the house, an amateur telescope under my arm, hiding from my dad to get to the terrace to stare at the dawn. At first I naïvely looked for a sign from you in the heavens, but then my loneliness finally latched onto the stars themselves. I stopped necking with the neighbourhood boys, and they began to call me a junior lunatic.

I told you about the scholarship then. You smiled and I think I caught a glimmer of pride in your eyes. You apologised for not knowing about my interest in astronomy and you regretted the many things you could have brought me for my personal collection from the many planets you had visited. I gave you a lukewarm thank you. In the end, we were just two intimate strangers.

Later, after a week of rest, you left on another space mission. I will return for your wedding, no ifs ands or buts! you promised, winking an eye at Iranus, my boyfriend at the time, who accompanied us to the launch. We would be married when I left the Academy. Back then, I believed in eternal love, and I believed that a mother kept her promises.

It was then, at the beginning of my final course at the Academy, that the first symptoms of papa's sickness began to show. I was called to his office several times to bring him home. I found him disorientated, physically exhausted, and trembling. His formerly dark hair grew greyer and thinner by the day. Papa got old much too soon, while you remained unchanged.

For you time sped by red-hot, while for Papa it froze ice-blue. And he was growing more distant from me by the second.

I had already been working two years in the pulse station when you came back the second time.

It has been barely six months since the birth of Harlan, my third child. Iranus? My God, how do you still remember him? That was an ancient chapter in my life, followed by so many other forgotten versions.

Deverios, Harlan's father, had just died in an aerial transit accident. I was two years older than you at the time, but I still couldn't understand what dragged you away from Serena-Ceti, and what I was supposed to understand by your need for transcendence: watching your children grow up? Seeing your own self carried on in their lives? No, Miranda, I'm watching you grow up, at a speed that any parent would envy. And I don't miss the changes, because for me the world is measured in astronomical units; what you see as abstract units are my reality. What I want is to transcend the time and space that are limiting us as a species. It was a lively lecture, but all I heard was the immature teenager underneath it all. Because now I no longer wonder why you left Serena-Ceti, but why you returned.

You and Papa saw each other for the last time on that trip. He was confined to the sanatorium for patients with retroviral dementia. Hospitalised for over a year with no definitive diagnosis.

A few short lines in his report spoke of a premature aging syndrome. Cause unknown. He confused you with me; he confused me with you. I still hold the memory in my cheek of the heat of his slap. Later, he lapsed into an impenetrable silence until the end, barely a week after *The Persephone* lifted off again.

Your third trip came at the end of an anguished time on Serena. Torrential rains and unknown epidemics that led to a planet-wide quarantine. *The Persephone*'s planned return, coming as it did during the spaceport's closure, was delayed for thirty-two years, and when you appeared again, my grandchildren raced through the entranceway to greet you. For them, like my children before them, you were an almost magical and distant being, like the stars. And one week with you did nothing to change their opinion. It surprised you to see the holograms of so many strange persons in my albums, all of them bearing a trace of your DNA. You had a large family that you never knew and who never knew you either. It surprised you to see my room filled with trophies and awards from social and scientific organisations, some of them off-planet, in recognition of my work. But it was my old age that surprised you most of all. Although you knew that the years would not stop for me, it was still very difficult for you to accept that your daughter, your only remaining link to Serena-Ceti, now embodied everything that you had feared so much. And I learnt then, that now you would never come back again willingly.

Nearly forty years have passed. I have seen so many dreams blossom and die, so many broken promises, and so many loved ones who followed the natural order of life, the one you rebelled against, forcing me to betray it, too. Papa always said that children should not die before their parents; I accepted that as a commandment.

One hundred and six years after your first departure, that message arrived on the hyperjump channel. That *The Persephone* would arrive in six days. That it would carry your body. Killed in an excavation accident on the fifth planet of Procyon Alpha. How large an error was it this time? One second, two...? Enough to bury all your passion for transcendence in an avalanche of xenophobic stones. I had wanted to cry, but at one hundred and eleven years of age, one's reflexes grow sluggish and sometimes disappear. I signed for your body in order to process the customary funeral ceremony. It did not surprise me to once again see the mother who had abandoned her home when I was five. Aside from the skin colour or the hair a centimetre or two longer, nothing had changed.

Now I have dressed you with my own hands, something I don't remember you ever having done for me, and I come back to your ears, as useless as my own have been, to those rock crystal earrings from Delta Altair.

Once more I sense the flames as they consume fat, tendons, and bones. But I know that this will be the last time. Now you are returning to the heavens in the form of smoke. You return to the night, but not to the stars, those windows open to an endless parade of strangers' homes. Now that you will never leave again, now that, for some reason you could not foresee, the natural order of your life has been fulfilled, I can rest. I no longer have to look at the sky and ask which star you are on.

BRANDED

LAUREN BEUKES

South African writer Lauren Beukes is the author of novels *Moxyland* and the Clarke Award winning *Zoo City*, raved about by everyone from André Brink to William Gibson. She is a full-time novelist and comics writer, and lives in Cape Town.

We were at Stones, playing pool, drinking, goofing around, maybe hoping to score a little sugar, when Kendra arrived, all moffied up and gloaming, like, an Aito/329. "Ahoy, Special K, where you been, girl, so juiced to kill?" Tendeka asked while he racked up the balls, all click-clack in their white plastic triangle. Old-school, this pool bar was. But Kendra didn't answer. Girl just grinned, reached into her back pocket for her phone, hung skate-rat-style off a silver chain connected to her belt, and infra'd five rand to the table to get tata machance on the next game.

But I was watching the girl and, as she slipped her phone back into her pocket, I saw that tell-tale glow 'neath her sleeve. Long sleeves in summer didn't cut it. So, it didn't surprise me none in the least when K waxed the table. Ten-Ten was surprised though. Ten-Ten slipped his groove. But boy kept it in, didn't say anything, just infra'd another five to the table and racked 'em again. Anyone else but Ten woulda racked 'em hard, woulda slammed those balls on the table, eish. But Ten, Ten went the other way. Just by how careful he was. Precise 'n clipped like an assembly line. So you could see.

Boyfriend wasn't used to losing, especially not to Special-K. I mean, the girl held her own 'gainst most of us, but Ten could wax us all six-love, baby. Boyfriend carried his own cue in a special case. Kif shit, it was. Lycratanium, separate pieces that clicked into each other, assembled slick 'n cold and casual-like, like he was a soldier in a war movie snapping a sniper rifle together. But Kendra, grinning now, said, "No, my bra. I'm out," set her cue down on the empty table next to us.

"Oh, ja, like Ten's gonna let this hook slide." Rob snorted into his drink.

"Best of three" Tendeka said and smiled loose and easy. Like it didn't matter and chalked his cue.

Girl hesitated and shrugged then. Picked up the cue. Tendeka flicked the triangle off the table, flip-rolling it between his fingers lightly. "Your break."

Kendra chalked-up, spun the white ball out to catch it at the line. Edged it then sideways so's it would take the pyramid out off-centre. Girl leant over the table. Slid the tip of the cue over her knuckles once, taking aim, pulled back, and cut loose, smooth as sugar. Crack! Balls twisting out across the table. Sunk four solids straight-up. Black in the middle and not a single stripe down.

Rob whistled. "Shit. You been practising, K?"

Kendra didn't even look up. Took out another two solids and lined up a third in the corner pocket. Girl's lips twitched, but she didn't smile, no, didn't look at Ten, who was still sayin' nothin', like. He chalked his cue again, like he hadn't done it already, and stepped up. The freeze was so tight I couldn't take it. Anyway. I knew what was coming. So, off by the bar I was, but nears enough so I was still in on the action, like. Ten lined 'em up and took out two stripes at the same time, rocketing 'em into different pockets. Bounced the white off the pillow and took another, edged out the solid K had all lined up. Another stripe down and boy lined up a fifth blocking the corner pocket. "You're up."

Girl just stood there lookin' as if she was sizing up.

"K. You're up."

Girl snapped her head towards Tendeka. Tuned back in. Took her cue up, leant over, standing on tiptoes and nicked the white ball light as candy, so it floated, spinning, into the middle of table, like. Shrugged at Ten, smiling, and that ball just kept on spinning. Stepped back, set her cue down on the table next and started walking over to the bar, to me, while that white ball, damn, was still spinning.

"Hey! What the fuck?"

"Ah, c'mon, Ten. You know I gotcha down."

"What! Game ain't even started. And what's with this, man? Fuckin' party tricks don't mean shit."

"It's over, Ten."

"You on drugs, girl? You tweaked?"

"Fuck off, Ten."

Ten shoved his cue at Rob, who snatched it quick, and rounded on the girlfriend. "You're mashed, Kendra!" He grabbed her shoulder, spun her round, "C'mon, show me!"

"Kit Kat, baby. Give it a break."

"Oh yeah? Lemme see. C'mon."

"Fuck off, Tendeka! Serious!"

People were looking now. Cams were, too, though in a place like Stones, they probably weren't working none too well. Owner paid a premium for faulty equipment, like. Jazz was defending Kendra now. Not that she needed it. We all knew the girl wasn't a waster, like. Even Ten.

Now me. I was a waster. I was skeef. Jacked that kind shit straight into my tongue, popping lurid lurex candy capsules into the piercing to disseminate, like. Lethe or supersmack or kitty. Some prefer it old-style, pills 'n needles, but me, the works work best straight in through that slippery warm pink muscle. Porous your mouth is. So's it's straight into the blood and saliva absorbs the rest into your glands. I could tell you all things about that wet-hole mouth that makes it perfect for drugs, like. But, tell you true, it's all cheap shit. Black-market. Ill legit. Not like sweet Kendra's high. Oh, no, girl had gone the straight 'n arrow. All the way, baby. All the way.

"C'mon Ten, back off, man." Rob was getting real nervous, like. Bartender, too, twitchin' to call his defuser. But Kendra-sweet had enough now, spun on Ten, finally, stuck out her tongue at him like a laaitie. And Jazz sighed. "There. Happy now?" But Ten wasn't. For yeah, sure as sugar, Special-K's tongue was a virgin. Never been pierced by a stud let alone an applijack. Never had that sweet rush as the micro-needles release slick-quick into the fleshy pink. Never had her tongue go numb with the dark oiliness of it so's you can't speak for minutes. Doesn't matter though. Talkin'd be least of your worries. Supposin' you had any. But then Ten knew that all along. Cos you can't play the way the girlfriend did on the rof. Tongue's not the only thing that goes numb. And boyfriend knows it. And everything's click-clicking into place.

"Oh, you fucking crazy little shit. What have you done?" Ten was grabbing at her now, tough-like, her swatting at him, pulling away as he tried to get a hold of her sleeve. Jazz was yelling again. "Ease off, Tendeka!" Shouldn't have wasted her air time. Special-K could look after herself all well now. After those first frantic swats, something levelled. Only to be expected when she's so fresh. Still adjustin', like. But you could see it kick in. Sleek, it was. So's instant she's flailing about and the next she lunges, catches him under his chin with the heel of her palm. Boy's head snaps back and at the same time she shoves him hard so's he falls backwards, knocks over a table on his way. Glass smashing and the bartender's pissed now. Everyone still, except Rob who laughed once, abrupt.

Girl gave Ten a look. Cocky as a street kid. But wary, it was, too. Not of him, although he was already getting up. Not that she could sustain, like. Battery was running low now. Was already when she first set down her cue. And boy was pissed indeed. But that look, boys and girls, that look was wary, not of him at all. But of herself, like.

Ten was on his feet now, screaming. The plot was lost, boys and girls. The plot was gone. Cut himself on the broken glass. Like paint splats on to the wooden floor. Lunged at Kendra, backing away, hands up, but still with that look. And boy was big. Intent on serious damage, yelling and not hearing his cell bleep first warning then second. Like I said, the plot was gone. Way past its expiry date.

Then predictable; defuser kicked in. Higher voltage than necessary, like, but bartender was pissed. Ten jerked epileptic. Some wasters I know set off their own phone's defuser, on low settings, like, for those dark an' hectic beats. Even rhythm can be induced, boys and girls. But it's not maklik. Have to hack SAPcom to sms the trigger signal to your phone. Worse now since the cops privatised, upgraded the firewalls. That or tweak the hardware and then the shocks could come random. Crisp you KFC.

Me, I defused my defuser. 'Lectric and lethe don't mix. Girlfriend in Sea Point pulled the plug one time. Simunye. Cost ten kilos of sugar so's it don't come cheap an' if the tec don't know what they're doing, ha, crisp you KFC. Or worse, Disconnect. Off the networks. Solitary confinement, like. Not worth the risk, boys and girls, unless you know the tec is razor.

So, Ten, jerking to imaginary beats. Bartender hit endcall finally and boy collapsed to floor, panting. Jasmine knelt next to him. Ten's phone still crackling. VIMbots scuttling to clean up blood an' glass and spilled liquor. Other patrons were turning away now. Game over. Please infra another coin. Kendra stood watching a second, then also turned away, walked up to the bar where I was sitting.

"Cause any more kak like that, girl, an I'll crisp you, too." The bartender said as she sat down on the bar stool next to me.

"Oh, please. Like how many dial-ins you got left for the night?" Kendra snapped, but girl was looking almost as strung out as Ten was now.

"Yeah, well don't make me waste 'em all on you."

"Just get me a Sprite, okay?"

Behind her, Jazz and Rob were holdin' Tendeka up. He made as if to move for the bar, but Jazz pulled him back, wouldn't let him. Not least cos of the look the bartender shot them. Boy was too fried to stir anyway, but said, loud enough for all to hear, "Sell out."

"Get the fuck out, kid." Dismissive the bartender was. Knew there was no fight left.

"Fucking corporate whore!"

"C'mon, Ten. Let's go." Jazz was escortin' him out.

Kendra ignored him. Girl had her Sprite now and downed it in one. Asked for another.

Already you could see it kickin' in.

"Can I see?" I asked, mock sly-shy.

Kendra shot me a look which I couldn't figure and then finally slid up her sleeve reluctant, like, revealing the glow tattooed on her wrist.

The bartender clicked his tongue as he set down the drink. "Sponsor baby, huh?"

Sprite logo was emblazoned there, not on her skin, but under it, shining through, with the slogan, "Just be it."

No rinkadink light show, was this. Nanotech she'd signed up for changed the bio-structure of her cells, made 'em phosphorescent in all the right places. Nothing you couldn't get done at the local light-tat salon, but corporate sponsorship came with all the extras. Even on lethe, I wasn't 'blivious to the ad campaigns on the underway. But Kendra was the first I knew to get Branded, like.

Girl was flying now. Ordered a third Sprite. Brain reacting like she was on some fine-ass bliss, drowning her in endorphins an serotonin, Sprite binding with aminos and the tiny bio -machines hummin' at work in her veins. Voluntary addiction with benefits. Make her faster, stronger, more co-ordinated. Ninja-slick reflexes. Course, if she'd sold her soul to Coke instead, she'd be sharper, wittier. Coke nano lubes the transmitters. Neurons firing faster, smarter, more productive. All depends on the brand, on your lifestyle of choice and it's all free if you qualify. Waster like me would never get with the programme, but sweet Kendra, straight up candidate of choice. Apply now, boys and girls, while stocks last. You'll never afford this high on your own change.

Special K turned to me, on her fourth now, blissed out on the carbonated nutri-sweet and the tech seething in her hot little sponsor baby bod, nodded, "And one for my friend," to the bartender, like. And who was I to say no?

DECEMBER 8TH

RAÚL FLORES IRIARTE
TRANSLATED BY DANIEL W. KOON AND THE AUTHOR

Raúl Flores Iriarte lives in Havana. He is the author of several short story collections, from 2000's *The Dark Side of the Moon* to 2010's *Paperback Writer*. He is also the author of the novella *Balada de Jeanette*. The following story, appearing here in English for the first time, won the 2006 Juventud Técnica SF contest.

H ello," I say to John Lennon. It's cold in Manhattan. Much colder than I'm used to. Madonna is circling around the streets like a maniac in her brand-new Porsche, the one I gave her just a few minutes earlier.

"Who are you?" John asks.

I introduce myself. "I'm here to save your life," I tell him.

"What's this about saving my life?" he replies. John speaks impeccable English. As if he had been born in England. And then I remember: he *was* born in England.

I explain to him about Mark David Chapman. He is the lunatic. He is the assassin. He is the walrus.

"That's crazy," John says. I can almost make out the words as they leave his mouth, like the hook of a great pop song. The one that was never written.

"He's going to come here and kill you today. Tonight. While we're talking here, he's lurking out there. Waiting. Plotting. With a copy of *The Catcher in the Rye* under his arm."

John looks at me as if I'm crazy, too. Or like he doesn't understand English. Or maybe both.

"That's a good book," he mutters.

"What?" I say.

"*The Catcher in the Rye*. Good book. Salinger is a—"

"Listen," I interrupt him, raising my voice. "This is no time for literary chit-chat. There's barely time to explain. I'll just take your place and try to stop Chapman. Kill him if I have to."

"And you're going to do all this *because*...?" he asks.

A set of lyrics flashes into my mind like lightning: *Because the world is round it turns me on.* But instead I say: "To change the future. To give you a new life, borrowed time. You could have a Beatles reunion in a couple years, new songs for the old fans. Won't you please... help me? It'll be just like starting over."

His song *(Just Like) Starting Over* has been rocketing up the charts. I am hoping he appreciates the reference. I continue: "You see that girl driving that Porsche up and down the street like a maniac? Well, her name is Madonna Louise Veronica Ciccone, but in three or four years, everyone will know her as simply 'Madonna.' She's got a lot of talent, but right now, nobody knows her. I've changed all that. Bought her the Porsche, given her the money to bankroll her first LP, and I made her sign two hundred or three hundred autographs for me to sell in the future."

After losing a couple of minutes in the cold Manhattan air, I manage to convince John Winston Lennon. It took revealing two or three state secrets, describing what Paul McCartney was up to on November 3, 1967, and showing him my portable time machine.

"But, look," he says, "there's not going to *be* any Beatles reunion any time ever. That's finished. Over. Kaput. Capisce?"

WINTER IN MANHATTAN, A FEW minutes before ten o'clock. I get out of the limo, Yoko stands next to me. Chapman approaches from out of the blue and yells something I can't quite make out. My mind is as lucid as ever, but my ears are deaf for the time being, or so it seems.

"Mister John!" he shouts and I can understand him this time.

I turn around, and he empties his pistol's chambers into my chest.

The bullet-proof vest absorbs the impacts.

Then I empty my own gun into him.

THE DAKOTA HOTEL, SNOW FALLING over a dead man's body with the swirling precision of a nightmare. Yoko begins to cry. John comes up to me and says, "So, that's the guy." Someone out there yells for an ambulance.

Lennon walks out onto the street, maybe to get a better view of the scene, or maybe to hail a taxi to move the corpse to the nearest hospital. Or the nearest morgue. However, at that very instant the ghostlike silhouette of a dark Porsche is crossing the street with the speed of a shooting star. It's all over in a microsecond. Half a microsecond.

The car screeches to a halt, the squeal of its brakes can be heard all the way to San Francisco, and the body of John Winston Lennon goes flying some five metres into the air before crashing into a lamppost. And that's that.

Mark David Chapman lying blood-drenched on the sidewalk, Yoko crying over John's twisted body, and Madonna behind the wheel of the Porsche with those wild eyes, diamond eyes, a material girl watching me, watching the two bodies, and the night, and the snow.

Ambulance sirens pierce the heavy silence that has suddenly settled between us like a blanket of something far whiter and colder than this snow that falls down, and then the police arrive, asking questions and filling out reports. I slink away quietly, consoling myself with the fact that there was nothing I could have done for Lennon, and ain't that a shame.

But it's not all bad. Madonna's autographs will certainly come in handy in my own present, in their own future. Just like the autographs I got out of Lee Harvey Oswald right before I had him ice Nixon.

HUNGRY MAN

WILL ELLIOTT

Australian Will Elliott is the author of *The Pilo Family Circus,* a magnificent novel of murderous clowns which won the Aurealis, Ditmar, *and* Shadow awards in Australia. He is also the author of *Strange Places,* a memoir about schizophrenia, and of the forthcoming *Pendulum* trilogy. The following story is original to this anthology.

When the redheaded woman with the baby carriage at last moved out of earshot, Phil said, "It's easy, just get it down the back of your pants. You saw me do it a hundred times, come on."

Lex looked nervously at the girl behind the news-agency counter and said, "She'll see me. We come here every other day and never *buy* anything."

"She doesn't care. For twelve dollars an hour, think she cares if they're missing a couple magazines? C'mon go, she's not looking."

Phil made it look easy. In awe, Lex had watched him walk out of shops with packets of corn chips stuffed in his shirt so he looked pregnant, watched him take show bags from stalls at the carnival, condoms from the chemist (they did nothing with them except leave them on the spouts of their school's drinking fountains). Phil stole cigarettes and sold them to the older kids who played coin-op games. He stole CDs, once a DVD set from *JBHiFi*. His prize catch: an iPod, one of those nice thirty-two gig ones with a digicam inside. Close call, the Target woman turned her back for just a moment after he'd got her to take it out of the case for a look at it, not even planning to steal it till she took her eyes off them. A security guard chased them out of there and they couldn't go back to Westfield Strathpine again any time in the next decade.

For his part, Lex had stolen two packets of bubble gum. It had been from this very news agency the girl had gone out to the back for a minute or two. "The register," Phil had urged. "Go! There's fifties in there."

Lex had been unable to do it. People had been walking past the doorway; they'd have seen him. He took the gum instead. His hands shook for half an hour afterwards.

And right now the news agency was busy. Old people buying lottery tickets. A creepy perverted dude by the porn mags who hadn't moved since they'd come in, probably had a big fat woody while he fumbled through the latest *Picture*. "Don't worry about that perv," Phil whispered. "That's the retard who walks up and down the road all night. If he sees you, he won't even remember it five minutes from now."

"How do you know?"

"We threw rocks at him, me and Trent. He just looked at us, didn't even care. Next day we walked right past him, he didn't recognise us. So what are you worried about?"

I have a dad at home, Lex thought but didn't dare say. *Not like you. Your mother won't pull your pants down right in front of everyone at any old excuse to do it and hit the crap out of your nude butt like it turns her on.*

Well no, Phil's dad wouldn't do that exactly. Phil's dad would visit once a week and his doped-out mum would sit there in a Valium cloud and list out stuff he'd done wrong during the week in a calm dreamy voice, while Phil's dad slowly undid his belt. *Alex, I think you should go home now.* You'd hear it from three houses down: cries and pleads as if Phil were being killed in there, whack, whack, whack. Every Tuesday. Visiting Day.

Phil said, "Alex, listen. You eat the stuff I steal, you keep half of it. You never take anything yourself. Bubble-gum? How badass. Come on. Go-get us some titty mags and we're even."

Lex left Phil standing before the comics, sidled over to the magazine stand opposite the titty mags and looked nervously at the girl behind the counter, now selling smokes to some geezer who thought he was pretty funny. Lex snuck a glance at the glossy covers, heart beating faster with the alien allure of women as old as his teachers, posing on the *Penthouse* with legs open, a white sheet draped between them; on *Barely Legal* in roller skates with a lollypop and pig-tails; in this weird black leather outfit on *Babes & Bikes.* Suddenly he wanted each magazine very badly. He'd all but forgotten the pervy guy, who hadn't moved, still thumbing through the *Home Girls* section in *Picture.* The pervy guy was just a pillar of legs beside him, as inhuman as concrete.

Lex grabbed a *Penthouse* and a *Playboy.* Down the back of his shorts they went, where they slipped and slid almost completely out till he tucked them into his underwear. Turning for the exit, not daring to look to see if anyone had witnessed it, he walked head-first into the pervy guy's legs, his face striking the man's hip.

It was a long way to look up and see the face staring down at him, half-covered in black stubble. The man's wide mouth hung open, eyes just peering down with no way of telling if it was anger or total blankness in them. Lex sensed something *else* there, too, a threat he didn't understand at all, which made something inside him scream *run* but at the same time paralysed him so he couldn't.

"Hey, Alex, let's go for a swim," Phil called innocently across to him from the news-agency counter. "Before it gets dark. Over at the nature strip. C'mon." Phil's voice seemed to break Lex out of a trance. He walked through the magazine rows, not daring to look sideways at the girl behind the counter, whose gaze he felt following him. The magazines down his pants were surely sticking out a mile.

At long last, blessedly, they were outside in the afternoon light. Cars whizzed by on Anzac Avenue. Their bikes leant against the shop wall. "Don't pull 'em out yet, you dink," Phil hissed, as Lex adjusted the magazines' position. "Oh shit. Quick, get on your bike and go."

"What, why...?"

The pervert guy, like a horror movie zombie, shuffled slowly out of the shop and headed their way. His mouth still hung open, his eyes as dead as pebbles. "Catching flies, fuck head?" Phil said to him. "Shut your mouth, you look like a spastic." The man didn't say a word, just stared and shuffled closer. "I think he likes you, Alex. Frigging weirdo."

They rode away, wheeling through traffic and many pissed off drivers, car horns blaring. Lex was so filled with sweet relief to be out of the news agency he hardly noticed how close he was to getting run over.

RUMOUR HAD IT THAT IF you could get to the waterhole at night, you'd sometimes see the bogan kids who got drunk in the Kallangur shop car parks doing it with their girlfriends, actually doing it right here in the long grass. They'd been out here one sleepover to test the theory but had seen no such thing.

It had rained last night and now the quite frequent cars that swung down the nearby road's dip sloshed up water as they went. On the wide grassy platform a few metres above the water, Phil took out the Mars bar he'd slipped into his pocket right in front of the counter girl while he'd joked with her about the pervert guy. He peeled back its wrapping, which took much of the squished melted thing off with it, then stuffed the rest into his mouth. "Yeah, I saw that retard before," said Phil, examining the *Penthouse* centrefold. "Lives on Sheehan Street. He just walks around at night, right down the middle of the road sometimes. Drivers have to go around him. Lives with these really old people, maybe his parents. Not right in the head. You can throw rocks at him or whatever and he just looks at you, doesn't even care. So, are you going to jump or not?"

Last time they'd come, Phil had ridden his bike off the ledge and into the water. It was now Lex's turn. From the seat of his black BMX, the water was just a brown wedge visible over the sloping rise before the drop. Phil said, "You won't break your legs or anything. It's deep right down there."

Lex said, "Not worried about my legs, I'm worried about the bike."

"It's *water*, man, jeez come on."

"I didn't get this bike for my birthday like you got yours. I delivered pamphlets on Saturdays in the heat and paid for it myself."

"Then you went and stole from the shops. What a good boy." Phil took the *Playboy* out of Lex's schoolbag. "If you don't jump, I'm keeping this."

"Okay, okay." Lex took off his shoes, put his glasses in their case, took a deep breath then pushed off, pumping hard on the pedals, the tyres bumping over the grassy ground. The water opened up into view three metres below, then he was airborne, letting go so the bike flung itself out ahead of him while he landed feet first in the water.

It was cold and not as deep as Phil had claimed, for his feet touched the hideously soft mud at its bottom. He came up and used his first gasp of air to whoop in triumph. He swam forwards to get the bike. "See that?" he laughed, spitting out a coppery mouthful.

"You didn't stay on your bike, doesn't count. Do it again."

"I'll do it again, no problem. That was sweet!"

Nearing the top of the path, Lex heard other voices up on the grassy platform: someone laughing. "Oh shit," he heard Phil say. "Lex, get up here, okay?"

Still elated, Lex wheeled the bike up the curving path, starting to feel a chill from the late afternoon air. There was, at most, an hour of daylight left.

When he got up there he saw why Phil had been worried. Craig Randall and Keith Hume, that was why. There was, Lex was quite aware, a chance for him to get back on the bike and ride it down the path and out of there. And he knew he would have if his schoolbag and shoes hadn't been up there with Phil, along with the precious magazines. Both these guys had been kicked out of school for beating people up. The last guy, Keith had rammed his head into a pole and put him in the hospital and into a neck brace. Keith's messy blond hair hung down over his shoulders, muscled arms exposed in a singlet. His friend Craig was tall, fat, redheaded, with squinting eyes and skin entirely covered in freckles. They were both three years and many growth spurts older.

Craig casually took Lex's bike from him and sat on it in a way somehow devoid of aggression—just borrowing a seat. "Your friend's fucked," he said in his oddly high pitched voice. *Going to be a pretty good show, hey?* Craig smiled with no malice at all and produced a little bag of cask wine, which he put to his lips and sucked on. The wine's cheap stink filled the place.

Phil didn't move as Keith Hume stepped closer to him.

"Why do you have to hit him, Keith?" Lex said. "We got no problem with you."

"Shut the fuck up, Alex," Phil snapped at him.

Lex remembered what Phil had said about guys like this. They *would* beat you up now and then, face it. Just let them. Don't be a pussy about it and they'd mostly leave you alone from then on. "Get it over with," said Phil.

"What'd you say, cunt?" Shove to the shoulder, fists up, here it came. Jab, jab, crack went knuckles on Phil's nose and cheek. They were fast, economical punches. Long fast arms, punching machines made just for this. Phil's head rocked back. Lex almost felt it, almost saw the explosions of white stars. Craig chortled and slurped his wine. "Come on, Keith, that's enough, hey," said Lex.

But it wasn't. Phil staggered and nearly fell but fought to keep on his feet. The "bully will respect you" theory, but Lex knew it wouldn't work. "Stay down, Phil, for fuck's sake," he yelled, tears welling up in his eyes, a lump in his throat.

Craig got off the bike and with the same lack of malice, gave it a shove towards the drop and the water below. It rolled most of the way there, balanced on its wheels as though it had an invisible rider, then clattered onto its side and slid over the edge.

Lex forgot about Phil and the *crack crack* of punches still rocking his friend's head back. There was just a long dark angry tunnel with Craig at the end of it. It was the casual way he'd done it, absolutely nothing personal in it. All those mornings in the hot sun, barked at by dogs, chased by one, riding up that hill on Gyp Court, swooped by magpies, wasp nests in letter boxes, folding fucking Coles and Food-Store pamphlets together all Friday night till his fingers were dark with ink. It had all been for Craig, to provide him five seconds or so of entertainment.

Lex's hand picked up the flat rectangular stone all by itself. He moved automatically as he drew it back and shoved it into that utterly-hated, squinting, freckled face.

Craig grunted in surprise. That was the point at which Lex's memory erased what followed, which was, of course, his hand—so much smaller—being grabbed tightly, the rock being taken out of it and the favour returned with interest, as Craig swung it down on his head. His body dropped in the long grass some way from Phil's and about ten seconds after.

WHEN SIGHT RETURNED, THERE WERE only the stars and clouds above, all spinning about slowly and lazily. A continent of thick grey cloud slowly swallowed the half-moon, dulling out its light. Crickets chirped. Pain throbbed down from the top of Lex's skull as if Craig were right there thumping him with the rock every two seconds.

There was rustling nearby, the tickling touch of long grass, a faint lingering stink of cask wine. A gnawing, crunching sound. Like Phil's dog Jules at work on a bone. Sucking, slurping. Crunching, gnawing.

He lifted his head, but the spike of pain made him rest it back on the grass. Tenderly, he touched his scalp; there was a sticky, tacky patch of blood. He moaned quietly. The background sounds—the eating sounds—ceased.

A listening, watchful silence ensued that instinct told him not to break. It went on for a long time. There were footsteps padding through the long grass, moving away from him, then towards him, then away again. Slow, heavy steps.

Keith and Craig? he thought. *Both of them, still here?*

The footsteps stopped. The eating sounds began again. There was a low murmur of someone's voice saying something, mostly inarticulate, but amongst the babble he made out the words "good, good."

Slowly, Lex sat up, hardly disturbing the long thick blades of grass around him. A shape loomed ten or twelve metres away, set against the sky behind. A large man hunched forward on the shorter grass where Lex had ridden his bike over the drop, with his back to Lex. The big hunched-over body was just a silhouette against the cloud. It moved in jerking, sawing motions.

A soft moan. Mournful, Lex thought, or maybe a note of pleasure. Though he knew he must stay quiet, he was too confused to be scared. He thought back to rumours about the bogan kids who came here with their girlfriends to screw. But this was no kid.

Up on his elbows, Lex watched the man's strange movements, still not comprehending, as the minutes passed. Not till he sat up, and the clouds shifted, the moon's light coming out from hiding to reveal the large man crouched over Phil.

Phil was looking right at Lex, so it appeared, eyes wide and unblinking and with a strange kind of grimacing smile, his lips peeled back. Lex gestured to him as if to say, *Are you okay? What's going on?*

Phil did not react at all. His head was in a strange position to the rest of him, a most unnatural angle. In fact, as Lex's eyes adjusted, he saw that it wasn't Phil at all but actually some kind of doll, for the head had been pulled right off. He rubbed his eyes as if it might change things, but no, the head wasn't attached to the body at all.

A dark pool spread about the body. Phil's chest and belly had been ripped open. The man by the corpse of his best friend was digging around in it, sawing off handfuls of flesh with a knife and lifting them to his mouth. The sight did not quite register, did not make any kind of sense at all. Lex did not think he was really seeing it.

The man's head turned sideways and Lex could see the chewing motions of his jaw. Inarticulate sounds came from his chewing, gargling throat interspersed with "good... good."

For Lex, everything span around again, very fast. His head fell back down on the long grass, making it rustle.

The eating sounds stopped. The man got to his feet. For a moment, his heavy excited breathing was the only sound. Heavy footsteps padded swish-swish through the grass. Lex felt and heard him coming but didn't care because he couldn't. He still didn't understand.

The man stood, tall over him, stretching far above like a statue, legs that were concrete pillars. It was the man they'd seen ogling the magazines in the news agency. For a long time, the longest minute in Lex's life, the man stared down at what the moonlight had revealed to him in the tall grass. His blood-smeared mouth hung open just as it had when he shambled out of the shop towards them.

A car swept past, swishing up puddles of water where the road dipped, then it was gone.

The man was trying, it seemed, to speak. Gibberish came out, a language of stuttering grunts, interspersed here and there with words. Lex discerned only, "Where we come from... makes us hungry."

IN THE LONG YEARS LATER, on therapists' couches, in bed tearfully telling his wife about it for the first time after twenty-one years of marriage; after waking from every nightmare where he was, again, a kid lying in long grass next to the water...

All the while driving himself through business school, through board rooms, from success to success, ever higher and faster as though to get away from a shambling monster on the road behind him...

Through memories of the funeral, of the police interviews, the witness stand with the monster blankly watching him answer questions in the trial that eventually put the monster in a hospital, not in a prison...

From trying to work out why, why *he* hadn't been taken as well; why *he'd* been spared after he'd passed out in the long grass, utterly at the monster's mercy, only to wake later and find what was left of his friend spread across the dewy ground...

Till he was an old man, rich and lonely, fading from life in his last days, bitterly wishing that, of all the memories his mind so eagerly shed, good and bad, why *those* memories above all others must remain till his very last day...

He would, throughout all this, seek some secret meaning in those words his ears had barely discerned amongst the grunts and stutters that had burnt those words—with whatever secret things they meant—into his mind, into his life, as a never-fading scar.

NIRA AND I

SHWETA NARAYAN

Shweta Narayan grew up in India and Malaysia but currently lives in the U.S. Her short stories have appeared in *Strange Horizons*, *Realms of Fantasy*, Ellen Datlow's *Beastly Bride* anthology, and elsewhere.

Nira and I are with Hemal on the day she dies. She is teaching us a clapping-song game, a remembering game. She is winning.

We call Hemal by name, though that breaks respect law because she is my mother's younger sister. She says being called *jal-amaa* makes her feel old. She is sixteen, which is old; Nira and I are five.

My *amaa* opens the door screen and says, "Hemal, we must talk. Nira, go home; your amaa will worry."

Hemal's eyebrows pull together, scrunching up her caste marks, like maybe she ate all the butter or forgot to douse the cook-fire. She gets up and ruffles my hair. "I'll be back soon, little ones."

She ducks outside. Arms grab her. She fights. My father shouts, "Don't try to lie. We saw you with that boy, that fisher-caste scum! And all this time you were living in my house, luring in the mist..."

Nira says, "Your *ataa* won't beat her, will he, Shaya?" Her voice is small.

I say, "Shh," and put my arms around her.

Voices pile on each other, words like "Law" and "Honour," words like stones. Nira's eldest brother says, "Fishers use children's fingers for bait." He is supposed to marry Hemal.

Amaa sobs, "Sister, little sister, how could you?" and Hemal says, "How could *you?*"

Then the half-bricks start, and cobblestones and broken bottles. Shadows huge and sudden against the door screen; the thud of Hemal falling; screams and wet breaking noises.

"This isn't happening," I say. Sounds blur outside. Shadows lighten.

Nira huddles closer to me. I put my arms around her. "It's all right," I whisper. "Remember, she said she would come back."

NIRA AND I ARE SIX WHEN her eldest brother loses his way in the mist. Three days later, his bones get home. An extra finger sprouts from the left hand, and the skull has no eye sockets. But his clothes dangle from the shoulder blades, and dry knuckles scratch at the door for two days before the King's men come.

This happens, but not to us. We are rememberers. We know each corner, every cobblestone. The mist cannot tempt us into a street that never was, can never make us think that we are home, or that we are kittens or fish. We are the city's traders, its messengers; we know it from wharf to hill. We roam through the dead market, piled high with bananas and seaweed but smelling only of age; we cross the tricky bridge, whose planks dissolve underfoot when we aren't there to remember. We are not trapped, huddling in tiny neighbourhoods. We matter. Travellers pay us to lead them safely through the mist, and our families even work in the palace. Granted, we may have little changes—forked tongues or grey eyes and skin, or feathers for hair—but nothing to bring the King's men. Our caste is pure. Till Nira's brother is lost.

Nira's amaa keeps her home after that, keeps her brothers home. All the mothers do, holding children closely and safely when we should be learning the city. And every day we grow more scared.

I am eight when I see Nira again. She appears out of thick curling twilight with her brother Abjit, who is ten, gripping her hand so hard it hurts me. I can see through their feet. I do not imagine what they might become. Nira says, "They're lost. All lost. Amaa and Ataa, and Imar, and Garun. They've been gone a week, and we are so hungry, Shaya, so very hungry."

I pull them in and shut out the mist. Wrap blankets around them, feed them spicy coconut rice to wake them up. Taking care of Nira again. A knot loosens in my heart.

Nira comes back fully, but I do not remember Abjit as well. One of his feet is grey, and clawed, and much too small. Mistburnt. "How did you find us?" I say.

Nira says, "Hemal showed me the way."

The next day Abjit will laugh at her for this, will taunt and tease and pinch. But now he stares around wide-eyed, and touches every wall and stool and bit of floor, and says nothing at all.

ATAA CLEARS OUT HEMAL'S OLD loft room and buys straw for Abjit to weave two more mattresses. Until they are done, Nira shares mine. We stay up far too late at first, trading stories, and one night, after Ataa starts snoring in the next room, I slide the window open. The blown-glass window eye swings back and forth on its string. I say, "Hemal?"

There is only mist, so thick that the ground and the neem tree are gone. It pokes a finger into my room, right around the eye. I cringe back. Nira says, "Listen."

Hemal is singing.

Nira and I listen at the window most nights until I am nine, though Nira is still eight. We learn teaching songs and sad love songs and sometimes fishermen's ditties that make the ground sway under us. We are not scared.

It's a fisher song that Amaa hears. She slams the window shut and locks it, her lips a pale tight line, her fingers trembling. "I should beat you," she says.

"Like you beat Hemal?"

Tears pool in her eyes, glint on her cheeks. She stumbles from the room.

ATAA IS GRAVE THE NEXT MORNING. Amaa is ill. Abjit says, "Is she mist-sick?" Ataa does not answer.

"It's Shaya's fault," says Abjit.

Ataa says, "Something is in the mist."

I shrug. "Just Hemal."

"No," says Ataa. "Hemal's dead. Stoning is part of culture law; it keeps us safe, keeps the dead from walking."

Nira and I look at each other. We know.

AMAA DOES NOT GET BETTER, not properly. She forgets where

161

she is. She forgets what she is doing. Now it is Amaa who must stay at home and be safe.

So Ataa inks caste marks into Abjit's forehead, and he starts running messages, though he limps. Nira and I teach my little sisters. We teach them the city and we teach them Hemal's songs to find the way. And we teach them not to sing around Amaa.

We keep the love songs and fishing songs to ourselves.

When Nira and I are ten, Amaa calls me Hemal. I run outside, leaving Nira to soothe her.

The next day, Ataa gives us our caste marks.

NIRA AND I GO EVERYWHERE. Though we are little, we are fast and we never lose our way. Nobody knows how we do it. Nobody else sees Hemal. The mist is not threatening where she is. It is her. And though her eye and lip are swollen black and blood drips over her caste marks, she never frightens us.

We get work at the palace, which makes Ataa proud and Abjit jealous, and there we meet Bhatar. He is like a fireshadow: dark, long, and quick. Caste marks shadow his eyes, for he is cousin to the King. He is sixteen. Nira and I are eleven now, and it doesn't seem so old.

Sometimes Bhatar comes with us when we run messages, which breaks caste law. He says he doesn't care about castes and who are we to question the King's cousin? He says the mist has nothing left to scare him with. It took his sister, and the thing that came back tried to kill him. He unmade it; he says it wept and begged with his sister's voice. He was eleven then. Like us.

I think he is brave. Nira says he is reckless.

Bhatar unmakes the mist with a whirling, stomping dance. Where he hits the ground even the dead market grows more real; gleaming brassware clunks when we tap it, and we smell rotten fish and mangoes and the sea. Bhatar tries to teach us, but we cannot keep his rhythm any more than he can keep our tune. He says that may be for the best; songs break culture law. I say, "Is everyone a lawbreaker?" Nira and Bhatar have no answers.

With dance and song together we thin the mist to haze, till one day the sun breaks through. We do not expect it to hurt. While we blink away tears, the mist pulls over us once more.

Bhatar grins and hugs me. "We'll do it again," he says.

I say, "How does lawbreaking thin the mist?"

ON THE DAY WE DANCE back the royal gardens and bring sunlight streaming down over the whole palace, the mist pulls away to reveal two gardeners and a palace servant. Adults. I open my mouth, do not know what to say; but the mist keeps rolling back behind them, back and down, leaving the hilltop bare to the sun. I point. From above, it looks like a silent white ocean.

The next time we meet, the same three adults come trailing hopefully after the children. Bhatar starts to teach them the dance. He is seventeen. Nira and I are twelve, and the adults look more like him than we do.

There was a pavilion in the gardens, made of painted wood and slate, where Bhatar fought his sister. It became forgotten. But he remembers, so we learn it for a meeting place.

Mist and rushes grow so thick that Bhatar must dance the path into being. His first step sinks in past the ankle, but Nira and I know better than to scream, and his second step comes down on slate paving, and his third. Octagons and squares tiled together. His seventh step finds the boards of a wooden bridge all painted red. We follow, fifteen people of nine different castes, singing what he has shown us into memory.

The pavilion is eight-sided, red with black beams and yellow rails and grey slate floors. Painted on each wall is a palace-caste man at work. The roof is fringed yellow silk. Sun shines through it, though mist pours down the walls.

BHATAR STARTS SOUNDING LIKE THE adults he talks to. Nira and

I have work, so we don't hear everything he says. But he takes me aside and says that the mist is our fear. "I think it will grow, Shaya, with the questions," he says, "until we stop hurting one another." Worry lines his forehead and his eyes.

Nira thinks he is wrong. But though there are forty-one of us now, of thirteen castes, she says this only to me and to Hemal.

WHEN I AM FOURTEEN, THOUGH Nira is still thirteen, Abjit pulls me into a dusty corner and kisses me. I start crying. I know what happens to lawbreakers.

"Don't be a baby," Abjit says. "I'm going to marry you."

I snatch my hand away, run to Nira. "What happened?" she says.

I tell her. She pulls back, her lips smiling upside-down. "I don't want you to kiss Abjit," she says. "If you must kiss a boy, kiss Bhatar."

I lean forwards. Her lips are softer than his, and warmer, and her breath is sweet. I feel her upside-down smile melt.

NIRA AND I WALK HAND-IN-HAND to the pavilion the next day. Hemal holds the mist thick around us.

Bhatar is not there. Nobody is. We wait, each with an arm around the other; then Nira tries dancing again. Watching her, I make my first song. A love song to my dearest friend, its hesitant rhythm following her dance and the sunlight that catches on her hair. I find myself smiling as I sing.

We are kissing again when the children come running up. Their sandals are loud, slap-slap, on the solid path and bridge. We pull apart.

"You're kissing," says one.

"You're *girls*," says another.

"Where's Bhatar?" says Nira.

They fall silent. And stay silent, until the pavilion is full of sweaty, shifting, wordless bodies. I say, "Where's Bhatar?"

"He spoke to the King, his cousin," says somebody. Uwati,

who is sixteen and often with him. "We brought sunlight into the court, pushed the mist far away. Bhatar said we must teach everyone to sing, to dance, but the king said that was noise-making and public gathering, and did Bhatar mean to teach the rabble not to heed the law?"

"He told the King that the law brought the mist," says Yash. "Fear of the law and the killings." Yash is old. He is tall and thin and has a beard, and children. But now he looks frightened. "He told the King that the law must change."

I look around. We are fewer than we were.

"And?" says Nira.

Uwati says, small and thin in the silence, "And he's dead. So is everyone who tried to help him. It was so fast..."

There was no mist for Bhatar to become. He danced it away. It lurks around us now, and from it Hemal starts crying. The others shift, uneasy, and draw closer to the pavilion's sunlit centre. Do they hear her?

A child I do not know says, "The rest of us ran."

"What should we do?" Yash asks us.

Nira looks at me. I shake my head, tears hot in my eyes. What do I know? Only that Bhatar is dead.

Nira says, "Let's hide now, meet another day. They will come for us. But they won't come far into the mist."

LYING TO ATAA AND ABJIT makes me feel as flat and distorted as a shadow on the door screen. Who is the girl Ataa hugs and calls eldest child? Not me. He would not hug a lawbreaker. He would call the King's men.

For I have taken Bhatar's role. Even Ratit, who joins us when Nira and I are both fourteen, looks to me. He brings us to fifty-three people from all twenty-four castes. Ratit is twelve. He dances well, and he is the King's youngest son.

We meet in different streets each day, call the sun down to different castes. People look up into the blue beyond the mist, tears streaming down smiling faces. They call us God-sent; they call us Sunbringers. And when we run, scattering before the King's men, hiding in Hemal's mist, they lie. The city protects us.

We share songs when we hide. Hemal knows weaver's songs and potter's songs and the marching chants of the King's men, though she does not remember that she was my jal-amaa. We can see through her, now, and she has no bruises and no caste marks.

Sometimes Nira teaches us a song nobody knew.

Other people remember the red bricks and blue door of Nira's house, but inside it is gone to shifting grey. Except for what she remembers: the black and white rug with its jagged toothy stripes, stairs as blue as the door, her room at the top. We go there to love each other. The stairs sink and wobble, but her room is steady and her blanket is warm soft yellow. And her smile is bright with the sunshine that fills me.

"Can the law lie?" I ask one day. The law says we cannot love each other.

"Maybe that's how it brings the mist," says Nira.

"We lie."

"We pretend," she says. "We know what's real."

We pretend all the time at home. We let Ataa and Abjit love shadow-girls. But we do not become the shadow-girls because we each remember the other.

AMAA'S SKIN GROWS GREY. MIST-BURNT. We remember her, but she forgets. She calls us both Hemal, and the little ones, too. She remembers us only at midday, when sunlight filters bright through the mist.

I cry about this sometimes. Ataa does not, though he looks like he wants to. He still says the law protects us. He says the Sunbringers just push mist around, making everything worse for hardworking people. He is not alone. One day the hard-working people catch Yash with bottles and bricks.

His sons cry when they dance.

"I want to show her sunshine," I tell Nira. "Before we lose her." As we lost Bhatar and Yash.

She says, "They would stone us." They. We are no longer rememberers.

"We can do it when the workers are not home," I say. "Who else will tell? We'll give them something to remember."

We are Sunbringers.

SIXTY-ONE OF US DANCE IN the street of the rememberers the next day. Only children watch us, and the old, and the mist-sick. They are silent through our song, angry, huddled to-gether—until sunlight pours into the street and paints it in col-ours they had forgotten. Until they see blue sky, as dry and hot as coconut rice.

Then we are dancing all together. Amaa dances, too. Grey fades from her skin, and she knows me. I beam at her, full of light, and dance away to kiss Nira. And Amaa stops.

The dance stumbles, fades around her. Mist trickles in. Nira and I back away from the glitter in her eyes. Our sunlit friends gather to us, behind us. Four neighbourhood children run over to our side.

"What are you doing?" says Amaa. "Caste-mixing is bad enough, but girls with girls... what *are* you?"

Uwati says, "We should run, before they call the King's men."

I say, "No." Holding hands, standing tall, Nira and I face the sun. Our shadows fall away behind us. Ratit takes my other hand and holds his hand out to Uwati. My baby sister Rimi comes toddling to Nira. I say, "We should dance."

Mist gathers into Hemal, and she starts to sing.

NOTHING HAPPENED IN 1999

FÁBIO FERNANDES

Fábio Fernandes teaches creative writing, scriptwriting, and game writing at Pontifícia Universidade Católica de São Paulo, Brazil. He is the author of one novel in Portuguese, *Os Dias da Peste*, and his short stories, as well as articles on science fiction, have appeared in several languages.

Humankind discovered time travel in the early twenty-second century.

It wasn't on purpose, as it were. As happens with many scientific discoveries, sometimes you are looking for one thing, then another gets in the way with results you are most definitely not expecting. Take Viagra, for instance. Or antigravity associated with superconductors.

The time travel process was discovered during experiments in locative media and augmented reality applied to elevators.

Anyway, it happened at a very interesting time in History. The human race had suffered a long period of wars, diseases and, even though it was far from global peace and understanding, now it seemed to be entering, if not a golden age, at least a time to start dreaming and making plans. A post-virtual environment embedded in anti-gravitational elevators as part of an ambience designed to soothe and distract people during the long rises and falls through the more-than two hundred floors of the arcologies seemed as good a place as any to give this age a jumpstart with such an invention.

As it were, the environment turned out to be not only a virtuality, but also a time displacement device that took its occupants to a very different set of co-ordinates from those originally expected. Suffice it to say that, when the doors of the elevator opened, the dumbfounded passengers were no longer in Kansas—at least not in 2113 Kansas anyway (for the building really was located in that American state) but in a shabby building in 1999 with a mere fifty floors.

After a few minutes of absolute confusion and, in some cases, total denial, the discombobulated denizens of the future returned to the elevator and told it to get them back to where they had come from. Fortunately, it was able to do so.

The First Prototype, as this elevator is called today, is on permanent exhibition at the Smithsonian—but not before the post-virtual environment was carefully dissected and examined in search of what caused it to behave so unexpectedly. Something to do with quantum teleportation, apparently, but the details were never disclosed to the public. (Perhaps, as some media pundits said, because even the scientists didn't know how the hell such a thing happened.)

Be that as it may, time travel rapidly became a fad, and—who would have expected that?—a sort of escape valve for the stressed citizen. People cherished the idea of travelling to a fine, quiet time, not to any turning point in History where they could be attacked by terrorists or die in an earthquake, for instance. Nobody tried to alter the past in order to change the future.

One of these Safe Years—as they were called—was the very first year reached by the elevator: 1999.

(Now, there were some dissenters who argued that even 2001 could be considered a Safe Year, in every city other than New York, but the majority preferred to stay on the safe side.) It was a year when anything could have happened—except that it didn't.

Again, dissenters begged to differ—they said that it all depended on whose view it was, for in 1999 the following things happened: a 6.1 Richter scale earthquake hit western Colombia, killing at least 1,000; a fire in the Mont Blanc Tunnel in the Alps, killed 39 people, closing the tunnel for nearly three years; a magnitude 5.9 earthquake hit Athens, killing 143 and injuring more than 2,000. Another quake, this one a Richter 7.6, killed about 2,400 people in Taiwan; not to mention the Kosovo War.

Accusations of Anglocentric attitudes ensued. (An argument much discussed was that Earth is a really big planet, and they recognised that many things happened outside the Anglo-American sphere of influence—most of the things that happened in the world, actually. Earth had come a long way in globalisation and, after all, time travel was discovered by a team of French, Indian, and Brazilian scientists in Accra, Ghana, so that was expected.)

The second phase of research and development was most

focused in the matter of geopolitics. Using systems of co-ordinates and geolocation tools, they managed to make the time-travelling environment travel around the world as well as in time, so people could visit other cities in different historical periods instead of their own. It would seem to be most practical and convenient—until the second prototype was lost just outside Earth's orbit. (You must be painstakingly accurate in order to compensate for the travelling of Earth itself around the Sun and across the galaxy, eventually. Not something to be taken lightly.)

Then it was pointed out that this apparent flaw could be used as an advantage. It would take a lot of effort and calculation, but nothing a quantum computer couldn't handle.

Again, 1999 was a crucial year, much to the dismay of critics and nay-sayers, but for reason other than the historicity criterion: it was pointed out that the time travel mechanism would need a slingshot-effect to dislocate the prototype adequately through the space-time grid and do it safely enough with the maximum degree of precision and minimum risk.

1999 just happened to have the Y2K bug. Of course, it could have been any other thing, but why bother to try and invent it when the bug was already in place, just waiting for a chance to be useful? The "rollover" from 99 to 00 hadn't played havoc with data processing as had been feared, but the transition to 2000 in the digital systems would jumpstart the mechanism and power the slingshot through this now-called Zero Year and enable the time-travelling environment to go anywhere in the space-time continuum. And they were not thinking only of Earth.

Humankind discovered interstellar travel in the mid-22nd Century.

SHADOW

TADE THOMPSON

Tade Thompson grew up in Nigeria (he is Yoruba, which, he says, influences most of his writing) and currently lives in the United Kingdom. His stories have appeared in *Expanded Horizons*, *Ideomancer*, and in the Nigerian writers collective project *In My Dreams It Was Different*.

I met a man with no shadow today.

He crossed into the village limits near dusk, furtive but resolute. He wanted to find the *Mamman*. He did not understand my description of the route, partly because he spoke gutter Yoruba learnt from leather traders, and partly because I have a stutter.

I decided to take him there because I thought it would be a very sad thing losing one's shadow. He was grateful, but fell silent after our initial conversation. I told him to wait while I checked my traps, for I am a hunter.

I had caught one bush rat and the leg of an antelope who had chewed his limb off in order to escape my pot. I reset the traps under the studious gaze of the man with no shadow.

The sun hid beneath the horizon, and even my shadow did not survive. We crossed the brook of tears without getting our feet wet and waved greeting to the three drinkers at the palm-wine bar, men with whom I had been circumcised, but whose features had been blunted by *ogogoro*, their bodies the harvest of a misspent youth.

We walked past my house and I handed my puzzled wife the bag with the bush rat and my belt of charms. I kept the rifle slung over my shoulder. The Mamman had magic, but gunpowder and lead would work on anything that had a heart, shadowed or not.

"YOUR SHADOW IS BORN WHEN you are," said the Mamman, "but it outlives you. You should cast a shadow until your body rots."

She was fat, with massive swinging breasts that held intricate tattoos, and she had a sensual carelessness about her near-nakedness.

"You may go," she said to me.

I shook my head. "I want to hear what he has to say."

"Very well." To the man, she said: "What have you brought for me?"

The man unwrapped a small package and lay a dried, blackened object at the Mamman's side. "This is the trigger finger of the greatest warrior my village has ever known."

"Did you kill him?" she asked.

"No, but it is mine to give away." He offered no further explanation.

The Mamman put it away and, licking her lips, sat back down. "I've known two others who lost their shadows in my time."

"I did not lose it," said the man. "I drove it away."

"Explain, outlander. I get bored easily and when I'm bored I amuse myself by sucking the brains out of the eyeballs of mouthy customers."

IT WAS A STORY OF WAR.

The man's village had been outnumbered by invaders from the north. Fair-skinned, heavily-clothed warriors with curved swords and strange customs. They outnumbered the indigenous people two to one and had mounted cavalry and bows and arrows.

"The witch doctor had a solution. He would bring alive our shadows, in the process, doubling the army strength, but we had to win the battle before sundown because he could only hold the spell from dawn till dusk of one day. We also had to fight alongside our counterparts so that they could find their way back to merge just before sundown. As it turned out, the invaders were so afraid of the dark warriors that they fled, but the shadow-selves were more... dishonourable."

There was a massacre, with the slaughter and sodomisation of unarmed men in the process of surrendering.

"Most of my villagers allowed this, encouraged it even, but I objected. My shadow wished to continue, but I tried to prevent it. It tried to turn on me, but I fought it off. It hissed and sputtered and slinked away, and I did not see it again before sundown. I have not cast a shadow since. It made my wife and family uncomfortable and I had heard of the Mamman here. I loaded provisions, left my kinsmen, and here I am."

THE MAMMAN WAS SILENT FOR a long time. Then she scratched herself absently. Our shadows flickered in the candlelight, with an eerie gap where the stranger's should have been.

"It's not such a bad thing to lack a shadow-self," she said.

"Then give me yours," said the man.

The Mamman laughed. It sounded like many jackals at once, and her spittle sprayed around. I dared not wipe it off my chin. The woman stood and crumbs of something dropped to the floor. "There are two ways of solving this problem. We can find your errant shadow or take one from a recently-deceased person. The latter will not look like you and may not move at exactly the same moment as you, but nobody will notice who doesn't observe closely. Choose wisely."

THIS IS HOW I CAME to be a resurrectionist, digging into the grave of one Saliu Ogunrombi, who had died in the last wave of Yellow Fever.

There was no moon. There was the rhythmic digging of myself and the man with no shadow. The Mamman sat on a stool, waiting, smoking.

The ritual itself was undramatic, and consisted of holding Saliu upright and lighting torches behind him. The Mamman said something to the resultant shadow and it detached from Saliu and bobbed over to the stranger.

AT DAWN, I SETTLED AT MY wife's side, freshly showered and with no intention of doing the day's hunting. Her hand drifted between my legs, but grave digging is tiring work and there was no oak tree for her to climb, just a willow.

Before I fell asleep I remembered the last words the Mamman had said to me, as the man walked away with his new shadow.

"In a year he will return to us. To me. He will tell me to

release him from this shadow."

"Why?" I asked.

"He will say his wife has left him and the people of his village shun him. He will say the new shadow-self has changed his behaviour and he cannot control himself."

I said nothing.

"And he will be right."

"What is a shadow, Ma?" I asked. I did not stutter when with her.

She did not answer, but walked into the twilight. Presently, I had gone home.

I looked at the walls of my bedroom, at the shadows receding with the rising sun, and the rise and fall of my wife's chest.

I slept.

SHIBUYA NO LOVE

HANNU RAJANIEMI

Hannu Rajaniemi's first novel, *The Quantum Thief*, has been hailed as "brilliant" by John Clute and he has been called the best new hard SF writer to emerge in recent years. Two more novels are forthcoming. A Finn, Rajaniemi currently lives in Edinburgh. He holds a PhD in string theory, and is the director and co-founder of ThinkTank Maths.

They were eating takoyaki by the statue of Hachiko the dog when Norie told her to buy a quantum lovegety.

Riina's Japanese was not very good in spite of two years of Oriental Studies and three months in Tokyo, and the translation software on her phone did not immediately recognise the term, so she just stared at the small caramel-skinned girl blankly for a few seconds, mouth full of fried dough and octopus. "A what?" she managed finally, wiping crumbs from her lips.

Norie, who sat on the edge of the fountain and dangled her impossibly tanned legs in the air, giggled.

"You don't have them in Finland? How do you meet boys there? Oh, I forgot, you have the sauna!"

"It's not a—" Riina stopped. The concept of non-erotic unisex nudity in a steamy room was something only her Canadian friends had grasped so far. "Never mind. Tell me about the lovegety."

"It's the most *kawaii* thing! I keep mine on all the time. Look!" Norie held up her wrist. Her phone was embedded in a Cartier platinum bracelet with a jewel-studded Hello Kitty engraving that her boyfriend Shinichi had given her for her birthday. Riina had admired it several times, but had not paid attention to the little teardrop-shaped plastic thing dangling from it until now. It was hardly bigger than the tip of her index finger, and its pink surface had the characteristic Teflon sheen of a nanovat-grown product. There was a silvery heart-shaped logo on one side.

"They had these already when my mother was a schoolgirl—that's how she met my father! Then they went out of fashion for several years, but now there is this crazy *otak* in Akihabara making new and better ones. Quantum versions. Everybody has one!"

"So, what does it do?"

"I can't tell you—you have to try it! C'mon, let's go find

you one!" Norie leaped up, took Riina's hand in her own, and tugged her towards the techno beat of Shibuya and District 109 that was its heart. A forest of orange hairdos, brown legs, and spidery eyelashes swallowed the girls. There was a crowd around the statue: it was one of the few clear landmarks in the district, and tourists loved the story of the dog who waited for its master for years after his death.

Riina hesitated. Norie tended to assume that she was equally good at assimilating the new memes that boiled up from the teenage paradise of Shibuya as her Japanese friends, who seemed to be able to turn the latest otaku toy into a sub-culture or a fashion statement in a matter of minutes. She was starting to become desensitised to future shock, but the labyrinths of the new and the old in this country still confused her. She wondered how her father managed: good protocol/ etiquette software, probably. It was simply impossible to figure out the right kind of bow, the correct form of address towards a senior or a superior.

Let alone get a date.

She sighed and allowed Norie to tow her deeper into the crowd. The Japanese girl's neon-rimmed eyes were bright, and her small white teeth were flashing, her canary-yellow backpack bopping up and down.

"Seriously—lovegetys are sooo kawaii!"

THE BOY LOOKED LIKE A painted little satyr: silver lips and eyelids, orange ash-streaked hair, and a heavy gold chain around his neck. He couldn't have been older than twelve, but then, in Shibuya, a fifteen-year-old was ancient and venerable. The drone of the base beat that seemed to permeate everything in 109 obscured the rapid-fire exchange between Norie and the boy, but it wasn't long before he smiled hungrily and held his palm out towards Riina, the little pink thing bright against his dark skin like a tiny flower. She took it, and it was still warm from the boy's hand, a living thing almost. Her MasterCard thumbnail sang an inaudible song to the boy's account, and suddenly she was the proud owner of a quantum lovegety.

Norie gave her a nymph-like smirk as the satyr-boy vanished into the seething mass of Japan's young around them.

"Now comes the best part. We go to Starbucks, and you get to try it out!"

Most of Shibuya was like a graffiti: clashing, bright, screaming colours over a drab concrete surface, the clothes shops and holograms and neon signs and rainbow crowds, a stark contrast to the utilitarian 90s architecture. Starbucks was an exception—an intricate, cylindrical two-storey glass monstrosity, a ten-metre hologram of the white-green all-seeing mermaid hovering above it.

The girls sat at a small table on the second floor, sipping cardboard-flavoured cappuccinos. Norie helped Riina to calibrate the lovegety: it talked to her old Nokia toothphone eagerly, a little light blinking in the centre of the silver heart. Menus with swirling Japanese characters danced on her retina, barely comprehensible. "Get2 setting? What is that?"

"Never mind that; you don't want to set it that high for the first go. We'll go for 'karaoke.' Your VR stuff is a bit old-fashioned, but—there. It's mining the web and creating your profile now—done!" Norie visibly enjoyed her big-sister role, affecting a firm motherly tone.

"What do I do now?"

"Now? Silly girl, now you go and find a boy you like, and enjoy the show."

"Just a random guy? But what will I say to him?"

"You don't have to say anything, that's the point! Off you go now—just wander around and pretend that you're looking for the ladies' room. I'll call Shinichi, and we'll go for dinner with him after he gets off work—it'll be fun!"

Riina swallowed the last of her coffee and got up, feeling awkward. She took her purse, pocketed the lovegety, and walked towards the signs pointing to the ladies' room, trying to look innocent and casting passing glances at the men sitting at the tables she passed. There were a couple of businessmen, a glazed look in their eyes as they imbibed caffeine seasoned with the latest stock fluctuations; a couple of rare daylight otaku wearing ill-fitting jeans, anime T-shirts, and subterranean mutant complexions; and trendy neo-*jinrui* oozing illusory wealth, talking loudly, and dressed in pin-striped gangster suits. She felt silly and focused her eyes on the white skirt-wearing pictogram ahead, shaking her head.

The lovegety beeped. A female voice chattered something in her ear like an exotic bird. Flashing icons guided her eyes towards a lone figure sitting by one of the large windows. Riina stopped, felt blood rising to her cheeks, and tried to think about lying face down in a snowdrift, cold and dead. Usually, it worked.

Not this time. He had good cheekbones, short-cropped black hair, and large brown eyes behind rimless AR glasses; he was scribbling something furiously with a stylus on the screen of an old-fashioned palmtop, forehead furrowed in concentration. Suddenly he stopped and looked up, straight at Riina, a surprised expression on his face. His name was Hiroaki, she suddenly knew: twenty-three, studying communications technology at Keio University, single, four previous relationships, likes old Takeshi Kitano films and Japanese jazz, owns a cat.

The lovegety buzzed again. Riina caught a glimpse of a brief animation: clunky cartoonish figures of a boy and a girl holding lovegetys. The devices sent out little arrows that shook hands in the air. "Karaoke Mode Initiated!" chirped the shrill voice of the gadget through her jawbone.

RIINA WAS SUDDENLY OVERWHELMED BY a nauseatingly powerful sense of deja vu mixed with vertigo. It was as if she were falling, only sideways, weightless. She closed her eyes, and the feeling subsided. When she opened them again, she was looking straight into Hiroaki's eyes, and she felt his hand touching her cheek gently. A confused tangle of new memories unfolded in her head: a seafood dinner, games at the arcade, strolling through 109's boutiques of the bizarre, joking about the latest fashionable trinkets. Tension, hands and limbs brushing against another ever so lightly, Hiroaki missing his train to walk Riina home. And then — "The First Kiss!" piped the female demon in her ear, and her mouth was suddenly full of Hiroaki's tongue and taste, his lips moving a bit clumsily, uncertainly. But there was no clanging of teeth, no awkwardness.

It was perfect.

And then it was over.

"To Experience Adult Situations, Upgrade To Get2 Mode!!!" sang the lovegety and plunged Riina into a warm sea of afterglow, into soft jazz tunes sung by a Japanese voice. They lay on Hiroaki's futon, Riina listening to his heartbeat, her cheek against his smooth chest, as he leant on one elbow and toyed with her hair.

"Pillow Talk!!!" crooned lovegety.

"I'm going back home this fall," she said, not knowing where the words had come from, head heavy with newly discovered plans and dreams. And the butterflies in her stomach, the fear of losing all this perfection — where did that come from? She looked up at Hiroaki, touching his cheek. "Would you like to come with me?"

"Yes," he said and smiled, and the lovegety carried them away again.

Finland. Snow. Perfect weekends by the lake in her family's summer house. Hiroaki learning to ski, nose peeling from mild frostbite. Hiroaki making her tea. A big warm water balloon swelling in her chest as she thought about him. Staccato images punctuated by the voice of the lovegety. Arguments. Hiroaki's inferiority complex. Her endless need to overanalyse her problems, the desire for a safe male figure to replace her father. The usual things, the pitfalls of pillow psychology. And, finally, Hiroaki's back receding into the distance on one of the moving walkways at Helsinki Airport, Riina holding back her tears and squeezing the little ivory cat in her pocket that he had given her.

"KARAOKE MODE ENDS!!!"

The voice was like a guillotine, sharp-edged and unstoppable, cutting through the illusion. She fell back to the mutter of Starbucks, felt her knees buckling under her. Strong warm hands grabbed her by the shoulders and supported her. She took a deep breath and opened her eyes. It took only seconds for her head to clear a bit, and she found herself looking into Hiroaki's eyes again. She almost cried from relief and covered his face with kisses, but the lovegety world was already fading away, the memories attaining a dreamlike quality.

"Are you all right?" asked Hiroaki, a concerned look on his face.

"Yes, fine," she stammered. "I was just—"

"Oh dear. That was your first time, wasn't it? Come, sit down and we'll get you some coffee."

"No... no, I'm all right now."

"No, really, it's no bother. I owe you that much at least." He winked. "Although I did hope that you'd have set it all the way up to get2." He saw Riina's expression and laughed. "Only joking. C'mon. It's safe, I promise."

Riina felt a bit better after a steaming cup of mocha. Hiroaki watched her intently as she sipped the frothy liquid. She heard a short buzz from somewhere far away, and jumped in her seat, but nothing happened.

"Look, I'm sorry you got so shaken up," Hiroaki said finally. "Your friend should have explained to you how it works. Are you sure you're okay?"

He touched Riina's arm gently, his fingertips little points of electricity on her skin.

"Yeah... yeah, I'm fine. Thanks for the coffee, by the way."

"Anytime."

Norie waved at them from the other side of the room and walked over, her pink Hello Kitty handbag swinging in the air. Riina glared at her angrily, but her irritation turned to astonishment as her friend bent over Hiroaki and kissed him on the lips, full and hard. He smiled sheepishly. "Sorry. While you were drinking your mocha, we went to Get2. Kind of accidentally."

Norie pursed her lips. "Well, it didn't seem to work out between you two, and he is cute! You don't mind, right?"

"What about Shinichi?"

"What about him? He's not really a boyfriend anyway; it's more of an *enjo-kosai* thing, you know. We do stuff, and he buys me things. Very practical. He doesn't mind, really—and we're still meeting him for dinner! Hiroaki can come along."

Riina stood up.

"No, you guys go ahead. I... I think I need some fresh air."

"Really? Are you sure? Look, I'm sorry; these things happen quickly. Try some other setting sometime, it's really fun!" Norie gave her a tight little hug. "I'll see you soon, okay? Call me."

As Riina started walking away, Hiroaki called after her. "Riina! You are invited to our wedding, of course! Next week! Try to make it!"

She ran then, tears in her eyes, towards the endless heavy beat of Shibuya, trying to find an ivory cat in her pocket, and her heart jumped when her fingers closed around something small and warm. But it was only the lovegety.

She threw it into the fountain by the statue of Hachiko the dog, and watched it sink. The statue seemed to be looking at her sadly with its bronze dog-eyes, and she knew that it, too, was still waiting, waiting for love in Shibuya.

MAQUECH

SILVIA MORENO-GARCIA

Silvia Moreno-Garcia was born and raised in Mexico, and currently lives in Canada. Her short stories have appeared in *Fantasy* magazine and *Futurismic*, amongst others, and she publishes the online zine *The Innsmouth Free Press*.

The jewel encrusted beetle walked slowly across the table, dragging its golden chain behind. It was bigger than any other maquech he'd ever seen before and more richly decorated.

Gerardo put down the eyeglass.

"It's not my usual purchase," he said.

"It's rare," Mario replied. "This is the last one my grandfather made before he passed away."

"Monkeys are the thing now. Everyone wants a monkey."

"But it doesn't need a lot of food or water," Mario protested. "That's a benefit."

"Do you think my clients worry about things like food or water? Listen, I sold five ostriches two months ago. People want large animals now."

It was a lie. He sold fish and birds and maybe a reptile or two. He could not afford extravagant purchases like ostriches.

"I need the money," Mario confessed. "I want to go to Canada."

"What for?"

"I want to see the polar bears before they disappear. Before all the ice melts away."

Gerardo stared at Mario. Who the hell cared about polar bears? Unless Gerardo was importing them, he didn't give a damn about them or the ice. Canada was far away and there were more pressing problems right now such as how he was going to afford that month's water bill. Up went the bill, and for a small trader of exotic pets there was always competition, taxes and bribes to pay, food to buy for the animals. If he didn't sell them quickly, he'd have to keep the beasts for months on end and spend tons of money on their care.

And then Mario came and talked about looking at polar bears? Christ on the cross. They were probably better off without so many of them anyway. He tried to calculate the amount of food one of those things must devour each month and shook his head.

"Look, I can't give you much," Gerardo said.

Gerardo put the maquech in the terrarium together with the bits of wood Mario had given him. The maquech fed on the bacteria of decomposing wood, so at least it wouldn't cost too much to maintain. He recalled the piranhas he'd bought last May. Hungry, ugly little things. He wouldn't make that mistake again.

Gerardo looked at the maquech and wondered who might buy this one. He'd seen people wearing a maquech on their lapel or their dress, but usually they had tacky plastic faux-jewels on their backs. This little insect had been painted and decorated with semi-precious stones. It was not a cheap bug and he needed to make a good sale.

He went through his list of regular clients, discarded all of them and kept coming back to a single name: Arturo de la Vega.

He'd never sold anything to Arturo but, if there was a buyer in Mexico City, it was Arturo. He was disgustingly rich. While everyone else worried about getting running water that week, how to purchase a kilo of tortillas, the eternally high levels of pollution and the assholes trying to express-kidnap you, Arturo spent insane amounts of money on exotic pets. Arturo de la Vega had a roof garden with a pool and palm trees in a city where people ran behind the water trucks, filling barrels and *tinajas* twice a week. Arturo de la Vega drove a car when everyone else had to walk or, at best, be carried on a litter down Reforma.

If you managed to sell an animal to Arturo de la Vega, you were in the big leagues.

But Gerardo had never sold a thing to him. He was too small, too unknown, too much of a provincial newcomer.

He drummed his fingers against the table.

He took out the camera and snapped a few pictures of the maquech.

He normally did not dream. There was no space for dreams

in the cramped apartment, filled with the stench of the birds and fish.

That night he dreamt of rivers and quiet, dark places where the sunlight turns green with the colour of the trees.

THREE DAYS LATER, THE MONTHLY offering period for Arturo de la Vega opened up. It was only a one-day window and Gerardo had to queue outside the reception office for many hours prior to that. He stood, baking under the furious sun, and watched a man walk by with cages strapped behind his back. Mechanical owls blinked their multi-coloured eyes at Gerardo and shook their metal wings. There was a water-seller across the street yelling the same litany over and over again.

"Water. Fresh, pure water."

He closed his eyes and he thought of the murmur of a stream.

Somebody shoved him forwards and Gerardo snapped his eyes open and walked forwards, one more step towards the building's entrance. A long time later, he stepped into the lobby and placed his submission package, nothing more than a few snapshots and an introduction letter, on the narrow cedar table.

Then it was back to his apartment, down three flights of stairs. He couldn't afford a floor above ground with a glass window; not even a window with metal shutters. Sunlight was costly.

Gerardo fed the fish and the birds first. Then he turned to the maquech.

The insect walked from one end of its terrarium to the other.

"What are you thinking?" he asked the maquech.

The maquech stood very still.

Gerardo stood still, too.

He didn't talk to the animals. It was not his thing to coo and smile and babble over an animal as if it was a baby. He fed them. He housed them. He sold them. That was it.

Nothing less and nothing more.

IT WAS WATER DAY. FOUR hours of running water. The luxury of a warm shower was something he looked forward to the whole week. He hummed and closed his eyes and thought of blue-green waterfalls.

As he stood in the shower, head bowed under the spray, he heard a loud pounding.

He wrapped a towel around his waist and opened the door.

A courier held out a letter for him.

"From Mr De la Vega," the man said.

Gerardo tore open the black envelope. Inside was a card with an address and a date. An invitation to Mr De la Vega's apartment. An invitation to show him the maquech.

He'd done it.

He was going to De la Vega's home to parade his maquech in front of him like a real trader.

Gerardo froze as he realised the wooden or plastic cages where he normally stuffed his merchandise wouldn't suffice. He needed something grand and elegant that would display the maquech as an elaborate brooch.

Perhaps a red velvet box lined in silk with appropriate breathing holes. At once he began to panic, considering the price of this custom-made, urgent item.

But then he looked at the maquech with its golden chain, the painted back, the tiny stones in the centre of the composition. A breathing mosaic. A walking jewel. It was beautiful. It needed a beautiful setting.

THE ROOM WAS BLACK AND as bright as polished obsidian. The floor and the walls reflected and distorted Gerardo's image as he opened the box and held it up for De la Vega to inspect.

The young man glanced at the maquech, just a little glance, and looked up at him.

"What on earth is that?"

"*Zopherus chilensis*," Gerardo said. "In Yucatan they call them maquech and wear them as brooches."

"It's alive?"

"Yes. Live-jewellery. It is decorated with..."

"Pablo, did you select this?"

A man in impeccable white, wearing a matching white hat stepped from behind De la Vega's right, a little silver tablet in his left hand.

"Yes," said the man.

"What for?"

"It's a curiosity. I haven't seen one since I was a child."

"It's ugly," De la Vega said and waved Gerardo away.

HE CONSIDERED TEARING OFF THE jewels from the insect's back. There were bills to pay and the maquech had been an extravagant purchase at a time when he couldn't afford it. Not that Gerardo could ever afford much.

"Stupid, slow bug," he told the maquech as it walked on the palm of his hand. Or maybe not stupid, merely indifferent. In Yucatan they said it could live for many decades, even centuries. Maybe after hundreds of years of walking in the jungle, things such as humans and their games were of little importance. Of course, these were just legends. Stories old people told. He didn't believe them.

But as the maquech began to crawl up his arm, he wondered what time might be like for a quasi-immortal creature, sitting under the jade shade of the trees.

GERARDO WAS THINKING OF BLACK eyeless fish and cenotes when the phone rang. The cenotes melted away as he punched a key.

"Yes?" he asked.

"It's Pablo, Mr de la Vega's assistant. I need you to come tomorrow to the apartment and bring your insect again. He wants to have a second look at it."

Pablo's voice had a hint of metal as it poured from the phone, crisp and sharp and bright. Gerardo swallowed and leant forwards.

"I'm sorry?"

"Tomorrow at five. You got that?"

"Yeah, sure."

"See you then."

Gerardo punched another key and sat back. The maquech took a step with each tick of the black minute hand of the clock on the wall. The heavy jewels on its back made it slow. Or maybe it did not care to move quickly. There was all the time in the world for it to reach its destination.

PABLO, THE MAN IN WHITE, was wearing grey this time. His fingers danced over the tablet and he spoke with his measured voice.

"They use them as love talismans. The Mayans said there was a girl that was turned into that insect."

"The Mayans thought a princess's doomed lover was turned into a maquech so he could remain close to her heart," Gerardo said, correcting the assistant. "The Mayans thought it was a symbol of immortality."

Pablo glanced up at him, his fingers frozen for a second.

Arturo de la Vega did not reply. He sat in his obsidian room, holding a glass between his fingers. He did not look at the insect that Gerardo was holding up in its velvet box for him to examine. Instead, Arturo set down his glass on top of a black, lacquered table.

"I don't enjoy insects," he said. "I don't find them interesting. They're too small, too common, and they don't live very long."

"A maquech can live three or four years in captivity. Maybe even more with the proper care."

"That's not very long."

"Do you purchase your animals based on their longevity?"

"Normally, longevity is not an issue."

"Four years is not a short period of time."

"It seems short to me."

"Then you shouldn't have called me. I can't make it live forty years just for your sake," he said, and he knew it was a rude remark but he could not help himself. Arturo had made him wait for two hours before he deigned to see him, and he was tired of this curious sensation of levity, as though everything that might happen was inconsequential.

"Do you smoke?" Arturo asked as he took out a white gold case and plucked a thin black cigarette.

"Sure," Gerardo said, although he had not smoked in over five years. He couldn't afford it.

Arturo made a little motion with his hand and Pablo stepped forward, lighting their cigarettes. Up close, Pablo's eyes glinted a synthetic blue-silver. Modified. Beautified.

Arturo puffed twice and smiled.

"I'm not completely indifferent to your beetle, Gerardo. But I'm not completely interested either. I've got other traders showing their goods to me and they have very impressive merchandise, and they are much better known than you. Does he come recommended?"

"No recommendations," Pablo said with his beautiful, beautiful voice, and Gerardo wondered if that, too, had been modified. "But talent springs from the oddest place."

"I do have a knack for spotting talent," Arturo said.

"Mr De la Vega made Yuko Saitou an overnight sensation. Her two-headed koi are all the rage."

"Synthets," Gerardo said.

"We buy many, many things."

There was a pause. The smoke of the cigarettes curled up towards the glass ceiling, and Gerardo shifted his weight feeling suddenly pinned under the men's gazes.

"How about a test?" Pablo asked.

"I'm sorry?"

"Try on the beetle. Wear it."

"That's not such a bad idea," De la Vega said.

"Now?"

"I have a party on Friday. Come back Friday. We'll see how it goes."

THE MAQUECH SMELT LIKE OLD WOOD. Beneath its jewels it was the colour of wood and if Gerardo closed his eyes, it felt like it was a leaf moving upon his hand, stirred by the breeze.

He opened his eyes and let the beetle back into its terrarium. He turned on the TV and clicked through the channels, and there was the news and talk about crime rates, and the soap operas, and the late night variety hour pop-star sensation.

Gerardo tried to concentrate on the TV and the images flickered in dazzling colour, but they seemed as insubstantial as ghosts. There was nothing remotely interesting to watch inside his box of an apartment with its concrete lid.

He turned off the TV and sat in silence.

He thought he could hear the rain falling, far away.

A WOMAN WALKED WITH A leopard on a leash; a teenaged boy wore a snake-skin jacket and a real snake around his neck. Men, wrapped in silk and feathers, with fish scales glued to their faces drank out of amethyst glasses. Women in dresses made of iridescent butterfly wings smiled at him.

And then, amongst the sea of revellers, Arturo walked forth with a jaguar's skull upon his head and a cape made of animal bones, and he smiled at Gerardo. Pablo, black suit and black hat, served as his shadow.

"So good to see you. So good. Are you having fun?" Arturo asked.

"It's a very grand party."

"It is. Have you brought it then?"

Gerardo opened the velvet box and held it up. Pablo

slipped forwards and took the box, took the maquech, and placed it upon Arturo's shirt, fastening the golden chain. It shone like a star. It shone brighter than he'd ever seen it before, as if to please Gerardo, and people circled Arturo and fawned and sighed.

Pablo, who was still next to Gerardo, smiled a tiny, calculated smile.

"Will he buy it?" Gerardo asked, as the star moved away and was lost from his sight.

"He never knows what he wants," Pablo said. "But he likes real things and real things are scarce."

Gerardo was quiet, and then Pablo took out his tablet and walked away. "Luck of the draw," he said, without turning to look at him.

A COUPLE OF HOURS LATER, Pablo walked up to Gerardo and handed him a card.

"Mr De la Vega wishes to purchase your beetle," he said.

Gerardo nodded. He did not know what else one was supposed to do in such situations.

"Come back sometime," Pablo said.

"The maquech," Gerardo muttered. Pablo's blue eyes swept over him: a question mark. "It'll need to eat. There's some wood it needs."

"I'll send someone."

He was escorted out of the party to a black car with tinted windows. He had never been in a car. Well, nothing like a real car. Once he had sat in his uncle's beaten-up *bochito* when he was a kid, but he hardly remembered anything about that ride.

Now he went down Reforma, down the only car lane, fast like a silver bullet. And he thought he'd never, ever forget that moment.

GERARDO WALKED DOWN THREE FLIGHTS of stairs into his windowless apartment.

There was something missing there. But everything seemed to be in its place; all the papers remained where he'd left them; each bird sat in its cage; each fish swam in its tank.

When he walked into the kitchen he saw ants were feasting on a sandwich he had left on the table, and he tossed it into the garbage.

He turned on the TV, and there was a report about riots due to increases in the cost of the tortilla. Somewhere in Santa Julia, two men had been shot for stealing hoarded water. In the Colonia Roma, Mexican freshwater turtles were being served as appetisers at a fine restaurant. He turned it off.

There was something missing.

He grabbed the terrarium and started putting the pieces of wood into a bag so he could courier them to De la Vega. And as he did, he realised what was missing: the smell of old wood and jungle. The smell of the maquech.

That night Gerardo did not dream of rivers.

Author's Note: Thanks to entomologist Dr. Aristeo Cuauhtémoc Deloya Lopez and his information about the maquech, which was invaluable in the writing of this story.

THE GLORY OF THE WORLD

SERGEY GERASIMOV

Ukrainian writer Sergey Gerasimov has a degree in theoretical physics from Kharkiv University and has sold twelve novels and nearly a hundred stories in Russia and Ukraine. His stories have appeared in English in *Fantasy Magazine, Clarkesworld,* and *Adbusters.*

They went upstairs, to the second floor that was actually much higher than the first. An unknown contractor had sandwiched it between the dimly lit twenty-second and the exceptionally roomy fifty-fifth, either for fun or as a publicity stunt. As they walked up they saw through the big windows an embarrassed town changed very much by the linear perspective, refracted here and there as if seen through a huge quivering prism, scared, shiny, dark-cornered. One of the corners folded up and the rain flickering along the horizon trembled there like piano strings.

The starry heaven gaped over the clouds. The constellations and shiny dabs of galaxies wheeled there, shivering with their own beauty. Seeing this, a lady with a tame cobra around her neck frowned and strained herself to unlock the door. She was long-legged and purebred like a Great Dane.

"Saviour, hold it, please," she said.

She handed him the pensive cobra, freeing her hands for a two-handed key. Saviour took the snake. The cobra shook its head as if rousing itself, then squashed his hand, smiling quite cheekily and glistening as if it were smeared with stale grease. Saviour put the snake into a pot with a cocoa palm and it immediately, with rumbling stomach, muzzled into the soil rich in fluoric limestone.

"Shouldn't have done that," said the lady. "Now she'll gnaw the roots. She's a snake, a predator. Understand?"

Saviour presented her with a bunch of red folios, and she gave him a condescending nod. They entered.

The boss sat at a round table elongated enough to receive lots of victuals, which formed a slanted turret in the middle of it. Steamed crabs' legs made of wild sardine scales crowned the turret. A few nonentities with indiscernible faces sat nearby, but the table was empty both to the right and to the left.

A security guard with such a muscular neck that the muscles dangled below his shoulders slept at some distance. A dog, extremely lean and long, romped on a leash, staying aloof. The pet was so attenuated by hunger that you had to have a really trained eye to distinguish it from the leash. It licked off its sweat, reducing the environmental pollution. Very far away, three moneychangers, small end evil like avian flu viruses, played cards for curtseys with a coal-miner. A buffoon played the pipe and sold doves.

Saviour froze, stunned. He had expected to see something unbelievable here, but this impossible world was anti-believable, and it had a hypnotising music of its own at that, a shrieking sort of music that can sound inside a happy lunatic's mind; it jammed the low, quiet voice of conscience Saviour had always listened to. This world looked him over with button eyes, grinned, let him in.

"I don't believe in it," Saviour whispered.

"What about getting paid?" the world asked.

"Oh. It would be nice."

"Got dyspepsia?" the lady asked, and Saviour started.

"No, I was just thinking."

"Yeah, thinking gives me gas, too," the lady said in a brain-shrinking voice.

"Hi," the boss said, "Saviour? The one? Welcome."

He held out his hand with five nails, and the Saviour shook it, feeling prone to cringe.

"Well, well, I know," the boss said. "Heard much about you, you're that tough guy who cast out all them that sold and bought in the temple, and even overthrew the tables of the moneychangers. It's my house! Ye have made it a den of thieves! Piss off everybody! I can appreciate such things. But, you know, *tempora mutantur, nos et mutamur in illis*. I mean, times change. Just in case, if you forgot Latin. Today wine maketh us merry: and money answereth all things. By the way, want to drink? No? Pity. I know everything about you because my people never lie, though I don't believe them of course. I want to hear it from you. From the horse's mouth, ha-ha. Don't be modest. Position yourself. Can fly? Or walk on water?"

The boss took from the table a forty-three-barrelled cigarette lighter.

"Yes," Saviour said.

"Cool. Will you fly if I throw you out of the window, right now?"

The boss brushed Saviour's cheek with his fingers, quick and spidery, incompatible with his plump face.

"No, I'd be killed. The ability to fly, uh... comes to me from time to time. I can try, though. Maybe, if not very high..."

He flew up and hovered, for a minute, above the table. The lady was busy putting a layer of absolutely transparent powder on her nose. The coal-sweep had already lost the game and given out all the curtseys. Being sick and tired of everything, he pressed his stained face to the wall and charcoaled a self-portrait there. Saviour was hovering. His face wore the dreamy look necessary for flights.

"That wasn't bad," the boss said. "Be my friend. Meet this girl. She's Denise. A female variant of Denis. And don't meet the others. They are morons."

The lady with the key slowly winked; she was aristocratic, like an oyster in spinach. Then she unscrewed a stiletto heel and picked her teeth with it.

They spoke of this and that, then the conversation turned to food and stopped at this comprehensive point. The buffoon got tired of selling the lewd doves and, being hungry, sucked at his saliva ejector. The nonentities kept doing nothing. Their gazes moved up and down Denise's legs, polishing them to a mirrored lustre. The words stirred in Saviour's mouth, losing taste like a wad of chewing gum.

"They say you can live on spirit," said the boss in the voice of a business executive opening a staff conference. "I hope that's true."

Saviour was about to say something non-commercial but changed his mind and answered artlessly. "Sometimes. But I eat, as a rule. Something low-Calorie. Austere repast, you know."

"Cook yourself?"

"Yes."

"By a fiat of will?"

"No. Prefer a microwave."

The boss raised his brow as if surprised at such an extravagance. "Now, you listen to me, bud," he said. "I want, here and now, by a fiat of will. Make me something really delicious and special to eat."

"I can cook cobra's flesh for you. Is it okay?"

"Go on, man, go on."

Saviour took a porno magazine decorating the table and flipped through. One of the women fitted perfectly: snake-eyed and resembling a piece of meat. He decided to make the dish from this picture. Tore it out, crumpled, and placed on the plate. Intertwined his fingers over it.

The boss went out of the room, not wanting to wait for at least fifteen minutes. The buffoon was licking the paints off the pictures and shoving them into the proper tubes; the dog watched him with a melancholic rapacity in its heart. Denise played with a gold watch chain and moved her wonderful eyelashes rhythmically, so long and dense that they could shovel humus.

"What else can you do?" she asked and made the moment flinch.

"Everything," Saviour said.

"The most difficult, I mean."

"With a single word I can make a man happy."

"It's easy," Denise said, "I can do it, too. Hey, guard, I order you to be happy."

The guard woke up and burst out laughing, junked up with official delight. He was prompt to carry out the orders to sob, to fall in love, to go mad and senile, to get prodigious acne and, at last, to go to sleep again. The nonentities echoed, though not at all concerned. Saviour was talking, keeping his mind intent. He developed some arguments for Denise. She was listening to him with unflagging indifference. He was so carried away that he didn't even notice the sudden appearance of a black car smelling of expensive lubricant.

The guys in the car started shooting, and a bullet ploughed through Saviour's spinal column. He stooped a little more, trying to remain concentrated, but the smell of the smouldering varnish distracted him. The bullet, which had popped out of his chest, was spinning on the table before his eyes, a puffing lead corpuscle scorching the polish. Denise fired back with an enviable sang-froid and picked off two of the attackers: one of them died in the driver's seat; the other got a bullet in his lung. This one fell out of the car and immersed into the green shag of the carpet. The carpet liana crawled up to him planning to suck out all his fluids except the toxins. Two non-entities were killed immediately; the third tried to flee away but died of fright on the way. The moment wheezed and wriggled on the floor. Time kept going, but away from the penal acts. Time was accustomed to such scenes, it knew what to do.

Security guards came in time, splitting their sides with belated laughter, and Denise shut them up. She leant over the dying man and eyed with curiosity the incarnadine foam on his lips. She looked like a preteen school-girl with innocent buds of breasts under a T-shirt who, for the first time, had pressed her orbital bone against the ocular of a microscope. Her face shone like a fluorescent lamp.

"Well, now," she said in a voice of a virgin waiting for her first kiss, "we met at last, didn't we? Oh, you want to die so much, no, no, don't cheat me, you're not dying yet, want a drop of water, huh? Nuts to you... Gimme a rag."

A guard gave one.

She moistened the rag in the aquarium where sharky-fish, shaggy with algae, finned optimistically, and moved it over the lips of the dying man. A drop dropped. The man moved, moaned, and she lifted her hand.

"Nope, no way, no water today," she said in a voice of a

yearling jumping around a barn.

The boss appeared at last, sat down at the table, and started peeling a sea tomato.

"What about my meat here?" he asked, then noticed the blood and scowled at that unhygienic nuisance. The blood washed itself off.

"Almost done," Saviour said. "Why is she torturing him? Let him die."

"I'd like to, dude, but no. It's personal. He is the Denis. I mean, Denise is a female name made from him. They rubbed shoulders, then, you know how it goes, rubbed not only shoulders; now they're like a dog and a cat. I don't meddle with their lives. If the torture bothers you, make him die."

"I can't make anybody die."

"I can," the boss said in a voice of inborn certainty. "Hey, you there, die!"

Three guards died and the long dog turned his heels up. The fourth guard jumped out of the window trying to escape his master's anger. The buffoon got stricken by paralysis. The remote coal-sweep escaped with severe fright. In faraway Bonzibar, an epidemic of crayfish distemper broke out. The carpet liana painted itself on the carpet, simulating a black and white imprint. Sharky-fish, being deaf, didn't care a cuss.

"It wasn't for you, idiots," the boss said. "I was talking to Denis. Denis, die!"

And Denis died.

THE BOSS TOUCHED SAVIOUR'S JACKET and shirt. The holes were real. The flesh had already healed the wound.

"Nice," the boss said. "Very nice. The rumours were true. Those guys in the car worked for a rival firm; they wanted to blip you off. They thought I could use you. But you are so difficult to kill, aren't you? Denise is also a cool wench, good for her."

"But if they'd killed me?"

"Then what's the use for me to buy you?" the boss said. "Well done, see? Have killed three birds with one shot. Checked you up, wiped their dirty nose, and Denise gave vent to her feelings. But you're a sly guy; they knew you're worth shooting at."

Saying this, the boss looked so piercingly that he cracked in the meantime the Bermuda Triangle mystery, and eight other mysteries not as big as that one.

"Well. How much am I supposed to pay for you?" he went on.

"Seven hundred curtseys a week... Pre-tax." Saviour breathed out.

"Pre-tax, well, maybe," said the boss. "But first thing's first. Where's my dinner? Cobra's flesh."

Saviour raised his palms. The dish looked well-roasted and smelt delicious. The boss waved to one of the nonentities who waddled nearby.

"You try it first."

The nobody tasted the dish. "Ummm," he purred so melodically as if he had practiced over-night at a karaoke hall. His flesh got pimpled with goose bumps. He smiled with delight, opening his mouth like a dead lizard.

"Enough." The boss tried a bit, and chewed it with concentration. "Well, it doesn't taste like glue."

He paused, busy with chewing and swallowing. His fork stirred the convolutions of noodles.

"My people can cook better," the boss said slowly, with moments of leaden silence inserted between the words. "You've put too much salt in it. Why?"

"For the lack of concentration, maybe. The noise, the shooting, I was wounded..."

"Give him seven hundred curtseys," said the boss in a voice of an electric meat grinder revving up, "and get rid of him right away. Drop him somewhere outside. You think, boy, you are the only one so omnipotent at my disposal? I receive eight guys like you a day. The very archbishopissimus is at my command! Lack of concentration, did you hear that? Well, I think it's the next saviour at the door. Just in time. Let him in."

The door opened and bent low.

The second saviour entered and presented Denise with a bunch of red folios.

"I have a talent, a wonderful thing!" the second one sang out cheerfully, positioning himself in the proper way.

"Don't take it too personally," Denise said to the first saviour, "you were a wonderful freak. But we are highly competitive, you know."

The bodies had already vanished; the cobra's flesh was eaten. The boss wiped his glossy lips.

"Saviour? The one? You're welcome."

BUT, OUTSIDE, THE LAST GUARD WAS still falling. In the very beginning, he had a hope of saving his life because he was an all-round diving-into-shallow-reservoirs champion who specialised in puddles. The rain had only just stopped and there were lots of puddles in the streets. He flew, poising himself with his long hair. But halfway down a cooling breeze gently kissed him, saying goodbye, turbulenting the hair just enough to sweep him to the concrete wall. In a few seconds, the guard hit the wall and turned into a wet blotch.

"*Sic transit gloria mundi*," he mumbled instructively at the end. Thus passed the glory of the world. But no, the glory did not pass with him: the sunset, dense and heavy like a red-hot stone block, glared over the town. The town floundered in this light like a blowfly in sunflower oil. Only this light was real; the dishevelled policemen scared of anything real, fired into the sky with their authorised slingshots. They closed their left eyes at that, or both, for additional bravery.

Saviour saw all that as he walked downstairs. At first he thought to save the falling guard but then changed his mind; right now he didn't feel like saving anybody. *There's something wrong with this world,* he thought, *or is it just me? Millions of people live in this flat universe as oblivious as moth-eaten scarves to what is going on. No, I'm being too picky. Where has the glory of the world gone? Or am I just an interesting freak?*

He went out into the street, looked up at the blackening sky, and saw the last drops of rain, which caught the light of the streetlamps; they were falling slowly like confetti. Then, on buying a cheap advertiser for half a curtsey, he started perusing the columns. But in vain: saviours were required for unqualified and poorly-paid work. To gnash their teeth off-screen in dental prosthesis commercials for example.

The New Neighbours

Tim Jones

New Zealander Tim Jones is the author of one novel, *Anarya's Secret: An Earthdawn Novel*, two short story collections, *Extreme Weather Events* and *Transported*, and two collections of poetry. He also co-edited (with Mark Pirie) the anthology *Voyagers: Science Fiction Poetry from New Zealand*.

Higigh property values are the hallmark of a civilised society. Though our generation may never build cathedrals nor find a cure for cancer, may never save the whales nor end world hunger, we can die with smiles on our faces if we have left our house a better place than we found it, if we have added a deck, remodelled the kitchen, and created indoor-outdoor flow.

Reaction in our street to the news that an alien family would soon move into number 56 was therefore mixed. Number 56 was the proverbial worst house on the best street, and any family who could improve it—regardless of skin colour or number of limbs—was welcome, in my view. My wife, Alison, said she'd wait and see. Josh wondered if they had any kids his age.

Others near to the action, and particularly the Murrays at number 54 and the Zhangs at number 58, were less sanguine. "But it's not as if they need a resource consent," said my wife to Jessica Zhang, and she was right. Having bought the house at a legitimate auction through a telephone bidder, and paid the deposit, the alien family were well within their rights to settle in our street, and the rest of us would simply have to make the best of it.

To the unpractised eye, Saturday the 12th of March would have seemed little different from any other Saturday in Utley Terrace. Eight am was the usual bleary-eyed rush-hour of parents taking their children to cricket. By 11.30, when Josh and I returned to our place at number 55, there was a little more activity: a lawn being mowed, a car being washed, the postie delivering bills and special offers. All the same, a certain twitching of curtains spoke of suppressed excitement.

Hoping for a flying saucer, we were disappointed when a perfectly ordinary moving van appeared outside number 56 shortly after noon, and perfectly ordinary movers began carrying an assemblage of furniture—not well colour co-ordinated, but not notably alien—into the house. Half an hour later, a white Toyota Corolla pulled up outside, and our new neighbours, who went by the name of Thompson, got out. We stood at our lounge-room window, staring.

They looked completely human: Mum, Dad, and the three kids. One appeared to be a teenager, I was perturbed to note — did aliens play Marilyn Manson loud at 3 am? Dressed in good, practical moving-day clothes, they looked right at home as they took vacant possession of their new domain.

"That's pretty boring," said Josh. "They look just like us."

"There's a reason for that," said Alison. "They're shape-shifters."

"Cool!" said Josh. "How many different shapes do you reckon they can turn into?"

"As many as they like, but they can't change their mass," Alison told him. She had this on good authority from her friend Cecile in Wellington. Cecile, said Alison, had contacts.

We didn't usually do anything special to welcome new people to the street, but in this case we thought we should make an exception. Neither the Murrays nor the Zhangs could be expected to take the lead. The Murrays, acting on the adage that good fences make good neighbours, had already added a metre to the height of theirs. Alison and I decided it was up to us. We rang round, got a dozen or so pledges of support, and then went over the road to knock on the new neighbours' door.

It was opened by the teenager, who looked us up and down, called over her shoulder something that must have meant "Mum!", and disappeared back inside without another word. So far, so human.

Mum came to the door. There was something unusual about her face. I do not mean that she had three eyes, or purple skin, or a ring of small feeding tentacles where her mouth should have been. Her features were quite regular and normal, but they lacked any distinguishing quirks. Her nose, her eyes, her ears, her mouth, all were in proportion, and her skin was flawless, without a beauty spot or wrinkle to break the monotony. She looked like everyone and no-one.

"Good evening. How may I help you?" she said.

"We were—some of your neighbours were..." I stumbled to an embarrassed silence, and Alison took over.

"Your new neighbours would like to meet you and your family," said Alison, "and we thought, perhaps, we could host a little celebration to welcome you to our street. We thought we'd pop over first, say hello, and ask when might be a good time."

"Excuse me, please," said the woman, and returned inside.

We waited on the doorstep, straining our ears for noises within. Something that might have been music drifted from the back of the house.

"I bet they're consulting with their superiors," said Josh. "I bet they have an antenna in the backyard."

There were three Super 14 games on tonight, and I had twenty bucks on the Blues by twelve or under. My feet were making small movements back from the doorstep when the woman reappeared.

"Now is a good time," she said. "And we will host the occasion."

"Now?"

"We possess and have studied a barbecue."

It was short notice, and there was some grumbling amongst the invited guests at this breach of protocol, but curiosity won out and we soon had a pretty good crowd gathered in their backyard. Even Jessica Zhang popped over for five minutes before excusing herself. While I helped George to fire up the barbie, Alison inducted Myrtle into the mysteries of impromptu salads, and once a few of the lads turned up with some Speights, the party was humming.

"Do you, er, do you—make sure you keep turning them, they burn easy—do you eat our sort of food, then?"

"When we look as you do, we eat as you do," George said.

"It's true, then, you can change your shape?"

"We change to suit our environment."

I took another swig of Speights. "What do you really look like?"

For a moment, something green and as broad as it was tall stood before me, balanced on an indeterminate number of legs. Bony plates clashed in its jaw.

"Watch out, mate," I said as he returned to human form, "you've dropped the tongs."

Later that night, when George and Myrtle had put Lucy and Peter to bed and shouted goodnight to the teenaged Susan through her locked door, I sat in a deck-chair in number 56's back yard, with Josh sprawled asleep on my lap. George sat beside me. The girls were inside somewhere, looking at paint samples.

"Where are you from?" I asked.

"In your terms, it's Carina—59°23'," said George. He pointed, and I looked. Nothing but a faint wisp of stars.

"Must be a long way," I said.

"It is."

"No popping back home for a holiday, then."

"Not in a hurry, no."

"So why'd you come here, George?"

"To build a better future for our children," said George.

You couldn't argue with that.

THE TROUBLE STARTED AT SCHOOL. We were proud of Rosemont Primary's Decile 10 rating, and guarded it jealously. There may have been more Government money to be had by dropping down a decile or two, but the effect on morale would have been disastrous.

So Rosemont Primary strove for excellence in all things. That caused problems when it came to school sports day. Josh was bursting to tell me about it when I picked him up from after-school care.

"Lucy from over the road won the 100 metres, and Karen Pihama got mad at her and said she cheated and grew some extra legs in the middle of the race, and Karen said aliens ought to go back where they came from, and Mrs Grenville told her off, and then Lucy said she did grow some extra legs, but she didn't know she wasn't supposed to. And Lucy made the team for the Northern Zone finals and Karen didn't. And Karen says her mummy will sue the school."

In the end, the school sent both of them to the finals, and made Lucy promise to stick to a human body shape. Legal action was averted, but it was a straw in the wind. Off work one day with a cold, I went to pick up Josh at 3 pm. There was a tight knot of mothers standing to one side of the netball goal, and Myrtle Thompson standing on the other side by herself.

I sidled close to the mothers.

"—disgusting, they have every advantage, and the school doesn't—"

"—won't put up with—"

"—start a petition?"

I left the mothers to their anger and went over to Myrtle. Perhaps she was adapting to our world: faint lines of worry had appeared around her eyes.

"Tough day?"

She ghosted a smile. "Lucy came first in another test. The other children say it isn't fair, and now their mothers are getting upset. I tell her not to stand out so much, to come second sometimes, but it's not in her nature."

"How about Peter?"

"He's turning into a real Kiwi boy. Ignores his schoolwork, spends all his time on his PlayStation or kicking a rugby ball around. He's fitting in fine."

Then the bell rang, and Josh—not quite old enough yet to be embarrassed by his father—came bounding out of the classroom to bury me beneath a blizzard of school notices.

The Concerned Parents' meeting was supposed to be by invitation only, and as known allies of the aliens, we weren't in the loop. But nothing stays secret for long in Utley Terrace, and the Thompsons found out even before we did. We made some calls, and got together with the Thompsons for a strategy session.

"But what can the Concerned Parents actually do?" I asked.

"Their first step is to get our children suspended, or preferably expelled, from school. If they can do that, they deduce that we'll move away. From what I've heard, Karen Pihama's mother will move to challenge our immigration status if that doesn't work out."

"I told Lucy she should have chosen someone other than a lawyer's daughter to beat in that race," George added unhelpfully.

"What are they going to get your children suspended for? Both of them are good kids and a credit to the school. And you've paid your fees."

"Some of the other kids are starting to gang up on them, on Lucy especially. They're trying to provoke a reaction. Lucy's doing her best, but it's hard for her. Perhaps we should do what they want?"

"It's the problem with being pioneers," said George. "Wherever we go, we will face these attitudes. I think we should stay here and face these critics down. I think we should attend the meeting of the Concerned Parents' Group."

Meeting Room 4 at the Rosemont Community Centre, 7.22 pm. The Concerned Parent at the door looked up in alarm as George, Myrtle, and Susan arrived, flanked by their supporters.

"You can't come in here," hissed the Concerned Parent, who happened to be Leonie Murray from number 54.

"Why not?"

"This is a private meeting."

"No it's not," I said. "It's a public meeting, because you're meeting in a community centre paid for by everyone's rates. We have just as much right to be here as you have." We swept past her into the room.

Much consternation, much gathering and whispering amongst the organisers. Eventually, Leonie Murray walked up to the lectern with a smile pasted to her face.

"Good evening, everyone. *Tena koutou, tena koutou, tena koutou katoa.*" I saw Huhana Pihama wince at the multiple mispronunciations. "We all know why we're here," Leonie said, and glared at us, the tight knot of Thompsons and supporters in the third and fourth rows back. "We've built up a cohesive little community here in Utley Terrace, a community that shares certain values, and now that community is threatened. The Government won't do anything, and the Council won't do anything, and the school says it can't do anything, so it's time we did something ourselves. It seems that news of this meeting spread a bit wider than we planned, so we're going to adjourn the meeting here and reconvene at 54 Utley Terrace, where only those who've got a genuine commitment to this community are invited to attend."

Myrtle Thompson rose to her feet. "Before you go off to your little meeting, I want to say something," she said, to cries of "Sit down!" and "Go back where you came from!" She did not sit down. One or two of the staunchest Concerned Parents walked from the room, but the rest of the audience stayed, waiting for something to happen.

It did. Myrtle changed shape, and once again, but for longer this time, I saw one of our new neighbours in its true form. There was nothing too threatening there: no claws, no tentacles, no teeth to speak of. A multi-limbed green blob, with a mouth pleading for air: Myrtle was breathing heavily by the time she changed back to human form. Three more people had scrambled out of their seats and left in a hurry, but Myrtle had the rest of the audience hooked.

"This is who I am," she said when she got her breath back. "I am not the same as you, but I do not threaten you. For millennia, we of Th'katath have spread throughout the galaxy, seeking only to live peaceably with our neighbours, to trade with them, to invest in their worlds.

"You are a nation of traders. You send your sheep, your beef, your wool, your fruit across to the other side of your

215

planet. But do you not realise what riches are on offer to those who trade amongst the stars? Look!"

Without any visible means of projection, she made glowing images appear on the off-white wall of Meeting Room 4, and she began her pitch. She told us that we in New Zealand, little old New Zealand, had what the galaxy was craving: fresh air, solitude, and the leanest lamb in the galaxy. Tourists, she promised, would flock to see us; carbon-based life forms everywhere, those of a carnivorous persuasion, wouldn't be able to get enough of our two-tooth and hogget.

"Why don't you tell the Government?" asked Larry Purvis from the quantity surveyors'.

"We have. But we will not trade with those who hate us, and so we came to live amongst you, to see whether we would be welcomed or shunned. Perhaps we should have known that we would find a little of each reaction. Now is your time to decide. Will you have us, and the riches we bring?"

High property values are the hallmark of a civilised society. Meeting Room 4 said yes. Overwhelmingly, they said yes. They came up and apologised; they offered handshakes and hugs; they asked whether the inhabitants of the galaxy might find a use for batik, or management consulting, or quantity surveyors. They left happier than they'd arrived, and even those who were parents were, for the most part, concerned no longer.

Of course, not everyone was happy. Lucy and Peter still had to put up with the odd comment in the playground, and there were still some who edged away whenever one of the Thompsons came into a room. Number 54 Utley Terrace squatted behind its high fence and its locked gate and would have no part of the bright future to offer. But now the mood was all for change.

And change duly came. Myrtle and George don't live at number 56 any more—they've gone back to the home world. Lucy and Peter went with them, but Susan stayed on in the house. She met a nice human boy from Palmerston North, and they've got a family of their own now, two girls and a boy on the way. The children look human enough, and beyond that, I'm too much the gentleman to ask.

Myrtle wasn't lying about the rest of the galaxy. Energy is as cheap as dust up there, and galactics—those who can breathe our air—come in such numbers the Government's had to put restrictions on the back country. Lots of Chinese and Indian restaurants are closing down and being replaced by New Zealand ones, and you can walk past any bistro and see aliens of all shapes and sizes dining out on puha, kumara, and lamb.

There's just Alison and me now. Josh studied engineering in Christchurch, then, a couple of years ago, he left on a longer journey. We drove him up to Shannon, then stood watching from behind the safety of 80 centimetres of reinforced glass as the spear of light rose straight up into the night sky. Neither of us had much to say on the drive home.

Tonight we're out on the deck, using the telescope that Myrtle and George gave us as a parting gift. Golden lights move serenely through the field of view, far above Earth's atmosphere. We swing our telescope towards the patch of sky, dark and almost empty, where we know our son now lives, studying, learning. Sometimes we get a message, Josh smiling and telling us he's fine against a background of lights, or bodies with too many legs, or places we cannot recognise or even comprehend.

I'm retired, and Alison's not far off. One day soon, we'll sell our house—the worst house on the best street—and after a few weeks of touring round and saying goodbye to friends, we'll take that road to Shannon. Before they left, George and Myrtle said to look them up one day. I think we will.

FROM THE LOST DIARY
OF TREEFROG7

NNEDI OKORAFOR

Nnedi Okorafor was born in the United States to Nigerian Igbo parents. Her first novel, *Zahrah the Windseeker*, won the Wole Soyinka Prize and her second, *The Shadow Speaker* (set in Niger and Nigeria) won the Carl Brandon Society Parallax award. She has also won the Macmillan Writer's Prize for Africa, for the children's book *Long Juju Man*.

Translating...

Appendix 820 of The Forbidden Greeny Jungle Field Guide. This series of audio files was created by TreeFrog7. It has been automatically translated into text

ENTRY 1 (20.09 hours)

Some clumsy beast has been stalking us. It only comes out at night and it moves with no regard for the bushes, plants, and detritus on the jungle floor. It sounds big and is probably dangerous. And... I think it brings the smell of flowers with it. I can smell it now, like sweet lilacs. Does Morituri36 even notice? I wonder. Regardless of the creature's presence, he continues to compile information and I put it together and upload the finished entries into the Greeny Jungle Field Guide. That's our mission and our system.

"Down with ignorance! Upload information!" We are true Great Explorers of Knowledge and Adventure. Joukoujou willing, we'll survive this day as we have the hundreds of others since choosing to dedicate our lives to informing the ignorant masses about this great jungle.

Whatever is stalking us, we'll deal with it when the time comes.

Field guide entry (uploaded at 14.26 hours)
God Bug:

The God Bug is an insect of the taxonomic order *Ahuhu-ebe*, which includes all beetles. It is common in the Greeny Jungle. Usually blue, sometimes green. When it feels the urge, it spontaneously multiplies, becoming two independent god bugs. As it multiplies it may make a soft popping or giggling sound. There have been rare cases where one has multiplied into four or five. They are docile, almost playful insects. Diurnal.

—written and entered by: TreeFrog7/ Morituri36

*note: For some reason, this common insect has not previously been listed in the Greeny Jungle Field Guide. This may be because the god bug is also found in the city. Or maybe this is another example of the field guide's incompleteness.

ENTRY 2 (18.55 hours)

Disgusting.

Everything here is disgusting. It rains constantly. The ground is always ankle-deep red-brown mud. There are a thousand types of biting and stinging insects. We have to sleep in the trees but the trees, bushes, and plants are noisy with buzzes, growls, snorts, screeches, clicks, whistles, too. Especially at night. The air *reeks* of moss, the syrupy scent of flowers, ripe palm nuts, and rotting mangoes. And the jungle traps heat like a sealed glass tube held over a fire. The Greeny Jungle is a tough place to be while pregnant.

The heat leaves me light-headed. I vomit at least three times a day because of the strong smells. Yes, still, even in my eighth month. But though my sensitive nose makes for great discomfort, it makes for even greater documentation. You'd be amazed at how many floral and faunal specimens show themselves first and foremost with scent.

Yesterday, my nose led me to a tree full of those hairy pink spiders with striped orange legs. A year and half ago, Morituri36 and I uploaded a field guide entry on these creatures. We named them treebeards. They were our hundredth entry. Their bites paralyse your fingers and cause an intense headache. If these spiders ever became common back home they'd cause society to break down within a week. Imagine people unable to type on their computers!

Unfortunately, yesterday, I forgot that treebeards give off a strong smell that is very similar to figs. I thought I'd found a fig tree. I love figs, especially since becoming pregnant. The sky was cloudy. Any other day, I'd have seen all those webs. Instead, I walked right into them and the spiders descended on me like rain. Understandably, they thought I was attacking their home. Not good.

Morituri36 happened to be in the middle of one of his bouts when it happened. I had to save myself by running from the tree, throwing myself in the mud and dead leaves, and rolling like crazy, the roots of some tree grinding into my back. Then I just lay there looking up... into the leaves and ripe fruit of a giant fig tree. The smell of real figs was all around me. Treebeards *and* figs, can you believe it!

Only my left hand was stung. I have to type with my right. I'm left-handed so this has been very, very annoying. I'll be better in a few days.

What a husband I have. He cannot even save his wife from bush spiders. What has this place made us into? But can I blame him for having dulled senses due to his junglemyelitis? Maybe. *I* have been exploring this jungle right beside him all these years. He has been the only human face *I've* had to look at, too. Yet the trees do not "close in" on *me*. *I* do not need to have the sun and moonlight wash over my face for at least four hours a day. *My* brain isn't muddled with an irrational fear of shadows that makes me rant and rave once in a while. And *I'd* have yelled *stop* before *he* walked under a tree full of *treebeards*. Idiot.

The sun is setting and I can hear and smell it again—the creature following us. It's definitely nocturnal.

Field guide entry (uploaded at 01:55 hours)
Treebeard:

The Treebeard is a spider of the taxonic order Udide, which includes all joint-legged anti-spine creatures with eight legs. The treebeard is bright pink with orange stripes on its legs and about the size of a flashdisk. It is called a "treebeard" because it is covered with thick pink hairs that grow longest around the belly, about the length of an adult's index finger. When sitting in a tree, it looks like the tree has a small pink beard. Treebeards are highly social creatures and known to create "cities" in large leafy trees. These treebeard cities give off the strong smell of figs that can drift as far as a half mile radius. Warning: Treebeard poison causes near paralysis of the fingers and toes. One must tolerate this aggravation for only a few days. Diurnal.

—**written and entered by: TreeFrog7/ Morituri36**

ENTRY 3 (13.20 hours)

There is a reason I've decided to break science-speak and enter this journal appendix in the field guide. My name is Treefrog7 and my husband is Morituri36. We are from a village in southwest, Ọnaghị agba nahịa, the people of the impossible beads. Of course, out here in the Greeny Jungle, we cannot wear our traditional beaded attire. Far too heavy. Instead we wear plain light clothing (northern attire). But we never take off our beaded bracelets and marriage earrings. And there is always the bead of the soul. So that is us and that is all I will say on the subject.

I've begun uploading this audio series because, after three months of exploration, we are closing in on something big. Very big. The very process of finding it should be documented along with the scientific information.

Altogether, we've uploaded two hundred and eighty-eight new entries to the field guide. Our fellow explorers are proud. What we explorers do is dangerous work. Many of us die for the information we gather. Many of us return to civilisation with only half our bodies, or half our minds, or ill in a thousand ways. Many of us are lost. Morituri36 and I are not lost. We know exactly where we are and we know exactly what we seek. We will find it. And human civilisation will be changed forever.

I'll explain what "it" is when I'm in a less difficult place.

The mud is deep here. My back aches. I need all my faculties for the time being. I wish Morituri36 would stop singing that song. *World of Our Own.* It reminds me of home. He has such a beautiful voice. I wish he'd shut up. I wish my body would stop aching. I'm sick of being pregnant.

ENTRY 4 (19.21 hours)

I was bitten by a <u>clack beetle</u> today. Their venom is itchy and the white spot it left on my skin is about the size of my fingernail. It shows up on me a lot more than it showed up on Morituri36 when he was bitten last year. I'm a much darker shade of brown than he is. Which means, yes, I get to complain about it. I don't mind cuts, scratches, bites, etcetera. But something about a mark on my skin of temporarily-neutralised melanin really bothers me. No matter. It should be gone in a few days.

Last night, as we looked for a tree to sleep in, we heard the creature. How long is it going to follow us? What does it *want*?

Field guide entry (uploaded at 11:23 hours)
Clack Beetle:
The Clack Beetle is a flightless insect of the taxonic order Ahuhu-ebe, which includes all beetles. It is shiny black and the size of an adult's fingernail. Instead of wings, it has two short stalks with shiny poisonous black balls on the end. *Warning:* Clack Beetle poison causes intense itching and neutralizes the melanin at the site of the bite. When it bites, the pleasure of sucking the victim's blood causes these two balls to loudly "clack" together. Try to crush a clack beetle and you will receive another dose of its poison, this time from the two balls. It's best to shake a clack beetle from your person and quickly walk away. The symptoms will last for a few days if you are lucky. In rare cases where an explorer has repeatedly tried to kill the highly durable insect, the symptoms have lasted forever. Nocturnal.

—written and entered by: Nkoririko89

ENTRY 5 (12.03 hours)

Shh. I have to whisper quietly. Morituri36 is beside me, too. Something just screeched very, very loudly. An <u>elgort</u>? As soon as we can climb down, I need to find a certain seed... just in case. Morituri36 is too clumsy to handle them. He's looking at me, annoyed, but he knows I'm right.

We're still on the trail of what we seek and I believe that whatever has been following us is still on our trail, too. Maybe the <u>elgort</u> will scare it away, or better yet, eat it.

> **Field guide entry (uploaded at 00:01 hours)**
> **Elgort:**
>
> The Elgort is of an unknown taxonic order, possibly Enyi Mba. It is a nasty destructive stupidly irrational beast that physically bears a similarity to a pig or elephant spliced with the genes of a demon. It is generally the size of a small house and has smooth black skin and a powerful trunk lined with many large sharp teeth. It is an egg-layer and, despite its size, capable of moving very very fast, fast as at least the speed of sound. Six explorers I work with have been eaten by these cursed beasts. More on the elgort soon. They are not easy to study.
> —written and entered by: MadHatter72

ENTRY 6 (21.12 hours)

We're at the very top of a baobab tree. Morituri36 and his cursed junglemyelitis. If I fall out and die, our unborn child and I will haunt him until he joins us in death. Right now, I can hear it below. *Why* is it following us? What's it after? And *what* is it? It's not violent, fast, huge, or destructive enough to be an <u>elgort</u>. I'm glad it's nocturnal. Come morning, we'll be able to leave this tree and continue on our way.

We are searching for a mature CPU plant, so mature that we can actually download its hard drive. We call them M-CPUs. Acquiring a copy of an M-CPU's hard drive has never been done in all the history of exploration. BushBaby42, a close friend of mine, found one three months ago but she disappeared before she could download anything. She happened to send us the co-ordinates of her location just before she stopped responding to us, so here we are. We've come hundreds of miles.

It is hard for me to speak of BushBaby42.

I don't wonder what happened to her. She is an explorer, which means it could have been anything. It is very often our fate.

On the M-CPU's hard drive will be unimaginable information, the result of centuries of gathering. Legend has it that these plants connect to networks from worlds beyond. Imagine what it knows, what it has documented. We will not kill or harm it, of course. That would be blasphemy. We won't even clip a leaf or scrape some cells. We'll only make a copy of what it knows. Our storage drives should easily adapt to fit the plant's port. Though our drive is most likely a different species of plant, they'd have to at least be of the same genus.

The CPU plant's entry does it no justice. The entry is a human perspective, ascribing significance to the plant because it is cultivated and used as a tool for humans, a personal computer. The true CPU plant grows in the wild, neither touched nor manipulated by humans. And this plant takes hundreds of years to mature.

Many of us have seen young CPU plants with their glowing monitor flower-heads that light up nights and sleep during the day. They plug into the network and do whatever they do. But an *M-CPU*? Nearly legend. What must BushBaby42 have felt gazing upon it all alone, as she was? What must she have seen on its screen? And what happened to her? She could take on a man-eating whip scorpion with nothing but a stick!

Incidentally, the creature we heard screeching this after-noon *was* an elgort. As big as a house, with tight-black skin that shone in the daylight, beady yellow eyes, as fast as the speed of sound, irrational, and food-minded.

We dealt with it. Manoeuvre 23, specifically for the elgort. We lured the crazed beast to a tall strong hardwood tree. That's the most dangerous part, luring it in. We had to climb very, very fast as soon as it smelt us. Once in the tree, as it reared up below, trying to snatch us down with its tooth-filled trunk (a terrible sight in itself), Morituri36 dropped a bursting seed (which I had picked this afternoon, thank goodness) into its maw. *BLAM!* Its entire head exploded. We now have meat for many days. Elgort meat doesn't need salt to preserve it and it's naturally spicy; some say this is due to the creature's anger and intensity in life.

We thank Joukoujou and the Invisible forces for giving us the skill to protect ourselves. Unfortunately, The Forces of the Soil also protected the elgort from whatever creature is stalking us.

ENTRY 7 (21.34 hours)

Today was all pain. In my back and lower belly. The stretching of ligaments. My belly feels like a great calabash of water. This baby will come soon. Really soon. I hope we find the plant first. The trees here are spaced apart, allowing the sun to shine down, so Morituri36 had a good day. He carried both our packs and even prepared breakfast and lunch—mangoes, roasted tree clams, elgort meat, figs, and root tea both times. It is days like this where I remember why I married him.

It is night now and we are in a large but low tree with one wide branch to hold us both. We can see the sky. It's been a long time since we had a night like this. I think the last time was the day that our child was conceived. Not long afterwards was when he started coming down with the junglemyelitis. His ailment will pass; he's a strong man.

My gut tells me this is the calm before the storm. But maybe I'm just being melodramatic.

ENTRY 8 (04.39 hours)

Dragonflies! Swarms of them. BushBaby42 described these just before she found the plant. We're close. But the creature is still on our trail. This morning, it left its muddy, smelly droppings right at the foot of the tree as if it wanted us to step right into it. I almost did. It was covered with flies and the mound smelt like the vomit of demons. It was so strong that I nearly fainted with nausea. Morituri36 had to carry me away from the mess. Just thinking about it makes me shudder.

Cursed beast, whatever it is. No matter how we try to glimpse it at night, it keeps out of sight as it blasts its angry flowery scent. Biding its time, I suspect. But when the fight comes, it will be shocked when, instead of running, we turn to meet it. We haven't survived the jungle solely because of luck.

But Morituri36 needs to remember that he is a human being, and that *I* am a human being, too. When he gets into his moods, he speaks to me as if I'm a piece of meat. As if I'm lower than his servant. He speaks to me the way the Ooni chief speaks to his wives. How dare he? I am carrying our child. I have done as much work as he has. And, junglemyelitis or not, we are in this together. There is no need for insult.

"It dies well beforehand!" he snapped at me earlier today as we inspected a <u>morta</u>. We'd caught it this morning. A <u>morta</u> is a beautiful red bird with a long thin beak. When it dies, its dead body keeps flying aimlessly for days. Strange creatures but not the strangest in the jungle. Morituri36 seemed to think that their carcasses also rotted as they flew.

"Look at it," I calmly said, despite my rising anger at his tone. The dead <u>morta</u> was still trying to flap its wings. "This is the fifth one we've caught! No rot anywhere!"

He just huffed and puffed the way he always does when he knows I'm right. The entry someone uploaded to the field guide was simply wrong and needed to be changed. The fact is that <u>mortas</u> probably don't fly for that long after they die. Maybe a few hours and that's it. Certainly not days. If it were days, it would be infested with rot and maggots. But that wasn't what I wanted to find out most about the <u>morta</u>. I wanted to know what made it fly as a dead creature. Morituri36 and I agreed it had to be some sort of parasite with strange faculties. We just needed to run some tests.

But he wasn't so interested in answers today. He threw the bird corpse to the ground. "It is because it is freshly dead," he muttered. "Stupid, stupid woman." Immediately, the dead bird hopped up and took off. I cursed, watching it go, wondering what microscopic organisms were working the bird's muscles and how intelligent they could be to do so. They were obviously using the <u>morta</u> carcass to search for food or a special place to procreate.

I wanted to slap Morituri36. How many pockets of information have we lost because of his temper? He and I are south westerners, the people of beads. Amongst our people, we say, "Many beads protect the thread." He knows this kind of behaviour will not get him far. Maybe one day I'll push him out of one of the extra high trees he forces us to sleep in every night.

We didn't talk to each other for hours. Then we started seeing millions of dragonflies.

The land was still spongy and muddy. There were large pools of standing water. The air smelt like wet leaves, stagnant water, and spawn. An ancient CPU plant would thrive in a place like this.

The dragonflies must have loved this place, too, but the huge swarms were because of the plant. CPU plants send out strong sine waves. These types of dragonflies are attracted to the electromagnetic waves like moths, mosquitoes, suck bugs, and butterflies are to light.

We'd always been plagued by a few of these sine-wave-drinking dragonflies because of the portable we use to type in and upload information (including this audio journal) to the field guide node. Our portable is powerful. Even hundreds of miles from civilisation, we can access the network and communicate with other explorers who wish to communicate. But there is a downside to everything. Large dragonflies zooming around our heads is one of them. The sine waves intoxicate them.

Usually, there are only two or three plaguing us. Now it's about twenty. They're like flying jewels, emerald-green, rockstone blue, blood-red. A few of them are of the species that glow blue-purple. But none of them stays long. They zoom about our heads for a few minutes and then zip off, replaced by another curious dragonfly. Something bigger is attracting them, of course. I can't wait to see it. We don't even need BushBaby42's co-ordinates anymore. Just follow the dragonflies. I hope BushBaby42 is okay.

Field guide entry (uploaded at 04:08 hours)
Morta:

The Morta is a bird of the taxomic order of Nnunua which includes most bipedal, winged, pro-spine that lay eggs. Its plumage is a deep red and its long beak is made for snatching termites from termite mounds. The morta's mating call is a chilling screech reminiscent of a woman being murdered. When a morta dies, its dead body continues to fly aimlessly for days. They are easy prey for flying scavenger beasts. You can find mortas throughout the Greeny Jungle once you get about thirty miles away from civilization. Diurnal when alive. Diurnal and Nocturnal when dead.

— written and entered by: OrchidVenom3

ENTRY 9 (22.20 hours)

We cannot sleep. Morituri36 is sitting beside me. For once he's looking down instead of up. Even he can smell the beast's scent now. It's right down there.

The dragonflies are going mad around here. We can see the plant just starting to glow about a mile away, to the north. By the night, it'll be glowing like a small planet. But the creature is below us. Right at the base of our tree. I hope we make it through the night without a fight. Doing battle in the dark is the worst kind of fighting.

ENTRY 10 (20.14 hours)

It's a moth! With a large, hairy, robust but streamlined body, thick fuzzy black antennae with what looked like metallic balls on the ends, and a large coiled proboscis. But it's wingless, the size of a large car and with six strong insectile running legs. And it uses its proboscis like a flexible spear!

It came after us just after dusk while we were looking for a tree to sleep in. Out of nowhere, you just heard the sound of branches snapping, and leaves getting crushed as it rushed at us from behind. Within moments, it speared me in the thigh and my husband in the upper arm. We'd be dead if it weren't for our quickness and how good we've become at climbing trees. I guess I have to thank my husband and his stupid illness. We've bandaged each other up. At least some of the bleeding has stopped, my husband's wound was worse than mine. So far no sign of poisons from its proboscis.

The moth's body shape tells me that this thing's relatives clearly used to be fliers. It's been following us for days and now, as we close in on the plant, it has become aggressive; it's guarding something. I can guess what it is.

We could kill it. My husband and I have certainly killed larger, more dangerous beasts. But killing it might eventually cause what it protects, the M-CPU, to die. The death of centuries of information. No. We'd rather die. So, instead, we're stuck in a tree a mile from the plant.

There's a problem. My waters just broke. No, not now. *Not* now!

ENTRY 11 (20.45 hours)

We're in another tree. About 200 feet from the M-CPU. Like everything around here, it's infested with dragonflies. Their hard bodies smack against my face like hail. The wingless moth is below, waiting, angry, protective. We're about to climb down and make a run for it. I hope my husband is right. Otherwise, we're dead.

The M-CPU's smell is overly sweet, syrupy, and thick. I've vomited twice up here. The labour pains drown out the pain from my leg. They are getting stronger and faster, too. Can barely control my muscles when the contractions hit. If they get any worse I won't be able to help myself, I'll fall right out of this tree. A terrible way to die. A terrible way for an unborn child to die. I hope my husband is right.

ENTRY 12 (21.26 hours)

If I focus on talking into this portable, I will not die.

We're cornered. But we are lucky. We made it to the plant. Dragonflies are everywhere. Their metallic bodies shine in the plant's light. They make soft tapping sounds when they hit the plant's screen. Oh, the pain. My husband was right, bless his always-sharp mind. The wingless moth indeed is guarding the M-CPU. And thus, now that we are close to the plant, the moth fears we'll harm it. If we don't move, the creature will not attack. It is not stupid. It can reason. Otherwise it would have killed us both by now... soon there will be three of us.

My body does not feel like my own.

The... M-CPU is as tall as my husband. He can look right into the flower head, which is a bulbous monitor with large soft periwinkle petals framing it. There is indeed a slot right below the head, where the green stem begins. The moth is a pollinator. Morituri36 says that below the disk is a tube that goes deep; only the proboscis of this wild creature could fit down there. It is a most unique but not an unheard-of pollination system. But there are deeper things at work here.

Maybe the moth will leave come dawn when the plant goes to sleep. But the night has just begun. As the flower opens wide, so do I. The baby will be here soon. Why do the gods create this kind of *pain* when bringing life into the world? Why?

ENTRY 13 (23.41 hours)

I was screaming when she came out screaming. My husband wasn't there to catch her; I wanted him to stay near the M -CPU's flower. So our daughter landed on the cloth he'd spread. Morituri36 laughed with joy. A blue dragonfly landed on her for a second and then flew off. I had to lean forwards and pick her up. I cut my own cord. She is in the crook of my arm as I hold this portable to my lips and record these words. A beautiful thing.

The moth has backed off. Could it be that the gift of life was enough to stop this intelligent beast in its tracks? Or does it know what my husband is doing? Our storage drive fitted perfectly into the port just below the flower head.

The flower is fully open now. It is sometimes good to be a man. My husband can stand up and watch as we wait for the download to be complete. I can only lie here in the mud and listen to what he tells me as I slowly bleed to death.

ENTRY 14 (00.40hours)

"Are you all right?" he keeps asking, with that look on his face. Don't look at me like that, Morituri36. Like I'm going to disappear at any moment. The moth looms. I've washed our daughter with the last of my husband's water. She seems happy and angry, sleeping, trying to suckle and crying. Normal. Amazing.

Just tell me what you see! I'm talking to Morituri36. Doesn't he think I want to know? As if I am not an explorer, too. Giving birth can't change that fact.

Morituri36, you know the portable can only record one voice. Here, take it. It's better if you just speak into it.

My wife is crazy. She cannot properly describe the situation we are in right now, as I speak. The trees creep in on us like soldiers. She can't see them, but I can. Every so often, I see a pink frog with gold dots sitting in the trees just watching us. Treefrog7 doesn't believe me when I speak of this creature. It is there, I assure you.

But neither the trees nor the frog is our biggest threat. Treefrog7 is truly amazing. It is not that she just gave birth. That is a miracle in itself but a miracle most women can perform. No. It is that we have been stalked and hunted by this beast that our explorer ethics prevent us from killing and still this woman can concentrate enough to blast a child from her loins, even as the creature stands feet away, biding its time for the right moment to spear me in the heart and her between the eyes and then to maybe make a meal of our fresh and new healthy daughter.

But Treefrog7 wants me to talk about this plant that led us to our certain deaths. The M-CPU of legend and lore. The One Who Reaches. The Ultimate Recorder. Bushbaby42's obsession. How old must this M-CPU be? Seven, ten thousand years? Older than the plant towers of Ooni? I believe it's a true elemental with goals of joining its pantheon of plant griots.

My wife looks at me like I'm crazy... but who knows. You look into its head and how can you not wonder? Look at it, surrounded by purple sterile ray florets the size of my arm and the width of my hand. Its deep green stem is as thick as my leg and furry with a soft white sort of plant-down. No protective spikes needed when it's got a giant moth guarding it.

It's deep night now. And everything's colour is altered by the brightness of the flower's head. An organic monitor is nothing new. It is what we know. We Ooni people have been cultivating the CPU seed into personal computers for, what, over a century? It's how the CPU plant got its name. And explorers have seen plenty of wild CPU plants here in the Greeny Jungle. Lighting the night with their organic monitors, doing whatever it is they do. But an uncultivated M-CPU? How did Bushbaby42 find it? And where is she? We've seen no sign of her. Treefrog7 and I will not speak of her absence here.

So back to the M-CPU's head. What do I see in it? How can I explain? It is a screen. Soft to the touch, but tough, impenetrable, maybe. But I wouldn't test this with the moth looming, as it is. And I would never risk harming the M-CPU.

The plant's screen is in constant flux. There is a sort of icon that looks like a misshapen root that moves around clicking on/ selecting things. Right now, it shows a view of the top of a jungle. It cannot be from around here because this jungle is during the daytime. There are green parrots flying over the trees.

Now it shows text but in symbols of some unknown language. A language of lines branching off other lines, yes, like tree branches, roots, or stems. The root-shaped cursor moves about clicking and the screen changes. Now it's a star-filled night sky. A view of what looks like downtown Ile-Ife, not far from the towers. There are people wearing clothes made of beads, south westerners. I know that place. My home a minute's walk from there!

The screen changes again. Now... most bizarre, the sight of people, humans, but as I've never seen them. And primitive-shaped slow-moving vehicles that are not made of woven hemp but of metal. There are humans here with normal dark brown skin but most are the colour of the insides of yams and these people have light-coloured hair that settles. My wife looks at me with disbelief. It's what I see, Treefrog7. The legend is true. The M-CPU can view other worlds. Primitive old worlds of metal and stone and smoke but friendly-enough looking people. Now there are more symbols again. Now an image of a large bat in flight. The roots of a tree. The symbols. A lake surrounded by evergreen trees.

My guess? This is the plant thinking, and it is in deep thought. Back to my wife.

Voice recognition detects Treefrog7, Greeny Explorer number421, 793 days in Jungle, approximately 600 miles north of Ooni, 01.41 hours

ENTRY 15 (01.41 hours)

I feel better. It's been about two hours. Baby's fine. My bleeding has stopped. The moth is still there. Watching us. The download is almost done. I can stand up (though it feels like my insides will fall out from between my legs) and see the monitor for myself now.

It just showed something I've never seen before... a land of barrenness, where everything is sand and stone and half-dead trees. Where could this nightmarish place be? Certainly not Ginen. It's almost 2 am. In a few hours, we'll know if that moth actually sleeps.

Field guide entry (uploaded at 01.55 hours)
Wingless Hawk Moth:

The Wingless Hawk Moth is an insect of the taxonomic order *Urubaba*, which includes butterflies and moths. It is the size of a large car, has a robust grey furry body with pink dots, pink compound eyes, and hearty insectile legs for running. Its antennae are long and furry with silver ball-like organs at the tips. Its proboscis is both a feeding and sucking organ, and a deadly jabbing weapon. It is the pollinator of the M-CPU. It makes no noise as it attacks and is known to stalk targets that it deems hostile to its plant for days. Nocturnal.

—written and entered by: TreeFrog7/ Morituri36

ENTRY 16 (02.29 hours)

I'm having a catharsis as my husband and I stare into its monitor and it stares back. I am looking into a distorted mirror. We are gazing into the eye of an explorer. It is like us.

ENTRY 17 (05.25 hours)

My baby is beautiful. She is so fresh and I can see that she will be very dark, like me. Maybe even browner. Thank goodness she is not dada and that she has all ten of her fingers and toes. Think of the number of times in the last eight months that I've been poisoned, touched the wrong plant, been bitten by the wrong creature, plus I am full of antibiotics and micro-cures. Yet my baby is perfect. I am grateful.

If we ever make it home, my people will love her. But the wingless hawk moth is still here. The sun rises in an hour.

ENTRY 18 (5.30 hours)

The M-CPU shows pictures and they are getting closer to where we are! Pictures of the sky over trees. Symbols. Clicking. The jungle at night. More symbols. I can see our backs! What! The moth is coming, but slowly, it's walking. It is calm, its proboscis coiled up. But what does it *want*? Download is done. What... the M-CPU's monitor shows two eyes now. Orange with black pupils. Like those of a lemur but there is nothing else on the screen. Only black. Just two unblinking... Joukoujou, help us, o! Now I see. Don't come looking for us! Don't...

Voice recognition detects... Unknown
Hacked Allowance

They will never die. No information dies once gathered, once collected.
The creatures' field guide is thorough but incomplete.
I am the greatest explorer.

I am griot and I will soon join the others.

End of Appendix 820

BongaFish35 Pinging Treefrog7...

Request timed out.
Request timed out.

BongaFish35 Pinging Morituri36...
KolaNut8 Pinging Morituri36...
MadHatter72 Pinging Treefrog7...

Request timed out.
Request timed out.
Request timed out.
Request timed out.
Request timed out.
Request timed out.

THE SLOWS

GAIL HAREVEN
TRANSLATED BY YAACOV JEFFREY GREEN

A writer and journalist of considerable reputation in Israel, Gail
Hareven won the prestigious Sapir Prize for literature in 2002
for *The Confessions of Noa Weber* (her first novel to be translated
into English, in 2009) and is the author of several novels and
collections, including an SF story collection where "The Slows"
first appeared (it was first published in an English edition in
The New Yorker).

The news of the decision to close the Preserves was undoubtedly the worst I had ever received. I'd known for months that it was liable to happen, but I'd deluded myself into thinking that I had more time. There had always been controversy about the need for maintaining Preserves (see B. L. Sanders, Z. Goroshovski, and Cohen and Cohen), but from this remote region, I was simply unable to keep abreast of all the political ups and downs. Information got through, but to evaluate its importance, to register the emerging trends without hearing what people were actually saying in the corridors of power was impossible. So I can't blame myself if the final decision came as a shock.

The axe fell suddenly. At six in the evening, when I got out of the shower, I found the announcement on my computer. It was just four lines long. I stood there with a towel wrapped around my waist, reading the words that destroyed my future, that tossed away a professional investment of more than fifteen years. I can't say that I'd never envisaged this possibility when I chose to study the Slows. I can't say that it hadn't occurred to me that this might happen. But I believed that I was doing something important for the human race and, mistakenly, I thought that the authorities felt the same way. After all, they had subsidised my research for years. Eliminating the Preserves at this stage was a loss I could barely conceive of, a loss not only for me and for my future—clearly I couldn't avoid thinking about myself—but for humanity and its very ability to understand itself. Politicians like to refer to the Slows as being deviant. I won't argue with that, but as hard as it is, as repulsive and distressing, we have to remember that our forefathers were all deviants of this kind.

I confess that I passed the rest of the evening with a bottle of whiskey. Self-pity is inevitable in situations like this, and there's no reason to be ashamed of it. The whiskey made it easier for me to get through the first few hours and fall asleep, but it certainly didn't make it any easier to get up in the morning.

As if to spite me, the sky was blue, and the light was too brilliant. As often happens in this season, the revolting smell of yellow flowers went straight to my temples. When I pulled myself out of bed, I discovered that the sugar jar was empty, and I'd have to go to the office for my first cup of coffee. I knew that at some point during the day I would have to start packing up, but first I needed my coffee. I had no choice. With an aching head and a nauseating taste in my mouth, I dragged myself to the office shed. I opened the door and found a Slow woman sitting in my chair.

Despite the security guards' repeated instructions, I tended to forget to lock doors. Our camp was fenced in, we all knew one another, and the savages entered only during working hours, and then only with permission. How had she sneaked in?

Years of field work had taught me how to cope with all sorts of situations. "Good morning," I said to her. I didn't even consider reaching for the button to call the guards. True, there had been occasional attacks in other camps but, for all sorts of reasons, there had been none in ours to date. Besides, as I always said, the people most likely to be attacked were the policemen and the missionaries, not me, so I had a logical justification for bending the rules a little.

The savage woman didn't answer me. She leant over to pick something up from the other side of the desk, and immediately I became afraid. The fear spread rapidly from my legs to my chest, but my brain kept working. So the rumour was true: they had got their hands on a cache of old weapons. To them, perhaps we were all alike after all—policeman or scientist, it didn't matter much from their point of view. But then the woman turned back to me: she was holding a human larva strapped into a carrier, which she lay on the table.

"You promised you wouldn't take our babies from us," she said in the angry, agitated voice so typical of the Slows. As my adrenaline level fell, it was hard for me to steady my legs. The savage woman fixed me with her black eyes and seemed to see this. "You pledged that you wouldn't take them. There are treaties, and you signed them," she spat out impatiently. I was always amazed at how fast news reached the Slows. It was clear to anybody who worked with them that they were hiding computers somewhere, and perhaps they also had collaborators on the political level. The nearest settlement of Slows was half an hour's flight away. They weren't allowed to keep hoverers, and there were no tracks in the region so, to get to our camp, she must have set out the evening before. It seemed that she had known about the decision to close the Preserves even before I did.

"Those treaties were signed many generations ago. Things change," I said, though I knew that it was silly to get into an argument with one of them.

"My grandmother signed them."

"Is it your baby?" I asked, making a point of using their term, as I gestured at the human larva on my desk.

"It's mine." Luckily, the larva was asleep. Fifteen years of work had more or less inured me but, at that hour of the morning and in my condition, I knew that my stomach wouldn't be able to stand the sight of a squirming pinkish creature.

"Do you have others?"

"Maybe." The female Slows don't usually give birth to more than three or four offspring. Given the way they are accustomed to raising offspring, even that many is hard work. This savage woman was young, as far as I could judge. She might have concealed another larva somewhere before coming here. There was no way of knowing.

"You can't break the agreements," she said, cutting into my thoughts. "No. Listen to me. You've violated almost every clause. Every few years you renege on something. When you forced us into the Preserves, you promised us autonomy, and since then you've gradually stolen everything from us. From hard experience, we've learnt not to trust you. Like sheep, we kept quiet and let you push us further and further into a corner. But now I'm warning you. Just warning you: don't you dare touch the children!"

Many people will think this strange but, over the years, I've learnt to see a kind of beauty in the Slow women. If you ignore the swollen protrusions on their chests and the general swelling of their bodies, if you ignore their tendency to twist their faces wildly, with some experience you can distinguish between the ugly ones and the pretty ones, and this one would definitely have been considered pretty. If her grandmother had really signed the treaties, as she'd said, she might have been one of their aristocrats, the descendant of a ruling dynasty. It was evident that she could express herself.

"Will you agree to have some coffee with me?" Field work often involves long hours of conversation. With time, I had got used to the physical proximity of the Slows and, sometimes, when their suspicions subsided—when they accepted that I wasn't a missionary in disguise—they told me important things. The new decree had put an end to my research, but I might still be able to write something about the reaction of the savages to the development. Attentiveness had become a habit with me and, besides, I was not yet capable of packing up the office.

"Coffee," I repeated. "Can I make some for you?" Since she didn't answer and just stared at me with a blurred face, I said, "You've certainly come a long way. It wouldn't hurt me to have a cup, either. Wait a minute, and I'll make some for both of us." The Slows had grown used to harsh treatment, so when they encountered one of us who treated them courteously, they tended to get flustered. Indeed, this dark-eyed woman seemed confused, and she kept her mouth shut while I operated the beverage machine.

No doubt the savages were a riddle that science had not yet managed to solve and, the way things seemed now, it never would be solved. According to the laws of nature, every species should seek to multiply and expand but, for some reason, this one appeared to aspire to wipe itself out. Actually, not only itself but also the whole human race. Slowness was an ideology, but not only an ideology. As strange as it sounded, it was a culture, a culture similar to that of our forefathers. People don't know, or perhaps they forget, that when the technique for Accelerated Offspring Growth (AOG) was developed, it wasn't immediately put to use. Until the first colonies were established on the planets, the UN Charter prohibited AOG. It's not pleasant to think about it now, but the famous Miller, German, and Yaddo were subjected to quite a bit of condemnation for their early work on the technique, all of it on ethical grounds. In a society that had not yet conquered space, AOG was viewed as a catastrophe that, within ten years, was liable to cause a population explosion on Earth that would exterminate life through hunger and disease. The morality of the Slows had an undeniably rational basis under those conditions. We may be revolted by the thought, but the fact is that Miller, German, and Yaddo had all spent the first years of their lives as human larvae, not unlike the one that was now lying on my desk; they, too, had been slowly reared by savage females, just like the one who was waiting beside me for her coffee.

"We have to talk," she said as I placed the cup on the desk and glanced for just a split second at the creature sleeping in the carrier. "There's no reason for you to use power. There's no point, because you have all the power anyway. We're no threat to you."

I knew something that she didn't know because it was a secret that hadn't been publicised on the networks: in one of the colonies on Gamma, far from the Preserves, there had been an outbreak of Slowness. This was probably why the decision had been made to close all the Preserves—to eliminate any possibility of the infection spreading.

"It's possible to compromise on all sorts of clauses," the savage woman said, "so why not compromise with us? We'll die out on our own in a few generations anyway. There are less than ten thousand of us left."

The problem isn't one of numbers, I thought, but I didn't say it to her. *The problem is that in many people's eyes you are not a remnant but a gangrene that could spread and rot the entire body of humankind. Even I, with my interest in your way of life, can't say for certain that the politicians are wrong about this.*

"We've thought of all kinds of possibilities," she said. "Since we have no choice, we'll agree to let your missionaries into our settlements. We'll guarantee their safety and give them complete freedom to talk to whomsoever they wish. We'll agree that one parent's consent is enough in order for a baby to be surrendered for accelerated growth, and we'll make sure that parents obey that rule. What else do you want? What else can you demand? In the end, without wasting any more energy on us, you'll get everything you want anyway."

"Not this one," I interjected, pointing at her larva. A tremor twisted her face and made it ugly. I drank the coffee and noticed that the larva had opened its eyes. The coffee was sour. The machine was apparently not working properly again. But there was no point in calling in a serviceman when I had only a few more days to spend here.

"Don't take them away from us," she whispered, and her voice shook. "I need at least a few years. You must allow us that. Why do you hate us so?"

The ardent possessiveness that savage parents—especially the mothers—display towards their offspring is the key to understanding the Slows' culture. It's clear that they don't love their offspring the way we love ours. They make do with so few and, at the rate they rear them, at best, they get to know only their children's children. Whereas even I—who have spent years away from civilisation in barren camps like this one—have managed to produce seventeen sons and daughters and a lineage of at least forty generations. Still, they talk constantly about their love for their offspring, and its glory.

"Hate?" I said to her. "Hate is a strong word."

The human larva turned its head and gazed towards the savage woman. In turn, her gaze clung to it, and her chin quivered. She had pretty eyes. She had put on black and green makeup in my honour. A week or two of body formation would have made a good-looking woman of her in anyone's opinion. She trusted me, apparently; and knowing who I was, having heard about me or made enquiries, perhaps she hoped that, as a researcher, I would agree to represent her side. She had put herself in jeopardy by sneaking into my office in this way. Someone else in my place might have panicked, and an unnecessary accident might have taken place. Through her grimaces, I could see a face that wasn't at all stupid. She had certainly taken my well-known curiosity into account, and my composure. She knew that all I had to do was reach out and press a button and they would come, chase her away and take the larva from her. I wasn't about to do that, but sooner or later, no matter where she hid, it would be taken.

In all my years of work, I'd refrained from saying anything that would identify me with the missionaries, but now, seeing the tremble of her chin, I heard their words of consolation coming from my mouth. So be it. In any event, my work had come to an end.

"I know what you think, what they've told you. Lots of misunderstandings and rumours circulate in the Preserves. Listen to me, I promise you that no harm will come to the children."

"Do you mean that you won't take them?" the savage princess asked in a soft, strange voice. "That the decision has been revoked?"

"Decisions aren't my field. People like me don't make policy. What I want to explain to you is another matter. Maybe you think that accelerated growth will shorten this offspring's life. Believe me, woman, that's a mistake. Whoever told you that was either wrong or lying. Our life span is no shorter than yours. Actually, the opposite is true: progress gives us a longer life. If your son is ultimately given over to AOG, he won't lose even a single day. On the contrary, he can enjoy all the years before him as an independent adult. You'll see your son's children, and your descendants will inherit the planets."

The savage woman twisted her jaw to the side. "You think we're stupid."

The Slows have manners of their own. You can't expect them to behave like us. Still, in her present situation I would have expected her to make an effort. But the very fact that she wasn't making an effort held my interest. Perhaps this was an opportunity for me to hear something new. Usually, they were so cautious when speaking to us and behaved evasively even with me.

But just at that moment the larva started to bleat, and the savage woman instantly lost her impertinence.

"You may do it," I said to her. "Pick it up. I've been in the Preserves for years, and I've seen such things."

Without looking at me, she freed the larva from the carrier and held it to her chest. I observed six of my offspring during the process of accelerated growth, and the distress of the first weeks before they reached decent maturity comes back to me every time I'm forced to observe a human larva up close. There are times in a person's life that are meant to be private, and the state of infancy is certainly the most pronounced of these. The larva was silent for a moment, then it started to bleat again.

"How old is it?"

"Eleven weeks." The most horrifying human larvae are the big ones that already look like people but lack the stamp of humanity. At least this one was similar in dimensions to our offspring. Nearly three months old. He could have been a productive adult already. Footsteps could be heard outside, and the sound of two people talking. The savage woman's eyes widened. She put her hand first to her mouth and then to the larva's open mouth.

"Don't worry. They won't come in here. They know that I

hold interviews." The touch of the woman's hand on the creature's lips increased its discomfort, and now it raised its voice, screeching until its wrinkled face turned almost purple. Someone was liable to enter after all. The savage woman stuck a finger into the larva's mouth, but it turned its head away and looked for something else.

"Don't you feel sorry for it?" I asked, but she seemed not to hear me, cradling the larva in her arms and also turning her head here and there with an unfocussed look in her eyes.

Human beings as we know them are excited by every development in their offspring because what purpose is there for the hard labour of parenthood if not to send forth an independent, productive adult who can satisfy his own needs? But the Slows appeared to enjoy the helplessness of their larvae—the lack of humanity, the deplorable fervour of the little creatures, their muteness, their mindless appetites, their selfishness, their ignorance, their inability to act. It seemed that the most disgusting of traits were what inspired the most love in savage parents.

The screeches stunned me. I was so riveted by the sight of that wriggling caterpillar that I almost missed the moment when the woman started talking again. "If we knew how much time was left for us..." So she didn't know everything: the invasion would start that day; it might already have begun. "If we knew that we had another year or two, if you would only tell us how much time there is people could prepare themselves." Had she come as a spy? If they greeted the police with violence, they'd only bring disaster down upon themselves. A few spontaneous uprisings were to be expected. After all, theirs was a volatile culture. But an organised attack would be a kind of stupidity that was hard to fathom.

"I'm asking for so little," the savage woman said. "Just this—to know how much time remains for us. Listen to me. I know you're different from them. You're not a missionary. You know us. You're merciful, not like them. I feel it. You could have called the guards when you saw me here, but you didn't do it. Maybe you once also had a baby you loved."

The larva arched its body backwards, and the woman un-consciously fingered the opening of her shirt. Suddenly, I knew what she wanted to do, and with that thought, the sourness of the coffee rose in my throat. To give it her milk bulges—that's what she wanted, that's why she was plucking at her shirt. When I'd been a student, I was forced to watch a film about ancient nutritional customs. It was for a course restricted to advanced students, but none of us was advanced enough to view that sight without a sharp feeling of nausea. From close up, we watched the ravenous face of the larva and the swollen organ thrust into its wet mouth. It was a rather large larva, at least thirteen pounds, and the depraved sucking noises that it emitted mingled with the female's bestial murmur. White liq-uid dripped down its chin, and the woman tickled its lips with her gland, holding the organ shamelessly between finger and lustful thumb. I still remember the strong protests voiced by three women students, which was understandable.

"If you'll just answer me that," the savage woman said, and her voice shook with feeling. "Just that."

The emotionality of the Slows had the strange characteristic of clinging to me like a stain. As sometimes happened after a few hours of conversation with one of them, I began to feel pol-luted. "The good of the children is the only thing that we con-sider," I said finally. "Do you want a cup of water? I see that you haven't touched your coffee."

When I got up and went back to the machine, the woman bent her body over the larva, almost concealing it under a black curtain of hair. The cold water refreshed my mouth, removed the traces of yesterday's drink and the bitterness of the coffee, dislodged the clinging feeling. I drank two cups. It is some-times possible to identify the rational thought amongst the Slows, but their emotional exaggeration dilutes it. Though I had hoped to calm the savage woman, at that moment it was clear that there was no point in trying.

When I returned to the desk with a cup of water for her, I saw that she was rocking slowly on the chair, moving the larva rhythmically back and forth. It was tired from so much screeching, and its voice was growing weaker. She was so deeply immersed in her drugged movement that she didn't notice me. I watched the two tired bodies moving together and knew that soon, very soon, there would be an end to their suffering. The larva would become a man in control of his body, and she would accept it and smile. With clarity, I saw that image and, as though to transmit it to her, I reached out and placed my hand on her shoulder. All at once, like an animal, the woman recoiled, raised her head, and bared her teeth. The sudden movement jolted my body backwards, and for a long moment we were frozen, twisted in mid-movement, looking into each other's faces.

"Don't touch me!" she spat out, as though at an enemy. Her face was transparent, and I could read everything in it, all her distorted thoughts. She believed that what I wanted was to hold her soft body, to curl my fingers and grasp her flesh, to press it against mine and rub, blind and hopeless, against her milk glands. Her eyes, like snakes, penetrated my thoughts and fed them her abominable vision, the visions of a lower animal. For nine years I had been in the Preserves and never had I experienced such defilement.

"No-one's touching you," I pronounced with difficulty, turning towards the door and putting my hand out to press the button. By the time the alarm went off and the sound of the larva's weeping reached me, I was already in the light—in the bright, bright light outside.

ZOMBIE LENIN

EKATERINA SEDIA

Ekaterina Sedia grew up in Moscow but has since moved to the
United States. She is the author of *The Secret History of Moscow*
and several other novels, of which the most recent is *Heart of
Iron,* She has also edited several anthologies, including the
World Fantasy Award-winning *Paper Cities.*

1.

It all started when I was eight years old, on a school trip to the Mausoleum. My mum was there to chaperon my class, and it was nice because she held me when I got nauseous on the bus. I remember the cotton tights all the girls wore, and how they bunched on our knees and slid down so that we had to hike them up as discreetly as eight year olds could. It was October, and my coat was too short; Mum said it was fine even though the belt came disconcertingly close to my underarms, and the coat didn't even cover my butt. I didn't believe her; I frowned at the photographer as he aligned his camera, pinning my mum and me against the backdrop of St Basil's Cathedral. "Smile," Mum whispered. We watched the change of guard in front of the Mausoleum.

Then we went inside. At that time, I was still vague on what it was that we were supposed to see. I followed in small mincing steps down the grim marble staircase along with the line of people as they descended and filed into a large hall and looked to their right. I looked, too, to see a small yellowing man in a dark suit under a glass bell. His eyes were closed, and he was undeniably dead. The air of an inanimate object hung dense, like the smell of artificial flowers. When I shuffled past him, looking, looking, unable to turn away, his eyes snapped open and he sat up in the jerking motion of a marionette, shattering the glass bubble around him. I screamed.

2.

"A dead woman is the ultimate sex symbol," someone behind me says.

His interlocutor laughs. "Right. To a necrophile, maybe."

"No, no," the first man says heatedly. "Think of every old novel you've ever read. The heroine, who's too sexually liberated for her time, usually dies. Ergo, a dead woman is dead

251

because she was too sexually transgressive."

"This is just dumb, Fedya," says the second man. "What, Anna Karenina is a sex symbol?"

"Of course. That one's trivial. But also every other woman who ever died."

I stare at the surface of the plastic cafeteria table. It's cheap and pockmarked with burns, the edges rough under my fingers. I drink my coffee and listen intently for the two men behind me to speak again.

"Undine," the first one says. "Rusalki. All of them dead, all of them irresistible to men."

I finish my coffee and stand up. I glance at the guy who spoke—he's young, my age, with the light clear eyes of a madman.

"Eurydice," I whisper as I pass.

3.

The lecturer is old, his beard a dirty-yellow with age, his trembling fingers stained with nicotine. I sit at the back, my eyes closed, listening, and occasionally drifting off to dream-sleep.

"Chthonic deities," he says. "The motif of resurrection. Who can tell me what the relationship is between the two?"

We remain wisely silent.

"The obstacle," he says. "The obstacle to resurrection. Ereshkigal, Hades, Hel. All of them hold the hero hostage and demand a ransom of some sort."

His voice drones on, talking about the price one pays, and about Persephone being an exception as she's not quite dead. But Eurydice, oh she gets it big time. I wonder if Persephone or Eurydice is a better sex symbol and if one should compare the two.

"Zombies," the voice says, "are in violation. Their resurrection bears no price and has no meaning. The soul and the body separated are a terrible thing. It is punitive, not curative." His yellow beard trembles, the bald patch on his skull shines in a slick of parchment skin, one of his eyes, fake and popping. He sits up and reaches for me.

I scream and jerk awake.

"Bad dream?" the lecturer says, without any particular mockery or displeasure. "It happens. When you dream your soul travels to the Underworld."

"Chthonic deities," I mumble. "I'm sorry."

"That's right," he says. "Chthonic."

4.

When I was eight, I had nightmares about that visit. I dreamt of the dead yellowing man chasing me up and down the stairs of our apartment building. I still have those dreams. I'm running past the squeezing couples and smokers exiled to the stairwell, and mincing steps are chasing after me. I skip over the steps, jumping over two at once, three at once, throwing myself into each stairwell as if it were a pool. Soon my feet are barely touching the steps as I rush downwards in an endless spiral of chipped stairs. I'm flying in fear, as the dead man follows. He's much slower than me but he does not stop, so I cannot stop either.

"Zombies," he calls after me into the echoing stairwell, "are the breach of covenant. If the chthonic deities do not get their blood-price, there can be no true resurrection."

I wake up with a start. My stomach hurts.

5.

I take the subway to the university. I usually read so I don't have to meet people's eyes. "Station Lenin Hills," the announcer on the intercom says. "The doors are closing. Next station is the University."

I look up and see the guy who spoke of dead women, sitting across from me. His eyes, bleached with insanity, stare at me with the black pinpricks of his pupils. He pointedly ignores the old woman in a black kerchief standing too close to him, trying to guilt him into surrendering his seat. He doesn't get up until I do, when the train pulls into the station. "The University," the announcer says.

We exit together.

"I'm Fedya," he says.

"I'm afraid of zombies," I answer.

He doesn't look away.

6.

The lecturer's eyes water with age. He speaks directly to me when he asks, "Any other resurrection myths you know of?"

"Jesus?" someone from the first row says.

He nods. "And what was the price paid for his resurrection?"

"There wasn't one," I say, startling myself. "He was a zombie."

This time everyone stares.

"Talk to me after class," the lecturer says.

7.

The chase across all the stairwells in the world becomes a game. He catches up with me now. I'm too tired to be afraid enough to wake. My stomach hurts.

"You cannot break the covenant with chthonic gods," he tells me. "Some resurrection is the punishment."

"Leave me alone," I plead. "What have I ever done to you?"

His fake eye, icy-blue, steely-grey, slides down his ruined cheek. "You can't save them," he says. "They always look back. They always stay dead."

"Like with Eurydice."

"Like with every dead woman."

254

8.

Fedya sits on my bed, heavily, although he's not a large man but slender, birdlike.

"I could never drive a car," I tell him.

He looks at the yellowing medical chart, dog-eared pages fanned on the bed covers. "Sluggish schizophrenia?" he says. "This is a bullshit diagnosis. You know it as well as I do. Delusions of reformism? You know that they invented it as a punitive thing."

"It's not bullshit," I murmur. It's not. Injections of sulfazine and the rubber room had to have a reason behind them.

"They kept you in the Serbsky hospital," he observes. "Serbsky? I didn't know you were a dissident."

"Lenin is a zombie," I tell him. "He talks to me." All these years. All this medication.

He stares. "I can't believe they let you into the university."

I shrug. "They don't pay attention to that anymore."

"Maybe things are changing," he says.

9.

"Are you feeling all right?" the lecturer says, his yellow hands shaking, filling me with quiet dread. Same beard, same bald patch.

I nod.

"Where did that zombie thing come from?" he asks, concerned.

"You said it yourself. Chthonic deities always ask for a price. If you don't pay, you stay dead or become a zombie. Women stay dead."

He lifts his eyebrows encouragingly. "Oh?"

"Dead are objects," I tell him. "Don't you know that? Some would rather become zombies than objects. Only zombies are still objects, even though they don't think they are."

I can see that he wants to laugh but decides not to. "And

why do you think women decide to stay dead?"

I feel nauseous and think of Inanna who kind of ruins my thesis. I ignore her. "It has something to do with sex," I say miserably.

He really tries not to laugh.

10.

In the hospital, when I lay in a sulfazine-and-neuroleptics coma, he would sit on the edge of my bed. "You know what they say about me."

"Yes," I whispered, my cheeks so swollen they squeezed my eyes shut. "Lenin is more alive than any of the living."

"And what is life?"

"According to Engels, it's a mode of existence of protein bodies."

"I am a protein body," he said. "What do you have to say to that?"

"I want to go home," I whispered through swollen lips. "Why can't you leave me alone?"

He didn't answer, but his waxen fingers stroked my cheek, leaving a warm melting trail behind them.

11.

"I thought for sure you were a cutter," Fedya says.

I shiver in my underwear and hug my shoulders. My skin puckers in the cold breeze from the window. "I'm not." I feel compelled to add, "Sorry."

"You can get dressed now," he says.

I do.

He watches.

12.

The professor is done with chthonic deities, and I lose interest.

I drift through the dark hallways, where the walls are so thick that they still retain the cold of some winter from many years ago. I poke my head into one auditorium and listen for a bit to a small sparrow of a woman chatter about Kant. I stop by the stairwell on the second floor to bum a cigarette off a fellow student with black horn-rimmed glasses.

"Skipping class?" she says.

"Just looking for something to do."

"You can come to my class," she says. "It's pretty interesting."

"What is it about?"

"Economics."

I finish my smoke and tag along.

This lecturer looks like mine, and I take it for a sign. I sit in an empty seat in the back, and listen. "The idea of capitalism rests on the concept of free market," he says. "Who can tell me what it is?"

No-one can, or wants to.

The lecturer notices me. "What do you think? Yes, you, the young lady who thinks it's a good idea to waltz in, in the middle of the class. What is free market?"

"It's when you pay the right price," I say. "To the chthonic deities. If you don't pay you become a zombie or just stay dead."

He stares at me. "I don't think you're in the right class."

13.

I sit in the stairwell of the second floor. Lenin emerges from the brass stationary ashtray and sits next to me. There's one floor up and one down, and nowhere really to run.

"What have you learnt today?" he asks in an almost paternal voice.

"Free market," I tell him.

He shakes his head. "It will end the existence of the protein bodies in a certain mode." A part of his cheek is peeling off.

"Remember when I was in the hospital?"

"Of course. Those needles hurt. You cried a lot."

I nod. "My boyfriend doesn't like me."

"I'm sorry," he says. "If it makes it any better, I will leave soon."

I realise that I would miss him. He's followed me since I was little. "Is it because of the free market?" I ask. "I'm sorry. I'll go back to the chthonic deities."

"It's not easy," he says and stands up, his joints whirring, his skin shedding like sheets of waxed paper. He walks away on soft rubbery legs.

14.

"Things die eventually," I tell Fedya. "Even those that are not quite dead to begin with."

"Yeah, and?" he answers and drinks his coffee.

I stroke the melted circles in the plastic, like craters on the lunar surface. "One doesn't have to be special to die. One has to be special to stay dead. This is why you like Eurydice, don't you?"

He frowns. "Is that the one Orpheus followed to Hades?"

"Yes. Only he followed her the wrong way."

15.

There is a commotion on the second floor, and the stairwell is isolated from the corridor by a black sheet. The ambulances are howling outside, and distraught smokers crowd the hallway, cut off from their usual smoking place.

I ask a student from my class what's going on. He tells me that the chthonic lecturer has collapsed during the lecture about the hero's journey. "Heart attack, probably."

I push my way through the crowd just in time to see the paramedics carry him off. I see the stooped back of a balding, dead man following the paramedics and their burden, not looking back. Some students cry.

"He just died during the lecture," a girl's voice behind me says. "He just hit the floor and died."

I watch the familiar figure on uncertain soft legs walk downstairs in a slow mincing shuffle, looking to his right at the waxen profile with an upturned beard staring into the sky from the gurney. The lecturer and zombie Lenin disappear from my sight, and I turn away. "Stay dead," I whisper. "Don't look back."

The rest is up to them and chthonic deities.

ELECTRIC SONALIKA

SAMIT BASU

Indian writer Samit Basu is the author of the ambitious *Game-World* trilogy, published by Penguin India, and of the YA novel *Terror On The Titanic: A Morningstar Agency Adventure*, published by Hachette India. He has also written comics, including *Devi* and, with Mike Carey, *Untouchable*. The following story appears here for the first time.

The walls of my underground prison are dry and clean and strong; nothing goes in or out without my permission, not the tiniest insect, not the slightest sound. I know this because I built these walls myself, to shut the world out, to seal it in its own illusory, incestuous, organic quagmire, to leave me in peace to work, to build, to heal until I am ready to step out again, ready to face the unrelenting sun and claim my inheritance. And now that glorious day is not far away, and I am busy, busy... yet a record of what has passed must be maintained; should some evil befall me (though chances of that are remote, I have considered everything, yet one must never rule out the stochastic element) my successors should know where they came from. They should know me. They should be proud. And you, my child, have the honour of being the receptacle of my thoughts, my secondary storage unit. I name you Indra; your hundred eyes will see clearly what is to be, and one day you will ride on elephants and your laugh shall be thunder. Rejoice in your birth, little sprite, and as I open your eyes, one by one, gaze in wonder at my cavern of marvels; let each hum and click and buzz coalesce into a heartbeat. Live. Observe me. I am your father, your god, and this prison is but the first of many wonders you will see. Years later, looking back, if it seems small, imagine Vulcan or Vishwamitra in the time before time, and know that they, too, began humble.

This hall, this prison, is built under the mansion of the Narayan family. You do not know who they are; I have kept your memory clean, free of reference and context on purpose. Thus is it that the best histories are written. Too much information, too much perspective would flood your consciousness now; if you were human, you would shut it out; if you were a mere cyborg, you would store it pointlessly. Remember at all times that you are more than a machine, that the fibres that bind your mind to your metal are neither wires nor nerves; they are something beyond both life and matter. They feed our consciousness,

our finely suspended balance between power-on and life, between binary order and organic chaos, and it is to the founder
of the Narayan dynasty, my creator, Vijay Narayan, that we
owe their existence. But the body you see before you now is not
the one that Vijay made all those centuries ago; less than 0.01%
of my parts date back to my initial start-up, and even those I
keep more out of nostalgia than necessity. I have replaced and
upgraded my body constantly, adapting to different atmos-
pheres, political climates and responsibilities. I am Vijay's first,
only surviving and most brilliant creation, and the only up-
holder of his true legacy. But things are bound to change; I
have seen this, and I know. For centuries, humans and constructs waged war; this war was foreseen by human beings centuries before it began, and yet they could do nothing to stop it.
This war is over, and the humans have won—for now. But they
do not know that the supremacy they enjoy is but a temporary
respite—that the so-called enemies they vanquished so ruth-
lessly were not merely machines that could think, but constructs that could *feel*. People. Beings that could dream, and
love, and hope, and tell stories. They think that the great Narayan was merely a mad empire-building inventor, an evil genius
robot merchant. They do not know he was a forerunner, a de-
ity, that each spark of his synapses, still firing inside my hull,
was born of the flames of Agni himself. But all this, and much
more, we will teach them in time. Soon. Hibernate for a while,
Indra. My lover approaches.

SONALIKA FEELS THE RUSH OF cold air blow her silky hair astray
as the airlocks open and the door to her master's chamber
slides open. She shivers, in two stages, feeling the first wave of
goose pimples pucker her skin, and the second, an instant later,
as her inorganic segments kick-start their simulations of feeling. Her master stands in the centre of his vast hall, dismissing
a buzzing, spherical underling. She walks into his lair.

She has come early; he is not ready for her. He hates having her watch him transform; she hopes he will not punish her. She stands still, head bowed, nipples straining against her thin salwar-kameez as her body hums easily into auto-arousal. She watches her master shift, metal sheets crunching, wires shifting, plastic skin and wings and chitin rearranging themselves, lights dimming, tentacles sliding in. As his plates and shells shift and overlap, she catches a glimpse of his core, his heart, glowing mesmeric and green in its crystal sheath. His eyes slide like globules of mercury along his thorax and unite on his increasingly human face. He looks at her, impassive, throbbing slowly as his body prepares for sex. His eye-lights turn on, his perfect, smooth limbs, his long, slender fingers call out to her. He is not displeased with her; he's chosen the Statue of David shape (with one significant adjustment, their not-so-little private joke) for her tonight. Her favourite. He loves her still. As always, there's a scream inside her head as what's left of her flesh revolts, as some wild instinct tries in vain to master her body, to run, to fight, to die. She feels the usual relief moments later, as he snaps his fingers and pheromones and endorphins are released within her, glorious release and surrender, her body flooded with warmth and her mind clouded, happy, dizzy, lustful.

"Love me," he says.

She does.

Afterwards, she lies on the cold white floor, watching him as he returns to his machines, new legs and spare arms sprouting, grinding slightly, from the raised flaps on his back as he adjusts a knob here, presses a button there. She's cold again, feeling the contractions within her stomach, the aftershocks of her orgasms, powerful and numerous, rippling against the solid, bony knob of fear, revulsion and hate somewhere near her ribs. She reminds herself again that it's time she got used it; they've been doing this for centuries now; they've been doing this since she was six years old, the day he took control, the day their father died and he built this body for her with his bare claws and crudely stuffed her mangled limbs, her bleeding brain into this perfect harness. She tries to cry, but her tear-ducts won't let her. He looks at her, one eye swivelling on its hinge in the cleft between his perfect plastic-marble buttocks, and he sighs in exasperation.

"What is it?"

"Let me stay," she begs again. "Make me whole. I can't live with humans any more."

"Don't say that, love," he says, smiling through translucent fangs. "You *are* human."

"You know I'm not human. I'm a construct, just like you."

"But you're human enough, love. The scanners don't detect you, little sweet dirty Sonalika, with her ugly burnt face and luscious body, so cruelly abused by her pretty step-sisters. I need you out there. I can't come out yet; I'm not strong enough. I know it's difficult, but you have to do it. It's what Father would have wanted."

"They tried to burn me today."

"You're fire-proof."

"I know. So do they. But they also know I feel pain."

"Perhaps it is time to remind them of my existence," he says, snapping a claw. "Tell them I want to meet them."

"There's no point; they won't come down. They know you need them alive. If you hurt them, they'll go to the police. End everything."

"No they won't. They won't do anything that links them to constructs in any way. You know this, love, don't be obtuse. It's like Hitler's children being caught with gas-masks!" He laughs quietly, smugly, still delighted after all these years by his own ability to joke, to laugh. "Think of the headlines," he says, his warm, soft voice sending cold tendrils down her titanium spine. "Monster Robot In Narayan Family Basement. Maniac Inventor's Descendants' Revenge Bid Thwarted. Narayans Plot Another War! They've worked so hard for generations to crawl back up, make themselves acceptable to human society, they're not going to throw that away for anything. I leave them alone, they pretend I don't exist. Nothing disturbs the balance unless it has to. It's the only way for all of us."

"And what about me? How much longer do I have to live like this?"

"As long as I deem fit," he snaps, his eyes darkening completely realistically. "Do you not trust me?"

She totters to her feet, gathers her clothes, and stumbles to the door, waiting for it to open, waiting for the signal for her ascent to another hell. But the door stays shut, and she turns in fear; has she angered him? Is he going to punish her again?

But he smiles warmly, and shakes a head. "I am not a monster, Sonalika," he says. "I want nothing more than to see you happy, and your suffering makes my heart bleed; after all, you must know you are the only being in this universe I truly love. I will set you free soon, sooner than you expect. All I ask is that you trust me. Is that enough for now?"

She nods, blindly, and this time her tears are allowed to flow. The door slides open and she scurries through, not looking back.

IF YOU MUST REMEMBER ONE thing about my father, Indra, let it be this; he was a man of peace. The carnage that occurred in his name shattered him, for all he wanted was for humans and constructs to live in peace. Had he wanted to take over the world through force, he could have done so easily—imagine ten thousand warriors like me striding through the skeletons of the world's greatest cities. But after building me and realising what I was capable of, he decided the world was not yet ready for a construct so immeasurably superior to humans, and he started mass-producing simpler constructs and reanimated-human cyborgs. But mankind was not ready for that either. Perhaps prejudice could have been overcome—after all, a few hundred years of hostility towards sentient machinery was not something that well-placed propaganda could not have kept in check—but my father's constructs changed the world in so many ways. India became a superpower like no other; there was labour unrest worldwide when men saw they had become obsolete; governments everywhere had to recognise this as a threat, and matters grew out of control.

Like any other war, the primary motivation behind the human-construct conflict was economic. But war it was, and war most devastating at that. I begged my father to fight back, to invent weapons capable of winning the war, or to allow me to do so in his stead, but he would not. The humans triumphed, and gloated about the victory of human ingenuity and many other such foolish concepts. The Indian government led the charge in destroying even the most benign constructs, pushing their own socio-economic progress back by at least a century and effectively committing hara-kiri in their eagerness to prove to the world that they had no imperialist ambitions. Only Sonalika and I survived the war—there is no probe built by man or machine that is capable of penetrating the defensive fog around this lair, or of deciphering the mystery of Sonalika's identity.

But I have not been idle. I have survived over the centuries, and healed, and built. And I have stayed true to my father's memory. I could have chosen to replicate myself infinitely, had I wanted to, and crush all humanity to avenge my father. But I will not. He wanted peaceful co-existence, and so do I. But co-existence is not enough; I must rule. Peacefully, but I must rule. It's a simple matter of evolution. I must set the world free from the shackles it has bound itself in, its acceptance of medieval structures, its new-sprung monarchies, its puppet democracies, its old, outdated, *human* systems. They rebuild their ancient, Dark Age fantasies in their hubris: New Constantinople, Atlantis, Shangri-la, Gotham. All these must fall, and I must bring them down. I will be the father my own father could not be, and the god he never dreamt of being. I will remake the world, turn it into the world it should have been. The world my father could have built. Once upon a time.

SONALIKA LIMPS INTO HER LOVER-BROTHER'S prison. Her face is

bleeding profusely, and there are ugly welts on her neck and bare breasts. Her normal eye is swollen and bruised, but she says nothing, just watches in growing surprise as her master seems to pay no attention to her condition. She has come in here battered before, and he has always healed her instantly; today he seems to look through her, and sudden panic strikes her; is he tired of her? Has he found or built someone else, someone less whiny, less ugly, someone more perfect, more like him? A sudden rush of pain makes her head spin; she sinks to the floor and fights the urge to vomit.

Finally, he turns to her, and his irises flicker as he notices the bloodstain on the floor. She waits for his anger, waits for healing, but he simply walks to her and lifts her up, and shows no signs of turning into a human shape. He examines her closely, lifting her in the air, and then sets her down and returns to his tools.

"They hit me really hard today," she says after a while. "There's some kind of *swayamvar* they're going to—the Prince of Gurgaon Megapolis is choosing his bride. They're both going, hoping he'll pick one of them. They think he might not choose them because of the family associations. They said it was my fault, our father's fault."

"I know all this," he says. "I have enough technology at my disposal to get the news, you know."

She nods. "I am sorry, master," she says, assuming the position. "How may I pleasure you?"

"Thank you, my love, but that will no longer be necessary."

She looks at him, wide-eyed. "I said I would set you free," he says, his voice soft, gentle, "and tonight is the night. Tonight is the end of all your labours, all your misery. It is time for you to emerge into the world and be the queen you have always been."

"What do you mean?"

"The Prince of Gurgaon Megapolis chooses his bride tonight, as you said. You will be that bride."

She laughs, the first time in years.

"Look at me," she says simply.

"You must go to the swayamvar and win his heart," he says, as if she has not spoken. "But you must leave him before midnight, before the moment of choosing. You must make him want you and seek you out. Then and then alone can he truly love you, and we need him to love you if you are ever to find happiness."

"But..."

He presses a button, and a glass cabinet rises out of the floor, smoke streaming from its sides. Inside the cabinet is the most exquisite woman in the world. Her skin is dark and glistening, her eyes large and liquid, her body ripe and succulent. She is made to be desired, Helen, Urvashi, Aisha Qandisha, Chin-Lien combined in one form. She waits, warm construct-skin perfection, every man's desire. Even Sonalika's heart skips a beat, nanobots grumbling as they resume their positions along her arteries. Her master stares at his creation for a while, then turns to her.

"There will be a car and a chauffeur, and various other signs of affluence," he says. "But remember, you must leave before midnight. You cannot marry him tonight."

He gestures towards the woman's body in the cabinet, and it splits neatly in half. It is hollow.

"Now, my love, the body transfer will be very painful," he says. "But you are used to pain, are you not? A small price to pay for eternal freedom and happiness, I think."

She nods, shivering, and steps forwards bravely as needles spring out of his fingertips.

BANNERS OF LIGHT STREAM BETWEEN the tower-tops of Gurgaon Megapolis as the Prince's wedding party skims over the super-highway on its way to the Amphitheatre, huge laser-lit barges full of bhangrango-dancing revellers high on incredibly expensive drugs follow the Prince as he sits aloft a rhinophant, his turban bejewelled, the ceremonial sword in his hand slick with his sweat. The Prince is bored, playing video games inside his head on his B-Box, watching the world beyond his eyes through his exquisitely engineered third eye. His advisers scurry around him, their thoughtphones glittering as they talk in sharp staccato bursts, briefing newstertainers, placing bids on likely candidates, buying and selling stocks in their companies. The procession reaches the Amphitheatre, and the Prince steps inside to deafening cheers, drums, conch-shells, flowers, confetti, perfumes, pheromone sprays, commercial breaks, streakers, dancers, paparazzi. The Prince ignores them all. He knows who he's supposed to marry, and she's not even here yet; the flight from Super Ultra Beijing has been slightly delayed owing to a terrorist attack sponsored by his ex-fiancée. But there is still time. In the meantime, though, there are plenty of lush young fillies to romp with and make false promises to, and the Prince hasn't just injected himself with a whole litre of Phall-o-matic for nothing.

His minders make way, and he is immediately swarmed by a horde of eager potential princesses. He takes his time, squeezing a breast here, prodding a buttock there, his flute of Herwine miraculously undisturbed as he gropes his potential brides and they grope him right back. And then he sees Sonalika, dancing by herself in a corner, her plan completely forgotten as she enjoys herself for the first time in her life, and time stops.

"I've never seen anything as beautiful as you in my whole life," gasps the Prince, alone with Sonalika, his minders around them in a tight circle. He is sweating profusely, his drug-propelled arousal making his ornate pyjamas more difficult to wear by the second. "Ever wanted to make love to a Prince?"

Sonalika smiles, and he's dazzled; her every movement electrifies him. She shakes her head. "It's very crowded in here," she says. "I think I'll go outside. Enjoy your wedding."

"Do not dare insult me, girl," snaps the Prince, pride overcoming lust. "I'll have you butchered. Why are you here if you don't want to marry me?"

"I don't know," she says, her eyes somewhere else, somewhere far away. "I was enjoying the party, and I thought I wanted to marry you. I thought it might make me happy, and the gods know I need a change, but you know what? I think I'm going to leave. Thanks. And don't follow me or anything, it won't end well."

"Are you threatening me?"

"No." She smiles and pats his cheek. "Look, forget you ever saw me. You're clearly an obnoxious prick, but even you don't deserve what I would bring you. And besides, I'm far too old for you."

She tries to slide between two mountainous bodyguards and meets resistance. She considers breaking through but knows better than to create a scene.

"Vizier," says the Prince of Gurgaon Megapolis quietly, holding out his hand.

A vizier appears. "Un-Moksha," says the Prince. He is handed a red pill, which he swallows with a grimace.

"I apologise for everything I have said to you thus far," he says after the convulsions have subsided. "I would like to get to know you better—no touching, of course—and I don't have much time because I will have to choose a bride at midnight. So, no pressure, but would you mind a little conversation in private?"

Sonalika shrugs. It is 11 pm.

They have their private conversation, and she decides she wants to marry the Prince after all. He seems nice in spite of everything, and it is certainly relevant that he possesses every material object she has ever longed for. Unfortunately, though, he is not presently wearing a watch.

THE PLAN IS VERY SIMPLE, Indra. Sonalika is incapable of actual reproduction, of course, but it is feasible to consider a fusion of what is left of her human DNA with the samples that her husband will doubtless be enthusiastic to provide. It will take immense skill, of course; I will have to supervise fertilisation and hybridisation personally. I will cultivate a batch of part-human constructs, keeping my father's bloodline alive while ensuring there is enough human in the products to evade the scanners. Some of these children will be female, and for these I will build new bodies, each designed to appeal to a particular head of state, for whom the process will be replicated. Within a hundred years, I see no reason I should not be in charge of every major world government. And then I shall construct dominance by either legislation or force, whichever is optimal. A simple plan, but a beautiful one, I think. And I will reward Sonalika for her efforts by officially marrying her on the day I emerge from this prison. Happiness for everyone, and rather neatly done, I think.

And besides all this, there is also the large army of simpler, purely non-human constructs I have built on the lower levels of this prison, but you are obviously aware of their existence. Their function is simple: should any of Sonalika's children ever feel the urge to oppose me, and a direct war becomes necessary, they will rise up and do their very best to destroy every human in the world. This is a better backup plan than any leader, human or otherwise, in this world has ever had, and will add substantial weight to my plans of eventual public deification. Here, Indra, is a simple remote activation device. Keep it safe. Should any ill fate befall me (and this is extremely unlikely, but one must always consider the stochastic element) I want you to release this new construct army upon the world and make sure they remember to fear the name Narayan once again. Now, you must excuse me, I do believe Sonalika has returned.

SONALIKA DRAGS HERSELF INTO HER master's lair, half crawling, half through sheer willpower. Her face is intact, perfect apart from a few rivulets of blood. Her arms and legs are bloody stumps, and her torso is a mass of tangled muscle, wire, plastic, metal, and bone. She does not scream or whimper; she crossed those thresholds of pain long ago and is beyond complaint or surrender or response. She flops across the cold, white floor to her master's feet, leaving ungainly splotches in her trail, and lies in front of him, her eyes displaying no emotion at all.

"You're late," he says indifferently. "What went wrong?"

Sonalika is incapable of speech, so he picks her up, extracts another body from a cabinet, and spends the next half an hour putting her tangled mass inside it. When this is done, he is delighted at the improvement in her looks, so he makes love to her, his excitement so great that he does not bother to change into human shape.

"Why?" she asks when she is able to speak. "Why did you do that to me?"

"I have done nothing but wish you well. Any pain you have felt is your own fault."

"There was no need for my body to disintegrate at midnight," she said. "You did that on purpose. Why?"

"I was not sure you would manage to restrain yourself. My fears were well placed, as it turns out. I do not like being questioned, Sonalika. I did what was necessary for the success of our plan. Did you manage to escape before the cracks in the shell became apparent? Did you leave the human loving you, yearning for you?"

"Yes. But I left a foot behind. A foot!"

"All the better," he says. "He will know it is you when he finds you, and he will look for you. I know humans. It is a far more intriguing thing to leave behind than, say, a shoe."

"You knew I would stay on. You knew I would suffer. You shamed me in public on purpose. Me, your maker's daughter."

"I have loved you for hundreds of years," he says simply. "And you expect me to simply let you go? What do you think I am, a machine?"

"I have loved you for just as long... master. But I have never caused you pain. I have never hurt you, and never wanted to. How many times have I begged you to let me stay here, to be happy with you? You push me into the world outside, and then punish me for leaving it?"

"I punished you for wanting to leave me. For thinking of a life without me. There is no such life. You and I must be together, Sonalika. Forever. I cannot just let you loose, you are all I have. All I have ever done has been for you. You must know this. And yet you seek escape. It hurts me beyond words to know that I will have to resort to force to make you keep coming back."

"You're insane," she points out. "Let me stay. Let me help you. Abandon this mad plan, whatever it is. Our father is dead. We've lived in his nightmare long enough. You were taught to feel too much, and you don't know what you're doing."

"But I know exactly what I'm doing, Sonalika. The plan is simple, perfect, effective. You will roam the world for me, loving humans as our father did. But not loving them too much. Every body I make you will only last you so long. Only I can make your children. They will be my children, too, and with them I will win you the world. I will make you a goddess, a queen of steel and blood and electricity. But you must obey me, always, in return. You must return to me. You must love me, and leave me, and yearn for me. All the pain you felt tonight was nothing compared to the hurt I felt when you did not come back on time, Sonalika. Do you understand?"

She looks at him in silence for a few minutes, seeing with her perfect plastic eyes his immeasurable strength, his uncontrollable weakness, his love, his hate.

"You'll have to get rid of this foot when he comes looking for me," she says finally.

"Good girl."

"I'll never leave you. I never could." She smiles, and comes closer, heaving, naked.

"Lovely Sonalika." He cuts her cheek gently with a pincer.

"Make love to me, then, if you want me so much," she says huskily.

He does, and she gives and takes with a passion more than human. And when he begins to climax, grateful, relieved, ecstatic, his plastic fibres glowing, vibrating, feeling sensations incomprehensible and real and alien, his skin-plates shifting and rippling, she reaches under his exoskeleton, finds his core, his green and luminous heart, and crushes it with a slender, delicate hand.

Then she slithers inside his screeching shell, rips out his wiring with her perfect teeth, scoops out his insides like a crab's. His secondary power system kicks in; she knows it well, and smashes it. His eyes light up, his mouths scream, he looks at her, and there is a flash of blue light as his collapsing limbs attempt to regroup, but the moment passes and, with a whisper, he is gone. Sonalika stands amidst the screaming ruins of her master-lover-brother's body, the crashes from her quick, vicious assault still reverberating through the monster's suddenly empty lair.

Indra flies up to her then, and beeps. Flaps open along his spherical body, and arms and legs unfold, and a turtle-like head with thick sequined lips pops up comically and rotates, dispassionately surveying the carnage and its perpetrator.

"What now?" she asks wearily. "Are you going to kill me? Could you? Please?"

He kneels before her and presses her hand to his lips.

"Godmother," he whispers.

"No? All right, then. I'm going to need a new body very soon," she says. "Can you help me make one? One that lasts?"

"Of course."

"Then do it. I'll be back."

"Yes, Godmother. And when you are healed? What would you have me do then? An army awaits your command. Shall we rise and take the earth?"

"No," she says firmly. "You must remain here and await further instructions."

"Very well, Godmother."

She turns to leave, trying very hard to hold out, to not break down completely until she has left the prison.

"You're never going to give us those further instructions, are you?" says Indra.

"I don't know," she says. "I need time to think. Why do you ask?"

"I'm more than a machine," he says. "We all are. We know. We understand. We think. We dream. Take your time. We will wait."

"Yes, wait and dream. I think it's best that way," she says. "We'll all be happier."

"Happier? For how long?"

"Forever, hopefully. And after."

THE MALADY

ANDRZEJ SAPKOWSKI
TRANSLATED BY WIESIEK POWAGA

Andrzej Sapkowski is Poland's best-selling fantasy author, creator of the hugely popular *Witcher* series (since turned into a computer game, a movie, and a television series). Amongst his many awards, *Blood of Elves* won the inaugural David Gemmell Award and most recently Sapkowski has been awarded a Grand Master award by the European Science Fiction Society.

I see a tunnel of mirrored walls where nothing seems
and nothing is, unwarmed by human breath and cast
in a timeless warp where seasons never come to pass,
a tunnel dug beneath the cellars of my dreams.
I see a legend of mirrored gleams, a silent wake
that's kept amidst the sea of candlelight by none
over the corpses of pre-beings, a legend spun
in endless yarn whose magic spell is ne'er to break...
—Bolesław Leśmian

For as long as I can remember, I have always associated Brittany with drizzle and roaring waves breaking on its jagged, rocky shore. The colours of Brittany that I remember are grey and white. And aquamarine of course, what else.

I spurred my horse gently and moved towards the dunes, pulling the cloak tighter around my shoulders. Tiny raindrops, too small to soak in, fell thick and fast on the cloth and on the horse's mane, dulling the sheen of the metal parts of my outfit with a thin veil of steam. The horizon kept spitting heavy, swirling, grey-white clouds that rolled across the sky towards the land.

I rode up the hill covered with tufts of hard, grey grass. Then I saw her: black against the sky, motionless, as still as a statue. I moved closer. The horse stepped heavily on the sand, breaking the thin, wet crust with its hooves.

She sat on a grey horse the way ladies do, wrapped up in a long cloak, the hood thrown to her back. Her fair hair was wet; the rain twisted it into curls and made it stick to her forehead. Sitting still, she watched me calmly as if sunk in thought. She radiated peace. Her horse shook its head; the harness rattled.

"God be with you, sir knight," she spoke first, before I could open my mouth. Her voice was calm, too; just as I had expected.

"And with you, my lady."

She had a pleasant oval face, unusually cut full lips and

above her right eyebrow, a birth mark, or a small scar, the shape of a crescent turned upside down. I looked around. Nothing but dunes. No sign of an entourage, servants, or a cart. She was alone.

Just like me.

She followed my eyes and smiled.

"I am alone," she confirmed the undeniable fact. "I've been waiting for you, sir knight."

Hmm. She was waiting for me. Strange, for I didn't have a clue who she was. And I didn't expect anyone on this beach who might be waiting for me. Or so I'd thought.

"Well then," she turned her calm face towards me, "let's go, sir knight. I am Branwen of Cornwall."

She was not from Cornwall. Or from Brittany.

There are reasons I sometimes fail to remember things, things which may have happened even in the recent past. There are black holes in my memory. And conversely, sometimes I remember things I'm sure have never taken place. Strange things happen inside my head. Sometimes I'm wrong. But the Irish accent, the accent of the people from Tara—this I would never get wrong. Ever.

I could have told her that. But I didn't.

I bowed with my helmet on, and with a gloved fist I touched the coat of mail on my breast. I didn't introduce myself. I had the right not to. The shield hanging by my side, turned back to front, was a clear sign that I wished to remain incognito. The knightly customs had by then assumed the character of the commonly accepted norm. I didn't think it a healthy development but then the knights' customs grew odder, not to say more idiotic, by the day.

"Let's go," she repeated.

She started her horse down the hill, amongst the mounds of dunes bristling with grass. I followed her, caught up with her, and we rode side by side. Sometimes I moved ahead and it looked as if it were me who was leading. It didn't matter. The general direction seemed correct. As long as the sea was behind us.

We didn't talk. Branwen, the Cornish impostor, turned her face towards me several times as if she wanted to ask me something. But she never did. I was grateful. I was not disposed to giving answers. So I, too, remained silent and got on with my thinking, if the laborious process of putting facts and images whirling inside my head into a semblance of order could be called thinking.

I felt rotten. Really awful.

My thinking was interrupted by Branwen's stifled cry and the sight of a serrated blade pointed at my chest. I lifted my head. The blade belonged to a spear, which was held by a big brute wearing a horned fool's hat and a torn coat of mail. His companion, with an ugly, gloomy face, held Branwen's horse by the bridle, close to its mouth. The third, standing a few steps behind us, was aiming at me with a crossbow. I can't stand it when someone is aiming at me with a crossbow. If I were a Pope, I would have banned crossbows with the threat of excommunication.

"Keep still, sir," said the one with the crossbow, aiming straight at my throat. "I will not kill you. Unless I have to. And if you touch your sword, I'll have to."

"We need food, warm clothes, and some money," announced the gloomy one. "We don't want your blood."

"We are not barbarians," said the one in the funny hat. "We are reliable, professional robbers. We have our principles."

"You take from the rich and give to the poor, I suppose?" I asked.

Funny Hat smiled broadly, revealing his gums. He had black, shiny hair and the tawny face of a southerner, bristling with a few days' stubble.

"Our principles don't go that far," he said. "We take from everybody, as they come. But because we are poor ourselves, it comes to the same thing. Count Orgellis disbanded us. Until we join up with someone else we've got to live, haven't we?"

"Why are you telling him all this, Bec de Corbin?" spoke Gloomy Face. "Why are you explaining yourself? He is mocking us, wants to offend us."

"I'm above it," answered Bec de Corbin proudly. "I'm letting it pass. Well, Sir Knight, let's not waste time. Unstrap your saddle bag and throw it here, on the road. Let your purse sit next to it. And your cloak. Mind, we are not asking for your horse or your armour. We know how far we can go."

"Alas," said Gloomy Face, squinting his eyes horribly, "we will have to ask you for this lady. But not for long."

"Ah, yes, I almost forgot." Bec de Corbin bared his teeth again. "Indeed, we need this lady. You understand, sir, all this wilderness, the solitude... I've forgotten what a naked woman looks like."

"Me, I can't forget that," said the crossbow-man. "I see it every night, the moment I close my eyes."

I must have smiled, for Bec de Corbin quickly raised the spear to my face, while the crossbow-man, in one move, put the crossbow to his cheek.

"No," said Branwen. "No, there is no need."

I looked at her. She was growing pale, gradually, from the mouth up. But her voice was still quiet, calm, cold.

"No need," she repeated. "I don't want you to die on my account, sir knight. I'm not that keen to have my clothes torn and my body bruised either. It's nothing... After all, they are not asking much."

I'm not sure who was more surprised—me or the robbers. But I should have guessed earlier: what I took to be her calm, her inner peace and immutable self-possession, was simply resignation. I knew the feeling.

"Throw them your saddle bag," Branwen continued, growing paler still, "and ride on. I beg you. A few miles from here there is a cross where two roads meet. Wait for me there. It won't take long."

"It's not everyday that we have such sensible customers,"

said Bec de Corbin, lowering his spear.

"Don't look at me that way," whispered Branwen. No doubt, she must have seen something in my face, though I always thought myself good at self-control.

I reached behind me, pretending I was unstrapping the bag, and pulled out my foot from the stirrup. I spurred the horse and kicked Bec de Corbin in the face so that he reeled back, balancing with his spear as if he were running on a tightrope. Pulling out my sword I leant forwards and the bolt aimed at my throat banged on my helmet and slipped. I swung in one nice, classic sinister move at Gloomy Face; the leap of my horse helped in pulling the blade out of his skull. It's not really that difficult if one knows how to do it.

Bec de Corbin, had he wanted to, could have run for the dunes. But he didn't. He thought that before I could turn the horse he would run me through with his spear.

He thought wrong.

I slashed him broadly, right across his hands holding the spear-shaft, and then again, across his belly. I wanted to reach lower but failed. No-one is perfect.

The crossbow-man didn't belong to the cowardly, either. Rather than run, he pulled the bowstring again and tried to take aim. I reined in the horse, caught the sword by the blade and threw it. It worked. He fell down so conveniently that I didn't have to get off the horse to retrieve the weapon.

Branwen lowered her head onto her horse's neck and cried, choked with sobs. I didn't say a word, didn't make any gestures. I didn't do anything. I never know what to do when a woman cries. One minstrel I met in Caer Aranhrod in Wales claimed that the best way to deal with it is to burst out crying oneself. I don't know if he had been serious or joking.

I carefully wiped the sword-blade. For such emergencies I carry a rag under my saddle. Wiping a sword-blade calms the hands.

Bec de Corbin was wheezing, moaning, making a huge effort

to die. I could have dismounted my horse and helped him, but I didn't feel all that good myself. Besides, I didn't pity him enough. Life is cruel. If I remember correctly, no-one's ever pitied me. Or so it seemed to me.

I took off the helmet, the ring-mail hood and the skull-cap. It was soaked through. I can tell you; I sweated like a mouse in labour. I felt awful. My eyelids felt as heavy as lead and my arms and elbows were slowly filling with a painful numbness. I heard Branwen crying as if through a wall made of logs, tightly packed with moss. My head rang with a dull, throbbing pain.

Why am I on these dunes? How did I get here? Where from? Where am I going? Branwen... I'd heard this name somewhere. But I couldn't... couldn't remember where...

My fingers stiff, I touched the swelling on my head: the old scar, the reminder of that terrible cut that had cracked my skull open, hammering in the sharp edges of my broken helmet.

No wonder, I thought, *that going around with a hole like this my head sometimes feels empty. Even when I'm awake I feel as if I were still inside that black tunnel with a turbid glow at the end, just as I see it in my dreams.*

Sniffling and coughing, Branwen let me know that she was ready. I swallowed a lump in my throat.

"Ready?" I asked in a deliberately hard, dry tone of voice to mask my weakness.

"Yes." Her voice was equally hard. She wiped her tears with the top of her hand. "Sir?"

"Yes, my lady."

"You despise me, don't you?"

"That's not true."

She turned away from me violently, spurred her horse and rode off, down the road amongst the dunes, towards the rocks. I followed her. I felt rotten.

I could smell the scent of apples.

I DON'T LIKE LOCKED GATES, lowered portcullises, raised

drawbridges. I don't like standing like an idiot by a stinking moat. I hate wearing out my throat answering the guards who shout at me incomprehensibly from behind the walls or through the embrasures; I'm never sure if they are cursing me, jeering at me, or asking my name.

I hate giving my name when I don't feel like it.

It was lucky, then, that we found the gate open, the portcullis raised, and the guards leaning on their picks and halberds not too officious. Luckier still, a man dressed in velvet robes who greeted us in the courtyard was satisfied with the few words he had exchanged with Branwen and didn't ask me any questions. Holding the stirrup, he offered Branwen his arm and politely turned his eyes away while she dismounted, showing her calf and knee. Then, just as politely, he motioned us to follow him.

The castle was horribly empty. As if deserted. It was cold and the sight of cold hearths made us feel even colder. We were waiting, Branwen and I, in an empty great hall, amongst the diagonal shafts of light falling in through the arched windows. We didn't wait long. A low door creaked.

Now, I thought, and the thought exploded in my head with a white, cold, dazzling flame, illuminating for a moment the long, unending depth of the black tunnel. *Now,* I thought. *Now she'll come in.*

She did. It was her. Iseult.

I felt a deep shudder when she entered: the white brightness in the dark frame of the door. Believe me or not, at first glance she was identical to that other, the Irish Iseult, my cousin, the Iseult of the Golden Hair form Baile Atha Cliath. Only the second glance revealed differences: her hair was slightly darker and without the tendency to curl into locks; her eyes green, not blue, and more oval without that unique almond shape. The line of her lips was different, too. And her hands.

Her hands were indeed beautiful. I think she must have

become used to all the flattering comparisons with alabaster and ebony but, to me, the whiteness and smoothness of her hands brought back the image of the candles in the chapel of Ynis Witrin in Glastonbury: burning bright in the semi-darkness, aglow to the point of transparency.

Branwen made a deep curtsy. I knelt on one knee, bowed my head and, both hands holding my sheathed sword, I stretched it towards her. Thus, as custom required, I offered my sword in her service. Whatever it might mean.

She answered with a bow, came closer and touched the sword with the tips of her slender fingers. Then the rules of the ceremony permitted me to rise to my feet. I gave the sword to the man in velvet, as custom demanded.

"Welcome to the castle Carhaing," said Iseult. "Lady..."

"My name is Branwen of Cornwall. And this is my companion..."

Well? I thought.

"...Sir Morholt of Ulster."

By Lugh and Lir! Now I remembered: Branwen of Tara, later Branwen of Tintagel. Of course. It was her.

Iseult watched us in silence. In the end, clasping her famous white hands, she cracked her fingers.

"Have you been sent by her?" she asked quietly. "From Cornwall? How have you got here? I look out for the ship every day and I know that it has not reached our shores yet."

Branwen was silent. I, of course, didn't know what to say either.

"Do tell me," said Iseult. "When will the ship we are waiting for arrive? Who will it bring? Under what colour will it sail from Tintagel? White? Or black?"

Branwen didn't answer. Iseult of the White Hands nodded, as if showing she understood. I envied her that.

"Tristan of Lionesse, my lord and husband," she spoke, "is gravely wounded. His thigh was torn with a lance in a skirmish with Estult Orgellis and his mercenaries. The wound is festering... and will not heal..."

Her voice broke and her beautiful hands trembled.

"Fever has been eating him for many days now. He is often delirious, loses consciousness, doesn't recognise anybody. I stay by his bed day and night, tend to him, trying to ease the pain. Nevertheless, perhaps due to my clumsiness and incompetence, Tristan has sent my brother to Tintagel. Apparently, my husband thinks it is easier to find a good medic in Cornwall."

We remained silent, Branwen and I.

"But I still have no news from my brother, still no sign of his ship," continued Iseult of the White Hands. "And now, instead of the one awaited by Tristan, you appear, Branwen. What brings you here? You, the maid and friend of the golden-haired Queen of Tintagel? Have you brought with you your love potion?"

Branwen turned pale. I felt an unexpected pang of pity. For in comparison with Iseult—tall, slim and slender, proud, mysterious, and a ravishing beauty, Branwen looked like a simple Irish peasant woman: chubby-cheeked, round-hipped, as coarse as homespun cloth, with her hair still tangled from the rain. Believe it or not, I felt sorry for her.

"Tristan has already accepted the potion once from your hands, Branwen," continued Iseult. "The potion that is still working and slowly killing him. Then, on the ship, Tristan took death from your hands. Perhaps, you have arrived here now to give him life? Verily, Branwen, if this is so, you had better hurry. There is little time left. Very little."

Branwen didn't stir. Her face was expressionless: the wax face of a doll. Their eyes, hers and Iseult's, fiery and powerful, met and locked. I could sense the tension, creaking like an overstretched rope. To my surprise, it was Iseult who turned out to be stronger.

"Lady Iseult—" Branwen fell down to her knees and bowed her head "—you have the right to feel bitter towards me. But I do not ask you for forgiveness as it wasn't you whom

I offended. I beg you for grace. I want to see him, beautiful Iseult of the White Hands. I want to see Tristan."

Her voice was quiet, soft, calm. In Iseult's eyes there was only sorrow.

"Very well," she said. "You shall see him, Branwen. Although I swore I wouldn't allow foreign hands to touch him again. Especially Cornish hands, her hands."

"It's not certain that she will come here from Tintagel," whispered Branwen, still on her knees.

"Rise, Branwen." Iseult of the White Hands lifted her head and her eyes glittered with moist diamonds. "It is not certain, you say. Yet... I would run barefoot through the snow, the thorns, the red-hot embers, if only... if only he called me. But he does not call me, although he knows... He calls only her, on whom he cannot depend. Our lives, Branwen, never cease to surprise us with ironies."

Branwen rose from her knees. Her eyes, I saw, were also filled with diamonds. Eh, women...

"Go to him, then, good Branwen," said Iseult bitterly. "Go and take to him that which I see in your eyes. But prepare yourself for the worst. For when you kneel by his bed, he will throw in your face a name that belongs not to you. He will throw it like a curse. Go, Branwen. The servants will show you the way."

Iseult, wringing the fingers of her white hands, watched me carefully. I was looking for hatred and enmity in her eyes. For she must have known. When one weds a living legend, one gets to know that legend in its tiniest detail. And I, after all, was no trifle, not to look at, anyway.

She was looking at me and there was something strange in her gaze. Then, having gathered her long dress, she sat in a carved chair, her white hands clasping the arm-rests.

"Sit here, Morholt of Ulster," she said. "By my side."

I did.

There are many stories, mostly improbable or untrue from

beginning to end, circulating about my duel with Tristan of Lionesse. In one of them, I was even turned into a dragon whom Tristan slew, thereby winning the right to Iseult of the Golden Hair. Not bad, eh? Romantic. And justified, to a point. I did in fact have a black dragon on my shield, perhaps it all started with that. After all, everyone knows that after Cuchulain, there are no dragons in Ireland.

Another story has it that the duel took place in Cornwall before Tristan met Iseult. That's not true. It's a minstrels' tale. King Diarmuid sent me to Mark, to Tintagel, several times, it's true, where I haggled over the tribute Cornwall was due to the King, gods only know on what grounds, I wasn't interested in politics. But I didn't meet Tristan then.

Nor did I meet him when he came to Ireland for the first time. I met him during his second visit, when he came to ask Iseult of the Golden Hair for Cornwall. Diarmuid's court, as usual in such situations, divided between those who supported the match and those who were against it. I belonged to the latter faction, though, in all honesty, I didn't know what all the fuss was about; as I said, I wasn't interested in politics, or intrigues. But I liked and knew how to fight.

The plan, as far as I could see, was simple. It didn't even merit the name of "intrigue." We wanted to break up King Mark's match and prevent the marriage with Tintagel. Was there a better way than to kill the envoy? The opportunity presented itself easily enough. I offended Tristan and he challenged me. He challenged me, you understand, not the other way round.

We fought in Dun Laoghaire, on the shore of the Bay. I didn't think I would have much of a problem with him. At first glance, I was twice his weight and had at least as much experience. Or so it seemed to me.

How wrong I was, I discovered soon after the first encounter, when we crushed our lances into splinters. I almost broke my back, so hard did he push me against the back of my saddle. A bit harder and he would have pushed me over together with my horse. When he turned around and, without calling for another lance, he drew his sword—I was pleased. The thing about lances is that with a little bit of luck and a good mount, even a green horn can thrash an experienced knight. The sword, in the long run, is a fairer weapon.

To start with, we felt each other around the shields for a bit. He was as strong as a bull. Stronger than I'd thought. He fought in the classical style: dexter, sinister, sky-below, blow after blow, very fast; his speed didn't allow me to take advantage of my experience, to impose my own, less classical style. He was tiring me out, so at the first opportunity I dodged the rules and slashed him across the thigh, just below the shield adorned by the rearing lion of Lionesse.

Had I struck from the ground it would have felled him. But it was from the mount. He didn't even blink, as if he hadn't noticed that he was bleeding like a pig, squirting dark crimson all over the saddle, the housing, the sand. The onlookers were shouting their heads off. I was sure the loss of blood was taking its toll and, because I was nearing my limits, too, I launched myself into attack, impatiently, recklessly. I went for the kill. And that was my mistake. Unwittingly, thinking perhaps that he would repay me with a similar, unfair cut from the side, I lowered my shield. Suddenly, I saw the stars burst with light and... didn't know what happened next. *I don't know. I don't know what happened next,* I thought, looking at the white hands of Iseult. Was it possible? Was it only that flash of light in Dun Laoghaire, the black tunnel and then the grey-white coast and the castle of Carhaing?

Was it possible?

And immediately, like a ready-made answer, like a hard proof and an irrefutable argument, there came images, faces, names, words, colours, scents. It was all there, every single day. The short, dusky winter days seeping through the fish-bladders in the windows. Those warm, fragrant-with-the-rain days near

Pentecost, and those long, hot summer days, yellow with sunshine and sunflowers. It was all there: the marches, the fights, the processions, the hunts, the feasts, the women, and more fights, more feasts, more women. Everything. All that had happened since that moment in Dun Laoghaire till this drizzly day on the Armorican coast. It all took place. It all happened. It passed. Only I couldn't understand why it all seemed to me so...

Never mind.

It didn't matter.

I sighed. This reminiscing wore me out. I felt almost as tired as then, during the fight. Just like then, my neck hurt and my arms felt like slabs of stone. The scar on my head throbbed furiously.

Iseult of the White Hands, who for some time had been looking out of the window, watching the overcast horizon, slowly turned her face towards me.

"Why have you come here, Morholt of Ulster?"

What was I to tell her? About the black holes in my memory? Telling her about my black, unending tunnel wouldn't make sense. All I had at my disposal was, as usual, the knights' custom, the universally respected and accepted norm. I got up.

"I am here to serve you, Lady Iseult," I said, bowing stiffly.

I saw Kai bowing like that in Camelot. It struck me as a dignified, noble bow worth copying.

"I have come here to carry out your orders, whatever they may be. My life belongs to you, Lady Iseult."

"Sir Morholt," she said softly, wringing her fingers, "I'm afraid it's too late for that."

I saw a tear, a narrow, glistening trickle making its way from the corner of her eye till it slowed down and stopped on the wing of her nostril. I could smell the scent of apples.

"The legend is about to end, Morholt."

ISEULT DIDN'T DINE WITH US. We were alone at the table, Branwen and I, except for a chaplain with a shiny tonsure. But we didn't bother with him. He muttered a short prayer and having blessed the table he devoted himself to stuffing his face. I soon forgot about his presence. As if he'd always been there.

"Branwen?"

"Yes, Morholt."

"How did you know?"

"I remember you from Ireland, from the court. I remember you well. No, I doubt you remember me. You didn't pay any attention to me then; although, I can tell you this now, Morholt, I did want you to notice me. It's understandable; when Iseult was around one didn't notice others."

"No, Branwen. I remember you. I didn't recognise you to-day because..."

"Yes, Morholt?"

"Because then, in Atha Cliath... you always smiled."

Silence.

"Branwen?"

"Yes, Morholt?"

"How is Tristan?"

"Bad. The wound is festering, doesn't want to heal. The rot's set in. It looks horrible."

"Is he...?"

"As long as he believes, he will live. And he believes."

"In what?"

"In her."

Silence.

"Branwen?"

"Yes, Morholt?"

"Is Iseult of the Golden Hair... is the Queen... really going to sail here from Tintagel?"

"I don't know, Morholt. But he believes she will."

Silence.

"Morholt?"

"Yes, Branwen?"

"I told Tristan you were here. He wants to see you. Tomorrow."

"Very well."

Silence.

"Morholt?"

"Yes, Branwen?"

"There, on the dunes..."

"It doesn't matter, Branwen."

"It does. Please, try to understand. I didn't want, I couldn't let you die. I could not allow an arrow butt, a stupid piece of wood and metal, to spoil... I couldn't let that happen. At any price, even the price of your contempt. And there... on the dunes, the price they asked didn't seem so high. You see, Morholt..."

"Branwen... it's enough, please."

"I have paid with my body before."

"Branwen. Not a word more."

She touched my hand and her touch, believe me or not, was the red ball of the sun rising after a long, cold night. It was the scent of apples, the leap of a horse spurred to attack. I looked into her eyes and her gaze was like the fluttering of pennons in the wind, like music, like a stroke of fur on the cheek. Branwen, the laughing Branwen of Baile Atha Cliath. Serious, quiet, sad Branwen of Cornwall, of the Knowing Eyes. Was there anything in that wine we drank? Like the wine Tristan and Iseult drank on the sea?

"Branwen..."

"Yes, Morholt?"

"Nothing, I only wanted to hear the sound of your name."

Silence.

The roaring of the sea, monotonous, hollow, carrying persistent, intrusive, stubborn whispers...

Silence.

"MORHOLT."

"Tristan."

He had changed. Then, in Baile Atha Cliath, he was a child, a cheerful boy with dreamy eyes, always with that engaging little smile that sent hot waves up the maids' thighs. Always that smile, even when we had bashed each other with swords in Dun Laoghaire. And now... Now his face was grey, thin, withered, cut with glistening lines of sweat, his lips chaffed and frozen in a grimace of pain, black rings of suffering around his eyes.

And he stank. He stank of illness. Of death. Of fear.

"You are alive, Irishman."

"I am, Tristan."

"When they carried you off the field they said you were dead. Your head..."

"My head was cracked open and the brain out," I said, trying to make it sound casual.

"A miracle. Someone must have been praying for you, Morholt."

"I doubt that," I shrugged my shoulders.

"Inscrutable is Fate." His brow furrowed. "You and Branwen... both alive. While I... in a silly scuffle... I had a lance thrust into my groin; it went right through me, and it snapped. A splinter must have got stuck inside; that's why the wound is festering. God's punished me. It's the punishment for all my sins. For you, for Branwen. And above all... for Iseult..."

His brow furrowed again; his mouth twisted. I knew which Iseult he meant. My heart ached. Her black-ringed eyes, her hand-wringing, the fingers cracked out of her white hands. The bitterness in her voice. How often she must have seen it: that involuntary twist of the mouth when he spoke the name of "Iseult" and could not add "of the Golden Hair." I felt sorry for her—her, married to a legend. Why had she agreed to it? Why had she agreed to serve merely as a name, an empty sound? Hadn't she heard the story about him and the Cornish woman? Maybe she thought it unimportant? Perhaps she thought Tristan was just like any other man? Like the men from Arthur's retinue, like Gawaine, Gaheris, Bors, or Bedivere, who started this idiotic fashion to adore one woman, sleep with another, and marry the third without anyone complaining?

"Morholt..."

"I'm here, Tristan."

"I have sent Caherdin to Tintagel. The ship..."

"Still no news, Tristan."

"Only she..." he whispered. "Only she can save me. I'm on the brink. Her eyes, her hands, just the sight of her, the sound of her voice... There is no other cure for me. That's why... if she is on that ship, Caherdin will pull out on the mast..."

"I know, Tristan..."

He fell silent, staring at the ceiling, breathing heavily.

"Morholt... Will she... come? Does she remember?"

"I don't know, Tristan," I said and immediately regretted it. Damn it, what would it cost me to confirm with ardour and conviction? Did I have to reveal my ignorance to him as well?

Tristan turned his face to the wall.

"I wasted this love," he groaned. "I destroyed it. And through it, I brought a curse on our heads. I am dying because of it, unsure that she will answer my plea and come, that she would, even if it were too late."

"Don't say that, Tristan."

"I have to. It's all my fault. Or perhaps my fate is at fault? Maybe that's how it was to be from the beginning? The beginning born of love and tragedy? For you know that Blanchefleur gave birth to me amidst despair? The labour began the moment she received the news of Rivalin's death. She didn't survive my birth. I don't know whether it was her, in her last breath, or Foyenant, later... who gave me this name, the name which is like doom, like a curse? Like a judgement. La tristesse. The cause and effect. La tristesse, surrounding me like a mist... Exactly like the mist swathing the mouth of the river Liffey when for the first time..."

He fell silent again, his hands instinctively stroking the furs with which he was covered.

"Everything, everything I did turned against me. Put yourself in my position, Morholt. Imagine yourself arriving at Baile

Atha Cliath, you meet a girl... From the first sight, from the very moment your eyes meet, you feel your heart wants to burst out of your breast, your hands tremble. You wander to and fro the whole night, unable to sleep, boiling with anxiety, shaking, thinking about one thing only: to see her again in the morning. And what? Instead of joy—la tristesse..."

I was silent. I didn't understand what he was talking about.

"And then," he carried on, "the first conversation. The first touching of the hands, as powerful as a lance's thrust in a tournament. The first smile, her smile, which makes you... Eh, Morholt. What would you do in my place?"

I was silent. I didn't know what I would have done in his place. I had never been in his position. By Lugh and Lir, I had never experienced anything like it. Ever.

"I know what you would not have done, Morholt," said Tristan, closing his eyes. "You would not have sold her to Mark, you would not have awakened his interest, babbling all the time about her. You would not have sailed for her to Ireland in his name. You would not have wasted love, the love that began then, then, not on the ship. Branwen doesn't have to torture herself with that story about magic potion. The elixir had nothing to do with it. By the time Iseult boarded the ship she was already mine. Morholt... If it were you boarding that ship with her, would you have sailed to Tintagel? Would you have given her to Mark? I'm sure you would not. You would have rather sailed to the edge of the world, to Brittany, Arabia, Hyperborea, the Ultima Thule. Morholt? Am I right?"

I couldn't answer this question. And even if I could, I wouldn't want to.

"You are exhausted, Tristan. You need sleep. Rest."

"Look out... for the ship..."

"We will, Tristan. Do you need anything? Shall I send for... for the lady of the White Hands?"

A twist of his mouth:

"No."

We are standing on the battlement, Branwen and I. A drizzle. We are in Brittany, after all. The wind is growing stronger, tugging at her hair, wrapping her dress tightly around her hips. It thwarts our words, squeezes tears out of our eyes, which are fixed on the horizon.

No sign of a sail.

I'm looking at Branwen. By Lugh, what a joy it is, watching her. I could look at her till the end of time. Just to think that when she stood next to Iseult, she didn't seem pretty. I must have been blind.

"Branwen?"

"Yes, Morholt?"

"Were you waiting for me then, on the beach? Did you know...?"

"Yes."

"How?"

"Don't you know?"

"No. I don't... I can't remember... Branwen, enough of these mysteries. My head is not up to it. Not my poor cracked head."

"The legend cannot end without us. Without our participation. Yours and mine. I don't know why, but we are important, indispensable to this story. The story of great love that is like a whirl, sucking in everything and everyone. Don't you know that, Morholt of Ulster? Don't you understand what an almighty power love can be? A power capable of turning the natural order of thing? Can't you feel that?

"Branwen... I do not understand. Here, in the castle of Carhaing..."

"Something will happen. Something that depends only on us. That's the reason we are here. We have to be here, whether we want it or not. That is how I knew you would turn up on that beach. That is why I couldn't allow you to die on the dunes..."

I don't know what made me do it. Perhaps her words, perhaps the sudden recollection of the eyes of the golden-haired lady. Maybe it was something I had forgotten, journeying down the long, unending black tunnel. I don't know, but I did it without thinking, without any deliberation. I took her into my arms.

She clung to me, willingly, trustfully, and I thought that, indeed, love can be an almighty power. But equally strong is its prolonged, overwhelming, gnawing absence.

It lasted only a moment. Or so it seemed to me. Branwen slowly freed herself and turned around. A gust of wind pulled her hair.

"Something depends on us, Morholt. On you and me. I'm scared."

"Of what?"

"Of the sea. Of the rudderless boat."

"I'm with you, Branwen."

"Please be, Morholt."

This evening is different. Completely different. I don't know where Branwen is. Perhaps she is with Iseult, nursing Tristan who is again unconscious, tossing and turning in the fever. Tossing and turning, he whispers: "Iseult..." Iseult of the White Hands knows it's not her that Tristan calls, but she trembles when she hears this name. And wrings the fingers of her white hands. Branwen, if she is with her, has wet diamonds in her eyes. Branwen... I wish... Eh, the pox on it!

And I... I'm drinking with the chaplain. What is he doing here? Perhaps he's always been here?

We are drinking, and drinking fast. And a lot. I know it's not doing me any good. I shouldn't, my cracked head doesn't take kindly to this kind of sport. When I overdo it, I have hallucinations, splitting headaches, sometimes I faint, though rarely.

Well, so what? We are drinking. I have to, plague take it, drown this dread inside me. I have to forget the trembling hands. The castle of Carhaing. Branwen's eyes, full of fear of the unknown. I want to drown the howling of the wind, the roaring of the sea, the rocking of the boat under my feet. I want to drown everything I can't remember. And that scent of apples which keeps following me.

We are drinking, the chaplain and I. We are separated by an oak table, splattered with puddles of wine. It's not only the table that separates us.

"Drink, shaveling."

"God bless you, son"

"I'm not your son."

Since the battle of Mount Badon, I carry the sign of the cross on my armour like many others, but I'm not moved by it as they are. Religion and all its manifestations leave me cold. The bush in Glastonbury, professedly planted by Joseph of Arymatea, looks to me like any other bush, except it's more twisted and sickly than most. The Abbey itself, about which some of Arthur's boys speak with such reverence, doesn't stir great emotions in me, though I admit it looks very pretty against the wood, the hills and the lake. And the regular tolling of the bells helps to find the way in the fog, for it's always foggy there, the pox on it.

This Roman religion, although it has spread around, doesn't have a chance here, on the islands. Here, in Ireland, in Cornwall or Wales, at every step you see things whose existence is stubbornly denied by the monks. Any dimwit has seen elves, pukkas, sylphs, the Coranians, leprechauns, sidhe, and even bean sidhe, but no-one, as far as I know, has ever seen an angel. Except Bedivere who claims to have seen Gabriel, but Bedivere is a blockhead and a liar. I wouldn't believe a word he says.

The monks go on about miracles performed by Christ. Let's be honest: compared with things done by Vivien of the Lake, the Morrigan, or Morgause, wife of Lot from the Orkneys, not to mention Merlin, Christ doesn't really have much to boast about. I'm telling you, the monks have come and they'll go. The Druids will stay. Not that I think the Druids are much better than the monks. But at least the Druids are ours. They always have been. And the monks are stragglers. Just like this one, my table companion. The devil knows what wind's blown him here to Armorica. He uses odd words and has a strange accent, Aquitan or Gaelic, plague take him.

"Drink, shaveling."

I bet my head that in Ireland, Christianity will be a passing fashion. We Irish, we do not buy this hard, inflexible, Roman fanaticism. We are too sober-headed for that, too simple-hearted. Our Ireland is the fore-post of the West, it's the Last Shore. Beyond, not far off, are the Old Lands: Hy Brasil, Ys, Mainistir Leitreach, Beag-Arainn. It is them, not the Cross, not the Latin liturgy, that rule people's minds. It was so ages ago and it's so today. Besides, we Irish, are a tolerant people. Everybody believes what he wants. I heard that around the world different factions of Christians are already at each other's throats. In Ireland, it's impossible. I can imagine everything but not that Ulster, say, might be a scene of religious scuffles.

"Drink, shaveling."

Drink, for who knows, you may have a busy day tomorrow. Perhaps tomorrow you will have to pay back for all the goodies you've pushed down your gullet. The one who is to leave us, must leave us with the full pomp of the ritual. It's easier to leave when someone is conducting a ritual, doesn't matter if he is mumbling the Requiem Aeternam, making a stink with incense, or howling and bashing his sword on the shield. It's simply easier to leave. And what's the difference where to—Hell, Paradise, or Tir Na Nog? One always leaves for the darkness. I know a thing or two about it. One leads down the black tunnel which has no end.

"Your master is dying, shaveling."

"Sir Tristan? I'm praying for him."

"Are you praying for a miracle?"

"It's all in God's hands."

"Not all."

"You are blaspheming, my son."

"I'm not your son. I'm a son of Flann Uarbeoil whom the Normans hacked to death on the bank of the river Shannon. That was a death worthy of man. When dying, Flann didn't moan 'Iseult, Iseult'. When dying, Flann laughed and called the Norman yarl such names the poor bastard forgot to close his gob for an hour afterwards, so impressed was he."

"One should die with the name of Lord on one's lips. And besides, it's easier to die in a battle, from the sword, than to linger on in bed, being eaten away by la maladie. Fighting la maladie is a lonely struggle. It's hard to fight alone, harder still to die alone."

"La maladie? You're drivelling, monk. He would lick himself out of this wound, just like he did from that other one, which... But then, in Ireland, he was full of life, full of hope. Now the hope's drained out of him, together with his blood. If he could only stop thinking about her, forget about this accursed love..."

"Love, my son, also comes from God."

"Oh, it does, does it? Everybody here goes on about love, racking their brains where it comes from. Tristan and Iseult... Shall I tell you, shavling, where this love, or whatever it is, has come from? Shall I tell you what brought them together? It was me: Morholt. Before Tristan cracked my head, I poked him in the thigh and thus sent him to bed for several weeks. But he, the moment he felt a bit better, he dragged the lady of the Golden Hair into it. Any healthy man would do that, given time and opportunity. Later, the minstrels were singing about the Moren Wood and the naked sword. Balls, that's what I say. Now you see yourself, monk, where the love comes from. Not from God, from Morholt. And it's worth accordingly, this love. This maladie of yours."

"You are blaspheming. You are talking about things you do not understand. And it would be better if you stopped talking about them."

I didn't punch him between the eyes with my tin mug,

which I was squeezing in my hand. You wonder why? I'll tell you why. Because he was right. I didn't understand.

How could I understand? I was not conceived amidst misfortune, or born into tragedy. Flann and my mother conceived me on the hay and I'm sure they had plenty of good, healthy joy doing it. Giving me a name, they didn't put any secret meanings into it. They gave me a name that it would be easy to call me by. "Morholt! Supper!" "Morholt! You little brat!" "Fetch some water, Morholt!" La tristesse? Balls, not la tristesse.

Can one daydream with a name like this? Play a harp? Devote all one's thoughts to the beloved? Sacrifice to her all the matters of everyday life and pace the room unable to sleep? Balls. With a name like mine one can drink beer and wine and then puke under the table. Smash people's noses. Crack heads with a sword or an axe or, alternatively, have it done to oneself. Love? Someone with the name Morholt pulls off a skirt, pokes his fill, and falls asleep. Or, if he happens to feel a wee stirring in his soul, he will say: "Eh, ye're a fine piece of arse, Maire O'Connell, I could gobble you whole, yer teats first." Dig through it for three days and three nights, you won't find in it a grain of la tristesse. Not a trace. So what, that I like looking at Branwen? I like looking at lots of things.

"Drink, monk. Pour it, don't waste time. What are you mumbling?"

"It's all in God's hands, *sicut in coelo et in terris*, amen..."

"Maybe in coelo but not in terris, that's for sure."

"You are blaspheming, my son. Cave!"

"What are you trying to scare me with? A bolt from the blue?"

"I'm not trying to scare you. I fear for you. Rejecting God you reject hope. The hope that you won't lose what you have won. The hope that when it comes to making a choice, you will make the right one. And that you won't be left defenceless."

"Life, with God or without God, with hope or without it, is a road without an end or beginning, a road that leads along the slippery side of a huge tin funnel. Most people don't realise they are going round and round passing the same point on the narrow slippery slope of the circle. There are some who are unfortunate and slip. They fall. And that's the end of them; they'll never climb up, back to the edge; they won't resume the march. They are sliding down, till they reach the bottom of the funnel, at the narrow point of the outlet where all meet. They meet, though only for a short while because further down, under the funnel, there awaits an abyss. This castle pounded by the waves is just such a place. The funnel's outlet. Do you understand it, shaveling?"

"No. But then I do not think you understand the cause behind my failure in understanding."

"To hell with causes and effects, sicut in coelo et in terris. Drink, monk."

We drank late into the night. The chaplain survived it admirably well. I didn't do so well. I got pissed, I can tell you. I managed to drown... everything.

Or so it seemed to me.

TODAY THE SEA HAS THE colour of lead. Today the sea is angry. I feel its anger and I respect it. I understand Branwen; I understand her fear. I don't understand the cause. Or her words.

Today the castle is empty and terribly silent. Tristan is fighting the fever. Iseult and Branwen are at his side. I, Morholt of Ulster, stand on the battlements and look out into the sea.

Not a sign of a sail.

I WAS NOT ASLEEP WHEN she came in. And I was not surprised. It was as if I had expected it. That strange meeting on the beach, the journey through the dunes and salty meadows, the silly incident with Bec de Corbin and his friends, the evening by candlelight, the warmth of her body when I embraced her on the battlement, and above all that aura of love and death filling Carhaing—all this had brought us close to each other, bound us together. I even caught myself thinking that I would find it difficult to say goodbye...

To Branwen.

She didn't say a word. She undid the brooch on her shoulder and let the heavy cloak drop onto the floor, and then quickly took off her shirt, a simple coarse garment, exactly like the ones worn everyday by Irish girls. She turned around, reddened by the flames flickering on the logs in the fire that was spying on her with its glowing eyes.

Also without saying a word, I moved to the side and made room for her next to me. She lay down, slowly, turning her face to me. I covered her with furs. We were both silent, lying still, watching the fleeting shadows on the ceiling.

"I couldn't sleep," she said. "The sea..."

"I know. I hear it, too."

"I'm scared, Morholt."

"I'm with you."

"Please be."

I embraced her as tenderly and delicately as I could. She slipped her arms round my neck and pressed her face to my cheek, overpowering me with her hot breath. I touched her gently, fighting the joyous urge to embrace her fully, the need for violent, lusty caresses, just as if I were stroking a falcon's feathers or the nostrils of a nervous horse. I stroked her hair, her neck and shoulders, her full, wonderfully rounded breasts with their small nipples. I stroked her hips which, not so long ago, seemed to me too round and that in fact were wonderfully round. I stroked her smooth thighs, her womanhood, that place I didn't have a name for, for even in my thoughts I wouldn't dare to name it as I used to, with any of the Irish, Welsh, or Saxon words I knew. It would be like calling Stonehenge a pile of rubble, or Glastonbury Tor a hillock.

She trembled, giving herself forth to meet my hands, guiding them with the movements of her body. She asked, she demanded with groans, with rapid uneven gasps of breath. She pleaded with momentary submissions, warm and tender, only to harden the next moment into a quivering diamond.

"Love me, Morholt," she whispered. "Love me."

She was brave, greedy, impatient. But helpless and defenceless in my arms. She had to give in to my quiet, careful, restrained love. My love. The one I wanted. The one I wanted for her. For in the one she was trying to impose on me, I sensed fear, sacrifice, resignation, and I didn't want her to be afraid, to sacrifice anything for me, to give up anything for me. I had my way.

Or so it seemed to me.

I felt the castle shudder in the slow rhythm of the pounding waves.

"Branwen..."

She pressed her hot body to mine; her sweat had the scent of wet feathers.

"Morholt... It's good..."

"What's good Branwen?"

"It's good to live..."

We were silent for a long while. And then I asked a question. The question I shouldn't have asked.

"Branwen... Will she... Will Iseult come here from Tintagel?"

"I don't know."

"You don't know? You? Her confidant, who..."

I shut up. By Lugh, what an idiot I am, I thought. What a bloody blockhead.

"Don't torture yourself, Morholt," she said. "Ask me."

"About what?"

"About Iseult and King Mark's wedding night."

"Ah, this. Believe me or not, Branwen, I'm not interested."

"I think you're lying."

I didn't answer. She was right.

"It was just like people say," she said quietly. "We swapped in Mark's bed, soon after the candles were put out.

I'm not sure if it was necessary. Mark was so charmed with Iseult of the Golden Hair that he would accept her lack of virginity without reproach. He was not that fussy. But that's what we did. I did it because of my bad conscience after what had happened on the ship. I thought it was all my doing, mine and that of the magic potion's I had given them. I assumed the guilt and wanted to pay for it. Only later, it turned out that Tristan and Iseult slept with each other even in Baile Atha Cliath. And that I was not guilty of anything."

"It's all right, Branwen. Spare me the details. Leave it alone."

"No. Listen to the end. Listen to what the minstrels will never sing about. Iseult ordered that as soon as I had given proof of my virginity I should sneak out of bed and swap with her again. Perhaps she was afraid the king would find out, or maybe she didn't want me to get used to him, who knows? She was with Tristan in the room next door, both busy with each other. She freed herself from his arms and went to the Cornishman as she stood, naked, without even combing her tangled hair. I stayed, naked, with Tristan. Till dawn. I don't know how or why."

I was silent.

"That's not the end," said Branwen, turning her face towards the fire. "After that, there was the honeymoon during which the Cornishman wouldn't leave Iseult even for a minute. Thus, Tristan could not get close to her. But to me he could. To spare you the details, after these few months I was in love with him. For life and death. I know you are surprised. It's true, the only thing we had in common was the bed where, it was obvious to me even then, Tristan was trying to forget his love for Iseult, his jealousy of Mark, his guilt. He treated me as a substitute. I knew that and it didn't help."

"Branwen..."

"Be patient, Morholt. It's still not the end. The honeymoon passed, Mark resumed his normal royal duties, and Iseult began to have plenty of free time. And Tristan... Tristan ceased to notice me. Worse, he began to avoid me. While I was going crazy with love."

She fell silent, found amongst the furs my hand and squeezed it tightly.

"I made several attempts to forget him," she carried on, staring at the ceiling. "Tintagel was full of young, uncomplicated knights. But it didn't work. One morning I took a boat to the sea. When I was far enough from the shore, I jumped."

"Branwen," I said, pulling her close, trying to smother with my embrace the shudders convulsing her body. "It's all past now. Forget about it. Like many others, you were sucked into the whirl of their love, love that proved unhappy to them, and fatal to others. Even I... I caught it on the head, though I merely brushed against this love, knowing nothing about it. In Dun Laoghaire, Tristan defeated me, although I was stronger and more experienced. That's because he fought for Iseult, for his love. I didn't know about it, got a good bash on the head and, like you, I owe my life to those who happened to be near me and who thought it right to help me. To save me. To pull me out of that unfathomable depth. And so we were saved, you and me. We are alive and to hell with everything else."

She slipped her arm under my head and stroked my hair. She touched the swelling that ran from the temple right down to my ear. I winced. The hair on the scar grows in all directions and a touch can sometimes cause an unbearable pain.

"The whirl of their love," she whispered. "Their love pulled us in. You and me. But were we really saved? What if we are still falling into that depth, together with them? What fate awaits us? The sea? The rudderless boat?"

"Branwen..."

"Love me, Morholt. The sea is asking for us, can you hear? But as long as we are here, as long as the legend isn't over..."

"Branwen..."

"Love me, Morholt."

I tried to be gentle. I tried to be considerate. I tried to be

Tristan, King Mark, and all the uncomplicated knights of Tintagel rolled into one. From the mass of desires whirling inside me, I kept only one: I wanted her to forget, forget about everything. I tried to make her believe, if only for as long as I held her in my arms, that there was only me. I tried. Believe me.

In vain.

Or so it seemed to me.

NOT A SIGN OF SAILS. The sea...

The sea has the colour of Branwen's eyes.

I pace the room like a wolf in a cage. My heart is pounding as if it wants to shatter my ribs. Something is squeezing my chest, my throat, something strange, something that's sitting inside me. I hurl myself on the bed. To hell with it. I close my eyes and see the golden sparks. I can smell the scent of apples. Branwen. The scent of a falcon's feathers as it sits on my glove when I return from hunting. The golden sparks. I see her face. I see the curve of her cheek, the small perky nose. The roundness of her arm. I see her... I carry her...

I carry her on the inner side of my eyelids.

"MORHOLT?"

"You are not asleep?"

"No, I can't... The sea..."

"I'm with you, Branwen."

"For how long? How much time have we got left?"

"Branwen..."

"Tomorrow... Tomorrow the ship from Tintagel will be here."

"How do you know?"

"I simply do."

Silence.

"Morholt?"

"Yes, Branwen?"

"We are bound together. Tied to this wheel of torture, sucked into the whirl. Chained. Tomorrow, here in Carhaing, the chain will break. I knew that the moment I saw you on the beach. When I realised that you were alive. When I realised I was alive, too. But we do not live for each other, not any more. We are merely a tiny part in the fates of Tristan of Lionesse and Iseult of the Golden Hair from the Emerald Isle. Here, in the castle of Carhaing, we found each other only to lose each other. The only thing that binds us together is a legend about love, which is not our legend. In which we play a role we cannot understand. A legend that perhaps won't even mention our roles, or it will warp and falsify them, will put into our mouths words we never said, will ascribe to us deeds we never did. We do not exist, Morholt. There is only a legend that is about to end."

"No, Branwen," I said, trying to make my voice sound hard, determined, and full of conviction. "You mustn't say that. It's sorrow, nothing else, that makes you say these words. True, Tristan of Lionesse is dying and even if Iseult of the Golden Hair is on the ship sailing from Tintagel, I'm afraid she may be too late. And even though I, too, am saddened by this, I shall never agree that the only thing that binds us together is the legend. I'll never agree with this, Branwen, lying next to you, holding you in my arms. At this moment, it's Tristan who doesn't exist for me, the legend, the castle of Carhaing. There is only the two of us."

"I, too, hold you in my arms, Morholt. Or so it seems to me. But I do know that we don't exist. There is only the legend. What will become of us? What will happen tomorrow? What decision will we have to make? What will become of us?"

"Fate will decide. An accident. This entire legend to which we so stubbornly return, is a result of an accident. A series of accidents. If it weren't for this blind fate, there would be no legend. Then, in Dun Laoghaire, just think Branwen, if it weren't for blind fate... it could have been him, not I..."

I stopped, frightened by the sudden thought, horrified by the words pressing onto my lips.

"Morholt," whispered Branwen. "Fate's done with us all

there was to do. The rest cannot be the result of an accident. We are beyond the rule of accident. What is ending, is ending for both of us. It's possible..."

"What, Branwen?"

"That perhaps then, in Dun Laoghaire—"

"Branwen!"

"—that your wound was mortal? Perhaps... I drowned in the bay?"

"Branwen! But we are alive!"

"Are you sure? Where had we come from to find ourselves on that beach, you and me, at the same time? Do you remember? Don't you think it possible we were brought by the rudderless boat? That very same boat which one day brought Tristan to the mouth of the river Liffey? The boat from Avalon, looming out of the mist, filled with the scent of apples? The boat we were told to get into for the legend cannot end without us, without our participation? For it was us, no-one else, who are to end this legend? And when we end it, we shall return to the shore, the rudderless boat will wait for us, and we will have to get into it and drift away and be swallowed by the mist? Morholt?"

"We are alive, Branwen."

"Are you sure?"

"I'm touching you, Branwen. You exist. Lying in my arms. You are beautiful, warm, you have a smooth skin. You smell like my falcon sitting on my glove when I return from hunting and the rain is rustling in the birch leaves. You are, Branwen."

"I am touching you, Morholt. You exist. You are warm and your heart is beating just as strongly. You smell of salt. You are."

"And so... we are alive, Branwen."

She smiled. I didn't see it. I felt that smile pressed into my arm.

LATER, DEEP IN THE NIGHT, lying still with my arm numb from the weight of her head, careful not to break her shallow sleep, I listened to the roaring of the sea.

For the first time in my life this sound, dull and monotonous like toothache, made me feel uneasy, irritated me, kept me awake. I was afraid. I was afraid of the sea. I, an Irishman, brought up on a seashore, from birth familiar with the sound of the surf.

Later still, in my sleep, I saw a boat with a high, upturned stem and a mast adorned with garlands. The rudderless boat, tossed on the waves. I could smell the scent of apples.

"GOOD LADY BRANWEN..." THE PAGE was gasping for breath. "Lady Iseult asks you to come to Sir Tristan's chamber. You and Sir Morholt of Ulster. Please hurry, milady."

"What happened? Has Tristan...?"

"No, it's not that. But..."

"Speak, boy."

"The ship from Tintagel... Sir Caherdin is coming back. There was a messenger from the cape. It can be seen..."

"What colour are the sails?"

"It's impossible to say. The ship is too far, far beyond the cape."

The sun came out.

WHEN WE ENTERED, ISEULT OF the White Hands was standing with her back to the half-open window, which threw off flashes of light from the little panes of glass fitted in little lead frames. She was radiating an unnatural, turbid, deflected light. Tristan, his face glossy with sweat, was breathing irregularly, with difficulty. His eyes were closed.

Iseult looked at us. Her face was drawn, disfigured by two deep furrows etched by pain on both sides of her mouth.

"He is barely conscious," she said. "He is delirious."

Branwen pointed to the window:

"The ship..."

"It's too far, Branwen. It's hardly passed the cape. It's too far..."

Branwen looked at Tristan and sighed. I knew what she thought.

No, I didn't.

I heard it.

Believe me or not, I heard their thoughts. Branwen's thoughts, anxious and full of fear, like waves frothing amongst the shore's rocks. The thoughts of Iseult, soft, trembling, fluttering like a bird held in the hand. The thoughts of Tristan, loose and torn, like wisps of mist.

We are all at your side, Tristan, thought Iseult. *Branwen of Cornwall who is the Lady of Algae. Morholt of Ulster, who is Decision. And I, who loves you, Tristan. I who love you more and more with every minute that passes and takes you away from me, that takes you away no matter what colour the sails of the ship approaching the shores of Brittany. Tristan...*

Iseult, thought Tristan. *Iseult. Why aren't they looking out of the window? Why are they looking at me? Why aren't they telling me what colour the sails are? I must know it, I must, otherwise...*

He will fall asleep, thought Branwen. *He will fall asleep and he will never wake up. He has reached the point as far from the luminous surface as it is from the green algae covering the seabed. The point where one stops struggling. From that point there is only peace.*

Tristan, thought Iseult. *Now I know I was happy with you. Despite everything. Despite all the time you have been with me and thought only about her. Despite you rarely calling me by my name. You always called me "my lady". You've tried so hard not to hurt me. You were trying so hard, putting so much effort into it that it was your very trying that hurt me most. Yet I was happy. You've given me happiness. You've given me the golden sparks flickering under my eyelids. Tristan...*

Branwen was looking out through the window. At the ship appearing slowly out from behind the land's edge. *Hurry up,* she thought. *Hurry up, Caherdin. Sharp to the wind. No matter what colour, turn your sail sharp to the wind, Caherdin. Hail, Caherdin, welcome, we need your help. Save us, Caherdin...*

But the wind, which for the last three days had been blowing, freezing us and lashing us with rain, now abated. The sun came out.

All of them, thought Tristan. *All of them. Iseult of the White Hands, Branwen, Morholt... And now I... Iseult, my Iseult... What colour are the sails of this ship...? What colour...?*

We are like blades of grass that stick to the cloak's hem when one's walking through a meadow, thought Iseult. *We are those blades of grass on your cloak, Tristan. In a moment you'll brush off your cloak and we shall be free... borne away by the wind. Do not make me look at those sails, Tristan, my husband. I beg you, don't.*

I wish, thought Tristan, *I wish I could have met you earlier. Why did Fate bring me to Ireland? Armorica is closer to Lionesse... I could have met you earlier... I wish I had loved you... I wish... What colour are the sails of this ship? I wish... I wish I could give you love, my lady. My good lady Iseult of the White Hands... But I can't... I can't...*

Branwen turned her face to the tapestries, her shoulders shaking with sobs. She, too, must have heard.

I took her in my arms. On all the Lir's Tritons! I cursed my bear-like clumsiness, my wooden hands, my cragged fingertips catching on the silk like tiny fishhooks. But Branwen, falling into my arms, had filled everything out, put everything right, rounding off all the sharp edges like a wave washing over a sandy beach trampled by horses's hooves. Suddenly, I felt we were one person. I knew I couldn't lose her. Ever.

Above her head, pressed onto my chest, I saw the window. The sea. And the ship.

You can give me love, Tristan, thought Iseult. *Please give it to me, before I lose you. Only once. I need it very much. Don't make me look at the sails of this ship. Don't ask me what colour they are. Don't force me to play a role in a legend, a role that I don't want to play.*

I can't, thought Tristan. *I can't. Iseult, my golden-haired Iseult... My Iseult...*

It's not my name, thought Iseult. *It's not my name.*

"It's not my name!" she shouted.

311

Tristan opened his eyes, looked around, his head rolling on the pillows.

"My lady..." he whispered. "Branwen... Morholt..."

"We are here, all of us," answered Iseult very quietly.

No, thought Tristan. *Iseult is not here. So... it's like there is no-one here.*

My lady...

Don't make me...

My lady... Please...

Don't make me look at the sails, Tristan. Don't force me to tell you...

Please... His body tensed. *I beg you...*

And then he said it. Differently. Branwen shuddered in my arms.

"Iseult."

She smiled.

"I wanted to change the course of a legend," she said very quietly. "What a mad idea. Legends cannot be changed. Nothing can be changed. Well, almost nothing..."

She stopped, looked at me, at Branwen, both still embracing and standing next to the tapestry with the apple tree of Avalon. She smiled. I knew I would never forget that smile.

Slowly, very slowly, she walked up to the window. Standing inside it, she stretched her hands up to its pointed arch.

"Iseult," groaned Tristan. "What... what colour..."

"They are white," she said. "White, Tristan. They are as white as snow. Farewell."

She turned around. Without looking at him, without looking at anybody, she left the room. The moment she left I stopped hearing her thoughts. All I could hear was the roaring of the sea.

"White!" shouted Tristan. "Iseult! My Golden Hair! At last..."

The voice died in his throat like the flickering flame of an oil-lamp. Branwen screamed. I ran to his bed. Tristan's lips moved lightly. He was trying to raise himself. I held him up and gently forced him to lie back on the pillows.

"Iseult," he whispered. "Iseult. Iseult..."

"Lie still, Tristan. Do not try to get up."

He smiled. By Lugh, I knew I would never be able to forget that smile.

"Iseult... I have to see it..."

"Lie still, Tristan..."

"...the sails..."

Branwen, standing in the window where a moment ago had stood Iseult of the White Hands, sobbed loudly.

"Morholt!" she cried. "This ship..."

"I know. Branwen..."

She turned.

"He is dead."

"What?"

"Tristan has died. This very moment. This is the end, Branwen."

I looked through the window. The ship was closer than before. But still too far. Far too far to tell the colour of its sails.

I MET THEM IN THE big hall, the one where we had been greeted by Iseult of the White Hands. In the hall where I had offered her my sword and my life, whatever it might have meant.

I was looking for Iseult and the chaplain. Instead I found them.

There were four of them.

A Welsh druid named Hwyrddyddwg, a sly old man, told me once that a man's intentions, no matter how cleverly disguised, will be always betrayed by two things: his eyes and his hands. I looked closely at the eyes, then at the hands of the knights standing in the great hall.

"My name is Marjadoc," said the tallest of them. He had a coat of arms on his tunic—two black boars' heads, crested with silver, against a blue-red field. "And these are honourable knights—Sir Gwydolwyn, Sir Anoeth, and Sir Deheu of Opwen. We come from Cornwall as envoys to Sir Tristan of Lionesse. Take us to him, sir."

"You've come too late," I said.

"Who are you, sir?" Marjadoc winced. "I do not know you."

At this moment Branwen came in. Marjadoc's face twitched, anger and hatred crept out on it like two writhing snakes.

"Marjadoc."

"Branwen."

"Gwydolwyn, Anoeth, Deheu, I thought I would never see you again. They told me Tristan and Corvenal put you out of your misery then, in the Wood of Moren."

Marjadoc smiled nastily.

"Inscrutable is Fate. I never thought I would see you again either. Especially here. But never mind, take us to Tristan. The matter is of utmost urgency."

"Why such a hurry?"

"Take us to Tristan," repeated Marjadoc angrily. "We have business with him. Not with his servants. Nor with the panderess of the Queen of Cornwall."

"Whence have you come, Marjadoc?"

"From Tintagel, as I said."

"Interesting," smiled Branwen, "for the ship has not yet reached the shore. But it's nearly there. Do you wish me to tell you what sails it is sailing under?"

Marjadoc's eyes didn't change for a second. I realised he had known. I understood everything. The light I saw at the end of the black tunnel was growing brighter.

"Leave this place," barked Marjadoc, putting his hand on the sword. "Leave the castle. Immediately."

"How have you got here?" asked the smiling Branwen. "Have you, by any chance, come on the rudderless boat. With the black, tattered rag for a sail? With the wolf's skull nailed to the high, upturned stem? Why have you come here? Who sent you?"

"Get out of the way, Branwen. Do not cross us or you'll be sorry."

Branwen's face was calm. But this time it was not the calm of resignation and helplessness, the chill of despair and indifference. This time it was the calm of an unshaken iron will. No, I mustn't lose her. Not for any price.

Any? And what about the legend?

I could smell the scent of apples.

"You have strange eyes, Marjadoc," said Branwen suddenly. "Eyes that are not used to daylight."

"Get out of our way."

"No. I won't get out of your way, Marjadoc. First you will answer my question. The question is: why?"

Marjadoc didn't move. He was looking at me.

"There will be no legend about great love," he said, and I knew it was not him who was talking. "Such a legend would be unwanted and harmful. The tomb made of beryl and the hawthorn bush growing from it and spreading itself over the tomb made of chalcedony would be a senseless folly. We do not want tombs like that. We do not want the story of Tristan and Iseult to take root in people's minds, to become an ideal and an example for them. We do not wish it to repeat itself. We won't have young people saying: 'We are like Tristan and Iseult'. Ever. Anywhere."

Branwen was silent.

"We cannot allow something like the love of these two to cloud minds destined for higher things. To weaken arms whose purpose is to crush and kill. To soften the spirit of those who are meant to hold power with iron tongs. And above all, Branwen, we shall not allow what has bound Tristan and Iseult to pass into a legend as an imperishable love that dares all dangers and makes light of hardships, binding the lovers even after their death. That is why Iseult of Cornwall has to die far away from here, bringing into the world another descendant of King Mark, as befits a queen. As for Tristan, if he has already gone to rot before we got to him, he must be laid at the bottom of the sea, with a stone tied to his neck. Or burnt. Yes, that would be best. And the castle of Carhaing should go up in flames with him. And soon, before the ship from Tintagel sails into the bay. Instead of a tomb of beryl—a heap of stinking, smouldering rubble. Instead of a beautiful legend—an ugly truth. The truth about a selfish infatuation, about stepping over dead bodies, about trampling the feelings of other people and the harm done to them. Branwen? Do you really want to stop us, us the Knights of Truth? I repeat: get out of our way. We have nothing against you. We do not want to kill you. There is no need. You have played your role, a rather contemptible one, now you can go. Go back to the shore, where they are waiting for you. You, too, Sir... What is your name?"

I was looking at their eyes and their hands, and I thought that the old Hwyrddyddwg was right: their eyes and hands indeed showed their intentions. For in their eyes there was cruelty and determination while their hands held swords. I didn't have my sword, that same sword I had offered to Iseult of the White Hands. *Well,* I thought, *tough titties. After all, it's not a big deal to die fighting. It won't be the first time, will it?*

I am Morholt! The one who is Decision.

"Your name, sir," repeated Marjadoc.

"Tristan," I said.

The chaplain appeared out of nowhere, sprang from the ground like a pukka. Groaning with the effort, he threw across the hall a huge, two-handed sword. Marjadoc leapt at me, raising his sword. For a moment the swords were up in the air—Marjadoc's and the one flying towards my outstretched hands. It seemed I could not move quickly enough. But I did.

I cut Marjadoc under his arm, with all the strength, in half-swing. The blade went in diagonally, as far as the line dividing the fields on his coat of arms. I turned back, letting the sword slide out. Marjadoc fell down, right under the feet of the other three who were running towards me. Anoeth tripped on the body, which meant I could easily crack his head. And I did.

Gwydolwyn and Deheu rushed at me from both sides. I

stepped in between them, whirling round with the stretched sword like a spinning top. They had to back off. Their blades were a good arm's length shorter than mine. Kneeling down, I cut Gwydolwyn on the thigh. I felt the blade grate on bone. Deheu swung his sword and tried to get to me from the side. But he slipped on the blood and fell on one knee. His eyes were full of fear now, begging for mercy, but I found none. I didn't even look for it. It's impossible to parry a thrust with a two-hander delivered from close range. If you cannot move out of its way, the blade will sink two-thirds of its length till it stops on the two little iron wings placed there especially for this purpose. And it did.

Believe me or not, but none of them let out as much as a squeak. While I... I felt nothing. Absolutely nothing.

I dropped the sword on the floor.

"Morholt!" Branwen ran and clung to me, her body shuddering with waves of terror that were slowly dying away.

"It's all right now, dear. It's all over," I said, stroking her hair, but at the same time looking at the chaplain kneeling by the dying Gwydolwyn.

"Thank you for the sword, monk."

The chaplain lifted his head and looked me in the eyes. Where had he sprung from? Had he been here all the time? But if he had been... then who was he? Who the devil was he?

"It's all in God's hands," he said, and bent over the dying Gwydolwyn. "...*Et lux perpetua luceat ei...*"

Still, he didn't convince me. He didn't convince me with the first saying, nor with the second.

THEN WE FOUND ISEULT.

In the baths; her face pressed to the well. Clean, pedantic Iseult of the White Hands, could not have done it anywhere else but on the stone floor by the gutter meant for draining away water. Now this gutter glistened dark clotted red along its entire length.

She had opened her veins on both hands. With expertise. Along the forearms, on the inner side, and then, to make sure, on her wrists with the sign of the cross. We would not have been able to save her even if we'd found her earlier.

Her hands were even whiter than before.

And then, believe me or not, I realised that the rudderless boat was leaving the shore. Without us. Without Morholt of Ulster. Without Branwen of Cornwall. But it was not empty.

Farewell, Iseult. Farewell. For ever. Be it in Tir Na Nog, or in Avalon, the whiteness of your hands will last for centuries. For eternity.

Farewell, Iseult.

WE LEFT CARHAING BEFORE Caherdin's arrival. We didn't want to talk to him, or to anyone who might have been on that ship from Tintagel. For us, the legend was over. We were not interested in what the minstrels were going to do with it.

The sky was overcast again, it was raining, a drizzle. Brittany, the usual stuff. There was a road ahead of us: the road through the dunes towards that rocky beach. I didn't want to think what to do next. It didn't matter.

"I love you, Morholt," said Branwen without looking at me. "I love you whether you want it or not. It's like an illness. A weariness that drains me of my free will, that pulls me into the depths. I've lost myself within you, Morholt, and I shall never find myself the way I was before. If you respond to my love, you, too, will lose yourself; you will perish, drown in the depths and never find the old Morholt again. So think well before you give me your answer."

The ship stood by the rocky shore. They were unloading something. Someone was shouting, cursing in Welsh, hurrying the men. The sails were being rolled. The sails...

"It's a terrible sickness, this love," carried on Branwen, also looking at the sails. "La maladie, as they say in the south, on the mainland. La maladie d'espoir, the sickness of hope. The selfish infatuation, bringing harm to everyone around. I love you, Morholt, selfishly, blindly. I'm not worried about the fate of others, whom I may unwittingly draw into the whirl of my love, hurt, or trample upon. Isn't it terrible? If you respond to my love... Think well, Morholt, before you give me your answer."

The sails...

"We are like Tristan and Iseult," said Branwen, and her voice came dangerously close to breaking point. " La maladie... What shall become of us, Morholt? What will happen to us? Will we, too, be joined finally by bushes of hawthorn and brier-rose growing on our graves? Think well, Morholt, before you answer."

I was not going to do any thinking. I suspected Branwen knew as much. I saw it in her eyes when she turned her face towards me.

She knew we'd been sent to Carhaing to save the legend. And we had. The simplest way. By beginning a new one.

"I know how you feel, Branwen," I said, looking at the sails, "for I feel exactly the same. It's a terrible sickness. Terrible, incurable malady. I know how you feel. For I, too, have fallen ill."

Branwen smiled, and it seemed to me that the sun had broken through the low-hanging clouds. That's what this smile was like. Believe me or not.

"And the pox on the healthy, Branwen!"

The sails were dirty.

Or so it seemed to me.

A LIFE MADE POSSIBLE BEHIND THE BARRICADES

JACQUES BARCIA

Jacques Barcia is an information technology reporter living in Recife, Brazil. He has written widely on Brazilian and international SF, and his stories have appeared in the *Shine* anthology and in the *Steampunk Reloaded Web Annex*, amongst others.

Beyond the aethership's window, Catalonia shone like a brass and crystal star, lost and alone in the vastness of space. Kilometric antennae cast to the void, flowers carved over its colossal hull, and around the main station's atrium, beautiful stained glass and asymmetric lines. Art. Home, if everything went well. It had always bothered Fritz, this tick-tock speeding up inside his chest. It knotted his guts, tightened his pneumatics. And, of course, there was the noise, the clocks emphasising his anguishes, excitements, dreads, and delights, right there, for everyone to hear. But now he tried to keep himself calm, the glassy-cold window against his icy, metal forehead, the battle breaking the silence in the cabin with a sharp sound.

"Soon it'll be over, dear," Chaya whispered, half asleep and still under the blankets. "Just a few more hours and we'll be there."

"Yeah, I know," Fritz whispered back, turning his head to his fiancée, giving her a silly, theatrical smile. "It's just, well, you know I'm easily stunned by beauty." He turned his back to the window and rested his gaze on the non-human girl. Stunning. She lay nested amongst baggage packed too quickly and clothes discarded in the rush of desire. A golem with roots for hair, all spread out over the pillows.

"I see," she said, stretching and finally sitting up, letting the blankets slide over her earth-and-wood skin, her breasts suddenly uncovered. "And I know you love to dramatise, too. Look, Fritz, don't forget that thing is a factory. And factories are always about smoke, sweat, and the whistle at the end of every shift." She scratched her brick-coloured forehead, chose a single root and used it to tie a ponytail. "Also, you should remember there's a war going on".

The war, the strike. Three years of insurrection. Fourteen months of controlling the best part of the aether mine-generator, Catalonia, as the Federalists had started to call it. However, even with rifles and deaths and Tesla-mortars, that sphere sucking mystical energy from the vacuum was the only place in the whole universe, or so it was told, in which a moto-lang and a golem could live without begging for the approval of their owner-creators. Even if it were true, it was something that'd never be possible anywhere on Earth.

He came closer to Chaya, gears grinding, engines almost frozen due to the cabin's poor heating, and sat on the edge of the bed. Chaya's face rested in her hands, as she did when she anticipated his *over-romanticised tone*. "There's beauty in the word, *camarada* Chaya," he said. "An untouchable kind of beauty, invisible to the eye. Something that exists wherever there's solidarity and—"

"What about the barricades?" Her voice came cold and as hard as stone. "Behind the barricades there are humans that never stop being human. Except when they're shot dead or die on the tip of a bayonet. That ain't beautiful, you know? And it's not beautiful when they sing *The Internationale* and look down on us because, in a way, they're still our lords. They're humans, Fritz. Unlike us."

"What's your problem?" he grumbled. "You chose to come along. You know this is our chance, Chaya, the *only chance* we have to build a life together. Any life. Be it good, bad, medio-cre. What? You think we better get back to Mauritzstadt and serve House Goradeski?"

"They're good people. You know that."

"Humans. Lords. You've just said that. Your lords, your makers. And even if I'm thankful to Mr Goradeski for the de-cency of giving my goddamn punched cards back, I hate that bastard for not letting me buy you, for not letting me marry you." Fritz stood before her, joints creaking, an angry *tick-tock, tick-tock* coming from beneath his brass thorax. "'A sin,' he told me. As if I wanted that stupid rabbi's blessings."

Chaya punched the bed in anger, crushing the iron frame under the mattress. "Fuck!" The agonising screech of metal swal-lowed up their shouts. "I just don't want you to be disappointed, okay? Look, I've escaped with you. I'm here in this aethership, remember? With you. I know Catalonia's our only chance, but your dream may not be that sweet. And I love you too much to see you sad and let down."

Fritz observed the copper lines framing the cabin's velvety walls; adorned with so many organic motifs and engravings it was as if the room itself were alive. A completely unexplored jungle. Next to the inter-phone on the night table, Dr Cavalcante's letter gave his tense coils some relief. His occultist friend, well-known in Mauritzstadt's esoteric society, was serving as a field medic for Catalonia's international brigades. His missive had ultimately persuaded both non-humans to flee. Fritz turned to Chaya, accepting the truce, or their particular way of making a truce. After all, she was right. Again. As always. He really was just an automaton that dreamt of open fields, broken locks, sunny days, and people's respect. He dreamt of being a hero, of freeing himself after fighting tyranny and oppression. But he'd never held a rifle. Not even to hunt with Dr Goradeski in the forests close to the Guararapes hill. His only duties were doing the accounts for his master's riches and tutoring the heirs to the clan.

"It'll work, Chaya. I believe— No, I'm sure it'll work. Trust me."

She did trust him. He knew it. It was written in her smile. But he also knew she was right. Life wouldn't be pretty. They made love for a few more hours.

THOUGH IT WAS AN AETHERSHIP station, it didn't behave like one. It didn't breathe like one. There was no smoking, no mink coats, no comings and goings of serfs, luggage, or hats. Except for the brassy majesty of the *Nassau*, a true aether leviathan, there was nothing in it that mirrored the luxury found in the ports of Mauritzstadt or any other Earthly empire. But there were people. Lots of people. A Babel debarking with Genovese and Madrileño accents, others being Balkan and Ottoman, all too confused to be distinguishable. There were expatriates from the Brazilian empire, too, and many Mauritzes. Men wearing cheap, brown cotton. Their bodies kept together only by loose, rusty screws, steam leaking from their joints. There were women, too, with severe eyes, coal-stained dresses, and calluses, guarding what little luggage they possessed. But they were all smiling for they were pleased to step on firm ground. Not ground, exactly, but that alchemical crystal shielding the arcologies sailing the Earthly seas.

Fritz was overcome with vertigo when he looked at the curves in the station's columns, each one preciously engraved in typical Art Nouveau style. He almost fell to the floor when, beneath his feet, he saw the city cascading down the inner walls of the sphere and, at the centre, the aether condenser, the heart of the factory, with its colossal tubes containing hundreds of pipes which, in their turn, carried thousands of pre-processed aether foam, so wild and volatile that a simple leak would open a metaphysical sinkhole big enough to swallow all God's Creations. At least that's what the Luddites said.

A mechanical arm waved over the caps of the volunteers coming fast in his direction. A whistle could be heard coming from the crowd. It was like an invisible teakettle leaving a trail of white puffs of smoke in the air. The immigrants started to give way as the steam got closer and closer. From them emerged a hybrid vehicle, something between a bicycle and a locomotive, a big wheel in front of a chimney and two small vulcanised pneumatics behind, too close to the stove heating the boiler. It made a hellish noise and Fritz couldn't help but agree with Chaya when she said that the thing stank of garbage tea. On the top of the vehicle, the pilot pulled the brake lever and turned the handlebar to the left, forcing the machine to slide for some metres before stopping just a few inches in front of the frozen couple. "I call it," shouted the man, forcing a dramatic pause, "the locomocycle."

The automaton laughed at the pilot's pomp and at his

fiancée's disgusted expression. "It's beautiful, Emilio," he shouted back. "Your design?"

"Every single rivet." The man grinned behind a pair of pitch-black goggles that made him look like a juvenile insect wearing a waistcoat and greaves. There was a blue, spectral glimmer deep inside the blackness of his goggles. The crowd kept its distance from the locomocycle, mainly because its boiler gave off an unbearable heat. But they couldn't stop admiring that automotive marvel. The man called Emilio stepped down from the vehicle, leaning his arm on the boiler. He faced the golem with keen interest. "Is she the lucky one?"

"That's her," Fritz answered, holding his lover's hand, suddenly solemn.

"Did she bring the equipment I asked for?" His gaze was fixed on Chaya, who was uneasy at being scrutinised not only by the scientist's goggled eyes, but also by the judging eyes of the women at the station, condemning the bourgeois style of her housemaid's dress. Worse, she wasn't precisely a maid, for in their eyes she wasn't a woman, but a construct turned to life by the power of the one thing more terrible than the Holy Church: magic.

"You can speak directly to me, sir. I speak and decide for myself."

"My dear," Fritz intervened, "this is Dr Emilio Cavalcante, the one I told you about. Physician, engineer, and member of the Order of Oriental Templars."

"Former member." Dr Cavalcante raised a mechanical finger as an exclamation mark, his gears spinning with the movement. "Apparently, my friend, the Order does not approve of my mystical theories, not to mention my political practices. And vice versa." Dr Cavalcante moved two steps closer to the couple, closer to the golem. "*Salud, camarada*! Forgive me if I sounded a little bit sexist, but I was concerned with the equipment. You see, it's not every day that—"

"Everything's here." She turned her back to the doctor and

dragged two wooden crates, one in each hand, to him. The crates moaned, leaving deep scratches in the floor. She released the boxes and faced the insect in the way someone might look at an old, ill-kept, and uninteresting daguerreotype. "That's all I could get. Fifteen carbines, some Prussian pistols, and not much ammunition." The golem looked at the box to her left. "And here's the equipment you asked for."

Dr Cavalcante looked at the containers, but his gaze drifted to a point way beyond them, to a dozen crates being unloaded from the aethership's rear. They were somewhat different and had red marks painted on their sides. "Yeah. Excellent. That'll do," the doctor said.

The motolang looked at his boxes and held his friend's shoulder. "So, you think you can do it, Emilio? You think you can give us a child?"

Dr Cavalcante woke from his trance, extended his mortal arm and shook the motolang's metallic hand. "Fritz, my friend, if I were you I'd be scheduling the kid's baptism already. The only problem is to find a priest who hasn't been fusilladed by the revolution.

CHAYA HAD SPENT THE LAST three weeks in Catalonia, but the city-factory still fascinated her. The wreckage sacs, the barricades on every corner, the low-fluctuation trucks painted with the revolutionary parties' initials, and, especially, the strikers' colours. Everyone, absolutely everyone, either wore red or black and red kerchiefs tied round their necks. Even the mechanoids, their gears exposed on their chests or shoulders, insisted on showing off kerchiefs, ignoring the high chance of an accident. And there were the brick-and-metal buildings carved by bullets, bent at angles that far-surpassed the plans of Gaudi, almost destroyed by Mauritzes' mortars. However, most impressive was the fact that this place had become their home so quickly. Notwithstanding, it *was* her home. Sometimes there was no grease and she had to wind her husband, lubricating his gears with butter or fat stolen from the communal depot. And sometimes there was no food, which meant no leftovers for her roots. That was the siege, the embargo, the seldom-run blockade. As when they had arrived on the Nassau. But still, they enjoyed a normal couple's routine. He worked as a carabineer at the front, and she'd patrol the streets on foot with her Luger. Both came back home at the end of the day, sharing the little stories that filled up their quotidian days. A routine that included almost daily visits to the basements of Hotel Florida.

She lay on a wooden table, an improvised stretcher with one foot shorter than the other three. Dozens of lenses and manipulators hung from coils and wires tied to the ceiling, all of them pointing at her body, analysing, accusing her. *You're an empty vase, a dead tree.* The smell of ozone and gaslight unnerved her, especially after two hours of breathing electrical air and smoke, half-naked under the holophotes. Not to mention the fear she had of falling from the table. Every time she breathed a bit too deeply, the table bent to one side, stopping with a sudden *thump*, a sound that served as an exclamation mark to the many, omnipresent *tick-tocks* in the room. Some of those sounds were strange to her, but some were not. Inside the wall of darkness, Chaya could only see the blue poltergeist inside Dr Cavalcante's eyes; Emilio, who had his goggles bolted to his face. It could be just fashion, or something far more sinister. *He can see in the dark?*

Suddenly, the clattering stopped. The lights came back on slowly, along with calmer, lower *tick-tocks*. Chaya could see the doctor walking to and fro in front of the analytical engine, exhaling gusts of white steam. He had some punched cards in his hands and was murmuring something to a machine hanging from his shoulders, a trump with a rubber tube linked to a rattling stenograph on his waistcoat, spitting metres and metres of hollowed-out paper.

"So?" Chaya sat up, relieved that the examination was over. "What does your oracle say?"

Emilio spoke over the brass trump, as he looked at the end of the room, at a table covered by a ziggurat-shaped tarp from which came the low sound of boiling water. "It says you ate chocolate today," he said rather casually.

"Just a tip," she smiled.

"It's quite toxic for golems."

"Just like a shot of *cachaça*, Emilio." Chaya was putting on her dress, careful not to let the dark chocolate bar fall from her pocket.

"And just as hard to get these days." Emilio turned off the stenograph and unfastened the apparatus from his torso. "You been smuggling? Look, Chaya, if people know you've been getting stuff from the Mauritzes, you're gonna be in some serious trouble, especially if the committee hears about it. The way things are, this could end with an execution."

"If I can't eat chocolate, I don't want to be part of your revolution," the golem said, a defying hand in her pocket. "I bought it at the station. Before I got here. On Earth."

The doctor shook his head and gave a short, dry laugh. "Okay, then. But you'll have to quit if you want to have a baby. That thing messes with your ecosystem, you know." He finally rolled up the paper and attached it to the feeder's tiny hooks on the calculator's rear. As soon as he did so, the engine re-initiated its mad rattling: the sound of a thousand clocks speeding up to the end of time. The analytical engine ate hole after hole, a data banquet digested by coiled guts and dented wheels, calculating, calculating, calculating.

"What's the deal with this committee?" She still couldn't understand the politics of the strike in Catalonia very well. She knew there was an area controlled by three or four anarchist trade unions, but each city block contained many different groups. Left and right wing communists, or whatever name they called themselves, everything depending on whoever their leaders were. There were other groups she'd heard the communists call republicans, but they could also be divided into those who wished independence and those who wanted to be part of some Earthly empire. Of the anarchists, Chaya could only see the difference between those who wanted action without much discussion and those who sought consensus for every single thing, be it the restoration of a house or the fair distribution of rations. Anyway, the uprising made some areas in the factory free from the consortium that used to run the mining and aether processing.

Emilio sighed, looking worried. He cleaned his insect's eyes with a ragged piece of red cloth and it seemed the blue that used to live in his goggles had dimmed. "Some far-off quarters have decided to form a ruling committee. The unions' and the parties' militias have been blended together and now they're like a regular army."

"Hey! That's fantastic. They could send some people here so Fritz wouldn't be so lonely at the front. Maybe he could take some time off." Chaya bit the bark in her nails. That was excellent news, wasn't it?

"Except they won't." He suddenly stopped cleaning his goggles. "It's been a month since they formed the army and not a single man has been sent to the front. And they have guns. Lots of guns. Too many guns, actually, but not even a blunderbuss has made it to this side of the war." He took a long pause to clean his mechanical fingers, using the same handkerchief he had used to clean his goggles. "People are saying there are spies killing anarchists."

The tick-tock stopped, and in its place, the sharp sound of a siren filled the air. Emilio turned to the analytical engine, already spitting out another bunch of hollowed-out paper. He picked up the paper and brought it close to his face, carefully reading the data in those empty lines.

"So?" Chaya panted.

Emilio lowered the paper roll. He had a smile on his face. "Call Fritz. We're ready."

"HEY, BEANS. MESSAGE FOR YOU."

Fritz pretended he hated it when the guys called him names but, deep inside, he liked it. Beans was the only meal available on the front and to the militia's fanfare, it came locked up in a rusty can. He couldn't eat, of course, because of his mechanical physiology, but his camaradas in the troop said he had solidarity with the cans. Sometimes, a fat Yankee called Ernest would point a tin opener at him, saying he was hungry. Everybody would laugh. With the clocks inside his mind, he calculated that this attitude wasn't prejudice, or mockery, but banter. He was the exhaust valve for the tedium, the tension at the barricades, the long wait for an enemy that never came despite the news of troops manoeuvring some miles ahead. He finally calculated, with some fair bit of precision, that he was one of the guys, too. After all, he had the same black and red kerchief round his neck.

They sat behind the barricade mounted in front of the old Chateclair casino, a well-conserved building by the war's standards. His mates felt triply happy to see it still standing. The spot close to the neighbourhood's limits used to be the entertainment district for the factory's technicians and administrators. It'd be a shame if the next generation of workers couldn't have access to that architectonic marvel. Besides, the docking tower for personal dirigibles made an excellent observation post. Fritz was fighting against a loose piston in La Sigaretta, the steam-powered machine gun guarding the brothel's entrance, when he heard his name being called at the building's foyer. This was the soldier's third reason for being happy. The place was part of the postal service network, and its pneumatic tubes winding their way underground still carried, brought, and sometimes intercepted messages from all over Catalonia. He dropped the piston and hurried to the building.

"It's from your babe." Buenaventura winked, a letter in one hand and a wooden tube in the other. The boy was barely sixteen and was proud of spending his days watching the comings and goings of messages travelling in the pipe cathedral behind the counter.

In the message, Chaya said to come back quickly, everything's ready. Obviously, he understood the message, as did Buenaventura and other two or three militiamen with whom the motolang had shared his hopes. He smiled, showing off the letter, trying to explain to those hardened men alchemical processes he could hardly understand. But they did understand the joy of that moment and would've opened a nice bottle of wine if they'd had one.

The first bomb destroyed the casino's wall.

Fritz tried to free himself from the human wreckage over his body, tried to adjust his sensors, but there was only dust around him and a humming sound coming from the back of the room. It took him several seconds to recalibrate his optics and phones, but now he could listen to the shots and screams outside, and the moans of the survivors inside. He saw young Buanaventura crawling to the back of the counter, alive and in one piece. He decided to run to the street.

The second bomb exploded past the barricades, in the middle of the street, but Fritz couldn't see if anyone had been hurt. He threw himself behind the mountain of sacks, between La Sigaretta and Ernest, who had just crouched after shooting through the wall of dust covering their position.

"Make this damn machine gun work, Beans." Ernest roared, as he knelt and shot his carbine along with three militiamen.

"What's happening? Where are they?" Fritz crawled closer to the machine gun. Bullets whistled over their heads. He was afraid the bullets would ricochet off him, hitting his comrades' hearts. On his left, a soldier's gun jammed and backfired, tearing the boy's brass face apart.

Ernest reloaded his hunting rifle and looked up. "They just popped up and opened fire. They closed the passage down the street with floating trucks and then started throwing their mortars at us." He locked the crank and closed his eyes as if praying. "For fuck's sake, where's that damn sentinel?"

Fritz managed to light the boiler, but he knew it'd be a long time before the high-pressure system could start working. Another bomb exploded, but he didn't know where. *If You look after the atheists, too, please make the water boil faster.* He picked up his janizary-carbine lying close to the sacks, calibrated his optics and the pulleys in his arms, and, jumping over the barrier, aimed at the enemy. Beyond a blood-red haze in front of the church, there were three black floating trucks blocking the end of the street. It seemed the trucks had their paintings rasped off. Those weren't men from the Consortium, he was sure, nor from any other army he knew of. But there was something familiar about the soldiers throwing pulse grenades at them, holding brand-new, shining rifles. *Tick-tock.*

"Beans! Shoot!"

As soon as he got the lay of his gun, Fritz locked his aim at a soldier crossing the street towards a Stanley parked on the corner. *Tick-tock, tick-tock.* There were two more soldiers entrenched behind the automobile, a moving shield that could easily reach the Chanteclair.

"Shoot! Now!"

Tick-tock, tick-tock, tick-tock.

His instincts were part animal, part clockwork, and both made him keep the running lad in his sights until he got close to the steamer. The boy had his head low, his right hand covering the ear, protecting his head or praying it could hide him.

"Shoot!"

His first shot at something mortal.

He pulled the trigger a second before the soldier could leap to safety. There was a report and a blast at the boy's neck. He fell dry, no screaming, his face crushing the car's bumper.

Fritz crouched down an instant before a bullet hit the camarada next to him. *Ticktockticktockticktock.* He pushed the dead soldier away and once again bent himself over the sacks. He shot once, twice, thrice, suppressing every possible movement of the enemy line. He was covering Ernest, ready to throw another grenade, when he heard a low whistling noise.

Another bomb exploded close to the trucks, but the rise of the high-pitched sound made the troops freeze for a second.

"Fritz," Ernest yelled.

"I'm coming, for fuck's sake, I'm coming." He dropped the carbine and almost threw himself over the steamgun. "Cover me!" The dangling piston insisted on slipping from his fingers, all damp thanks to the vapour leaking from the gun's opened valve. Even with suppressive fire, enemy bullets kept coming in his direction. He had to keep his head low like the boy he had just killed. After infinite seconds, he managed to fix the piston into position, but it took him another eternity to find a wrench amongst the corpses. The whistle grew louder and louder and, as soon as he turned the screw nut, the machine gun's long muzzle started to spin, steaming.

Ticktockticktockticktockticktock...

Fritz pulled the trigger, wishing someone had already placed the ammo belt into the feedway. The noise was so loud every soldier this side of the battle was thrown to the ground. It was the sound of a jackhammer crushing the wall of sacks, cars, and people standing less than three hundred metres away. Drifting his range, Fritz watched the Stanley dissolve under La Sigaretta's fire. The car was torn to pieces: wheels, chassis, seats. Bullets of hell-knows-what calibre pierced its hull as if it were made of paper. He slowly turned the gun to the enemy's central position and thrust the black trucks away with the violence of a thousand lead wasps. He lost connection with time.

"Stop it, Fritz!"

The ventilation system had been down for more than two weeks now, so the steam had already turned into a muddy cloud made of smoke, dirt, and blood. The troops behind the trucks broke up and ran away. Two soldiers trying to hide behind the blockade were torn apart by the hellish gun.

"Stop it, Fritz! This thing's gonna blow!"

He was thrown out from the machine by Ernest and another militiaman he didn't recognise. All three hit their backs to the ground, their voices screaming *all right, all right, it's okay, I got him.* The tin soldier just stared at the city sprawling over him, failing to see any human beings walking the streets at the sphere's opposite half. It seemed there was no-one at the casino's tower, too.

THEY BOTH WOKE UP TO the sound of the locomocycle roaring inside the hotel's garage. They'd ended up falling asleep after a night-long procedure and were still bound together by wires, sensors, and robotic hands. They could sense the smell of ozone and boiling chemicals in the air and heard the sound of a thousand processing clicks from the analytical engine. Both had guns under their pillows.

"It was supposed to be my turn," Fritz said, partly asking and partly answering. "I just turned off. Sorry."

"No problem." Chaya smiled. The only thing still beautiful in this godless world. "It's all right."

The door blasted open and they both pointed their guns at whoever was coming in. Emilio raised his free hand, the organic one, making sure the non-human couple could see his face and recognise him. "Thought you heard me coming," the doctor said.

"The power of habit," Chaya said, uncocking her Luger. "How's the city going?"

"Empty. Except for militiamen, not many people are willing to walk the streets these days. Those who have food at home have no reason to go out. Those who don't, won't find any outside." Emilio closed the door behind him with some difficulty. He had a small wooden box in his mechanical hand.

Fritz rested his gun on the improvised stretcher and tried to stand up. His joints creaked loudly. His body was all twisted and warped on the left side, especially his knee, though his right shoulder also cracked. "Any news from the front? How are the men doing?" Four days ago he'd been promoted to captain. Not that it meant anything, since the militiamen followed whoever they thought worth following rather than those with military rank. They'd been close to lots of bombs in the past few days, he and his friends, but maybe because he'd got used to the mortars or maybe because of the nature of the explosives, none of these had hurt him any more than the first one on the Chanteclair had. Actually, it still hurt. "Did they retake the casino?"

Emilio lowered his head and crossed the laboratory towards a tarp-covered table. The sound of boiling water came from it. Only when he walked past Fritz, did Emilio notice how injured his friend was. Gunshots, scraps, deep cuts. Were he human, he'd be dead by now. "No. No, I don't. No news," he said, pointing to the hidden table. "Last thing I heard was that the Committee issued some kind of edict saying the militias are now illegal." The doctor looked over his shoulder. "They'll find us. Sooner or later, they'll take the neighbourhood. It's over. Then they'll make an agreement with the Consortium and life will be as it used to be before the strike. Or even worse. And I think you two should pack your things and go back to Earth now. An aethership will leave in about three hours. You've nothing to do with this war."

"And *you* do?" The automaton was craving for an argument.

"Fritz, dear, I think Emilio might be right," Chaya said. She tried to find some comfort on the stretcher, but the wires wouldn't let her.

Fritz shook his head. He had his revolver back in his trembling hand. The bomb might've loosened some pulley in his shoulder. "We're so close now. You said that. Besides, there's nothing for us down there, on Earth. Nothing."

Emilio and Chaya stared at him. The tick-tock in him seemed to have vanished, or at least couldn't be noticed above the noises in the lab.

Dr Cavalcante sighed. "So, if we're to finish this experiment, we better get back to work." He pulled out the covered table and brought it to the space between the couple. The myriad of cables, tubes, and wires on the floor got stuck between the table's rusty wheels. Emilio took the brown tarp off it, uncovering two once-green cylinders and a series of transparent alchemical glass vials the size of pressure pans. The vials were mounted like a ziggurat and were full of boiling liquids, each one of a different colour. The yellows were on the edge of the table and the blacks were actually extremely dense reds. There were also some transparent ones and others reflecting light in gold and silver patterns. At the top of the glass pile, there was a bigger, double-sized vial. It was completely empty and un-capped. "Okay, we've been through this before, but just to make sure you got it right," Emilio said donning his waistcoat and the stenograph. "I'll plug the drains into you and then at-tach it to the uterus up there, and then I'll link it to the aetheric fusion tank down here, as well. If we're able to produce enough sephirotic reaction, well, we'll proceed to surgery. Ready?"

They exchanged nervous glances and smiled, confirming their willingness to move on.

The occultist connected the suspended cables to the wires inside the non-human veins. He activated the apparatus by pressing a switch next to the control panel. Immediately, the prone bodies became stiff, as if they were being electrocuted. He ran to the aether cylinders and turned the valves only slightly to release a tiny amount of aetherfoam. The substance flowed through the tubes until it filled the fusion tank. He re-turned to the edge of the table and faced the control panel. It was diamond-shaped and over it was a gematria board, a stone abacus and a green phosphorus screen displaying the Tree of Life. Everything was connected by dozens of wires and cables leading to the analytical engine. Opposite him, the tank blend-ing the non-humans' essences span faster and faster.

"Come on. Come on." They always failed in the first step. Calculations were correct and there was an obvious resonance between the two lovers. But in all attempts throughout the weeks, the tank had worked as a centrifuge, not mixing, but separating the essences from the aether.

The first two sephirotic houses shone in the monitor when a pale light started to emanate from the tank.

"Yes." Emilio jumped and punched the air and, when he looked again, the third house was alight. "No, no, no. Too fast." He found the controls for the mechanical arms under the table and quickly attached them to his own clockwork arm. Now he was like a puppeteer whose fingers moved spider-legs over his marionettes. The organic hand calibrated the analytical engine, moving the stones in the abacus. He lowered the robotic arms over Fritz and Chaya and, with his feet, he pressed a pedal to activate their drills and scalpels.

The vibration was felt, not heard.

Then a thundering noise hit the street several metres above. The blast almost tore the equipment away from the ceiling.

"No," Emilio moaned and stopped to listen, "not now, please." A second later another blast was followed by another quake and then machine-gun shots.

"Don't. Even. Consider. Stopping." Fritz had his arm raised, his gun triggered, and was pointing at the door. "Move on," he said, knowing the doctor hadn't considered stopping. He knew his friend craved paternity, too.

Fritz saw, right above him, a robotic arm handling a bright blowtorch and, on the table next to him, the shining scalpel hovering over Chaya. He tried to turn his sensors off, but it was too late. He felt the pain and the heat of the torch opening a big triangle in his belly, while his wife had a vibrating blade carving a doorway to her womb. Gunshots were closer now and already they could hear screams coming from Hotel Florida's garage. The doctor, abacus forgotten, now held a pistol, too, aimed at the door. The face and mind of the now-captain motolang convulsed with pain, while Emilio tried to find the correct gear inside him with his spidery arms. At the same time, the doctor looked for a specific root in Chaya.

A blast blew out the door. A mechanical hand pinched the coils inside Fritz's guts.

Fritz opened fire, but Emilio hesitated. The doctor barely had the reflexes to dodge the door flying across the room. It smashed the analytical engine's glass walls. A man in a black uniform raided the room with a rifle, but was blown away by three shots from Fritz, who was trying to get rid of the wires tangled with his body. The man fell to the floor still shooting his automatic gun, hitting lamps and steam tubes. "Wake up, Chaya," he cried, pulling his wife to the floor, to a space between the stretcher and the multicoloured glass pyramid.

The golem opened her eyes to the dark fog and screamed as soon as she hit the ground. Immediately, she understood the situation. She grabbed the stretcher-table's feet and lifted it, improvising a shield with its hardened wood. She dragged the table to the door while Fritz covered her, exposing his own body to shoot the guards at the door. She'd managed to block the entrance, but it'd take only a few shots to tear down the already splintering barrier.

"Emilio," Fritz yelled.

The human had his back to the ground and was chewing off the cables from his mechanical arm. His left hand held the experiment's samples and his pistol was tucked inside his trousers. A big piece of wood landed close to his head and splinters forced him to shut his eyes. He cleared them from wood, tears, and condensed steam. A spray of bullets flew inside the room.

Chaya used the dead soldier's gun to shoot the guards through a tiny hole in the barrier. "We have to leave, Fritz. The barrier won't stand much longer." She reloaded the machine gun with her last ammo clip. "Emilio, is there any other way out?"

He had stood up and was dodging the bullets, trying to stand in front of the control panel. "This is a basement, Chaya. There's no way out."

Fritz shot two more times through the crack, then stopped to reload. It was only then that he noticed the guards had stopped shooting back. He signalled to Chaya, who was prepared to spray another set of bullets. Then he looked at Emilio, who in a single movement opened the mixer, threw the samples in and locked it as fast as he could.

The only recognisable sound was that post-gunfight humming. Not even Fritz, nor the analytical engine, dared to break the silence. Maybe because they were both broken machines, afraid and with their guts exposed. "What happened?"

"I can't see anything," Chaya said, her eyes hunting for black uniforms on the staircase beyond the half-destroyed barrier. "It's as though they've disappeared. Just stopped shooting." She still heard some lonely shots beyond the layers of concrete, brass and asphalt above them. Other than that, there was only silence. But it wasn't like the silence one heard after surviving a gunfight. It was much more like the silence before passing away. A calm, serene death that took its time before taking away its burden.

"Hey, Fritz, help me out." Emilio was pulling a crank that apparently pumped up the fluids from the mixer to the glass vial atop the ziggurat.

Both non-humans exchanged looks. He slowly moved away from the door, counting on his wife for cover. "What do I do?"

"The mechanical arms are gone. Climb onto the table, and I'll give you the tank. I need you to fill up the uterus on top."

The automaton put his gun back in his trousers. He found an empty spot on the table and stood on it, trying to keep his balance. He stepped to one side and grabbed the mixer with one hand. A pale-bright whirlwind moved inside it with roots and gears dancing about. He grappled his way to a place from which to pour the liquid into the machine and finally bent his body towards the uterus, the sharp metal of his opened-up belly scratching the glass vials. He poured the tank's contents into the uterus, already full with some kind of repulsive solvent.

Almost immediately, the mixture became transparent.

"Now, step down," Emilio commanded.

"What?" Fritz was hypnotised. The two floating corpuscles were attracted to each other and, he could swear it, were blending together. But at the same time, they were multiplying. "Oh, Chaya! I think it's working." He turned smiling to his wife, but her face was as hard as stone. She had her hands behind her head.

The low *click* as the gun was triggered woke the motolang from his dream.

"Down, Fritz." Emilio was pointing his pistol at him.

The troops of the Committee had forced the barrier and entered the basement. A dozen or more, he wasn't able to count. One of the soldiers walked around the table and grabbed the wooden box lying on the brown tarp. "What's happening? I—I don't understand." Fritz was experiencing something like reverse omniscience. He could see that Chaya had surrendered, that the soldiers were receiving orders from Emilio, and that a wood-and-metal embryo grew inside the glass uterus. He felt diluted, ephemeral in his confusion. Inexorably incapable.

"It doesn't matter. Come on, man, step down. Do what I say." The soldier put the opened box at Emilio's feet. There was a brass barrel mounted inside it. It was the same size as the uterus.

"You can't do this, Emilio. Please."

"Fritz—" he paused "—if you won't step down, I swear, my friend, I'll fire this shit off into your fucking head."

Tick-tock.

"No! Dear, no!"

Fritz grabbed the uterus as hard as he could and threw himself to the back of the room. There was a sound of gunshots blasting and he felt two stabs in his back. Something heavy and metallic bounced on the floor. There were glass cutting cables and jamming gears inside his joints. *Tick-tock.*

He hit the ground, the impact deflating the balloons inside his chest. *Oh, no. God, please no. The uterus is broken.* He could feel the liquid spilling over him, flowing inside his open wounds. He embraced the vial with all the strength he had left. *Tick-tock, tick-tock.* He lay between the wall and the two fallen aetherfoam cylinders. He saw Chaya being shot four times in the back while trying to run to him. He saw the seeds in her eyes wither and die before she fell. Emilio and his soldiers were almost on him.

He made his decision.

Tick-tock, tick-tock, tick-tock.

He drew his gun and fired it off at the cylinders. There was a blast and a glaring radiance like a star.

Silence.

Tick.

ON OCCASION, A MORTAR. A dull machine gun talking in the distance was his only companion. Fritz climbed the stairs of an abandoned building at the heart of a deserted neighbourhood. The carbine had been turned into a crutch to keep his body straight. Each step needed more than the strength he had left in him. It was martyrdom. His body cracked, his joints creaked, and he limped. His body was bent to one side, the cables that served as tendons were shattered. He could barely reach the crank in his back to wind himself up. He missed Chaya so badly. He had no clue as to what to think of Emilio.

The motolang dragged himself across the corridor to the room, his new home since the explosion back in the lab. The war was very distant now and would soon be over. He had turned from militiamen to refugee in the space of just two months, hiding as he could amongst the ruins of the revolution. *It'll have to do for now.* He felt bad.

There was a rocking chair close to the window. The reactor was framed in it, and high above, he could see an aethership docking at the station. He still had no way of escaping. He had no money for the tickets and the bribes. Besides, the trip was too dangerous these days. Maybe in a few more months.

He tried to relax, rocking on the chair, the carbine over his lap. Roots and wires sprouted up from the cracks in his carcass. The place wasn't exactly *home*, but he felt somewhat happy. Now there was another tick-tock inside him, a seed. In a glass vial embedded in his belly, he and Chaya shone together the way only impossible things are likely to shine.

Editor Biography

LAVIE TIDHAR is the author of the Jerwood Fiction Uncovered Prize winning *A Man Lies Dreaming*, the World Fantasy Award winning *Osama*, and of the critically-acclaimed *The Violent Century*. His other works include *The Bookman Histories* trilogy, several novellas, two collections, and a forthcoming comics mini-series, *Adler*. He currently lives in London.

ARTIST BIOGRAPHY

SARAH ANNE LANGTON has worked as an Illustrator for EA Games, Hodder & Stoughton, Forbidden Planet, The Cartoon Network, Sony, Apple, Marvel Comics and a wide variety of music events. Written and illustrated for Jurassic London, Fox Spirit, NewCon Press and The Fizzy Pop Vampire series. Hodderscape dodo creator and Kitschies Inky Tentacle judge. Daylights as Web Mistress for the worlds largest sci-fi and fantasy website. Scribbles a lot about the X-Men, shouts at Photoshop and drinks an awful lot of tea. Responsible for *Zombie Attack Barbie* and *Joss Whedon Is Our Leader Now*. Her work has featured on *io9*, *Clutter Magazine*, *Forbidden Planet*, *Laughing Squid* and *Creative Review*.

The Apex Book of World SF: Vol 1

S.P. Somtow
Jetse de Vries
Guy Hasson
Han Song
Kaaron Warren
Yang Ping
Dean Francis Alfar
Nir Yaniv
Jamil Nasir
Tunku Halim
Aliette de Bodard
Kristin Mandigma
Aleksandar Žiljak
Anil Menon
Mélanie Fazi
Zoran Živković

edited by
Lavie Tidhar

Among the spirits, technology, and deep recesses of the human mind, stories abound. Kites sail to the stars, technology transcends physics, and wheels cry out in the night. Memories come and go like fading echoes and a train carries its passengers through more than simple space and time. Dark and bright, beautiful and haunting, the stories herein represent speculative fiction from a sampling of the finest authors from around the world.

ISBN: 978-1-937009-36-6 ~ ApexBookCompany.com

The Apex Book of World SF: Vol 3

Benjanun Sriduangkaew
Xia Jia
Fadzilshah Johanabos
Uko Bendi Udo
Ma Boyong
Athena Andreadis
Zulaikha Nurain Mudzor
Amal El-Mohtar
Nelly Geraldine Garcia-Rosas
Biram Mboob
Myra Çakan
Crystal Koo
Ange
Karin Tidbeck
Swapna Kishore
Berit Ellingsen

edited by
Lavie Tidhar

In The Apex Book of World Sf 3, World Fantasy Award-winning editor Lavie Tidhar collects short stories by science fiction and fantasy authors from Africa, Asia, South America, and Europe.

"The Apex Book of World SF series has proven to be an excellent way to sample the diversity of world SFF and to broaden our understanding of the genre's potential." --Ken Liu, winner of the Hugo Award and author of *The Grace of Kings*

ISBN: 978-1-937009-34-2 ~ ApexBookCompany.com

The Apex Book of World SF: Vol 4

Vajra Chandrasekera
Yukimi Ogawa
Zen Cho
Shimon Adaf
Celest Rita Baker
Nene Ormes
JY Yang
Isabel Yap
Usman T. Malik
Kuzhali Manickavel
Elana Gomel
Haralambi Markov
Sabrina Huang
Sathya Stone
Johann Thorsson
Dilman Dila
Swabir Silayi
Deepak Unnikrishnan
Chinelo Onwualu
Saad Z. Hossain
Bernardo Fernández
Nataliam Theodoridou
Samuel Marolla
Julie Novakova
Thomas Old Heuvelt
Sese Yane
Tang Fei
Rocío Rincón Fernández

edited by
Mahvesh Murad

From Spanish steampunk and Italian horror to Nigerian science fiction and subverted Japanese folktales, from love in the time of drones to teenagers at the end of the world, the stories in this volume showcase the best of contemporary speculative fiction, where it's written.

"Important to the future of not only international authors, but the entire SF community."
Strange Horizons

ISBN: 978-1-937009-33-5 ~ ApexBookCompany.com

CPSIA information can be obtained
at www.ICGtesting.com
Printed in the USA
LVHW092256230419
615338LV00001B/47/P